Naughty Astronautess

Naughty Astronautess

Glamour Galore

A Novel

Iory Allison

Author's copy
19/30

For Marianne

all my love

Iory

December 10, 2007

iUniverse, Inc.

New York Lincoln Shanghai

Naughty Astronautess

Glamour Galore

iUniverse books may be ordered through booksellers or by contacting:

iUniverse
2021 Pine Lake Road, Suite 100
Lincoln, NE 68512
www.iuniverse.com
1-800-Authors (1-800-288-4677)

Because of the dynamic nature of the Internet, any Web addresses or links contained in this book may have changed since publication and may no longer be valid.

This is a work of fiction. All of the characters, names, incidents, organizations, and dialogue in this novel are either the products of the author's imagination or are used fictitiously.

ISBN: 978-0-595-47804-0

Printed in the United States of America

Naughty Astronautess is dedicated to my dear friends, Phyllis Hanes and Joan Murphy. Without their considerable efforts of editorial expertise and their generous spirits, my astronautess and her Twinkle Star Ship would never have blasted off the launching pad. Thank you both again and again.

WHAT THE READERS *HAD* TO SAY

Betty Gets Her Digs In

Betty the Bounder
Marginal character of: *Naughty Astronautess, The Family Jewels*, etc.
Last seen lurking in the phone booth at the Follies Derrière

O.K. you guys, I gotta make this quick before that smart-ass author Mr. Iory gets back to his computer. But listen, I read his latest hogwash, *Naughty Astronautess,* and I gotta tell ya he has it all ass backwards as usual! I mean really, the schlub thinks of me as some kinda punching bag for all of his cheap jokes. And let me say, if he thinks my having a little drinkypoo now and then is such a side splitting yuck—then how about all those Romeritas he keeps knocking back at the Casa Romero night after night? What kinda sissy drink is a Romerita anyway? And as for his running joke, "Betty has spent a large chunk of her career selling leftover perfume samples at Filene's Basement," well think again dumbo, because the Basement is like over, Miss Thing. That is, it's closed, kaput, as in, no more! So get with the times....

Author's note: Betty's ranting has been translated into hacker's scrawl so deeply embedded into my computer that I cannot get rid of it, but please consider the source when reading the above attack. Betty has been known to mistake Lysol for Galliano. And what kind of sissy drink is Galliano anyway?

Ba Ba Bolts the Door

Ba Ba Rum Toddy
The Charma Karma Ashram
Pun—Jab, India

His Holiness Dilly Dally Rimpoché and I were reminiscing over a bowl of yak butter tea laced with Slivovitz about the good old days at the Portola, when much to our surprise, the profane volume, *Naughty Astronautess,* arrived in the mail from that hopeless disciple of mine Iory Allison. I was just about to toss the smut out the window when Dilly Dally, invoking the spirit of Milarepa to exorcise the demons seeping from the flimsy cover, was amazed to see the image of the "Astronautess" on the front cover. It would seem that there is a distinct resemblance to D. D. R.'s missing sister who was kidnapped by marauding Red Guard thugs during the Cultural Revolution. So naturally we were compelled to read the book. We had hardly started chapter 2 when we decided to bolt the door of the inner sanctum in order to protect our young monks, especially when we read about the antics of the monks at the Holy Fryer's Monastery in Somerville.

You may remember our last judgment was succinct and to the point when we said about *The Family Jewels*, "This book is clap trap in the extreme." Now we are not so sure D. D. R. is considering the esoteric ramifications of such an arcane mystery, and until more is revealed, the book will be banned from Bhutan to Brookline.

Tilly Wink Weighs *in on Naughty*

Tilly Wink
Literary Critic for
The Bumble Bee Beacon
Bumble Bee, Arkansas

Last time I encountered this *Glamour Galore* Trilogy thing I never thought that guy, Iory Allison, would have the gumption to make good his threat about writing a sequel to *The Family Jewels.* So imagine my surprise when my husband, Shadrach, of all people, brought home a copy of this outrage. He was still giggling from reading the absurd ending when he handed it to me but I only had to peek at the cover to know that trouble was in store.

I must admit to a certain amount of bias here because I got a mysterious call from some Betty the flounder (?), up in Boston, warning me not to read the blasted thing. How that screw ball got hold of my number is anyone's guess. But, you know, I really don't appreciate city slickers pushing me around so naturally then I wanted to read the story myself.

I am absolutely stumped! *Naughty Astronautess* has more odd ball characters then that Garrison Keillor ever thought about. I read it at a gallop, hardly taking a breath and Shadrach had to fix dinner which turned out to be Puerco Adobado, a recipe he got from actually calling the Casa Romero Restaurant all the way up in Boston, Massachusetts! He said that he read about it in the 'astronautess' book and had to try it. All I can say is the Puerco Adobado was a lot better than that song, "Scuba in Aruba." But besides the lousy lyrics, the book does have a lot of razzmatazz so read it and tell me what *you* think.

Sonia Schnable Spits It Out

Lucius Beebe
As channeled through the ouija board by
Madame Sonia Schnable
Literary Critic for
Mystic Messages

That darling boy, Iory Allison, has done it again and written a modern marvel! In my day at the *Herald Tribune* even I could not have gotten away with such a prank. I mean this charming ditty is an out and out Gay romp (all puns intended) I would observe, however, that although a great deal happens in *Naughty Astronautess* you couldn't really say it has a plot. I suppose that this is the case with most farces, but Mr. Allison twists one's mind in such obtuse directions that a good laugh is all that we can expect for an explanation.

Bunko Goes Bonkers

Bunko Lestrad
Editor of *The Police Blotter*
Boston, Massachusetts

I apparently made a serious mistake when reviewing the first volume of the *Glamour Galore* trilogy with far too much leniency. Now I am left asking myself, what price for a laugh? I had assumed that these books would be mysteries and as such they would have a moral and lawful resolution no matter what mischief the list of suspects were up to. But no, the author has dropped that pose and degenerated into pure farce. On top of that almost all the characters are guilty of various offenses from drug and alcohol abuse, larceny and bald-faced lies about almost everything.

I have ordered one thousand copies of the book for all my cadets to study in order to show them what kind of shenanigans we can expect from *those* kinds of people! As far as literary value, I would say that *Naughty Astronautess* has as much substance as laughing gas.

The Last Word, Again

Shirley Slurp
Avid Reader for
Silos and Commoner
On line hawker of excessive literary output

I am happy to report that Iory has outdone himself with *Naughty Astronautess*! He may also have undone a whole bunch of tightly made beds in the process. Expect the unexpected when you read this story of raw ambition tempered by completely unforeseen circumstances. And what a cast of characters! Although we met most of these loonies in the last book what we didn't know about them would fill an encyclopedia. This story makes mistaken identity seem like a natural occurrence as common as looking in the mirror.

CONTENTS

CHAPTER 1

▼

GODDESS OF GLAMOUR

Lilly Linda Le Strange sat at her dressing table, a shrinelike beauty bench that was draped with pink chenille swags over chartreuse plastic lace. Diva Le Strange was putting the finishing touches to her over elaborate toilette, and the results of her labor, a three-hour process of art-a-facial genius, was dazzling in the extreme. She puckered and smacked her lips triumphantly, which she had painted with more tender skill than Leonardo had ever lavished on his *Mona Lisa.* Even in her flimsy peignoir, barely covering her sturdy corsets, which without their lace and bows might have looked suspiciously like osteopathic appliances, Mademoiselle Le Strange was a goddess of glamour and one beguiling fairy.

However, this fairy was pissed! She had not been invited to the grand opening of the Essential Center Shopping Mall. Everyone who was anyone in Boston had been invited to that razzle-dazzle shindig, and Mademoiselle Le Strange was more than just anyone, she was a star. The current vehicle that bore her hefty weight amongst the celestial regions was, of course, *Glamour Galore,* the smash hit musical that had been playing to packed audiences for over a year at that outré watering hole, Club Crazy. Lilly's list of credits from decades of entertaining troops of thirsty revelers stretched beyond printable space in the Who's Who column of *Playbill,* so you know she was a star.

But why had our heroine been excluded from the festivities at the newly extended Essential? Why indeed! In response to this conundrum, which had been plaguing her precarious temperament, Mademoiselle Le Strange hurled a full bottle of *Poison* perfume at the wall of her dressing room. The *Poison* made a dark stain, bruising the innocent Minnie Mouse wallpaper as the vial shattered into a million odoriferous shards. But this act of violence only whetted the appetite for blood in our sizzling chanteuse.

The pink satin upholstered door of her dressing room flew open and a hard-boiled voice was heard to inquire, "OK bitch, what's the problem?"

"That worm George Wortheley!" bellowed Le Strange.

"Yeah, yeah, I know, Georgie boy's just fine when he's shelling out the dough, but God forbid he should forget his little tidbit, just for one night."

"I am not his little tidbit!"

"Well, there's no denying that 'cause little you ain't. And now that you mention it, there seems to be quite a lot more of you than I remember. What have you been doing? Eating that makeup or putting it on your face?"

Betty the Bounder, Lilly's dresser, was used to Le Strange abuse and she gave it back as hard as she got it.

"Shut the fuck up and bring me that dress!"

Betty proffered the undone garment and waited for the headliner to climb in. As Betty buttoned round the Diva's rotund bulges, she sniffed the air and asked, "Say, ain't that *Poison* I smell? Wow, forget I asked, just hand me a gas mask. Whaddja do, bathe in the junk?"

"No, I threw it against the wall."

"Lilly, you're supposed to daub perfume in intimate crevasses, not fumigate with it."

Betty knew whereof she spoke, having done time as the cosmetic and fragrance salesgirl at Filene's Basement for a large chunk of her career.

"If pest control was so easy, I'd wash the floor with that horse piss." hissed Lilly. "The worm gave it to me last week after the three hundred and fiftieth performance of *Glamour Galore.* I have tripled his investment over the last year, but do I get an invitation to his opening? Noooo. The bastard and that toothpick Rosalind are hosting the most fabulous event of the social season. What am I supposed do, stay home and knit?"

"Rosalind Wortheley is his wife, Miss Thing, what do you want from him? Marriage?"

"I want an invitation to the opening of the Essential Center Shopping Mall!" To emphasize her serious lust for that ephemeral scrap, she beat a militant tattoo upon the floor with her reinforced platform heels. These special pumps were said to have been designed after the pylons of the Tobin Bridge. When thumped so rigorously, they made a racket rather more raucous than a mere rat-a-tat-tat.

"Don't be silly, you have a performance to give, right here in the theatre."

"Listen QuasiModo, pipe down and zip up my dress. Then go down to the chorus dressing room and tell my understudy, Tallulah that she's gotta go on for me."

"But you're already in the dress, and besides, Tallulah, stinks."

"Well tell her to come up here and rub against that wall. That should take care of her B.O."

"I didn't mean she stinks. I mean she stinks, you know, she … uh … stinks."

"Listen, Betty, have you been drinking again?"

"Hey, sober and clean for 377 days and long, long nights. But it's a life second to none."

"Good because there are no more scholarships to the Betty Ford Clinic coming from me! Now as far as Tallulah's dress goes, she can wear my diamond-studded sheathe from last year's Dynasty Ball."

"Yeah, Tallulah and who else? That tent would flap in the breeze around her!"

"Well wrap her in foam rubber and stick her in it. Am I the only one with an imagination around here? For Christ sakes, fill her out with prostheses for all I care. This is her big chance! Now if you'll excuse me, I have an important phone call to make."

Mademoiselle Le Strange kicked the spangled train of her bejeweled gown with her left foot, clearing the way for the ejection of Betty, an act of force accomplished by an arm bulging with the strength of Hulk Hogan but delicately festooned with a sparkling collection of rhinestone bracelets.

*   *   *   *

Mademoiselle Le Strange sauntered over to her chintz-covered chaise where she flopped and wriggled her girdled bulk into its forgiving depths. Once settled there she could not help but notice the stained and gouged wallpaper where the vial of *Poison* had smashed.

Pangs of remorse tore at her conscience as she gazed upon the destruction her temper had wrought when she tossed the perfume bottle at the wall. Because of that olfactory projectile, the charming wallpaper whereon pretty little Minnie Mouse innocently cavorted now more closely resembled Sarajevo after the Serbian bombardment.

A tortured sob escaped La Diva when this resemblance struck her.

"What have I done? What am I about to do?"

Having thus painfully posed these rhetorical misgivings, Diva Le Strange was reminded of the slight and effrontery of being excluded from the opening-night festivities at the Essential Center Shopping Mall and she replaced her doubts with renewed bile.

"Sorry, Minnie, but tomorrow you're gonna be scraped off the wall," the Diva proclaimed ruthlessly, making a broad sweeping gesture of dismissal.

"I know it's my girlish ways that makes that worm, George Wortheley, think he can ignore me like this. It's really the little things, like Minnie Mouse wallpaper in my dressing room, that give a fluffy impression. Even after he rakes in the dough on *Glamour Galore,* he still considers me a mere defenseless damsel. I've got to be hard as nails. That's it! I'll lacquer the walls with red nail polish!"

Having solved her important decorating crisis, Lilly sighed with relief. After all, this was the cold, cruel world of business. What Lilly needed was a powerful new image—and one that would be paid for by George Wortheley. Yes, he would pay dearly for this slight.

But if truth be known, *Glamour Galore* was small patooties to a man like George Wortheley. If Diva Le Strange had been graced with a particle of introspective hesitation, she would long ago have asked the obvious question. Why would the CEO of the largest insurance company in Massachusetts invest in a transvestite review? But Diva Le Strange did not question. She just took the money and ran and ran and ran. Her show, *Glamour Galore,* was in fact enjoying one of the strongest runs in theatre history and giving no sign of letting up.

But Diva Le Strange, if nonanalytical, was no dope. She knew that George had several reasons for backing her show. His wife was the most convenient, if improbable explanation. Yes, strange as it may seem, Rosalind Wortheley was in stiff competition with her old prep-school chum, Cornelia Chilton, to be the hippest hostess of the young set. Unlike Cornelia, however, whose omnivorous social appetite ran the gambit from high society to high camp with occasional excursions into the realm of esoteric Buddhism, Rosalind's life before *Glamour Galore* lacked spice and pizzazz altogether. In fact, it would not have been inaccurate to describe the perfect young socialite's progression of days as busy, busy, busy—but also predictable, and thereby deadly dull.

Lilly figured she knew something about Rosalind, having culled a picture from the relentlessly gushing social pages. But Mademoiselle Le Strange had actual firsthand knowledge of some intimate and exotic tendencies of George's, which were in sharp contrast to his outward appearance.

George Wortheley's signature Armani suits were built to obliterate all reference to human anatomy, but they could not entirely disguise his formidable bulk.

On George, 210 pounds of steroidal musculature was more of a threat than a delight, but nonetheless impressive. His extracurricular vitamin therapy and the relentless regime of his personal power trainer, Herman Petiprick, had pumped George up to high threat while exacerbating his irascible aggression to constant snarl, an attitude that made many in the business world tremble. George also liked to brag to his locker-room buddies that he had three balls, although no one, to date, had actually beheld them.

But if they could see him as Lilly did, would they so easily concede to him such a heaping portion of success? Yes, he did look like a million bucks—his prematurely steel-gray hair brushing the collar of his custom shirts, growing so thick as to make Sampson jealous. Yes, he did have the facial features of a thirties movie star, sculpted, square, and straightforward, with a smile of supernaturally bright porcelain that actually winked with gleaming sparkle. But, was George really as straightforward, as he seemed? Lilly knew better. But what she knew best was how to give a show and how to make an entrance. If need be, she could also cause panic, pandemonium and hysteria at the drop of a hat, and toward that end she now plotted.

La Diva yanked the rhinestone earring—an ornament the size of a small chandelier—from her right ear. She impatiently jiggled this gaudy bauble, making a noise like rattling dice while she dialed memory 13 on her cell phone. Pressing that high-tech toy to her unencumbered ear, she waited for the line to be answered.

"Hello, you have reached the Radical Fringe hot line. We specialize in forced outings, disruptive demonstrations, and guerilla politics expressing the view from the far left. Radical Fringe promotes queer consciousness through the diversity of lesbians, gay men, bisexuals, transgenderists, sexual radicals and all those connected to challenging dominant relations around issues of gender and power, pleasure and community. Please leave a message after the beep."

Diva Le Strange rolled her eyes and sighed with exasperation as this propagandist rigmarole rambled on and on. But she held the line, knowing that the "Fringers" were her only hope of protection tonight. Finally, the tape beeped her cue to talk and she did not mince words.

"Paddy, you Southy hooligan, this is your mother! I know you are there, so pick up the fucking phone!"

"Oh, Hi Lilly. I was just screening the calls in case it was the FBI."

"Darling, after your last caper I am surprised the combined forces of all the armed services aren't after you."

"Oh, you mean when we kidnapped the MIT ROTC officer and then video-taped him in hooker drag soliciting new recruits on campus? Yeah, that was real effective theatre!"

"A feat worthy of the KGB. Now, enough of the alphabetic babble. Listen, before you get sent up the river for life, I have a job for you."

"Of course, Lilly. We owe you one for putting up bail for us after the Ritz meat-locker affair."

"OK, here's what I want you to do ..."

CHAPTER 2

▼

THE ESSENTIAL
INGREDIENT

An immaculately polished black Packard limousine, vintage 1938, eased its way to the front entrance of the Essential Center Shopping Mall. There, amidst the klieg-lit crowds, horn-blowing cabs, vulgarly attenuated stretch Cadillacs and general hubbub, the aristocratic automobile attained its destination with an urbane authority that left the other jockeying arrivals squeezed into second place.

From the black-lacquered vehicle, gleaming with polished chrome, hopped a chauffeur of strapping proportions. He was clad in dove-gray livery that struggled to contain his menacing brawn. His swollen chest was tightly buttoned into a double-breasted tunic of military cut, decorated proudly with a gold bar set with pink rhinestones spelling the name, "Butch." His legs were encased in black leather riding boots topped by flaring jodhpurs that accentuated his massive thighs. Butch took three long strides toward the rear passenger door of the magnificent conveyance and stood to attention, a tantalizing posture that perked the curiosity of the scrambling public. At that dramatic moment there appeared from the thickening crowd a commando unit of phantom warriors. With gymnastic flourishes a troupe of Mutant Ninjas bounced into the central area, clearing a space around the vintage Packard.

The result of this commotion was to draw all attention curbside. Included amongst the gawkers were Bonnie Bung and the Live on Five news team. She honed in on this paramilitary invasion with breathless anticipation of the scoop of the century.

Ms. Bung lunged forward, microphone outthrust, dragging her camera crew by their electronic leash. She charged ahead fearlessly in her quest to harvest the latest muck that life could disgorge.

As if on cue, an overly excited technician manning the klieg lights obliged Bonnie by focusing a blinding beam on the newscaster. The fickle public turned toward Ms. Bung and sent up a chorus of "OOOHHHs and AAAHHHs" in recognition of their TV town crier. Then, with a reverential hush reserved in a more pious era for appearances of the Pope or at least a dignitary as glamorous as Murphy Brown, the crowd shut up. Bonnie began her spiel by launching into an authoritative narrative of the events unfolding.

"Good evening, this is Bonnie Bung and the Live on Five news team reporting from the front entrance of the dazzling new Essential Center Shopping Mall. Tonight, record crowds have turned out to witness the latest addition to Boston's international market place, and there are celebrities galore. Hosting the event are Essential Insurance CEO, George Wortheley, and his dazzling wife Rosalind Cabot-Saltonstall Wortheley. Mrs. Wortheley is wearing a spectacular floor-length gown of gold tissue net over rustling magenta taffeta by Boston's own Alessandro Fortunata ..."

Bonnie's fashion bla-bla reached an audience of twenty thousand enthralled viewers. This fact was not wasted on Diva Le Strange who, although impatient to enact her own agenda, saw Bonnie's butting in as Divine Providence and a great opportunity. Lilly gave the nod to Paddy O'Punk, and instantly the Ninja Fringers went into action parting the rabble by means of ferocious acrobatic flips accompanied by a crescendoing war cry of searing terror, otherwise known as the primal scream. The resulting lacuna gave Lilly access to the limelight and Bonnie's camera crew. Diva Le Strange barreled down the fairway, making a forceful impression as the hot spots ignited her sequined gown like matter being shattered in an atomic reactor. La Diva stood beaming down at Bonnie, who was so taken aback by such splendor that for once in her career she was left sputtering and speechless.

"Darling, leave the stuttering routine to Hermione Gingold and give me that thing!"

Not waiting to be obeyed, the towering queen relieved the newscaster of her microphone and cheerfully warbled, "Hi darlings, my own dear lumps, this is your Diva, Lilly Linda Le Strange. Tonight I just had to be here to help George and Ross cut the ribbon at this fabulous new shopping venue, and let me tell you girls, it was not easy escaping all those clamoring fans over at the Club Crazy. As you all know, we are going into our second year of *Glamour Galore* and it is still the hottest ticket in town!"

By this time Bonnie had begun to recover her wits. She, of course, recognized Lilly right off and sensed a big scoop behind her unexpected arrival. The newscaster did not need to double-check the guest list to know that Lilly's name was conspicuously absent from that roster. Although diminutive in stature, Bonnie was no slouch, and she was accustomed to narrative command. Through years of experience in the ruthless combat of city streets she had developed an aggressive tendency that was nigh unto ferocious—a trait that was accentuated by her famous signature hairdo, so like a glossy helmet. Whereupon, not lacking in heaps of chutzpa, the newscaster grabbed for her mike. But Lilly knew all sorts of catty maneuvers, having been professionally launched in the brothels of Gomorrah where competition amongst the artists was, if anything, more ruthless than in Bonnie's urban byways. La Diva tossed the electric umbilical cord from her right to her left hand, casually stretching the wire well above Bonnie's reach. Simultaneously her right leg kicked the sparkling train of her dress behind her. This dismissive movement wound the cord firmly round her massive frame, leaving poor Bonnie leaping like a frustrated Pekinese snapping at a biscuit. All at once, the newscaster realized the unseemly nature of her cavorting. She came to earth with the full weight and fury of a woman foiled.

"Cut!" she screamed a blistering command.

Bonnie's rage was so awful that everyone froze in Gorgonic paralysis. All except Lilly, who, with one gargantuan limb, festooned by blazing rhinestone bracelets, flung the mike back at Bonnie and stomped off in the direction of the front door.

CHAPTER 3

▼

STORMING THE TOWER OF POWER

The entrance of Lilly Le Strange into the front hall of the Essential Center Shopping Mall was no mere pedestrian stroll. First off, she was preceded by the acrobatic antics of the Ninja Fringers who, having seen far too many Kung Fu movies, fairly flew into the foray. This troop of a dozen radical gay activists, lead by Southie's own Paddy O'Punk, did more than act up. They bounced beyond all boundaries. In their efforts to assault and reform the politically incorrect, the Fringers wore a distinctive costume. This consisted of a green plastic carapace strapped to their front and back as well as knee, elbow and wrist guards of the type made for Rollerblading. All of this protective armor was fitted over spandex body stockings of submarine green. Their identities were further obscured beneath sleek helmets fitted with tinted Plexiglas visors, thereby lending the Fringers a striking resemblance to insectile turtles.

Lilly's bodyguard of zoomorphic zealots burst through the several doors of the Essential Center with a gymnastic routine that would have made Cirque du Soleil jealous. They assumed a stance of attack, all the while emitting threatening growls. No one was arguing with them.

In swept Lilly, striding atop her platform pumps that added an unassailable advantage of stature. She further supported herself in the grand manner by use of a gold-headed staff, fully six and a half feet tall. Armed with this halberd, she swaggered to the center of the foyer and paused to survey the surroundings.

"Nice work boys, now stick close to Mama 'cause the sparks are gonna fly."

Lilly didn't give the security cops time to recover before she and her entourage headed for the escalator. Once onboard that levitating ladder, she allowed herself a moment to digest the architectural refinements.

The glass-roofed hall, constructed in a Flash Gordon gothic style, was saved from being totally tacky by virtue of its titanic scale. Being able to see through the roof glass all the way to the top of the Essential Insurance tower some eighty-four stories above made it seem even bigger.

"Very Hollywood actually. Now I wonder if this is what Ronnie had in mind for his Star Wars space station," mused Lilly.

Paddy interrupted La Diva's ruminations to report, "Security pigs closing in ahead, Lilly, what do you want us to do?"

Sure enough, a gaggle of thugs in cop drag were frantically jabbering into walkie-talkies, presumably calling for reinforcements but otherwise looking rather nervous and unconvincing.

"Don't give 'em time to fart!" barked Lilly. Her battle cry gave full license to the Fringers' overexcited aggressions, and the group charged up the escalator. At the base of the escalators, behind them the Gay Men's Chorus was assembling in the grand foyer. They had been cleverly enlisted by the management to lend credence to the advertising hype, which described the Essential Center with the shameless slogan, "The heart of Boston now has a soul." It would of course be more accurate to have said about that phallic erection, the Essential Tower and the new swollen appendages at its base, "The prick of Boston now has balls."

Allowing these quibbles of questionable taste to slide by for now, let us return to the Gay Men's Chorus. This group of talented warblers, led by the unflappable maestro, Clovis Galicurchi, were not about to be upstaged by Lilly Linda or the Radical Fringers. They were there to sing and so they did, blasting forth with that famous message of joy, "I was glad when they said unto me we will go into the house of the Lord." This stirring bit of harmonic declamation had been composed for Elizabeth II's coronation at Westminster Abbey in 1952. Here, at the Essential, that grand ditty was serendipitously appropriate for the arrival of another queen of surpassing splendor, Lilly Linda Le Strange.

The grandeur of the music combined with La Diva's charge were such a compelling spectacle that the defensive stance of the security cops faltered. Their dilemma was articulated by one of the bunch, who remarked with unguarded perplexity, "What da Fuck?!" as the rest fell back into the crowd. This left a clear sweep of 225 yards of boutique-lined shopping mall for Lilly to strut her stuff.

La Diva's pylonlike pumps slammed against the polished granite floor with a percussive authority that drew everyone's attention. Her progress was also accompanied by gasps of undetermined emotions all the way down the line. The Ninja Fringers growled and snarled in the wake of her glittering train, providing an effective rear guard until one intrepid spectator of innocent years squealed with delight, "Donatello! Raphael!"

A small and fearless boy dashed after the parade, tugging at the green shell of one of the Ninja Fringers. As luck would have it, he had hit upon Gary Gardenia, whose true nature was less ferocious than the prescribed radical doctrine. Consequently Gary, stopped to give the kid an autograph, and being an accommodating fellow, gave his fan a pat on the head for good measure.

"Are you really, really Donatello? I'm Donny too, and I wanna be just like you!"

Gary Gardenia looked hard at the boy and said, "Cool man, gimme five."

The kid matched Gary's hand jive move for move and the Fringer thought, "Well kid, maybe you will be just like me."

Launched by the rush of Donnie's adoration, Gary did hand-over-head double flips back to the group around Lilly.

"Bye-bye, Donatello! Keep the faith!"

"Startin um sorta young, ain't ya' Gary?", quipped one of his compatriots.

"Fuck off punk! It's not like that. The kid thinks I'm his hero. I didn't want to wreck it for him, and besides, it feels kinda good."

CHAPTER 4

▼

OUTING WITH A VENGEANCE

La Diva's arrival at the Grand Court of the shopping mall, in her sparkling gown and towering grandeur was reminiscent of Brunhilde's return to Valhalla. One almost expected her to bellow forth a Wagnerian blast. There she stood, flanked by her escort of ferocious Fringers, her legs planted firmly apart, one arm cocked at the elbow with her fist pressed to her hip and the other hand firmly grasping her gold-headed staff. She thumped this mighty stick upon the newly polished floor, sounding an alarm that commanded a worried silence. A gasp of horror was heard as all eyes turned on the avenging Fairy.

Previous to her arrival, the assembled dignitaries had been relentlessly schmoozing and hurling kudos back and forth, in a grand slam volley of laudatory masturbation. They had gone so far as to present awards on subjects as diverse as business and humanitarian achievement, thereby implying a parallel linking these classically opposed poles where no similarity had ever been perceived before.

On an elevated dais were placed the highest echelon of Essential executives. They were headed by George Wortheley, who stood proud and wore the gorgeous Rosalind on his arm like a combat decoration won in that ruthless engagement called high society. Ross, fully accepting her position of reflected glory, had the same magical allure as a full harvest moon. Just to gaze upon the professional beauty was to be enchanted by her radiance supreme. Tonight was the achievement of all Rosalind's social ambitions, and for the occasion she had invested in a gown that had set George back some 40,000.00 smackeroos. Around her neck hung the solitaire diamond known as Glorious Dawn, a fabled gem once belonging to Marie Antoinette. One hoped that the brilliance of Glorious Dawn did not lead Rosalind to a similar fate as that of poor Marie. But what chance did Ross stand against the diabolical fury of Diva Le Strange?

Lilly did not mince words. She had everyone in the palm of her hand and now she was going to push the button.

"George Wortheley!" she proclaimed in a fearsome bass rumble that reverberated to the soles of everyone's shoes. "You made a big blunder when you neglected to invite me to this hoedown, George, because I know a great deal more about *you* than these folks! But I'm going to remedy that, George, and show them a side of you that none can imagine, most especially that toothpick with the ice cube around her neck, Miss Rosalind. Get a load of this, bitch. Your hubby in drag!"

With a fearsome yank, La Diva unfurled a poster-sized photo that had been cleverly wrapped around her staff. This graphic image clearly depicted Mr. George Wortheley, CEO of the Essential Insurance Company, husband, father, and pillar of society, luridly portraying the whore of Babylon.

Lilly's picture of George revealed him cavorting about in red satin panties, bra, garter belt supporting sheer black stockings, and the most amazing pair of six-inch-heeled "come fuck me" pumps that Fredrick's of Hollywood had ever produced. But the most astounding aspect of the photo was *not* the scanty costume or George's wanton posture or even the luxuriously cascading blonde wig he wore. The most astounding aspect of this photo was that George looked absolutely ravishing, and the triumphant grin on his face was a revelation of pure joy.

CHAPTER 5

▼

A FALLING STAR

Cornelia and Gyles Chilton were standing in the crowd that jammed the Grand Court at the Essential Center for the opening ceremonies of the new shopping mall. The Chiltons, brother and sister, were personal guests of Rosalind Wortheley. Cornelia had gone to prep school with their hostess, who subsequently had married George, the CEO of the Essential Insurance Company. The Wortheleys were also customers of the Chiltons antique and interior design business on Newbury Street in Back Bay. George and Ross were not, however, the favorite customers of the Chiltons. But they were big spenders so the Chiltons had cultivated a tolerance for the Wortheleys, one might almost say immunity.

"Don't look now, Cornelia, but Rambo's mother-in-law has just arrived. Foolish me, I thought this party was going to be dull," said Gyles with typical nonchalance, nodding in the direction of Lilly Linda.

La Diva stood across the hall from them in a combative stance that would have been the envy of the Green Bay Packers linemen.

"Oh, my goddess!" exclaimed Cornelia, recognizing the infamous star of *Glamour Galore*, "It's Lilly, but who are those creatures with her in that impossible green spandex?"

"Well, they're not the Swiss Guard, because glorious she may be, but Pope she is not." quipped Gyles.

"Perhaps, then, they're the Swish Guard? Because she sure is one grand queen."

As if to punctuate Cornelia's conjecture, La Diva pounded her staff upon the floor, putting a stop to all further speculation. Then Lilly unfurled her banner notoriously, wherein George was revealed wearing a brief costume and looking not altogether unlike Madonna in her sleaziest drag. But George had had the good taste to allow for a certain more girlish flourish in his version of a sizzler, by sporting a magnificent mane of blonde curls.

Lilly calmly affixed her scandalous poster to a handy pillar with the aid of juicy wads of bubble gum provided by a couple of her Ninja Fringers cohorts. While the Diva was thus engaged, a swarm of reporters and camera crews hurled themselves into the Grand Court shouting: "Who? What? Where? When? How?"

Disgraced, but never upstaged, Rosalind shrieked, "George!" screaming with the tortured martyrdom of the morally defiled.

She then toppled in studied slow motion from the brink of stardom, collapsing into the abyss of chaos. Her noggin bonked against the hard stone floor with a crack that made everyone present cringe and recoil.

In the horrified silence following Rosalind's fall, George sank to his knees on the floor beside the professional beauty. He easily held her in his strong arms and shook her vigorously, an action that only resulted in disarranging his wavy gray hair. But the beauty slept, and George, now stripped of his imperial command, growled with agony and remorse, "But Rosalind, I can explain!"

CHAPTER 6

▼

ESCAPE FROM THE JAWS OF OUTRAGE

Many questions were posed in the resulting hubbub created by Lilly's exposé of George Wortheley's transvestite tendencies at the opening of the Essential Center Shopping Mall. Lilly was immediately mobbed by the press descending upon her with a ravenous glee that would have made the furies blush. But Lilly had a question of her own, "How the fuck can I get outta here before they slap on the cuffs and drag my ass off to the hoosegow?"

She had not left the answer entirely to chance. In fact, Lilly's escape had been carefully planned. But the plan had been complicated seriously when the ever-stunning Rosalind collapsed, presumably under the impact of Lilly's revelations. In her fall Ros had apparently inflicted serious damage to herself, a conclusion drawn by all who gaped upon the lifeless sprawl at the base of the speaker's platform.

In the meantime, the Ninja Fringers, having been washed aside by the tidal wave of media news sharks, were floundering in the shallow waters at the edge of the crowd. Lilly, now frantic to be reunited with her escorts, curled her thumb and forefinger around her grimacing lips and let out a piercing whistle. This blast would have summoned both Beelzebub and the Boston Red Sox, had not the Fringers leaped to her aid first. Paddy O'Punk and his bunch attacked in a flying wedge formation that divided and scattered the pack holding La Diva at bay.

By this time George had recovered from his forced outing sufficiently to channel grief and remorse into his more normal mode of rage and revenge. He barked orders furiously to his minions, but as a result of having just witnessed their boss in drag, that gaggle hovered doubtfully at the mutinous edge of insubordination. This hesitation provided precious time for La Diva's contingent to beat a hasty retreat. So, pylon pumps and all, Lilly skidaddled out of there, surrounded by her phalanx of Radical Fringers.

The moment was intensified further by the deafening roar of propeller blades, as a chopper descended into the garden court just outside the glass atrium where all was panic and pandemonium whirling about the madly dashing Diva. Lilly hit the exit doors like a raging bull, and they flew open, tripping an alarm bell that seemed to scream warnings against any who would dare pursue. The chopper swooped down, creating a cyclone that whipped Lilly's sparkling gown in a mad dance. The wind storm did not, however, dislodge her wig—proving beyond a doubt La Diva's professionalism.

George's security guards, having conquered their doubts, dashed after and snapped at the very heels of the fleeing miscreants. Thus inspired, Lilly quickened her pace. On the very brink of disaster she dove into the chopper's plastic bubble, closely followed by frantic Fringers, one of whom clung to the dangling ladder as the conveyance shot up into the night sky. Unfortunately, Paddy O'Punk and several of his gang fell into the clutches of the security guards.

The pilot, Stanley Potsdam, one hunky number in a tank top and tight jeans, had known Lilly in Nam. Stan's chopper had been blasted from the skies by the Viet Cong and he had landed in the hospital where Lilly was a nurse. Stan figured he owed Lilly his life three times over because it was she who nursed his wounds, got him off junk and into a job stateside flying for WBZN as the traffic reporter.

"Sorry I was a bit late babe but there was a big jam on Storrow Drive I had to scope out."

"That's quite all right my dearest lump. I was running behind anyway because business got a bit outta hand down there and … OH FUCK! I've broken a nail."

"Here, Lilly, have a hit of this." From a pile of squirming Fringers at the back of the chopper, Gary Gardenia passed a joint.

"Ah, darling, how perfect."

"So, where to, Lilly?" asked Stan as he deftly maneuvered his craft amongst the blazing glass towers of Boston's big business.

"I'm not sure, Stan. What are the extradition laws in Aruba?"

CHAPTER 7

▼

ISLAND PARADISE?

"Aruba? Cornelia, I thought we were going to Bermuda! If I had known we were going to Aruba, I never would have agreed to come with you."

Gyles Chilton and his sister Cornelia were partners in an antiques and interior design business on Newbury Street in Boston's Back Bay neighborhood. Of the two, Gyles was the antiquarian and apt to be tightly and studiously focused on his subject. Cornelia, the interior designer of the company, was equally absorbed in her profession, although she also enjoyed a busy social life. Cornelia was in the midst of a break up with her long-time lover, Rita Rosenstein, and therefore had no partner to share her winter vacation with, so she had invited Gyles.

"You have used me, Cornelia. I agreed to come only because I felt sorry for you when you broke up with Rita, and you would be all alone on your vacation. I did not bargain for Aruba! I have made appointments with the curator of the Bermuda National Trust to visit their historic houses on a special tour."

"Gyles, please, you're causing a scene, give the lady your ticket and passport and let's get on with it."

"But I don't want to go to Aruba ... it's ... it's ... tacky!"

"Gyles, you are such a snob! But I forgive you. You're really rather endearingly old-fashioned sometimes. Now give her your ticket."

"I am not a snob. You told me Bermuda and I have appointments to keep there. Anyway, what would I do in Aruba, go snorkeling?"

"We have historical museums in Aruba also." chimed in the helpful ticket agent trying to process Cornelia and Gyles at the counter of Boston's Logan Airport. "In the capital, Oranjestad, there is Fort Zoutman with the Willem III tower, and in Tanki Leendert there is the Rococo Plaza. And yes, Aruba has some of the best snorkeling in the Caribbean."

"Do you? The Rococo Plaza, huh?" Gyles hurled his sneering retort at the innocent clerk. "And what is the historical significance of Aruba?"

"Uh? ... well ... there is the largest desalinization plant anywhere." The young woman whose nametag read "Nadine" hesitated uncomfortably, trying to placate Gyles before concluding with the information, "and a pretty big oil refinery too ... I haven't actually been to the museums.... but...."

"Never mind him, he got up on the wrong side of the bed this morning. Here are our tickets, Nadine." Cornelia wrenched the documents from Gyles' grasp and handed them over along with both passports.

"That's all right Mrs. Chilton, flying can be tense for some people." Nadine was determined to be pleasant and professional.

"Ms Chilton actually."

"I'm sorry?"

"Ms. Chilton, I am Mr. Chilton's sister."

"Oh, I thought you mentioned your bed? And I assumed that you meant...."

"Yes, I did mention it, but that was his bed, really." Cornelia breezed along heedless of her direction.

"And he was on your side?" Nadine was beginning to feel a trifle uncomfortable.

"I'm afraid he isn't on my side quite yet and that's the problem. But I am sure the Rococo Plaza will help."

Gyles sadistically ignored the convoluted web that Cornelia had snared herself in as he searched his pockets for his Sobrani cigarette box.

"Ms. Chilton I presume?"

This formal and polite inquiry was enunciated in cultivated tones by a strikingly handsome black man dressed in an impeccable three-piece suit.

"Yes," Cornelia replied with some surprise. "I am Cornelia Chilton."

"I am Claude Voit, Minister of Tourism and Transportation for Aruba. Congratulations on winning your luxury vacation to our sunny island paradise. We have booked you for the week at the five-star Aruba Royal Palms Resort and Casino, where I know you will be comfortable.

"Oh, Minister Voit, good morning! This is my brother, Gyles Chilton."

"Pleased to meet you, Mr. Chilton," said the minister. Radiating charm and savoir-faire, he flashed a winning smile at Gyles and shook his hand, then he returned his welcoming attentions to Cornelia, bowing over her outstretched hand with courtly grace.

"Please call me Claude," he said, "and forgive my formal appearance, but I have just returned from a short business trip to London. Now I am on my way home where we can all relax. I am so happy to have found you here this morning! After Nadine has checked you in, please do me the honor of joining me for coffee in the VIP lounge, and then we will be flying off together."

"How kind of you" was Cornelia's simple reply.

Claude Voit discreetly instructed Nadine in a brief whispered conference and gracefully ended the encounter with a nod and a smile guaranteed to melt an iceberg.

"So you see, Gyles, Aruba will have a great many unexpected delights." Cornelia's enthusiasm was stoked to high boil as she argued her case.

"Yes, Aruba is a most unexpected destination," Gyles replied ruefully.

"Oh come on, I saw you give Claude the once-over."

"Cornelia, I was looking at his suit, which was impressive indeed. Saville Row, unless I miss my mark, and made to order."

"Yeah right, and the smile, the dimples, the perfect skin, and all six feet two inches of Claude Voit completely escaped you."

"No, Cornelia, it did not escape me that Claude Voit is an attractive man. He also wears a prominent gold wedding band on his left hand. What *has* escaped me is a collection of rare eighteenth-century Bermuda cedar furniture and an opportunity to study the unique and important collections of the Trust."

"So you *were* checking him out. I thought he gave you a very warm welcome."

"Cornelia, the man is married. If anything, he was trying to get a peek down that skimpy outfit you're practically slipping out of."

"He was kissing my hand, or at least bowing over it. I thought the gesture was rather sophisticated and continental."

"Yeah, well, it's a good thing Rita didn't make it on this journey after all."

"That's not really funny, and you *are* a snob. Bermuda National Trust, indeed!"

"Ouch, I guess I deserved that. I'm sorry, I know Rita meant a great deal to you, but really, Corny, how come you're always springing these things on me?"

"I don't always spring things on you, Gyles, but sometimes you need encouragement. Because, after all, you have a slight tendency to be ... well ... stuffy."

"So, now I'm stuffy, because you invited me to Bermuda knowing full well that we were never going to go there. You let me make plans and appointments, and I suppose you are not interested in rare expensive furniture even though you jam your clients' homes full of the stuff."

"As an interior designer, yes I sell furniture. But I have no intention of obsessing about it on my vacation," Cornelia snapped at Gyles.

"Would you two please shut up and get on that plane."

"Val!" Gyles and Cornelia exclaimed in unison. A tall and lean young man stood before them, his eyes half hidden behind a heavy shock of blonde hair. He rested his weight on one leg, and on the opposite protruding hip he held flowers, candy and magazines.

"Here, take this junk outta my hands and kiss me quickly." Val handed over the loot, which included bouquets from Winston's Flowers for each sibling, two boxes of Godiva chocolates, a *Casa Vogue* for Cornelia and the latest Sotheby's auction catalogue for Gyles. Once unencumbered, Val took Gyles' cheeks in his large hands and voluptuously kissed his lover directly on the lips. Then he bent over Cornelia and chastely gave her pecks on both cheeks. "Now get going and cut out the bickering!" he ordered, smacking both their asses with his broad open hands.

"Val, you knew all along," accused Gyles.

"Ms. Chilton, Mr. Chilton, Minister Voit is waiting in the VIP lounge, if you would please follow me. I have your tickets and passports here, as well as your carry-on luggage." The ever-efficient Nadine stood to attention, bags in hand, waiting for the two travelers to follow.

Val shoved them off, waving cheerfully, and he blew Gyles an extra kiss.

CHAPTER 8

▼

DROPPING IN UNEXPECTEDLY

Gyles arranged himself on a chaise longue by the pool of the Aruba Royal Palms Hotel.

His electric-blue Speedo stretched tightly around his hips, well below his tucked navel. The spandex swelled substantially over his crotch, and just above the swimsuit a wedge of silken black hair climbed the golden skin of his rippling abs. His complete lack of winter pallor was the successful result of a Christmas present from his lover, Val, who had given him a subscription to the tanning booth at the Metropolitan Gym. Gyles had spread a thick terry-cloth towel over the woven plastic of his chaise, and from this comfortable vantage point he was checking out the action around the patio. Over his eyes he wore wrap-around dark glasses with iridescent blue lenses.

Surrounding the pool was a tropical paradise, complete with royal palms and draping flower curtains of orange and scarlet bougainvillea vines. Macaws with blue and yellow feathers perched in cages of scrolling ironwork that were tucked between giant-leafed philodendrons. Several splashing waterfalls, descending from elaborate rockery grottos were incorporated into the design. Gardenia blossoms floated in the crystal-clear waters of the swimming pool, where some guests were seated on submerged stools at the waterside bar. These determined vacationers had sidled up and were imbibing exotic rum concoctions, served in coconuts and garnished with tiny paper umbrellas, sliced fruit, and long, bending straws.

"I can see you've made yourself quite at home, Gyles. Here is your Sotheby's catalogue—you left it in the room." Cornelia breezed up to him like a soothing tropical wind. She was wearing a Balinese sarong tied around her hips with a transparent silk blouse provocatively covering her tiny bikini top.

"Oh, thanks. But I left it behind on purpose, I thought I would take a snooze in the sun. However, I am just as glad you brought the thing down, because now I can hide behind it. The cruise director was just over here soliciting my participation in a limbo contest. But if I did the limbo in this outfit I would probably be arrested for indecent exposure."

"What outfit?"

"I know. That's just what I mean. Val wants to go on a gay cruise to Costa Rica next year, so he has bought all these swimsuits from the Ah Men Catalogue for us to try out, and if you can believe it, this is one of the more conservative numbers. He has a leopard skin thong that is positively miniscule, and although it is completely outrageous, he, of course, looks so hot in it he might burst into flame."

"That's an accurate description of Val, whatever he's wearing."

"Yeah, and that tends to make me rather uneasy."

"Why on earth? If you've got it, flaunt it. What would you have him do—dress like a preppy?"

"No, I guess not."

"Meaning of course, yes, you would. Well, thank the goddess, Val never even heard of Brooks Brothers and natty bow ties."

"Actually, he has heard of Brooks Brothers. In fact, he used to turn tricks from that very block."

"What do you mean, turn tricks?"

"Just that, after the bars would close, he would hustle older men who would circle the block in their cars looking for rough trade."

"Oh, Gyles, I see what you mean, best not to encourage that kind of thing."

"Strangely enough, that is one thing I don't worry about anymore. Now that he is partners with Lucy Ann at the guest house, he hardly has time to breathe. He loves the work there and the guests love him. It seems that his success with 'the kindness of strangers' was due in large part to his genuine interest in most everybody. He is a good listener and he goes out of his way to help people. He's so proud of the old house and so glad to be a part of what he calls a respectable life. Now I am more jealous of his work than any potential rival. But still, I can't help myself from feeling ... well ... uneasy ... sometimes."

"Maybe you're right then, and Val could use a slightly more toned-down look. Since Lucy Ann and he are so successful at the guest house now, he can afford to go shopping. But I think Saks or Neiman Marcus would be more appropriate than Brooks Brothers. No, I've got it—when we get back, I'll take him around to Louie's and we'll find him a nice Italian suit, not too conservative, and he can wear it with a black cashmere sweater."

"Yeah, well forget it, because I bought him a pair of gabardine trousers for Christmas, nothing very provocative at all, but when he slid into them there was suddenly a new meaning to the term 'bubble butt.' No, Val is hopelessly sexy and I've decided to let him be."

Cornelia had deposited her beach bag on the tiled patio by Gyles, and carefully calculating the angle of the sun, she positioned her chaise to maximum absorptive advantage. She shed her sarong and blouse, leaving her pink bikini blinking brightly against pale skin. Then, digging in her bag she found a new tube of Bain de Soleil with which she slathered herself liberally. During this operation Cornelia resumed her train of thought.

"Now that Lilly is gone and *Glamour Galore* had to close, Val must at least have his nights free."

"You're right there, and I couldn't be more grateful. We finally have a life together, although he still keeps his stuff at his room in the guest house, and I guess that's OK, although I wish he would move in with me. But he is probably right, I would only smother him. I know you won't believe this, but I actually miss the Club Crazy and all those insane people. I was even warming up to Lilly, because she really seems to care for Val. He told me that she was the one who dragged him off the streets and shoved him into her shows as a dancer, just so he would have some income other than hustling. She encourages him, too, although I think she has her doubts about the guest house—and me, for that matter. In her rough way, Lilly *is* a kind of role model for him, because she's always working. Apparently, she's been on his case for years about safe sex, jamming his pockets full of condoms and these tiny bottles of mouthwash mixed with peroxide. She was the one who introduced him to the Fenway Health Clinic and insisted he be tested regularly."

Gyles lay back, eyes closed behind his dark glasses. As he relaxed in the sun and let the heat of Aruba soak into his body, he was more thinking aloud than talking with Cornelia.

Cornelia was a little surprised at the freedom of his revelations, and she never thought she would hear Gyles approve of Lilly Linda Le Strange. But then, the whole relationship between Gyles and Val was so volatile and unlikely, Cornelia knew at least part of the problem lay clearly in her brother's court.

Gyles' previous lover, John Trumbull, hovered in the periphery of his life, casting a long shadow into the present, where he could only return as a sad memory. John had died of AIDS only a year and a half ago. Cornelia suspected Gyles had never told Val. She knew this unmourned loss was a heavy weight that held down a mounting pressure inside him. Two proud men, standing together but alone, not knowing how to love each other.

These melancholy thoughts got Cornelia thinking about her own loneliness after her lengthy break up with Rita. Suddenly, a wave of loss tore into her womb like the cold empty spaces beyond the stars. Rita had been her anchor, her foundation. Now she was cast adrift … in….

"Aruba! I'm in Aruba." Cornelia shuttered and shouted out, forcing herself into the present.

"I can hardly believe it myself. How about a drink?"

So saying, Gyles sprang to his feet, tossed his dark glasses onto the chaise behind him and dove into the pool, all in one smooth movement. Almost immediately his sleek shining body shot back out of the turquoise water in a fountain spray of delight before the arch of his taut muscles slipped back again into the water. With several powerful strokes he arrived at the pool bar and perched on one of the submerged stools. Watching this display of male bravado, Cornelia was amused to see Gyles fish one of the floating gardenias out of the water and tuck it behind his ear.

"Well, I guess the boy's havin' a good time in spite of himself," murmured Cornelia as she reached for her tube of Bain de Soleil.

Just at that moment, a commotion was heard from the beach beyond the dense jungle barrier surrounding the pool area. Screams and shouts grew in volume and could be heard above the surf breaking on the sand and the artificial cascades splashing into the pool. Small children came running, squealing in high-pitched decibels. A deep, threatening roar from an unseen, demonic engine came rushing from nowhere, echoing against the concrete of the surrounding high-rise hotel. Above this terrifying bass rumble, from over the encircling royal palms—seemingly from the hot blue sky itself—came a yodeling Tarzan war cry, vacillating between several octaves. Everyone around the pool cringed and dove for cover, the elderly desperately cowering beneath raised arms and young couples clinging to each other as if for the last time.

A meteoric explosion hit the pool with the force of planets colliding. The resulting tsunami wave, traveling at the speed of light, deluged the entire surrounding pleasure garden. In an instant, everyone and everything was drenched. Two of the iron macaw cages were tossed against the rockeries and the panicked birds flew the coop, screaming and flapping in a flash of scarlet, blue and yellow. One tipsy, Mai Taied matron was miraculously saved from drowning by sliding fanny first into the surprised arms of the poolside bartender.

Then silence hung like a pall over the traumatized victims, as all eyes tried to focus on the emerging figure now bobbing on the considerable waves that agitated the waters of the diminished swimming pool.

"OOOOWWWWW ————WWWWEEEE!!! WHAT A FUCKIN' RUSH THAT WAS!!!!!!

Cornelia blinked away the river of water pouring from her limp hair.

"Lilly? Lilly Linda La Strange?" She asked incredulously.

Gyles who had withstood the flood by wrapping his arms around the trunk of a royal palm, miraculously still held his two Grand Caribbean rum punches in both determined fists.

"Why am I not surprised?" he inquired of no one in particular.

∗   ∗   ∗   ∗

Lilly—and of course it *was* Lilly, albeit a tad bit rumpled and more than slightly disheveled—was hauling herself out of the pool in a forceful manner reminiscent of Godzilla emerging from the primordial ooze. Gyles could not help but stare. Once fully grounded, Madame Le Strange, that infamous headliner, shook herself like a pooch, spraying yet more water in all directions. She then assumed a posture full of dignity, standing six feet four inches in her bare feet. La Diva demurely straightened the ruffled skirt of her Esther Williams one-piece swimsuit, which was gaily printed with schnauzers imbibing cocktails from stemmed glasses. Her massive upper body was squeezed into the flounced bodice, and her head was bound in a bathing cap that was affixed all over with wriggling rubber daisies. Unbuckling the chin strap of this latex bouquet and unpeeling its prophylactic membrane from about her head, she revealed an astonishing cascade of golden curls. These fell in luxuriant convolutions over broad, one might even say mammoth, shoulders. With conspicuous nonchalance, Lilly raked her long fingers through the silken tresses that fell heavily, snagging on the dark, hairy stubble that like a scythed cornfield, textured the upper part of her chest. Catching sight of her two Boston chums, one of whom seemed to be proffering exotic libations, Lilly bellowed forth in a full baritone, "darling lumps! Too Divine! I'd love a cocktail, how thoughtful of you."

Having delivered this simple but enthusiastic hello, she quickly quaffed the contents of both coconuts and tossed them over her shoulder.

CHAPTER 9

▼

DISHING WITH THE DIVA

"Cornelia, what is your brother not wearing?" Lilly stood on the balcony of the Sunset Suite, leering down at Gyles, who was standing by the pool.

"I can see why Vallisha is so completely swept off his feet! I mean, who would have guessed that underneath all those three-piece suits there lurked the hunk of the century?"

"Apparently, Val gave Gyles the Speedo. It does fit him well, don't you think?"

"A lot more than those monkey suits he's been hiding in. I mean, what's up with him anyway? I usta think he was ... you know.... kinda stuck up, but lately he's thawed out a bit, and now I can see he has really got quite a lotta potential, if not pure talent. By the way, have you got a microwave here? My stash got drenched in the splashdown." Lilly held out a soggy collection of joints in the palm of her hand.

"Lilly, you are a savior! Let me relieve you of those little darlings and yes, I am happy to report that the Sunset Suite comes equipped with *almost* everything, and now *you* have made that complete." Cornelia crossed the commodious living room to the galley kitchen tucked into the paneling of the wall, where she zapped the joints for a flash to dry them out. "You'll find extra towels in the guest bathroom down the hall to your right, so help yourself."

"Guest bathroom? What is this joint, the Taj Mahal?" Lilly continued to chat while searching for the bathroom.

"Listen, you little scamp, how did you manage all this?" The Diva reappeared, her head swathed in a terry-cloth turban that practically scraped the ceiling. She had donned one of the hotel bathrobes which, on Lilly, barely covered the essentials.

"You won't believe it, but I won the Firemen's Ball."

"Gonads? Yuck. I thought you were a high-class dyke."

"Not balls, silly, ball, singular, as in dance."

Oh, of course, so who did you do at the Firemen's Ball to win the keys to the royal suite?"

Lilly crossed the room and flopped down into the recesses of the sectional sofa, where she plucked the now smoldering reefer from Cornelia's hand. Cornelia was nestled into the other corner of the sofa, facing her friend. She was surprised to spy telltale signs of neglect sprouting from several places on the usually immaculately peeled Diva. Fascinated by this unexpected fuzz emerging from chin, chest, forearm and thigh, Cornelia began to appreciate the lengths to which Lilly went to accomplish her illusions.

"Lilly, you could make a nun's consecration sound lewd. I didn't do anything or anybody at the Firemen's Ball except buy a raffle ticket."

"That reminds me, what's the difference between a nun in a bathtub and a whore in a bathtub?"

"The nun has hope in her soul …" Cornelia delivered the answer with condescending dead pan.

"So you've heard that one. What about this: there's a grasshopper who goes in a bar.…"

"Lilly! What on earth were you doing being flung from a catapult into the pool at the Royal Palms Hotel? And for that matter, how and when did you even get to this island paradise?"

"You don't need to bellow, I am not deaf you know—gimme that joint and let me get my bearings here," Lilly took a big hit off the reefer. "First off, I was not flung from a catapult. Really, some of us have managed to maintain a modicum of dignity."

"You could have fooled me.…"

"Are you going to interrupt or am I going to talk?"

"OK. OK, but try to keep the dignity to a minimum."

"As I was saying, Stan and I were out for a test run in the paraglider—well, actually he was in the speedboat and I was on the sky sail—you see, we are practicing for my comeback in my new show, *Naughty Astronautess*."

"Stan? Stan who?"

"Stanley Potsdam."

"You know Stanley Potsdam, the Eye in the Sky from WBZN in Boston?"

"Sure, I know Stan. We go way back to Nam together."

"Lilly, you were in Vietnam?"

"I thought you wanted to know what I was doing in the pool."

"To hell with the pool, what were you doing in Vietnam? Entertaining the troops?"

"No, unfortunately not, I was patching up the poor slobs as they were blown off the battlefield in pieces. Stan was one of the lucky ones—there was enough left of him that we could actually sew him back together. But his brain was fried from junk. That was the real killer in Nam. That goddamed junky flew his fucking chopper through hell and back until one day they nailed him, so I knew he had some kind of special something deep inside him. But it took six months to get him clean. That was the *real* miracle! And then it was a good while longer before he could walk again."

"But Lilly, are you a doctor?"

"No, sweet pea, nothing that important, just a nurse. So anyway, I've always wanted to go to the moon, and Stan thought that since we're here in Aruba 'till the heat blows over back in Boston, I may as well go for it. He has an old Marine buddy with the local paragliding business—you should try it, Cornelia, it is sooo COOL!"

"Heights are really not my thing. Say, how about a drink?"

"Darling!"

Cornelia tightened her sarong as she peeled herself off the couch and headed for the bar to do the honors.

"Tell me about *Naughty Astronautess,*" she said as she shook a cocktail shaker filled with ice, rum and tropical juice to a calypso rhythm.

"I play the part of the first astronautess. I wanna be shot out of a cannon, across the theater. That's why I was practicing my free-fall from the paraglider into the pool. I'm gonna get Wally St. John to design me the most fabulous silver lamé space suit and I'll wear a platinum blonde wig, of course. I am not sure what the plot will be, but I *am* sure it will be one hell of an entrance. Say, this is one swell little drinky-poo, how 'bout you topping Mama off ... [Guzzle-Guzzle-Guzzle] ... Thanks, Doll face."

"So that's it?"

"Well, yes, that's it so far, I'll probably need a good acid trip to really come up with the rest of the story, but I don't want to jeopardize Stan's sobriety. We are living practically on top of each other down here, so to speak. I mean we're not an item, noooo … Stan has his fine points but he is not exactly my type, actually, not even close."

Although brave, Cornelia was not sufficiently foolish to speculate on what Lilly's type might actually be.

"When did you get here?" she asked instead.

"We've been here since that night at the Essential Center opening when I burnt all my bridges big time. I think that was about a month ago, now. What a scene it all was, I had no idea the wife would take it so bad. I hope she snaps out of it. After all, George was the one I was after, not the beautiful Rosalind, she just kinda got in the way."

"She's in serious condition."

"Yeah, I've been following the story in all the papers, and I must say that it is perfectly infuriating how sensational she looks in her glass coffin."

"That's not a coffin Lilly, it's a life support bubble, apparently the latest in medical developments. It was designed specifically for coma patients."

"What about that outfit she's wearing? That wasn't designed by no hospital doctor!"

"I know, I know, it's a bit much but Alessandro Fortunata was … is! Rosalind's favorite Boston designer. She has a standing order with him for a new ensemble each week, so he continues to churn out the clothes. He described last week's creation as a cross between Botticelli's "Madonna and Child" as seen at the Gardner Museum and Julie Andrews as Sister Maria as seen in *The Sound of Music*."

"Who knew the woman would look so completely ravishing wrapped in a starched tablecloth, even if it is the exact pink shade of cupid's bottom. I'll tell you one thing, George Wortheley doesn't deserve her. By the by, sweet pea, thanks awfully for whisking me up here to dry out and smoothing over all that flap with the security guards down by the pool. I seem to have upset a few of the guests. But, how come you have such pull around here?"

"We are the guests of Claude Voit, the Minister of Tourism and Transportation for Aruba, and Lilly you should see this man. He is nothing short of a god. I thought Gyles might be interested, but he says Claude is straight, more's the pity. Anyway, Minister Voit is courting the U.S. National Fire-fighter's convention for next winter, which apparently has a huge constituency, although one wonders who squirts the hoses back at home when the brotherhood goes on convention."

Lilly scratched her head, puzzling over Cornelia's narrative digressions.

"So, you see, Claude contributed this VIP Aruba getaway to the raffle at the Boston Firemen's Ball, because the chairman of the national convention is our own Chief O'Malley. I am a member of the Firemen's Ball committee that raises money for widows and children of the firemen, and by the way, I got involved in that venture because Rosalind Wortheley asked me—we went to Dana Hall together. Rosalind is the chairwoman for the committee because of the obvious connection between fires and insurance, which as you know is George's shtick. The committee members are expected to support the event, and so naturally I bought a bunch of raffle tickets and, Bingo! I won. Did you follow all of that? No? Well here, finish up this joint and it will all become clear. When the security guards downstairs by the pool realized I knew you, and they saw no one was actually hurt they must have been just as happy that we cleared out when we did."

"You know girl, you have a way with stories. Maybe you could help me with *Naughty Astronautess*."

"Oh, I don't know, Lilly. I may have a certain flair for words. Gyles calls it my Gracie Allen routine, and whereas I do love Gracie, I'm not really sure he means it as a compliment. No, your shows are true genius, I couldn't hope to even hold a candle to your creations. After all, who else would have come up with that idea of the dancing rhinoceros in the third act of *Glamour Galore?*

"Thank you, darling little lump, but I stole that bit directly from *Fantasia*, where the hippos are ballerinas on pointe shoes."

"Yeah, but in *Fantasia* they don't pole-vault off the stage on ten-foot-long shlongs!"

"Well, you know how boys love to play with their dicks, it just seemed natural."

No, Lilly, that's one thing I know nothing about and, if you don't mind, I'd rather stay blissfully ignorant on the subject. Now finish up your drink and let's go back to the pool. I feel in need of a dunk."

"You're on, doll face. I've gotta find Stan before he calls out the Coast Guard to search the reefs for my remains."

CHAPTER 10

▼

A POWER VISIT

Rosalind Wortheley lay quiet and still beneath her Plexiglas dome. This isolating apparatus allowed for life support systems without the use of intrusive and potentially scarring technologies or other invasive measures.

When the report of Rosalind's "fall from grace" at the opening of the Essential Center Mall had reached her devoted Mummy, Mrs. Adams Cabot Lowell Untermeyer—at the time enduring the rigors of a complete makeover at Rancho Miraculoso—the grand dame had screamed with apprehension, "Not the face!" Mrs. A.C.L.U. had always encouraged a vacant passivity in her daughter, therefore she was not unduly concerned with a trifle such as a coma. She was greatly relieved by the favorable reports that, no, "Not the face"—or, more plainly: no, the face was not damaged.

The most important consideration of Rosalind's condition, as defined by her dear mother, was to preserve, at all costs, her daughter's flawless beauty. Mrs. A.C.L.U. knew whereof she spoke when prioritizing the wealth management of such a valuable asset. After all, it had taken generations of selective breeding and a great deal of cash to produce and train a specimen as stunning as Rosalind. Mummy knew that the all-too-ephemeral quality of dazzling loveliness had to last through several husbands if Rosalind were to afford houses in Wellesley, Wiano, Lyford Cay, Mount Desert Island, etc., not to mention the prerequisite income to furnish such costly abodes.

From the confines of her suite at Miraculoso, Mrs. A.C.L.U. had commandeered a video conference call, and what a chilling spectacle that was to the huddle of specialists attending her daughter.

"Don't touch a hair on her head!" she commanded.

The medical team was at first baffled by this pronouncement until Miss Pring, the personal assistant to Mrs. A.C.L.U. explained.

"Mrs. Adams Cabot Lowell Untermeyer means for you to take extra special care to preserve and protect her daughter's, Mrs. George Wortheley's, appearance."

Dr. Alphonse Bucherelli, plastic surgeon of the team, scrutinized the patient barely disguising his glee. However, even he, with his seemingly endless resources of imagination, had to admit that there was no room for improvement in Rosalind's case. With a sigh of resignation and regret, he withdrew his active participation, while doubling his consulting fees.

*   *   *   *

The husband of the moment, George Wortheley was one hour and fifteen minutes late for his appointed meeting with Dr. Laskar Cobb at Brigham and Women's Hospital in Boston's medical district. This captain of industry, or at least insurance, barreled out of the oversized hospital elevator, followed by a tight mass of suited assistants, who as a group were variously preoccupied with cell phones, digital recorders, palm pilots, black berries and the like. This squad of robotic linemen formed a flying wedge slicing through the busy corridor heading directly for the reception desk of the private suites at the famed hospital. George was at the apex of the formation. Charging forward without pause, he barked aggressively at the receptionist behind the counter.

"George Wortheley to see Dr. Cobb."

Lillian Oppenheimer, the current victim of George's perpetual assault on humanity, took pardonable delight when she replied, "I *am* sorry, Mr. Wortheley, but Dr. Cobb left the ward an hour ago."

"Then get him back here, and if he keeps me waiting tell him to look for another sucker to pay for his new laboratory. In the meantime I'm going in to see my wife, although God knows why. I suppose it will kill five minutes while I wait for Cobb."

So saying, he stormed through the door of Rosalind's private suite without giving Miss Oppenheimer time to respond in any manner. The gaggle of assistants clogged the corridor outside Rosalind Wortheley's suite, cooling their collective heels.

"OK Rosalind, enough of this already! For Christ sakes, snap out of it!" George addressed the Plexiglas dome. "Listen, the kids are hollering for you day and night, although God knows why since I'm not sure you even know their names."

George was a firm believer in tough management techniques, and he laid it on thick when he thought it was necessary. Here Rosalind had been languishing in her coma for two months already, without any sign of returning to her role as professional beauty and society hostess, not to mention mother of two "darling pets," as Rosalind had been wont to gush when addressing Rosalind-Jane and George, Jr. Since his wife was currently incapable of response, George used his advantage to get his digs in.

"And what am I supposed to do with your mother? She came out of seclusion from Rancho Miraculoso a month ago, and all I get is," 'How do I look?'

"And then that faggot Alessandro Fortunata had the balls to call me at the office sniveling about *his* sleeping beauty and all that crap, in the meantime sending me the most outrageous bill for those rags you're wearing! When I told you to spend major money like the other wives, the shroud of Turin was not in the deal. You're supposed to be out there with me, looking good, smiling, shaking the hands and working the room. You have a role to play here, and I expect some return on my investment, you know. So, you've had your little snooze, now it's time to wake up and get your ass to the party."

Bereft of his prize possession, the ideal trophy wife, George was pissed. His initial chagrin and panic resulting from the debacle created by Lilly Linda, self-cast as the bad fairy at Sleeping Beauty's christening, had all but been forgotten. But whereas Rosalind was still literally reeling from the impact of that revelation, George had long since dismissed it as yesterday's news. Aided and abetted by an army of corporate bullies, he had worked overtime to suppress the truth of the matter: fiction had usurped reality, and George emerged smelling like a rose.

The great man was now ready to get on with it and was chomping at the bit. He had lost all patience with Rosalind, something he never really had to begin with.

CHAPTER 11

▼

AFTER-DINNER CONVERSATION

After a peaceful dinner at the Kontiki Cave restaurant, Cornelia and Gyles had retired to comfortable deck chairs on the broad Loggia that encircled the lobby of the Royal Palms Hotel. This spacious corridor with its tall beamed ceilings and progression of lofty arches was hung with white canvas curtains that rippled gently in the evening breezes wafting in from the now dark waters of the surrounding ocean. A series of terraces planted with lush tropical foliage led down to the water gardens surrounding the pool. This lavish playpen was protected by a phalanx of royal palms that separated the hotel from an immaculate stretch of sandy beach. As the bending fronds tossed and rustled in the trade winds, an enticing whiff of jasmine mingled with the soft evening air.

"You know, Stan, this joint ain't half bad" was the remark heard from the adjoining deck chairs.

"I thought you told me Lilly was staying in a grass shack on the beach, Cornelia?" Gyles whispered rather too loudly.

"That's what she told me. How do you know it's her, now?"

"Come on, dearest, who else has those distinctively dulcet tones, not to mention the truck driver lingo?"

"I guess it's a smaller island than we thought. But don't complain, she's a one-woman traveling entertainment committee, and besides, I'm curious to meet Stan."

"Stan who?"

"Tiny LUMP! Is that *you* lurking in the shadows?"

Lilly appeared, larger than life, looming over Cornelia and Gyles. She wore lemon-yellow toreador pants that revealed every nuance of her sturdy gams. Shoved onto her bare feet were pink Plexiglas mules, through which could be glimpsed plump digits so like jumbo shrimp that one wondered whether the red tips were the result of a pedicure or cocktail sauce. Her blouse was a Hawaiian shirt printed with coconut palms that was tied tight beneath her ample bosom. The exposed midriff revealed a surprisingly defined musculature, decorated with a decal tattoo of a sinking pirate ship placed just above her navel.

"Is that brother of yours here clogging up the arteries? Yes, there he is, the closet hunk, darling, shove over. Mama wants to snuggle in. Stan, be a sweet thing and haul one adose nifty little loungers over here, and you may as well get one for yourself."

"Thanks for the invite, babe but now youse got some company, I'm headed for the casino. Hey, I'm Stan Potsdam. You must be the swells from Bean Town her majesty's been jawing about, pleased to meetcha."

Stan proffered a mighty mitt for Gyles to shake and waved a smart salute in Cornelia's direction.

"Aw, Stan, don't be so anti social. You can at least stick around for a minute. Cornelia is a fan of yours and wants to say hi."

No can do now, babe. Maybe tomorrow we'll go skiing. Did youse see Le Strange flying today? Jeez the broad's a natural. But right now I got a date with Lady Luck, so sayonara, folks."

"OK, you big lug. But leave us the dope." Stan tossed a slim cigarette case in Lilly's direction and beat a hasty retreat.

"Sorry about Stan, he's a little jittery in company. He likes to keep busy. Nothing personal. So, Gyles, I hear you scored big time with your Frothingham secrétaire at Skinner's last week." Lilly posed her considerable girth and brawn with graceful poise as she casually fired up a joint and peered at Gyles.

"Lilly! You can't smoke dope here! And how the hell did you know about the Frothingham secrétaire anyhow?" Gyles was always coming unhinged in front of Lilly, much to his discomfort, which was of course her intended strategy.

"Sorry, darling, I forgot myself for a moment," a bald-faced lie if ever there was one, but for Lilly there was no shame. "Quick, have a hit and then we'll snuff it."

Cornelia eagerly obeyed and passed the J to Gyles, who, with resigned exasperation, took a deep hit then pinched the end with wet fingers and handed the remainder back to Lilly.

"Now put that away and explain yourself."

"Explain what? That an unemployed drag queen can know something more about life than nail polish and lipstick?" This line was delivered with trembling indignation.

"I can see this is going to be like pulling teeth, but, yes, that rather sums up my train of thought."

"It's like this—my broker belongs to the club Le Pli at the Heritage Building and his trainer is the boyfriend of the curator of American furniture at Skinner's." Lilly blinked limpid eyes at Gyles in a manner intended to convey allure and beguilement, but this spasm more closely resembled a nervous tic.

"Who is your broker, Lilly?" asked Cornelia simply.

"Now wait a minute!" snapped Gyles, "who is your broker? Indeed!"

"What's the problem, chump? A drag queen can't have a stockbroker, either? That privilege is only reserved for snooty-patooty Wasps maybe? Well, sweetheart, lemme tell you, there ain't nothing sacred about the stock market, and while we're on that subject, I'll have you know that I lost five thousand smakeroos on Chichester & Chilton Bank stocks last month, and that's the last time I'll ever waste my money on your lousy family."

Gyles burst out laughing in spite of himself and kept at it for some time. When finally he could control himself, he plucked the dead joint out of Lilly's fingers and refired it with his Cartier lighter. Then taking a deep drag he shook his head and passed the reefer back to Madame Le Strange.

"Lilly, you constantly amaze me. I nearly lost all the funding reserved for my purchase of the Frothingham Secrétaire because of that wrinkle in the blasted market, and what a complete disaster that would have been!"

"Gyles, I am glad we are all seeing eye to eye at the moment," Cornelia interjected, "but do you think that's wise? If you want to smoke a joint, why don't we all go on up to the Sunset suite and relax in private?"

"No, little sister, let's join big Stan in the casino. I think Lilly is absolutely right, I need to loosen up a bit."

"OK, big shot, glad you're seeing the light now, but let's not get thrown in the slammer just yet." So saying, Lilly relieved Gyles of the remains of the contraband, tucked it in her stash and put that in her beaded purse. She proffered a limp wrist and waited to be plucked from her deck chair.

CHAPTER 12

▼

SPOOKS IN THE CASINO

The three friends drifted toward the Jungle Casino where Lilly, commanding the middle ground, teetered slightly on her mules and Gyles bravely offered her a steadying arm. The lobby entrance was a half story above the casino floor, affording an overall view of the vast gambling den, where all the supporting columns were swathed in fantasy versions of tropical trees.

"This looks like a cross between Brighton Pavilion and the temple of Karnak." observed Cornelia.

In the canopy of the spreading branches radiating from these "trees," there were perched oversized sculptures attempting to impersonate toucans and macaws, thereby supporting the jungle theme. But the real attraction was the infinite collection of gaming tables stretching as far as the eye could see, where everything from craps to blackjack was being offered. Here and there were also roulette wheels intended to add some class to the proceedings. Each table was presided over by a male or female croupier. They all achieved sexual neutrality with their identical black tuxedo trousers and pleated white shirts with black satin bow ties. Their collective demeanor was as lively as lobotomized zombies, but their shifty eyes calculated loss in an instant as well as the occasional but temporary win. Otherwise, the croupiers efficiently raked piles of colorful chips back and forth across the green baize in response to the throw of the dice, spin of the wheel or deal of the cards.

To further tempt that elite populace known as the High Rollers to indulge in delusions of suspended belief, otherwise called games of chance, there was a special raised alcove. This dais was furnished with thronelike chairs surrounding a highly polished mahogany table that stood on a thick carpet that was woven with a vaguely Persian design. These regal accommodations were cordoned off by a marble balustrade, behind which baccarat was the vice intended to consume fortunes. But this evening, the High Rollers were conspicuously absent, leaving plenty of room for the rabble who were enthralled by the slot machines blasting forth a cacophonous jangle of noise that could over stimulate a corpse, if need be.

On the right side of the casino stretched a cocktail bar, lavishly constructed of tropical woods, marble and polished brass. The bar-back bleachers held an encyclopedic collection of booze bottles that included every brand known to civilized man, and it was rumored that there might even be a semi narcotic voodoo potion, if you knew what to ask for and were prepared to pay for it.

Above the bar was an enormous, ersatz rendition of Henri Rousseau's famous painting of the gypsy in the jungle, called *The Dream*, depicting a dark-skinned nude woman stiffly perched on a Victorian love seat that is nestled in tropical foliage. In any other circumstances this bit of whimsy would have been a definite eye-catcher, but in the Jungle Casino, all eyes were riveted to the game at hand no matter how slight.

Lilly, Cornelia and Gyles stood at the top of the stairs musing over the comedy below until, by unanimous clairvoyance, they realized their need for cocktails to clear their scrambled minds. They had temporarily forgotten why they were in the Jungle Casino in the first place. This was indubitably the result of Lilly's killer dope; so to the bar they repaired for some restorative libations.

"There's Stanley now, sitting at the blackjack table." Lilly casually pointed to the pilot in the crowd.

"He seems to have attracted quite a crowd of his own, Lilly, but that's not the blackjack table. It's got to be craps he's playing. Can't you see him throwing the dice?" Cornelia asked.

"Darling, it could as easily be Skin the Cat for all I know about gambling. After that last J, I'm lucky to remember my own name. As a matter of fact, I had forgotten all about Stan until just now, when I saw him over there."

"You too? I thought I was loosing my mind to tropical torpor."

"I don't know nothin' 'bout torpor, doll-face, tropical or any other brand, but the weed was Maui Wowie."

"Well, that explains it all then."

"Explains what?" asked Gyles, handing them each an overfull sidecar cocktail in a stemmed glass. This may have been an admirable feat of balancing on Gyles, behalf, but more of a challenge than a gift for Cornelia and Lilly.

"Oh, nothing, Lilly has just picked out Stan, over there at the craps table."

"Oh, yeah, that's why we're here, I almost forgot. I've got to fetch my drink from the bar."

As Gyles returned to the bar, Lilly and Cornelia cast knowing glances at each other and Cornelia repeated the name "Maui Wowie." Then, grabbing at the proverbial straw, this time conveniently provided by the conscientious bartender, they greedily sipped their drinks.

"OK, here I am. Now, what did you say about Stan?"

"That he has attracted an adoring public, which must indicate his success in the realms of chance."

"If that's supposed to bait me into disbelief and surprise at your grammatical eloquence, I am not biting. I have already been sufficiently lectured on the equal abilities of drag queens, so I get the picture. How do you like the sidecars?"

"No need to get testy, your hunkiness. The drinks are *divine,* thanks a bunch!"

"Talking about pictures, get a load of the gypsy in the jungle, either I'm hallucinating or she's about split in two."

Cornelia's exaggerated blinking and eye-rubbing gestures directed all attention to the painting over the bar, which, amazingly enough, had begun to part in the middle and recede into the oversized frame that now began to resemble a proscenium arch. Above the hubbub and hurrah of the casino could be heard the brassy crescendo of a four-piece rumba band being brought to a boil by a conga rhythm section of compelling pluck. As the painted gypsy disappeared into the wings, a small stage apron slid forth, loaded with a wildly enthusiastic combo in identical outfits featuring oversized sleeves made from multiflounced layers of pink and green satin. Their skin-tight trousers of gleaming white linen rose sleekly all the way to mid chest. An alto and tenor sax blended perfectly with a trumpeter, all rolled into one beat by the frenetic conga drummer.

"Good goddess! It's the ghost of Xavier Cugat!" exclaimed Cornelia.

"Yeah, all they need now is Carmen Miranda, or was it Abby Laine." Lilly remarked, gazing with jealousy at the band on their neat little stage perched over the bar.

"I think your wish is about to come true, Lilly, here she comes," Gyles announced.

Although Carmen she was not, there was enough sparkle radiating from this heavenly body to ignite the big bang all over again, or, more simply put, on came the shooting star.

*   *   *   *

I was goin to Bermuda, but landed in Aruba,
Scubee-doobe-doobe-do
When you scuba in Aruba, watch out for barracuda!
Scubee-doobe-doobe-do.
If you're going to play the tuba, don't do it in Aruba,
Scubee-doobe-doobe-do....

*   *   *   *

"Cornelia and Gyles could hardly believe their ears or their eyes.
"Not exactly the stuff of legend."
"No, not exactly, I think those lyrics must have been written by Cheech and Chong."
"The music sounds a bit like one of Elmer Fudd's special compositions."
"Yeah, but look at her outfit. That's a work a art," Said Lilly, surprising them. "You know, she reminds me of someone, but I can't quite remember ... now who could that have been?"

La Diva trolled the dim recesses of her memory, while she studied the fine points of the singer's costume. It was definitely high drag, reminiscent of the surrealist creations that Elsa Schiaparelli might have cooked up after chowing down on an omelet of magic mushrooms. In fact, a culinary motif was the dominant decorative device of the costume.

The mysterious singer wore, for some unexplainable reason, a chef's coat made from red-checked linen of the type most often seen on café tables in Italian restaurants. This garment was miraculously tailored to follow her voluptuous figure, and she wore it provocatively unbuttoned at the top, revealing her daring décolletage. The shoulders were decorated with epaulets in the form of frying pans full of eggs sunny-sideup. These were made from black oilcloth and colorful felt. The coat was toggled down the front with forks and spoons of mismatched Art Deco patterns, which were sewn onto the checked fabric. Her rumba skirt, also of cheery red checks, hugged her shapely hips tightly, traveling an incredible distance all the way down to the floor where it frothed in a train behind her, foaming with a plethora of pink and green satin ruffles that matched the sleeves of the band members. Drowning in this sea of waving fabric could be glimpsed platform shoes made from aluminum coffee percolators. From the singer's ears dangled upside-down salt and pepper shakers that rained beaded fringes—one of pearls and one of black onyx representing the respective seasonings. On her head she wore a wig constructed of vermicelli arranged in savory swirls.

What any of this had to do with "Scuba in Aruba" was an esoteric mystery of cabalistic obscurity. But sing she did, and as she warbled her bouncy ballad she shook a pair of oversized maracas with the vigor of a mixing machine at the paint shop.

Lilly's gaze was transfixed by the raucous rumba queen on the tiny stage. There was something about this dame that teased the edge of her memory to a puzzling degree of frustration. She chomped on her cocktail straw while ruminating on this conundrum, and feeling in need of further inspiration she knocked back the remainder of her sidecar. This jolt of the sauce lubricated her synapse into smooth working order and then it came to her in a flash: "Urna! Urna Flamanté—but, you're dead!"

The riotous rumba ruffling up the airwaves was instantly silenced by La Diva's bellowing shout. An uneasy silence suspended all ordinary animation in the casino, even interrupting the rabble's relentless worship of the golden calf. Moses would have been gratified by such a reaction, but Stanley Potsdam was not.

"Hey, your majesty, do you mind? I'm on a roll over here!"

∗   ∗   ∗   ∗

If Lilly was shaken by the appearance of an apparition from her past, the rumbatic chanteuse aboard the "gypsy" stage was completely undone by the encounter. Was this really Urna Flamanté? And if so, who the hell was she anyway? But the lady in question did not stick around to give any interviews. She shuffled off, stage-right, as fast as her percolator platforms would allow, which in this case was remarkably fast.

The rumba musicians, finding themselves unencumbered by the "Scuba in Aruba" routine, gleefully resumed their merry-making with an old gaucho folk song known popularly as "Rumpus in the Pampas." But Lilly was hearing none of that, and without skipping a beat herself, she hoisted and heaved her brawn up onto the bar with amazing alacrity and began thumping her purse against the golden proscenium framing the musicians' lair.

"Urna Flamanté, you get your sorry ass out here and explain yourself!"

The gaggle of mixologists tending to the thirsty retreated to the far end of the bar, where they cowered in shock and disbelief. Lilly's assault didn't seem to faze the band, nor did it recall Urna for any encores or solo bows. The immediate response to Lilly's performance was the gathering of a swarm of security guards, swooping in from all directions. This time, the protection of Cornelia and Gyles was not enough to keep the authorities at a discreet distance.

La Diva was unceremoniously plucked from the bar of the Jungle Casino and dragged through the lobby of the Royal Palms Hotel by the considerable efforts of seven strapping men, three of whom had been highly decorated Green Berets. But altogether, they were hard-pressed to subdue the kicking and screaming of La Diva. The only gratifying consequence of the struggle was when one of Lilly's plastic mules flew through the air and landed in the mango margarita of Mrs. Merryweather Coldbottom, whose appearance was not improved by wearing her cocktail.

Lilly's escort tossed her into the gutter in front of the hotel, but, like Brer Rabbit in the briar patch, she had been born and bred there, so deep chagrin was not forthcoming. Instead, she resumed her accustomed dignity of six foot four inches and, bracing herself against the pole of the hotel's front awning, she removed her remaining mule from her left foot and handed it to the doorman.

"Darling, call me a cab."

The doorman was about to demur when his eye caught sight of the $50.00 bill stapled to the instep of the shoe.

"Sure thing, Miss!" His whistle split the calm night of paradise.

CHAPTER 13

▼

MISSING-PERSON SEARCH

A brawny plumber in a gray jumpsuit and Red Sox baseball cap stopped to check in at the security desk of the Royal Palms Hotel service entrance. He lugged a battered tool box in his left hand and a smoldering stogy in his right.

"Yo, here 'bout the sink." barked the plumber.

"What do you want?" shot back the crisply uniformed guard behind a thick glass partition.

"Got a call to clear a plugged sink" was the vague reply.

"You're not the usual guy, let's see some ID."

The security guard was well trained. The plumber stuck his cigar in a corner of his mouth and began a laborious search through the many pockets of his jumpsuit. This routine fumbled along producing bubblegum and wrenches but no ID until at last he threw up his free hand in a gesture of disgust and snatched a battered picture ID hanging from a long bee-bee chain around his neck. He briefly flashed it in the guard's direction.

"Jeez, the wife says I'd forget my head...." The plumber resumed his puffing vigorously.

OK, OK, big guy, but you gotta toss the stogy." The guard waved a manila file trying to clear the cigar stench that had invaded his booth.

"But this is Cuban! It's pure gold! I ain't tossing this baby."

"Suit yourself, but there is no smoking beyond this point" stated the guard with finality and satisfaction.

"Buncha fuckin' fairies," muttered the disgruntled plumber as he rubbed the ash end of his cigar against the rusty top of his toolbox. He stashed the offending butt in a pocket riveted to the upper arm of his jumpsuit, where there was already a collection of screwdrivers.

"Ok, Sarge, the clock's tickin', lemme in."

The guard buzzed the outer door open and the workman barged in, leaning his weight against the heavy swing of the door. He stooped to retrieve his drain snake, wound around its crank wheel. This allowed enough time for the guard to get a good look at the crusty plumber. He was puzzled by the hairy stubble growing on the plumber's chest and arms as if sprouting new growth after having been singed.

"That must explain the eyebrows too, just growing back. It's a good thing I made him put out that cigar, or he'd set us all on fire," the guard thought to himself. Then he went back to reading the contents of the manila folder that held last night's security report. This reported an incident involving some drunk climbing on the bar in the casino.

The plumber stopped at the water cooler down the hall and sucked in a deep draft. He swirled the clean water around his mouth and spit it down the drain. Then he extracted a small canister of violet breath freshener from another of his equipment pockets and spritzed liberally.

"Yuck, those stogys stink like a dog's ass!" Having thus refreshed himself, he and his heavy equipment rattled on down the corridor. He looked for the back-stage dressing room, but after having searched this way and that, he ended up in a seemingly empty control booth, where a long bank of TV monitors spied on every corner of the now-empty casino.

"Whoops, absolutely the wrong place to be, no need to wallow with the pigs." So saying, the plumber tip toed out the door, or at least as much as one could tip-toe, carrying forty pounds of plumbing equipment in each hand. But the physical burden was not the worrying factor for our plumber, it was the element of stealth that really taxed his capabilities, because he was not at all practiced in the subtleties of being unobtrusive.

"Hold it right there, mister!" a disembodied voice commanded with authority. The plumber adopted a defensive attitude of hostile contempt, a role not far from his true nature.

"How the fuck do I get to backstage?" he demanded, "I'm supposed to clear a drain!"

"You're way off the mark, buddy. Now, let's see some ID"

From the half-light of the control room emerged a uniformed security guard, equal in height to the towering plumber. A bulletproof vest padded his solid bulk, and a prominently displayed pistol hung from his equipment belt.

"Hey man, what's the hassle?" the plumber waved his picture ID "The guy at the back door let me in, but now I'm lost. So where's backstage?"

The guard proceeded with caution but no hesitation as he approached. He shined a flashlight on the clouded plastic covering the identification card.

"Albert Mellenoffsky, huh? Drain Magician, huh? You clog it, we clear it. Cute. Well, let's clear up this little bit of detail. What are you doing in the security booth?"

"Trying to get out and on my way."

"So you say, but let's check with the controller to see what orders have been dispatched today. As far as I know, all our plumbing is done in-house."

"Hey, officer, here, look at this. It's the fax we received this morning ordering your job and you can see by the rest of the list I've got a lotta drains to drill today, so cut me some slack and tell me where's the dressing room."

These lines were delivered with the authentic whine of William Bendix, Stanley Norton and Josephine—just the right combination of TV plumbers to convince the guard—who was impatient to get back to the copy of *Hustler* jammed into his back pocket.

"Down the stairs, take a right, and your first left. But, don't go wandering around anymore, and remember, I can see everything from Command Central, so don't think you're alone."

As the guard turned back to the bank of monitors, Al caught a glimpse of some impressive knockers prominently featured on the glossy page protruding from his rear pocket.

"Give my regards to Debbie from Dallas," muttered Al as he clanked his way toward the elusive hinterland of backstage.

He went down a dim staircase, then right, and left, and finally arrived at a nondescript metal door marked with a tarnished star. Without knocking, he muscled his way into the room, where he plunked down his tool chest and drain snake.

"Drain Magician."

His greeting got no reply. He was alone in the tiny dressing room, which was bursting with costumes hanging from a rack in the middle of the room. One wall was hung with a long mirror, circled by bare light bulbs. Beneath the mirror ran a white Formica countertop with four metal folding chairs lined up in front. This side of the room must be for the band members, thought Al. The other half of the room was obviously reserved for the rumba queen, because her ruffled skirt was hanging on the costume rack along with the red-checked chef's coat.

The plumber rubbed his palms together in a classic gesture of gloating delight. He turned the visor of his Sox cap backwards on his head and got down to business, rummaging through the litter of items crowding the dressing table. The first thing that caught his eye was a vintage '50s makeup kit, covered in pink leather with black-trimmed edges. This collector's item attracted Al's attention not only because of its prominent position but also because of the gold monogram impressed in the pink leather: U.F.O.

"U.F.O.! I thought I had seen a ghost, not a Martian. But, come to think of it, she did look like something from outer space."

He fumbled with the clasp on the makeup kit, but it was firmly locked, and although he could easily pop it with a screwdriver, that would mess the thing up something terrible. Al might be an intrepid sleuth without scruple when it came to gathering information, but ruthless vandal he was not, so he left it alone. Moving on with his investigation, he found the platform shoes.

"Now, who on earth would have dreamed this one up? Coffee-percolator platform shoes, and, if you can believe it, old mattress springs are inside the percolators. I suppose that's what gives the old queen some extra bounce. But, what's this, a designer's label? No, I don't believe it! Let's see what lunatic created these festive sabots. Wally St. John!!?? So, the plot thickens. We'll get around to you later, Miss Wally, all in due time."

Al poked his sturdy index finger back amongst the rouge pots and powder puffs on the dressing table this time with complete disregard for the trail of disruption he left. He was distracted for a moment by a rhinestone bauble, and he couldn't resist holding it up to his own ear. The sparkling number he now posed with made a glaring contrast to the gruff plumber with the stubbly chin, chest, arms and eyebrows, reflected in the mirror. He heaved a melancholy sigh at the sight of his reflection. But his indulgent self-pity was quickly discarded when he caught sight in the mirror of a familiar item sitting on the top of the costume rack directly behind him. He turned around and took it off the shelf. His eyes narrowed with the weight of heavy ruminations as he nodded his head in recognition and surety. Stashing the item in his toolbox, he charged out of the dressing room, retracing his way through the maze of backstage corridors.

CHAPTER 14

▼

BACK AT THE GRASS SHACK

Albert Mellenoffsky let himself into the Grass Shack on the beach. It wasn't exactly what it seemed, nor was he. Once inside, he punched an alarm code into a discreetly placed key pad by the front door, tossed his electric key into a Lalique bowl on a blue glass table, and plopped down his heavy gear.

"Yo! That you, Al, wanna brew?"

"Don't call me that, you big lug. And no, I don't want a brew, thank you very much. I would much prefer a pink lady and a big fat joint!"

"Hey, babe don't blame me. It's the getup, you had me convinced."

"Oh, thanks, Stan. I didn't mean to snap atcha, but I've been hunting ghosts over at the Jungle Casino and I nearly got nabbed by the local pigs. Now, how about you shaking up the cocktails, while I take a dip in the tub."

"Right, babe but what exactly is a pink lady?"

"I'm not sure. It's sorta like a kick in the head dressed up in a nightgown. Call up Cornelia Chilton at the Royal Palms and ask her. You'll find her cell phone number on the pad by the phone. That fairy brother of hers is forever coming up with these cutsie concoctions. It's part of his charm, I guess, and now I'm hooked."

"So, why don't I go right to the horse's mouth and ask him? You know that guy ain't no fucking fairy, babe. I mean, I know he sucks dick and all, but hey, who am I to judge? He's got one impressive body and he *acts* like a regular guy."

"Stanley, are you getting a boner over Gyles Chilton? Let me be the first to tell you he's married to my son, Val. So lay off."

"Well, no, babe. You know me, I'm no queer. I just sorta thought maybe we could, you know like, shoot the shit sometime."

"Stanley, you have such a way with words. Go right ahead and call up lover-boy. But don't forget to ask him about the pink ladies. Apparently, I'm going to have to be totally tolerant around here, but as you say, who am I to judge?"

Albert Mellenoffsky left the room, shaking his head in disbelief.

"What *is* this world coming to?" he muttered to himself.

Having thus disposed of his philosophic misgivings, Al lumbered off to the master bath to shed his grungy disguise. First, he unzipped his jumpsuit all the way down to his hairy crotch. Then, winding up into a shimmy-shake that traveled from his shoulders down to his toes, he slithered from his plumber's drag like a snake molting. Next, he turned the hot and cold taps to fast flood, filling the Jacuzzi tub with steaming water. He added a huge squirt of Vita Bath and a load of Epsom salts sufficient to dissolve the tensions of his sleuthing exertions. Lowering himself into this fragrant froth, he heaved a heartfelt sigh—which in his case resembled a great blue whale spouting—and like that superb creature he dove into the watery depths.

After some lengthy moments of merging with the perfumed water, the tired body bobbed to the surface, wearing a bubble wig in a pompadour style piled high on its head. Even with a stubbly chin, Lilly Linda's glamorous allure was beginning to return.

"OK, babe Here's your pink lady. Where do you want it?"

"Oh, darling, pour it down my gullet and fire me up a joint."

Stan interpreted this order with caution. He handed Lilly her special cocktail glass. The stem of this commodious receptacle had a spun glass sculpture of a girl in a grass skirt. For her other hand he proffered a perfectly rolled joint of Maui Wowie stuck in a six-inch-long plastic holder in the shape of a crocodile.

"Darling, you *are* a divine lump! Snag the pouf from my dressing table, perch it over there in the corner and set yourself down. You exhaust me standing up all the time. You need to lounge more, Stanley."

The two old Vietnam buddies stewed for a while in companionable silence. Lilly sipped and puffed as her bubbles burst about her, making a comforting sound like queer Rice Crispies. Stan straddled Lilly's pouf trying to get comfortable while he sipped his coffee and read the sports page of the *Aruba Vacation Times*.

"So," Stan broke the silence, "did you get the dirt on Urna?"

"Would you believe? Vampires don't fart?"

Stanley puzzled over this one for a count of twelve, and then he lost it altogether. First he giggled, followed by lusty guffaws and then rolling laughter, ending with a coughing jag that shook the bamboo-paneled walls of the Grass Shack. Whatever he had been expecting had not prepared him for this. The man of steel nerves was reduced to a helpless kid. Finally, he was able to reattach his Marine demeanor of unflappable cool back on his face long enough to reply.

"Hey, babe, if you say so. I can sorta see how that works too."

Then considering the implications of Lilly's statement that vampires don't fart, he went back to laughing some more.

Lilly, flushed from her bath and enveloped in bubbles, beamed benignly at Stan. He was even sexier when he laughed, because his gleaming white teeth showed in his big square cheeks, so she liked to make him laugh. But, ham that she was, she also had a mystery to solve.

"OK, enough of the mirth, doll face, do me a favor. In my toolbox you'll find a play that I found in the dressing room of the Jungle Casino. Bring it in here. I've got some ancient history to study."

Stan straightened his massive legs, raising his butt from Lilly's pouf and sauntered toward the front door. He popped the lid of the toolbox and found a dog-eared manuscript, bound between cardboard covers, lying on top of wrenches and hammers. Printed on the cover was the title:

Vampires Don't Fart
A Melodramatic Musical in Three Acts

By
UFO & LLLS
A.K.A. Urna Flamanté O'Reilly and Lilly Linda Le Strange

CHAPTER 15

▼

BUBBLE, BUBBLE, TOIL
AND TROUBLE

La Diva was enjoying the massaging bubbles of her Jacuzzi tub while she perused the script, *Vampires Don't Fart*. It had been a long time since she had read this magnum opus, so she had a lot of catching up to do. The first aspect of this theatrical catastrophe, which struck her like a slam punch to the jaw, was how remarkably awful it was. As a matter of record, she could remember with chagrin and dismay how many people had made this exact remark, or words to that effect. "The show stinks," was one of the more blunt assessments uttered by—Reginald Pew, "that little prick from *Gay Windows*," as he was forever afterward referred to by Lilly and her inner circle. But, Mr. Pew was not alone when he dished *Vampires* to filth. A unanimous crowd had rushed to the same judgment, thereby racking the play permanently on the drain board of fabled flops. Lilly had stubbornly defended her collaboration with her esteemed mentor, Urna Flamanté, when she had said, "It does have *some* redeeming features." The same line of unfounded optimism was once uttered by Genghis Kahn's grandmother when first presented with the little monster. But, redemption was hard to locate in *Vampires Don't Fart* except, of course, for the title, which was the direct result of a horrific acid trip that had climaxed a month-long experiment with macrobiotic diet number seven. Whether it was the protein depletion from thirty days of rice cakes and green tea or the inherent lack of literary competence on behalf of the two authors, the question was a moot. The show lacked oomph, and this was the least of its shortcomings.

Lilly came to this sad and belated conclusion only through the perspective of time, and a heap of that commodity had slopped over the edge of the rainbow since she and Urna had penned their ditty.

"It must be fifteen years since we opened at the Frères Jacques Café in Bay Village. It seems like just yesterday," Lilly mused aloud, a habit of narration she practiced with or without an audience.

"I was a mere slip of a lass then, just back from Nam, and that dinky little stage was not big enough for the two of us to even fart, much less sing and dance together. That was the situation that inspired the title. How the vampires came in, I forget."

"Scuse the interruption, babe" said Stanley, poking his head around the door, "I thought I heard voices."

"You did, Stan. That was me. Stick around, you might as well hear all about it."

"What's this, true confessions? Sounds like you need some more pink lady"

"Never mind her. Plop yourself down and listen up." When Stan had complied, Lilly continued.

"I first met Urna at the barracks of Fort Pendleton when I was being discharged after Nam. She was Lieutenant O'Reilly then, Terry O'Reilly. I was kicking around, waiting for the brass to get their act together and process my papers. Lieutenant O'Reilly was undergoing a heavy-duty debriefing that was mysteriously dragging on and on. You remember how it was then, the whole fuckin' world was rotten and nobody believed nothin'.I went out drinking to a dump by the docks one night in San Diego, and the joint turned out to be a gay bar. It was the first time I'd ever been to a place like that, and, as luck would have it, they had some drag queens performing. Well, I was just fascinated. I saw these big showgirls, all sparkling in jewels. One of 'em even had a crown on her head and tons of feathers in *real* pretty colors. The dresses were magnificent, just like Barbara in *Hello, Dolly!* In fact, that was one of the big numbers they did that night, Don't Rain on My Parade. I didn't even know about Carol Channing in those days. Before the service, I was straight off the farm from Bumble Bee, Arkansas. Until that moment, I'd never even heard the word *glamour*. But, when I saw those queens, I knew there was something beautiful in the world.

"After the field hospital, I needed something beautiful something bad. You have no idea how fuckin' ugly a nineteen-year-old football player from Texas can be with half his face blown off. I'd been splattered with brains, blood and shit 'till

I felt like the dirtiest bastard on earth. After all the lies of war, I was desperate to find something to believe in. Hell, that's why I became a nurse to begin with, so I could do some good. Back in Arkansas, I had been at Veterinarian College preparing to go back home to the farm. But, when I registered for nursing, the Army snatched me up and paid for everything. But there is no healing in war, just patch 'em up, send 'em back and watch 'em die. You were one of the lucky ones, 'cause you were such a fucked-up junky you couldn't go back, so with you, I could do some good.

"Anyway, they did eventually send you back, and I was finally relieved. Boy, is that a joke. How can you be relieved after you've been wallowing in the rotting muck of war? Just like the hog farm back home, nothing pretty.

"I was on my fifth or sixth boilermaker at the Galaxies of Stars, that was the name of the bar, and out comes Urna Flamanté. She was as big as me, but beautiful, with the prettiest red dress made outta some soft, flowing stuff. I thought right then and there, 'I wanna be just like her. I wanna be noticed. I wanna be beautiful!'

"So, I got me a bottle of hooch and two clean glasses, and I went backstage. Suddenly, I could see a glorious future for myself, and I charged off to battle. But I was not ready to find Lieutenant O'Reilly wearing the biggest set of eyelashes I have ever seen in my life! Drunk as I was, I knew it was him right off, 'cause of the tattoo of the Marine emblem. Oh, yeah, it hadn't shown onstage, on account 'a the full-length white gloves. But, when I arrived backstage, Urna had peeled off her gloves and was daubing her wrists with gardenia perfume. She always said this calmed her after a performance. Lord knows she needed somethin' to calm down with, 'cause her version of 'Don't Rain on My Parade' was like a fast forward of Judy Garland, having just shot up a pint of crystal meth, staying all night and singing them all.

"I know, that's mixing up a whole buncha stories, but that was Urna, a real wearing blender of fantasy. When she saw me standing in the doorway of her dressing room, she really freaked, although I never knew it. She just reached for the bottle in my hand and glugged away. Later, much later, the truth came out. But, by that time, I was beautiful, too, and already believing in make-believe."

CHAPTER 16

▼

CHASING SHADOWS

The great big cabby, wearing a Boston Red Sox cap, filled the front seat of the tiny cab to overflowing—he could only squeeze in by popping out. This explained the hefty shoulder, mighty bicep and powerful forearm that protruded from the window on the driver's side of the cab. It did not, however, explain the hairy stubble reclaiming the man's hand and arm, starting at his meaty knuckles gripping the steering wheel.

The stage door of the Aruba Jungle Casino swung open and four lean Latin types in shark skinsuits filed out.

"Get in boys," barked the cabby. "I'll take you where you're going."

At four a.m., the weary musicians gladly accepted the convenient offer, never suspecting the need for caution. Stripped of their puffy arm ruffles, the now-svelte rumba contingent piled into the waiting cab—the last one in folding his long legs into the front passenger seat—then they sped off into the night.

"So, where to, dudes?" was a question that riled up a lengthy debate in rapid Portuguese, involving a lot of nasal diphthongs and slushing sounds. The result of this pow-wow was an address card being thrust at the driver.

The cabby snagged a pair of reading glasses hanging from a pink plastic cord around his neck, and perched the spectacles on his nose. He squinted at the printed address, holding the card at arm's length out the driver's side window to gain farsighted perspective. The result of this maneuver was a perilous swerve to the left, into the oncoming traffic, whereupon a glissando moan of harmonic horror arose from the endangered musicians. But the cabby quickly recovered his direction with a screeching of tires. He thrust the address card back at the cowering passenger beside him.

"Not to worry, *muchachos,* we're on the right track now. How's 'bout some soothing vibes to chill out with?"

The driver snapped on the radio to a hot salsa station, while the rumba men rushed through their prayers and desperately fired up four unfiltered cigarettes. The hot night air poured through the open cab windows, stirring up the thick clouds of cigarette smoke and the strong scents of the men's colognes.

"Say, ain't you boys the band at the Jungle Casino?" the cabby asked with studied casualness. However, the salsa on the radio provided the only response to this chummy inquiry.

"I caught your act the other night, and lemme say, guys, super *bueno*! I especially dig the dame with the big maracas, if you catch my drift. When is she coming back, 'cause I just can't get enough 'a her?"

The boys in the back seat were having none of that, and after another short conference in more rapid Portuguese, the man in the middle nudged a muzzle of cool steel against the right temple of the driver's head.

"*Bueno, muchacho,*" he said. "Turn right, pull over, and shut up."

Albert Mellenoffsky never argued with firearms. He turned his cab off the main road onto a side street, where he pulled up to the curb and came to a rocking halt. Smoking butts were flung from the open windows, immediately followed by the four men in uniform sharkskin suits. They side-stepped the tiny cab, but the one with the gun lingered close. He pointed the weapon at the left front tire, then squeezed the trigger. Meanwhile, the other three men had hailed a passing cab back on the main street. When it pulled over, all four piled in and sped off, leaving Al staring with a mixture of relief and frustration at his deflating front tire.

Albert Mellenoffsky reached for the dashboard microphone of his dispatch line. "Car 77, report your location," he spoke with the dull tones of a bored dispatcher.

"Just picked up a fare on Main Street going to the Heights," replied Stanley Potsdam into his mike as he rocketed through the Aruba night in a cab with four passengers.

"Car 77, after you deliver, go to the Grass Shack and pick up a party named Le Strange going to the airport."

"Roger, 10-4."

*   *   *   *

A figure in silhouette leaned on the terrace railing of a lavish villa that was perched in the dark hills, high above the glittering lights of the resort hotels below. A pulsating, greenish light, reflecting off the gently waving surface of a swimming pool, animated the tropical foliage surrounding the figure. Ice cubes jingled faintly against a highball glass, held in the grasp of a well-manicured hand. The shadowy figure scrutinized the lonely, winding road that climbed in a serpentine meander up the hills leading toward the villa. Agitated and impatient, the figure daubed a drop of Jungle Gardenia perfume onto her overheated forearm and rubbed the cloying scent into a spot where a faded tattoo lingered.

CHAPTER 17

▼

A LONG-DISTANCE CALL

Back at the Grass Shack on the beach, in the relative safety of her boudoir far away from the gun-wielding rumba band, Lilly reclined on a mountain of pillows that crowded her bed. Lurking by her side was a twenty-pound box of See's chocolate truffles, from which she plucked several hoped-for favorites and plopped them all into her gaping trap in one fell swoop.

Whenever Lilly had some serious thinking to do, she always required stimulating vices to stoke her mental processes. On her bedside table sat a tumbler filled with a lurid green liquid that resembled antifreeze solution but was nothing more than Gatorade. Stirring her drink with a chocolaty finger, Lilly sucked the goo clean with a satisfied smack and dialed international information.

"Hello, darling lump, this is Lilly," she purred to the operator. "I'm sorry to bother you so late, but can you give me the number for the Holy Fryer's Monastery? What? In Somerville, of course. What? Massachusetts, where else? Really, honey, you do ask a lot from a girl ... USA, if you must know! Now, enough of this shilly-shallying and get on with it!.... Listen, if you think *I'm* rude, you should talk to the rumba boys. I mean, they put a gun to my head and blew out my tire ... What's that got to do with you? Not a whole hell of a lot. Now, how's 'bout my number? ... Yes, Holy Fryer's Monastery on Prospect Hill, Somerville ... 617-333-6463. Thanks a whole bunch. Next time I need a molar pulled, I'll ask for you."

Lilly required a liberal dosing of Gatorade and another fistful of truffles to recover from her dalliance with the overseas operator. One can only imagine what the beleaguered operator needed after their encounter.

Knowing that the Holy Fryers were up at all kinds of ungodly hours chanting and praying and carrying on, Lilly dialed Somerville, heedless of the time.

"*Kyrie Eleison*, Holy Fryer's Monastery, God bless you."

"*Geshundeit* to you, too, fella."

"I beg you pardon?"

"Never mind, you're right, that was a pretty lame joke. Anyway, this is Lilly, I'm down here in Aruba, and I need to talk with Wally, so sashay your sackcloth down to cell 17 and snag the bugger for me, will you?"

"Miss Le Strange, is that really you?" An enraptured voice was heard to inquire with reverence and awe.

Lilly had deposited Wally St. John (pronounced Sin Gin) at the Holy Fryer's Monastery after an unfortunate incident, involving an overdose of ecstasy ingested by the unwitting Wally. Under the brothers' tutelage and care, Wally was brought back from the brink to full production mode, and regularly exported his zany designs from the basement of the cloister, which Abbot Acidophilus had generously made available as Wally's atelier.

Lilly was a respected patron of the Monastery, because every year she gave a wildly successful fund raising performance at the Club Crazy for the benefit of the brothers' retirement fund. This mounting trust had, by careful investment, been growing by leaps and bounds, and now easily subsidized half a dozen brothers dispersed around the globe to some of the more desirable vacation resorts. It was rumored that Brother Anthony of Podunk had made a killing with golf cart rentals from his condo bordering the Royal Golf Links in Bermuda.

"Yeah it's me, Lilly Linda, star of stage and screen, brought to you by the miracle of satellite dishing—I usta think that was reserved for queens only—but hey, this is one crazy world. Now, who's that? Dopey, Doc, Grumpy or Sneezy?"

"Miss Le Strange, always such a joker. This is Brother Jebediah. Life in the Hub is a horrible cross to bear without your ministry, Miss Le Strange. I don't know how we are going to make it through Lent this year. Abbot Acidophilus is threatening to cancel Carnival altogether, with you out of the country. None of us can even muster up the energy to flip a flapjack on Shrove Tuesday because of the prospect of life without our Lilly. And that means no witty liturgical passion plays, either. I can tell you, the brotherhood is in crisis. Brother Porgy slipped out of polyphonic plain song right into 'Nobody Knows the Trouble I've Seen' in the middle of Matins last Monday! When are you coming home?"

"Brother Jeb! Darling! Buck up! Where's your stiff upper lip? For Christ sakes, I thought you people were Neo-Druids or some such thing?—you're not even supposed to *have* feelings, much less show them."

"*Mea culpa, mea culpa*, the flesh is weak."

"Darling, don't remind me, I'm already wearing steel corsets. Next thing you know, I'll be forced into aerobics class. Now, listen, dolly face, I'd love to chit-chat all night witcha, and thanks awfully for the slobbering affection, but I gotta talk with Wally, so drag him down the hall and put him on the horn."

Lilly knew that Brother Jeb needed some time to carry out these instructions, so she tossed the receiver onto the pillows and took the opportunity to go pee.

✳   ✳   ✳   ✳

"Hello, is that you, Wally?"

"Wally St. John here, costumer to the stars—eat your heart out, Edith Head."

"Forget Edith, Wally, and tell me about the coffee percolator platform shoes."

"Say, how do I know this is the real Lilly?"

"Well, Wally, you may have a point there. I've been known to ask myself that very same question."

"Oh, you have, huh? Well, I guess that proves it then. Fire away. What is it you want to know? Something about coffee-percolators?"

"That's it? You believe me?"

"What the fuck am I supposed to ask? Your mother's maiden name?"

"My mother ain't no maiden!"

"Sorry, I shoulda known. Now, do you mind? What's this all about? I was in the midst of some very important business."

"Like what? Saying your rosary?"

"No! I was giving Brother Jonquil a blow job."

"Why didn't you say so sooner! Let's get down to business. Tell me about the coffee-percolator platform shoes you made for Urna Flamanté."

"Don' know."

"Don' know what?"

"Don' know nothin'."

"Yeah, then how come your designer label is plastered all over the little gems?"

"Whoops! Where did you say you were calling from?"

"Aruba."

"Whoops! Have you ever heard of Scarface Malone?"

"Who?"

"I gather you've run into Urna?"

"You could say that. But I would add that she's run out on me. Not to mention the fact she's supposeta be dead!"

"I'm not surprised. Listen, Lilly, this is one thing I know nothin' about."

"No, Wally, there are many things you know nothin' about, but this is not one of them. Who is Scarface Malone?"

"Whoops! Did I mention him?"

"Wally, do you want me to get Abbot Acidophilus to resume your flagellations?"

"You wouldn't dare, and besides, he won't do it anymore."

"Why not?"

"Because I told him I was beginning to like it, and asked for more."

"You sleazy whore."

"I learned it all from you, Le Strange."

"OK, Wally, you win. I'll send you an ounce of grass and twenty-five hits of ecstasy."

"He's her old boyfriend."

"Now, that wasn't so difficult. Let's hear some more."

"Scarface and Urna were in business together.... Lilly, you have no idea how dangerous ... I can't say more ... Nobody's safe ... anywhere...."

... Ugg ... Gurgl ... Gurgle ... Thump ... Bonk ... plunk....

The line went dead. Lilly guzzled her Gatorade, as a cold sweat broke out on her forehead.

CHAPTER 18

▼

WE'VE GOTTA GET OUTTA HERE

Stanley Potsdam parked in the garden court of the Grass Shack on the beach, pushed his cabby's hat to the back of his head, and wiped the sweat from his brow. Already the light of dawn was peeking over the ocean horizon, heating up another day in paradise.

From across the drive he beeped his electronic key at the front door, which swung open on noiseless hinges. Through the opening doorway rocketed an empty Kahlúa bottle that detonated with a frightening crash on the cobblestones of the court.

"What the fuck?" exclaimed Stan, startled and annoyed. As if to answer that unanswerable question, out staggered Lilly, disheveled, distraught and drunk.

"Stanley!"

"Lilly!"

"I thought you were murdered! Didn't you get my message? 'Pick up Le Strange party going to the airport?' We've gotta get outta here! Throw the bags in the trunk and step on it!"

Lilly was scantily clad in what might once have been a lace-trimmed negligee, but now more closely resembled the torn tissues of a bad dream. She dashed for the back seat of the parked cab. With mounting alarm Stan watched the vehement panic of La Diva, but what really disturbed him most about her performance was her wig. That confection of saccharine whimsicality, always firmly affixed to its home port, was seriously askew and listing to starboard.

Lilly fumbled with the car door, unable in her present condition to open it. Without complaint, Stan wisely performed the task for her and she wriggled into the imagined safety of the conveyance. Resignedly, Stan yanked the patent-leather visor of his cabby's hat down onto his forehead and climbed back into the driver's seat. Now installed within the steel confines of their escape vehicle with its glass partition separating driver and passenger in the manner of the inviolate sanctuary of a confessional, Stan gently prodded Lilly.

"OK, babe what's got your skirt in such a ruffle?"

"Oh, Stan, don't ask, just drive! Somehow, Scarface Malone has bumped off Wally, all the way back in Boston, while I was on the phone with the little fucker! I know Wally can be a real pain in the ass, but he was ... oh my God, he *was* ... a genius! Who the hell is gonna make my space suit costume now? *Naughty Astronautess* will be a flop!

This will be a repeat of that disaster, *Vampires Don't Fart,* and all because of that slut, Urna! Why can't the silly bitch stay dead? We gave her a swell sendoff funeral—at Mount Auburn Cemetery, no less! Have you any idea what a niche in that ultrafaboo columbarium costs? We had to give up booze and drugs for a whole month, scrimping and saving, just so Urna could mix with the swells. And let me tell you, in those days Betty was not sober or clean, and she whined and wailed for the entire thirty days. What I have already suffered for that no-account drag queen, Urna, is not to be imagined. Now she shows up in, of all places, Aruba. I mean, really, some people have no shame. And it turns out she's also had the bad taste to pick Scarface Malone as a boyfriend!

Those rumba thugs are no better. I only asked one itsy-bitsy little question about Urna, and bam! They pulled a gun on me, blew out my tire, and left me in some God-forsaken wilderness. I was sure they would plug me, too!!"

Stan hoped Lilly would blow off enough steam so that eventually she would return to a coherent state of mind. This may have been an unrealistic wish on his behalf, but Stan was a generous soul. He lit up a Lucky Strike and puffed away meditatively as he looked out beyond the tossing palm fronds surrounding the Grass Shack at the sun rising above the ocean.

Without either of the occupants of the cab realizing it, a swarthy character, laden down with tourist trinkets, stepped out of the foliage enclosing the garden court. The intruder, a presumed native vendor—or so one would suppose from his burden of cheap tourist trinkets—sidled up to the driver's side of the cab and brazenly jingled an abundant handful of shell necklaces at Stan.

"Buzz off, butt-in-ski, this is private property." Stan dismissed the peddler without regard, an incautious reaction in this drama of deepening intrigue. But Stan was hoping that Lilly would soon succumb to the effects of the Kahlúa and/ or whatever else she had imbibed, and pass out. Then he could catch some Zs of his own, trusting that everything regarding the mystery of Urna Flamanté could be sorted out later, after a good snooze. But he realized with frustration and dismay that this simple scenario was to be denied him, when the intruder leaned a snub-nosed revolver against his head and ordered in heavily accented English;

"Darlink, get out of the car and put your hands on your head."

The intruder seriously miscalculated his advantage when he disregarded the drunken Diva in the back seat. Lilly was most dangerous after a few cocktails, and at this moment she had a great deal more than just a few under her belt, even if that article of support was now but a torn bit of lace. With surprising stealth, La Diva reached out the back window behind the peddler. Drawing upon reserves of pith and brawn as yet untapped on this brightening day, she got him in a monster headlock and ruthlessly bashed his noggin against the polished steel of the car roof. The mysterious stranger went limp and collapsed in a heap of tinkling trinkets.

"Now do you believe me, Stan?" demanded Lilly, as she extracted herself from the back seat.

"We've gotta get outta here, pronto!"

Having delivered this unarguable pronouncement, she went into the Grass Shack to change.

CHAPTER 19

▼

STORIES THAT BIND US TOGETHER

Stanley strutted into the Grass Shack, following the trail of disorder that led to La Diva's inner sanctum. There, the high-strung star was in a dither, dumping the contents of all her drawers into a suite of vintage pigskin luggage. This was not a neat and orderly process.

"OK, Captain Courageous, forget the fluff and fury and haul your ass back out to the garden court. There have been some developments of an unexpected nature that require your attention.

"Skip the legalese, Stanley. I am going as fast as possible already, and all my attention is required right here. Have you seen my bathing cap? You know, the one with the wiggly daisies? And where the hell is my garter belt, anyway? I tell you, I will never travel without servants again. It was a big mistake leaving Betty behind in Boston. I can't find a blasted thing without her help."

"We were chased out of Bean Town by the cops and the Feds. There was no time to collect your false teeth, much less your maid."

"I do not now, nor have I ever needed false teeth, and Betty is my dresser."

"She is also the dizziest bitch alive, and while we are on the topic of life and death, you had better come see our mysterious visitor, Juan Valdez, before he breathes his last. The guy's fingernails are a suspicious shade of bright red and his gun is loaded with stinky perfume."

Lilly glared at Stanley. Although she was accustomed to the topsy-turvy world of Bohemian buffoonery, there were certain individuals whom she relied on absolutely. Stanley Potsdam was one of these rocks, and now she suspected even he must be cracked.

"Bright red? And really stinky?" was La Diva's cautious inquiry.

"Uh-huh, and an old Marine tattoo on his left forearm."

"Ooh-ooh, that combination sounds dangerously familiar to me. But I thought Juan Valdez was a hit man for Fathead Fabiano?"

"With a squirt gun?"

"I don't know what the world's coming to if even the godamed thugs turn out to be fucking drag queens. I mean, who is writing this script anyway?"

Lilly reluctantly abandoned her packing, such as it was, and grabbing a wrinkled kimono from the piles heaped into her open suitcases, she wrapped the gaudy garment around her and marched off toward the garden court.

Stanley watched from the front doorway of the Grass Shack as Lilly gingerly prodded the rumpled body lying on the cobblestones with her foot. A groan of agony rose from the undignified heap, while Lilly cautiously pried the gun from his cramped grasp. Sure enough, scarlet nails, Lilly recognized the notorious shade as "Temptations of Evil," and she shuddered involuntarily. The nails were long and meticulously manicured. She sniffed the weapon, which made a gurgling noise and released several drops.

"Channel # 5?! This ain't no gun, its plastic."

Now properly outraged by the crook, who probably wasn't one, Lilly prodded the body with less care, exposing the right forearm where a faded Marine tattoo, like an old bruise, disfigured the slim limb that had also been shaved of all its hair.

"So, we meet again, Miss Thing. And this is all the thanks I get for arranging a Class A funeral for you, and footing the bill for the entire event. You ungrateful slut, get up and explain yourself!"

Lilly prodded even more forcefully the splayed figure sprawled on the pavement, while she liberally spritzed his kisser with Jungle Gardenia perfume from the squirt gun. The result of these ablutions was a melting face. Appearances being not at all what they seemed, the odiferous squirt washed away the heavy face makeup on the recumbent figure, revealing it to be none other than Urna Flamanté.

"Darlink, one more squirt from that gun and you're dead meat."

"Why, Urna, so glad you could join us this morning. Forgive me if I don't invite you in, but I'm expecting the exterminators at any minute and I know how sensitive you are to DDT."

"Listen, La Strange, I've come to warn you. We are all in big trouble here. Fathead Fabiano and Scarface Malone are gunning for us all now, thanks to you."

"Is that right? And what are *they* using for ammunition? Shalimar or Nina Ricci?"

"OK, I made a joke, but my heart was in the right place."

"Listen, pudding face, the joke is on you, and if you don't believe me look in the mirror. The only place for your heart is transplanted back into the baboon where it came from. What do you mean by coming here and threatening Stan and me like this? I thought you were a suicide bomber. I nearly peed in my panties. And while we are in the complaints, and, comments stage, how could you have unleashed those Rumba hooligans on me? Do you know what they did? They held a gun to my head, shot out my tire and then left me to rot."

"Darlink, you are already rotten to the core. Anyway, you were the one who picked them up. Parading as a cab driver, indeed! They told me your driving nearly killed them and I am not surprised by that. You would be dangerous on roller skates much less driving a cab. So, here we go again. You're always sticking your head in where it's not wanted...."

"Is that so? Well at least I haven't stuck my head up my ass like you have."

At this point the reunion of the two temperamental artists unraveled altogether and their hissy fits degenerated into real fisticuffs. Stanley had to pull the combatants apart before they inflicted any real damage to each other.

"OK, broads, simmer down. Lilly, I know you're pissed, but let this number explain."

"Urna Flamanté, if you please. I am no one's number."

"Right, Urna, now we've got that established, let's go inside and hash the whole thing out."

"Oh, have you got some hash? Jeez, I haven't smoked dope since I was dragged to this Godforsaken dump, months ago. Scarface doesn't approve of drugs."

"Not that kind of hash, you dope." snapped Lilly. "What we want to know is the whole story. How come you're not dead?"

"Look, Urna," Stanley broke in, "that's not such a bad idea. I think Lilly could use a joint, but let's all go inside where Fathead's boys can't pick us off so easily."

Stanley obligingly lifted Urna's load of cheap trinkets off her burdened shoulders and urged his two companions into the relative safety of the Grass Shack.

Lilly, whose short-term memory had been warped by a lifetime played out in left field, was incapable of holding a grudge. She offered Urna her substantial arm and the trio trundled in, seeking the privacy of Lilly's boudoir.

Once inside Lilly's bedroom, Urna griped, "Darlink, you always were a lousy packer, but this mess is ridiculous."

Urna's organizational talents from years of performing on the road were disturbed by the chaotic piles bulging out of La Diva's luggage. She grabbed a handy jar of cold cream from the mess on the dressing table and quickly cleaned her face, then she rolled up her sleeves and got to work on Lilly's clothes.

Meanwhile, Stanley obligingly rolled up two huge bombers for Urna and Lilly. La Diva took this opportunity to resume lounging on her queen-sized bed, which really wasn't big enough for her and the packing operation.

"I take it you're wondering how I got here," began Urna, as she deftly folded Lilly's chemises with her joint firmly affixed to the left corner of her mouth.

"Let's take it back to that night you burned a hole through the stage and disappeared with the proverbial puff," Lilly ordered from her half of the bed.

"*Oy veh*! What a night that was. But it really goes much further back to the time we met at Camp Pendleton. You see, I was not exactly discharged from the service then. In fact, I was transferred to a special branch of the CIA."

Between puffs on her joint, Urna's hands swiftly brought order to the heaps surrounding Lilly on the bed, and her tale unfolded.

"Holy cow, how to say this? Lemme think, it came to the attention of military intelligence, and there's an oxymoron for you, that I had special skills and talents that, surprisingly enough, were needed for a covert operation, and here's how that developed.

"I had a buddy in Nam, Flaming Freddy. He was a real sick son-of-a-bitch, and it was his mission to clear the jungle with a flamethrower before the advance of the infantry.

"Anyway, while on leave back in Saigon, Freddy turned me on to some killer acid, which he got from his little sister who was a hippie in the Haight Ashbury. That night we went to a very festive and accommodating brothel, and as I started to come on and began tripping my brains out, I was irresistibly drawn to the brightly colored dresses hanging around my gal's room. As I got more and more loaded on Freddy's dope, I had less and less interest in the little lady, and more and more interest in her wardrobe. This was the dawning of my Age of Aquarius.

"By the end of the evening, I was transformed from a simple soldier to a fantastic lady of the night, complete with my own form-fitting Suzy Wong dress of bright green silk brocade and a gorgeous real hair wig, all magically whipped up by the local, all-night sweat shop. After that I couldn't get enough—acid or drag—and let me tell you, I assembled quite a nifty little wardrobe by the time I met you back in California. Lilly!" Urna broke off, "What on earth is this item?" She held the missing bathing cap aloft, pinched between two fingers. The rubber daisies wiggled in an unseemly manner.

"It's a condom for a whale," snapped Lilly, grabbing the mysterious item from Urna.

"Yuck!" replied Urna, succinctly expressing her revulsion and disapproval.

"Yuck yourself, Yolanda. I'll have you know, that's an original Oleg Cassini creation from his first couturier show at Dior. It's ultraretro."

"Oh, and I thought it was merely a retrofitted drain plug," volleyed Urna swiftly.

"Can we please get back to the story?" Stan asked. "I'm sorta in suspense here."

"Why, of course, young man," Urna willingly obliged. "Now where was I?"

"Peaking on acid in a whorehouse in Saigon."

"Ah, those were the days. Well, one night I was sitting at the bar of the Pink Pagoda, wearing the most stunning outfit encrusted with jet beads and silver sequins, and this big galumph on the stool beside me starts buying the drinks. At the time he looked OK to me, but apparently, I was already in the strobing phase of my trip because I thought the peculiar arrangement of his face musta been the LSD. But, when I woke up beside him the next morning, his face was still scrambled. That was my first real glimpse of Scarface Malone, and it was not a pretty sight.

"My tour of duty was almost up, so I figured I could go back to being Lieutenant O'Reilly and no one would be any the wiser. I did go back to the States and, almost immediately after that, to Pendleton for debriefing. But, instead of the usual group process, I was taken to a private office where agent Claude Voit, the slickest son-of-a-bitch you could ever meet, shared with me a photographic essay of my high times at the Pink Pagoda. The upshot of Claude's little blackmail scam was ... hmm ... come to think of it, I'd better fill you in on the details first:

"Scarface Malone and Fathead Fabiano had been chased outta Cuba by Castro, and so their lucrative gambling operation had, of course, come to a grinding halt. Scarface and Fathead moved their operation to Saigon, where they were mostly pushing junk to Uncle Sam's finest, which, understandably, pissed off the CIA.

"But Scarface had a pal from the old days in Havana, J. Edgar. Edgar used to take trips to Havana, where he could let down his hair, or what there was of it, and relax from the arduous job of blackmailing half the population of Washington, DC. Edgar, as you may have heard, was also a big drag queen himself, and Scar liked his women to come equipped with big dicks. Edgar and him got along just swell and, in fact, became an item for a while. Edgar collected dirt on everyone, like a Hoover vacuum cleaner, and because he was a close personal friend of Scar, no one wanted to mess with Scar.

"It was that smart-ass agent, Claude Voit's little brainstorm, that I should renew my acquaintance with Scar and get him to finance the Galaxy of Stars drag bar in San Diego, where I could report to that slime bag, Claude. That's when you stumbled into my dressing room, Le Strange, in urgent need of a complete makeover. By that time, I knew Scar's tastes perfectly, and the essential ingredient was *big*. He likes 'em big and well equipped. I figured you would do just fine, a nice boy just off the farm with stars in your eyes. But, after a while, when I got to know you, I learned your big secret."

"That's a very interesting story, Urna. Stanley, you darling lump, I feel a powerful thirst coming on. How's about you rustling up a batch of those pink lady cocktails for Urna and me?"

To emphasize the urgency of her request, Lilly actually hoisted her bulk off the bed and affectionately ushered Stanley out the door, which she slammed after him with rather too much energy. Then, with one sweeping pirouette, she turned on Urna.

"You're close to the brink, Flamanté." Lilly hissed menacingly, "Drop a dime on me, and your life with Scarface will seem like a trip to Disneyland. You swore never to tell a soul about my special ... inclinations. So, keep your trap shut, especially around Stanley!"

OK, OK, Le Strange, if you say so. But I don't see how you could possibly dream of fooling real queens."

Urna shook her head pityingly as she finished up the packing by trying to stuff a garter belt of over-generous proportions into a smallish side pocket in the last suitcase.

"If you don't mind, I will be wearing that, so don't go getting your greasy mitts all over my intimate apparel," said La Diva, snatching the foundation garment away.

"I don't mind a bit." Urna retorted. "In fact, I was wondering what the thing was—the harness for a parachute?"

"Never mind what this is. Just remember, button your lip about my true nature."

Stanley came back, laden with a tray carrying cocktails and a shaker.

"Yeah, babe two pink ladies. So, what happened next, Urna?" Did Scarface front you the dough for your club, or what?"

"Of course he did. Galaxy of the Stars is where Lilly got her start, along with many other young hopefuls. It's practically on the National Registry of Historic Sites."

"Yeah, but let's skip to fast-forward." Said Lilly impatiently. "What about your untimely demise? And how come you ain't dead?"

Urna and Stanley, both exasperated by Lilly's interruptions, glared at her with disapproval.

"I'll flesh out the details for you a bit later, Stan," Urna continued. "For now, let's just say that Scar took a real shine to me, and as long as I wore a leather hood without eye holes, I did not tremble at the sight of him.

"For a number of years, this arrangement satisfied everyone involved. I got to perform nightly in the most sumptuous costumes, with the support of a talented cast. The CIA and agent Claude Voit kept tabs on Scarface and Fathead. Scar had me as his main squeeze, as well as a fresh bevy of chorus girls to choose from. Fathead pushed a whole bunch of dope all over the place and raked in the dough.

"That brings us to that fateful night at the Club Crazy in Boston, where my tour was playing. That bogus obituary in *Gay Windows* was so far off, I thought it was a joke. There truly is a sucker born every minute. I mean, really, I read their account of the event and, Darlinks, that was more than a little far-fetched. How could anyone tap-dance fast enough to burn a hole in the stage and die? No, that myth was created by Reginald Pew, their supposed theatre critic."

"The little prick!" Lilly interjected.

"What really happened was, Fathead wanted Scarface to go to Aruba, where he had big plans to reopen his gambling operations and also cash in on the growing Colombian cocaine market. But, he knew Scar was hung up with me and my girls. So, Fathead sent his punks over to the club, and, yes, it is a small world, because one of them was none other than my old Marine buddy, Flaming Freddy, who was underneath the stage with his blowtorch. I could feel the heat rising from the stage, and I was doing my best to stay airborne and above it all with my famous fast footwork. Unfortunately, I was not half fast enough. The boards burned through before my act ended, so, poof, I fell through the fucking floor. I was just about burnt alive, except that, when I fell, my huarache slammed into that maniac Freddy, redirecting the aim of his blowtorch toward the other lug who then became one charred corpse, which everyone assumed was me. Meanwhile, I was dragged outta that hole during the panic over the fire and thrown into Fathead's waiting limo in the alley.

"I ended up a prisoner on this island paradise, with a fuck buddy who looks like sliced meat. Scar tried to make it up to me by putting in that dinky stage over the bar, where I could resume my performance schedule, and he installed me in a swanky villa up in the hills, but without the other girls from Galaxy of the Stars to help me distract Scar, the pressure has been awful.

Then you came along, Le Strange, and Scar thinks you're my Lesbian lover and his violent jealousy has him fit to be tied, or rather, he wants to tie me up and have his way with me. The Rumba Quartette are really CIA operatives, keeping an eye on Scar's operations and reporting to Claude Voit. But after Scar locked me up at the Villa, the Rumbites didn't have much to do, so José, their leader, got bored and found my old copy of *Vampires Don't Fart*. He passed it around to the other guys, and they all read it, or at least read selected passages. They figured it was really a coded message and that I was a double agent. Then, the script disappeared, and now they are after me too."

Urna drained her pink lady with one slurp and, without invitation, grabbed the cocktail shaker and sucked down the remainder of the concoction.

CHAPTER 20

▼

WHY DO YOU ASK?

Gyles sat contentedly smoking his Sobranie cigarette on the broad loggia of the Royal Palms Hotel. He looked out over the lush green gardens, at the ever-changing shades of the turquoise ocean sparkling so brilliantly beneath the hot, equatorial sun. As his week in Aruba progressed, he had given up all pretence of reading the auction catalogues and antiques magazines he had collected to stave off the possible boredom of life away from Boston. The tropical heat had all but melted his resistance to vacationing, so much so that he had not even noticed morning slipping into afternoon.

"Hello there, Mr. Chilton. May I join you?" Claude Voit's deep, rich voice asked with studied politeness.

"Yes, please do. And call me Gyles. Mr. Chilton is someone I left way behind in Boston." Gyles confessed his new freedom, proudly.

"Gyles it is, then, and likewise, please call me Claude," replied Minister Voit, smiling pleasantly.

Gyles, in his abstracted mood, studied Claude's features almost as if the man were a picture, and not a real person. Claude's flawless dark skin was accented with deep smiling dimples below his high cheekbones and a strong, square jaw. But his vivid green eyes were his most remarkable feature.

"I trust your stay in Aruba has been a pleasant one, Gyles. Did you get out to see the sights? The California Lighthouse perhaps, or the Dutch colonial architecture of Oranjestad, our capital? I think I am correct in assuming that you are interested in architecture."

"Yes I am interested in architecture, but no I didn't visit Oranjestad. Maybe next trip, but a week goes so fast. I mostly stayed at the hotel, although I did go snorkeling. I had no idea there were so many fish in the ocean. I saw huge clouds of fish. There must have been thousands of them swimming together, and at the slightest movement from me they would all surge off in a different direction. That must sound rather ridiculous to you, but I had never gone snorkeling before and I was amazed. The different fish are all so colorful, some of them seem to glow from within, like a neon sign. Have you seen the little barracuda that swim right beneath the surface of the water? Utterly fascinating."

"Yes, the snorkeling here is some of the best in the world."

"Other than that, I am afraid I didn't venture too far from the beach or the pool, but you know, I really rather enjoyed myself."

"You sound surprised. You certainly got a handsome tan."

"Thank you, and yes I was surprised. You see, I am not used to resorts. I usually go to England several times a year for my antiques business, and then to the continent. I was afraid there wouldn't be much in Aruba to interest me and, come to think of it, there really isn't. I don't mean to be rude, because the rest was a good thing for me. I didn't know how much I needed to relax and unwind."

"Yet you did have some lively companions while you were here. They must have kept you amused."

"Companions? My sister Cornelia is usually the more social one of us."

"And Miss Le Strange?"

"Oh, you mean Lilly. We have seen a lot more of her than I expected. In fact, I had no idea she was here at all."

"You've known Miss ... Lilly for some time?"

"Yes, but it's Cornelia who is really Lilly's friend. Although my partner and Lilly are uh ... also good friends."

"And you are not?"

"I don't have a great deal in common with Lilly Linda Le Strange. In fact, until this trip I really didn't know her very well."

"Lilly is an actress?"

"According to her, she is the greatest star in the galaxy."

"And you have your doubts?'

"No, not on that level. Lilly is a consummate performer. You should see her show *Glamour Galore*. It's a dazzling extravaganza. You know, she is really a man?"

Gyles dropped this bomb, hoping that Claude would be shocked and uncomfortable enough with the information to drop the subject, but Minister Voit had his own agenda to pursue.

"Yes, that much I do know. But, who is the fellow that accompanies him … uh … her?"

"Stanley Potsdam. Apparently, they are old friends, although they seem an unlikely pair to me. Stanley is Boston's Eye on the Sky traffic reporter."

Claude's eyebrows rose in question to this surprising revelation.

"He flies a helicopter and reports from the air on the traffic all over the city. I guess, in a way, he is rather a personality in Boston. He is a highly decorated veteran from the Vietnam War. Back home in Boston, he does a fair amount of charity sponsorship, supporting Clean and Sober Teens. Apparently, he has been in recovery, himself, for years."

"I am surprised to hear that." mused Claude.

"I know, so was I. We had coffee together yesterday morning, and we got to talking."

"Did he say where they were going?" asked Claude. Gyles thought perhaps this was going a bit too far, but gossip was an indulgence he secretly enjoyed, and once started it was hard to stop.

"Going? No, they are staying at a place called the Grass Shack, on the beach. But I suspect it's a whole lot more than that."

"More? In what way?"

"Well, how many Grass Shacks have electric keys, or any keys, for that matter? I once went to Lilly's apartment in Boston, and that was rather amazing."

"How so?"

"For starters, a Little Lulu doll was strapped to an armadillo shell in a rather suggestive posture, and that was the mailbox."

"Oh."

"Oh, indeed. So who knows what the Grass Shack is like?" Gyles was pleased with his brief sketch of Lilly Land, as Lilly's notorious home in Boston's South End was affectionately called. He hoped this would rattle Claude's smooth and polite exterior manner. But Claude Voit, it seemed, was not the conventional bureaucrat Gyles had supposed. Evidently, it would take a lot more than Lilly Land to upset his composure.

"Have they returned to Boston, then?"

"I … uh … thought they were here for the duration," Gyles improvised vaguely. He was becoming decidedly uncomfortable with the drift of the conversation, although he didn't know why. It had all been rather innocent, or had it?

"The duration? Of what?"

"Oh, nothing. It's just an expression. I was under the impression they would be here for some time."

"Perhaps they flew off to Venezuela for a quick trip. There are many tourist excursions to the mainland, which is only a short flight away. Did Mr. Potsdam mention anything of that nature when you were at coffee yesterday?"

"No, as far as I know, they are still in Aruba."

"Then you have not spoken with either of them today? Is it possible that your sister has spoken with Miss Le Strange … didn't you say they were close friends?"

"I don't know if I would say *close* friends. Cornelia has a wide array of acquaintances, that's all. Will you look at the time, Claude! I am so sorry, I would love to stay and talk with you, but I am scheduled for a massage right now, and that is something I really do need. It's been nice chatting with you, goodbye."

"What time *is* it, Gyles?" Claude Voit asserted himself in a subtle way.

Gyles automatically looked to his right wrist to consult his Rolex, but much to his chagrin, he had forgotten to wear his watch today.

✳   ✳   ✳   ✳

"Cornelia! Are you here?" Gyles flung his question in no special direction as he stepped into the Sunset Suite and locked the door behind him.

"Oh … Gyles! Yes, here I am. I was napping," came a sleepy reply from one end of the enormous sectional couch that snaked around the living room of their hotel suite.

"I just had the strangest chat with your friend Claude Voit."

"Did you really? I thought you might warm up to him, but how was it strange?"

"Now you sound like Claude—nonstop leading questions." Gyles was attempting to purge himself of any complicity in the gossip he had indulged in.

Cornelia sat up straight and looked at Gyles, her head to one side in silent question.

"I was having a cigarette on the loggia downstairs when, out of the blue, Claude Voit appeared and invited himself to join me. At first, I thought nothing of it. You know how it is around here, so marvelously warm and relaxing, even sultry. Anyway, I was half asleep and Claude kept grilling me about Lilly and

Stanley. I guess I rattled on a bit, although I don't think I said anything important. I don't clearly remember what all he asked me, but after a while it seemed
rather probing. Cornelia, have you ever seen the Grass Shack?"

"No. Why do you ask that?"

"Because Claude seemed inordinately interested, and he is under the impression they have gone away somewhere. Did Lilly mention anything like that to
you?"

"No, not a word. I know she was planning to open a new show when she gets
back to Boston, but I was under the impression that would be some time in the
future."

"Claude got me to wondering, because of his questions. Do you have Lilly's
phone number?"

"No, I don't think so ... oh, wait, Stanley called yesterday to get the recipe for
pink ladies. I can probably find it on my cell phone by looking up recent calls.
Wait a sec., and I'll see."

Cornelia unfolded herself from the comfort of the overstuffed couch and rummaged in her beach bag looking for her phone, which in due course she found.
She flipped it open and consulting the memory file "Yes, here it is," she
announced. "Do you want me to call? And if so, what am I to ask her?"

"Just see if anyone answers first, and if they are there, say we would like to
come over and see the Grass Shack."

Cornelia did as he asked, but the number rang and rang without any answer.

"Nope, no one at home, or at least no one is conscious over there."

"Don't say that Cornelia!" snapped Gyles.

"Why, Gyles, whatever is the matter? You sound really upset."

"I don't know, it's just that Claude Voit worries me, somehow. He was trying
to find out from me where Lilly and Stan were. Why me?"

"Oh, come on, Gyles, he was probably trying to get *your* number, not theirs."

"No, Cornelia, as I told you before, Aruba's Minister of Tourism has no personal interest in me."

"But, how do you know? It sounds to me as if he was intent on just that."

"That is exactly the problem. He sounded all very matter-of-fact and charming, but there was urgency to his questions that went much further than idle
chit-chat. Listen, do you know where the Grass Shack is? I think we should stop
by for a visit."

"I am not sure. Lilly always referred to it as 'the Grass Shack on the beach,'
and that is such a clear image that I could imagine the place—but, let me think—
did she actually mention where it was?" Cornelia paced the floor for a bit and

then stopped in place with her eyes closed, plumbing the depths of memory for a hint about of the location of Lilly's Grass Shack.

"Nothing is coming to mind, but maybe Stanley's friend with the paragliding business knows where it is."

"Brilliant! I remember Stanley mentioning his buddy, and I think I remember him saying this fellow was also a Vietnam veteran? Isn't it odd?"

Gyles went to the bar and opened a bottle of Perrier, which he sipped pensively.

"Isn't what odd, Gyles?"

"All these people are Nam vets, as Stanley would say. I wonder … Cornelia, let's go down by the beach and see if we can find Stanley's friend. It shouldn't be difficult, they are taking people up all day long, right in front of the hotel."

"Sure thing. But, let me put on some shorts and sandals. If I'm going to play Nancy Drew, I have to change out of my sarong."

Gyles pulled his dark glasses out of his curly black hair and slipped them over his eyes. As he sipped his Perrier, he filled his pockets with his wallet, lighter and a thin box of Sobrani cigarettes Then he and buckled his Rolex onto his right wrist.

CHAPTER 21

▼

MEANWHILE, BACK IN BOSTON

Val lugged two heavy Louis Vuitton suitcases down the front stairs of 283 Commonwealth Avenue. He was careful not to scrape the expensive luggage against Lucy Ann's lovingly polished banister or the delicately turned balustrades that decorated the grand Victorian staircase of the guest house. Behind him on the stairs, Mrs. Fitzgibbon cheerfully bubbled her appreciation and thanks, as Mr. Fitzgibbon dug deep into the breast pocket of his Brooks Brothers suit, searching for his wallet.

"Val, you have really made our stay here very nice," Mrs. Fitzgibbon enthused sincerely, as she watched the young man's shapely physique descending the soft carpeted stairs before her.

"Frank and I just love this historic old house. It's like staying in a museum, except everything is so comfortable and you can sit on the furniture. We've just never seen anything like it. Back home in Utah, we don't have much that's old, except shabby shacks and suchlike. Chilton House is a real find, and you can be sure we'll tell all our friends."

Mr. Fitzgibbon turned to Val and handed him three crisp twenty-dollar bills.

"Sally and I really enjoyed ourselves, Val, and we will be back next spring for the big game, so see you then and take care of Lucy Ann. That woman is a gem!"

"Sure will, Mr. Fitzgibbon. Bye, Mrs. Fitzgibbon."

"Don't you think Stella and Jim would just eat this place up, Frank?"
"Yes dear, now let's be off and let Val go about his business."

Upstairs, Lucy Ann peered out from the now-vacant second-floor bedroom to Commonwealth Avenue, where Val was helping their guests into the waiting Checker cab. Mr. Charley carefully placed the Fitzgibbon's luggage on an old army blanket that lined the trunk of his cab. He then closed the hood with firm, but quiet, pressure. As he circled around to the driver's side, he felt the gaze of his dear friend and, looking up, saw Lucy Ann in the window, waving.

✳   ✳   ✳   ✳

Lucy Ann's idea of running Chilton House as a bed-and-breakfast was a natural extension of her life's work as the housekeeper to the Chilton sisters of Back Bay and nursemaid to their two wards, Cornelia and Gyles. The Chiltons were one of the great Boston clans, incorporating all kinds of characters. Their family tree had roots that bore into the rot and compost of the human forest, as well as branches reaching into the bright heavens above. Lucy Ann's position within this tightly stratified history had been an obscure secret carefully guarded and only coming to light after the death of Florence Chilton. The unexpected and happy ending to this story came when Lucy Ann's "babies," Cornelia and Gyles, gladly recognized Lucy Ann as their true aunt and the rightful heir of 280 Commonwealth Ave. known in the family as Chilton House.

Lucy Ann proved her legitimacy beyond a doubt, by maintaining traditional Chilton routines in her home. She decided to run her bed-and-breakfast with the least amount of change, using the house as it was intended, with spacious entry halls, the grand formal dinning room, a double parlor, and a well-stocked library on the second floor composing the suite of public rooms. The old-fashioned kitchen and other service amenities were located in the basement floor of the old house. On the upper stories, guest rooms with private baths were arranged spaciously around the grand spiraling staircase.

Lucy Ann did, however, add several helpers to her staff. Val served as the live-in "Assistant Innkeeper" and her most trusted partner. Secondly, but just as important, Lucy Ann employed, "my Russian gals," Olga, Tanya and Katia, who helped with all the chores during the daytime.

The Fitzgibbons and other customers of Chilton House were enchanted by the opportunity of experiencing life in a nineteenth-century Boston townhouse, and the warmth and competence of the staff had all contributed to the prosperity of the enterprise in its first year.

*   *   *   *

Lucy Ann was happy to see Mr. Fitzgibbon tipping Val, who acknowledged the gift with a smart salute and one of his most wining smiles. He then carefully closed the cab door and waved a final farewell.

Back inside the house, Val bounced up the stairs two at a time, calling out and waving the bills in the air.

"HEY, Lucy Ann, looky what I got!"

Lucy Ann was already in the process of stripping the enormous old four-poster bed the Fitzgibbons had so lately vacated, but she paused to see Val's well-earned tip. She was not so much interested in the money—although this was important to her—as she was charmed by the pride and enthusiasm lighting up the young man's face. Lucy Ann never took Val's youthful strength and companionship for granted. His cheerful and competent support was a godsend to her, after so many years of lonely toil in this house that she had so recently and unexpectedly inherited. She frequently said silent prayers of thanks for his help.

"Those folks may be from Utah, but yet and still, they do know how to mind their manners. They left me a little something, too."

As a lifelong Bostonian, Lucy Ann was snobbishly surprised by signs of civility from any poor creatures not born and bred in the Hub.

"Great, when Mr. Charley gets back from driving them to Logan airport, we can all celebrate!"

"Child, this is no time to be throwing away your hard-earned money. That's supposed to pay for your computer classes at Bunker Hill College." Lucy Ann gathered the rumpled bed sheets in her long arms and headed toward the door.

Not having had much of an opportunity for an education herself, and knowing how dependent this had made her in life, she was acutely mindful of Val's need to go to college. She was trying to urge him in that direction by easy stages. To inaugurate this campaign, she had bought him a computer after he agreed to attend courses at the local community college. She hoped that he would be able to take over the office work for their growing venture. From what she could gather, that necessitated learning computer skills to deal with e-mail and the internet. At least, this is what Rita Rosenstein, her accountant, had told her.

"But, Lucy Ann, don't you remember this is our first anniversary—Chilton House is now, officially, one year old."

Val plucked the pile of sheets from Lucy Ann's competent arms and led the way toward the back stairs, where they both descended to the basement.

Lucy Ann was about to reply that one year was nothing compared to the lifetime of thankless labor she had already expended in this house. But she held her tongue, because the shadows and burdens of the past had finally been lifted, and her new life of sharing the family home with appreciative and paying quests had made the old household routines worthwhile. Val's energy and competence had contributed immeasurably to the success of their venture and confirmed her decision in choosing him to help. She had seen in him common sense and natural intelligence, but she also saw in him a great need for a home, family, and meaningful employment.

Lucy Ann and Val had each experienced a want of kindness in their respective pasts. Although of vastly different backgrounds, they had developed parallel determinations to be friendly and helpful in life. They had both known the aching hunger of loneliness and recognized this in each other, although with delicate consideration they never mentioned or spoke of these issues.

Val deposited the laundry in the hamper in the basement hallway, and then returned to the front hall to collect the mail before joining Lucy Ann in her immaculate old-fashioned kitchen. She was seated in her usual place at the head of the large, well-scrubbed oak table that dominated the center of the room. Two steaming cups of coffee and a plateful of pecan sticky buns filled the air with enticing aromas. Val handed Lucy Ann the pile of mail as he greedily reached for a pastry. He effortlessly lifted one long leg over the back of the antique Windsor chair and plopped himself down. Lucy Ann looked up from sorting the mail and gave a gently reproving look at his exaggerated athleticism. She was a stickler for proprieties. Then she absently handed him a picture post card and continued her sorting.

"Hey, get a load of this!" Val flipped the card and read aloud: 'Dear Val, apparently it won't surprise you by the picture that we are in Aruba....'

"Aruba?" Lucy Ann looked up in surprise. "I thought they were in Bermuda."

"That's 'cause Cornelia was trying to keep it secret from Gyles," Val chuckled.

"That ain't no way to be," said Lucy Ann shaking her head. "I taught her better than that. Never, ever, tell lies ... that's what I told her. Seems like just yesterday I had to set that child right on just this point. Now I come to find out...."

"It was the only way Cornelia could get him to go," said Val. And if she didn't tell the exact truth, she did it because otherwise he wouldn't stop working. And besides, she was lonely without Rita."

"That's no excuse. From what Rita tells me, it was Cornelia who called the whole thing off. Just wait till that little lady gets her butt home here. She's gonna hafta listen to a whole heap of instruction from her old Aunt Lucy Ann. I'm also a little scared that Rita won't want to work with us any more, so you see, you just gotta study that computer hard if we are going to survive."

"OK, OK, I hear you, and yes, I am studying, but you don't have to worry about Rita. She's on our side totally. I think maybe she really doesn't want to break up."

"Val, you know I try to understand your, ah, gayness, or whatever it's called, and Lord knows, I don't have a lot of experience with the ways of the heart, but …"

"What do you mean, not a lot of experience? What about the family and Mr. Charley?"

"Now, watch out, boy. As far as the family goes, it's only my babies and Miss Florence who ever gave me so much as a hug. The rest of those Chiltons and Chichesters treated me like dirt before, and they still do. Mr. Charley is none of your business, so don't you go getting any ideas 'bout him. So, what else does the card say?"

Val continued reading, "I think, however, it may be news that Lilly Linda is also in residence, stirring up her usual brand of riot and chaos. Aside from that, Aruba is surprisingly relaxing and the only thing that's missing is you. Be home next week, so watch out! All my love, Gyles. P.S. Corny sends her love to you and A.L.A."

"Oh, this is so sad," declared Lucy Ann, rattling and snapping the *Back Bay Gazette* newspaper for effect and attention. 'Mrs. Rosalind Wortheley remains in a stable but comatose condition at the Brigham and Women's Hospital, where she has been in intensive care since her accident at the opening night of the Essential Center last month.' That girl was the most beautiful child you have ever seen."

"Wow, you know Rosalind Wortheley?"

"'Course I do. Since way back, when Cornelia first brought that child home here from school. Rosalind was a sweet thing then, very polite, and Cornelia was taken with her for a while, but then Rosalind got a crush on Gyles and Cornelia was jealous. It was puppy love, really. The girls couldn't have been any more than eleven years old at the time, which would've made Gyles thirteen or fourteen. Poor boy, you could see him torn by his loyalty to Cornelia—he was always very protective of her—at the same time, he couldn't hide his fascination with Rosalind. She was a tall, skinny thing then and, well, she was just lovely, with long, golden hair and that little sort of weeping break in her voice. Gyles always liked beauty, wherever he found it, and Rosalind was truly a pretty girl. But she made a nuisance of herself, because, being spoiled and pampered, she figured whatever she wanted, she should have. Gyles and Cornelia were different from the other kids at their schools. He went to Deerfield and she went to Dana Hall, but they were very close, like a couple really. None of the three could sort out their feelings. How could they, being so young and all? It would have been more natural for them to just drift apart, but Rosalind wouldn't let go and although beautiful, she really wasn't very interesting for them. Over the years Gyles has let Rosalind get to him—he can be powerfully serious about trifles sometimes—but this is the only way she can get his attention so she keeps it up. But now, what can the poor woman do? She's like Sleeping Beauty in the fairy tale, and I guess she won't be bothering anyone anytime soon, except for that husband of hers. What's his name? George Wortheley? Who is he, anyway?"

"George Wortheley is the backer of *Glamour Galore*."

"Is that the show you were in?"

"Sure is."

"Well, I guess this is a small world, after all."

"And gettin' smaller all the time."

CHAPTER 22

▼

WHERE DID THEY GO?

Cornelia and Gyles cut through the poolside gardens, past splashing waterfalls miraculously issuing from high-piled rockeries, where collections of rare orchids and jungle greenery were gathered in profusion beneath the arched vaulting of the constantly swaying royal palms. They emerged from the dappled shade of this oasis onto the bright, sandy beach. There, in the near distance, waves of reflected heat distorted the images of gathering tourists like a desert mirage slowly undulating skyward. The heat of mid-afternoon was palpably strong, and the two siblings slowed to a crawl as they surveyed the stretch of fine-sand beach, looking for the paraglider. Young children squealed with the thrill of breaking surf, and concerned parents kept watch from beneath the protective shade of a phalanx of palapas, thickly thatched with dried palm fronds.

Wandering aimlessly amongst these bikini-bare tourists were fully dressed native vendors, laden with trinkets ranging from wind chimes made of thin-sliced agate to soft-woven ponchos purported to be alpaca. They were further encumbered with heavy collections of shell necklaces and macramé bracelets, knotted from brightly colored acrylic string.

"Gyles, how can those poor people carry all that stuff in this blazing heat?"

"I don't know, but even fully clothed they seem oblivious to the heat. You have to admire their stamina but sadly it must indicate a great need."

"Yes, apparently the entire world is not on vacation with money to burn, although one would never know it from the sheltered confines of the Royal Palms Hotel."

"Hold on, there they are!" Gyles pointed toward a curtain of undulating heat waves down the beach.

"Looks like bad TV reception to me, Gyles, how can you tell? Is it Lilly?"

"Not Lilly, at least, I wouldn't expect her up in the sky today. But some poor tourist is being dragged through the ether. Look up there." Gyles pointed above the band of soft-focus heat waves rising from the burning sand to a clear view of an oversized kite. Its red-and-white-striped sailcloth supported a dangling traveler from Sioux Falls, South Dakota.

"Oh, yes, I see now, and they are coming our way. I can see the boat pulling him now. Thank the goddess we won't have to walk that much farther down this beach. It's really hot."

"I think if we go down by the water's edge the boat will come pick us up. At least, that's what I saw them doing yesterday when I came down here for a cigarette."

"Yes, I think you're right, and I'd like to cool my feet from the burning sand. It's getting to me, even with sandals."

Cornelia and Gyles crossed the beach toward the mild surf lapping rhythmically along the shore. They stood watching as the striped kite with its lone passenger soared far above the sparkling bay. On the return journey from the distant end of the beach, the boat began to slow down, which lowered the airborne tourist in graceful slow motion to the surface of the bay. The drivers of the motorboat then made a tight circle, quickly retrieving their customer, and headed for the beach.

"Gyles, that woman looks more than a little rattled. Do you think she's OK? I'll tell you one thing, I would no more go up in that contraption than I'd fly to the moon!"

"I am relieved to hear that, because I was terrified you would want to prove your sisterhood by launching into the blue. I guess this means that you will not be accompanying the Le Strange Astronautess into the outer atmosphere."

"You've got that one right, but what do you mean by proving my sisterhood?"

"Don't get riled, Cornelia, I just thought that neither of us should feel compelled to go up. We are, after all, just trying to find Lilly and Stan."

Gyles waded into the water waving at the powerful speedboat that idled a little way offshore, dipping and rolling gently on the water. Cornelia couldn't hear what was said between them, but Gyles turned back in her direction and beckoned her to come along. She waded out to join him, but the small, foamy waves shook her balance and she just escaped plunging in, when two strong arms lifted her out of the water and into the purring boat. Gyles was hoisted next, and one of the bronzed men handed out life jackets as the driver revved the engines and cut a furrow through the sparkling surface of the water.

"Thanks for picking us up," Gyles shouted over the roar of the engine, "but we don't want to go up. We are looking for Stanley Potsdam and Lilly Le Strange. Do you guys know where they are?"

The man handing out the life jackets was wearing a Hawaiian shirt, printed with surfers riding curling waves, over knee-length bathing trunks. His companion was similarly decked out, but his shirt featured a full-blown luau complete with a long line of hula girls that swayed across his solid shoulders. The first guy mimed a "cut," with an ominous slice with his index finger across his neck, and the man at the wheel shoved the throttle into neutral. The boat slowed down and the bow dropped, level with the stern. In the contrasting quiet, the water gently lapped against the fiberglass boat. After a brief whispered conference, both men stared confrontationally at their two passengers.

Cornelia put a gentle hand on her brother's shoulder and took command.

"Hi, I'm Cornelia, and this is my brother, Gyles. We are friends of Lilly and Stans' from Boston. We know that they are staying at a place called the Grass Shack, but we don't know exactly where that is. I remember Stan mentioning he knew you from the Marines, so I thought you'd tell us where we can find them."

Cornelia finished up her speech with what she hoped was a winning smile, but this performance only elicited sullen stares in response.

"I know it all sounds a bit lame," she sailed on, "but we rather lost track of them, and we're due to leave the island tomorrow, first thing, so I wanted to say goodbye, and a few things like that."

The two men turned away and launched into a heated conference in rapid Spanish. Then the driver whipped out his cell phone from his oversized trunks and punched in a number.

"Buenos, Don Nemo," he said, continuing in Spanish. "Pepe and I have picked up two nosey gringos asking a ton of questions about Signor Stan and the big queen." After listening a moment, he answered. "Yes, there is a skinny little dame trying to lay on the sex appeal, and some guy, supposed to be her brother, who looks like he has a stick up his ass." He paused again. "Yes, Yes. Adios."

The driver snapped his phone shut, stuffed it back into his shorts, and barked a quick order to his companion, who motioned for Cornelia and Gyles to sit down and shut up with a quick slash of his finger across his grim lips. The engine revved abruptly, throwing the two siblings down hard on the back bench, as the boat took off with a roar across the bay into the blinding sun. Cornelia nudged Gyles in the ribs with her elbow.

"Ow! Cornelia, do you mind?"

"Gyles, I don't like the look of those guys. Where do you suppose they are taking us?"

"To Lilly and Stan I hope. That was the idea."

"Yeah, but I thought Stan said he had been in the Marines with these guys, and how could that be? "They look younger than me, but the Vietnam War ended the year before I was born."

"Oh, I see what you mean."

Gyles realized too late why he kept anything to do with Lilly at a safe distance.

The speedboat cut a white water scar across the bay and then rounded the point leaving the barrier wall of tourist resorts far behind. Even with the blustering wind ruffling his hair and flapping his shirt against his chest, a nervous sweat beaded Gyles' forehead as the relentless sun beat down upon them.

The coastline here, beyond the artificial oasis of resort gardens, revealed Aruba as an arid desert. The occasional divi-divi tree, looking more dead than alive, was the only relief to scrub brush and cactus. The surrounding ocean stretched on without limit to a distant horizon. Cornelia pulled a spare tee shirt from her beach bag and tied it over her head to shield herself from the blazing sun. At that moment, she caught sight of a gleaming black hump emerging from the sparkling equatorial waters.

"Terrific, now we are going to be rammed by Moby Dick and devoured by sharks!"

"Wasn't Moby Dick a white whale?" remarked Gyles, dryly.

"Then you see it too? Thank the goddess. I was afraid I was hallucinating. Gyles, if we get out of this one, I'm never going to smoke another joint in my life, especially not from Miss Lilly Le Strange!"

As Cornelia was making resolutions of sobriety and covenants with the Almighty, a demonic sea monster was rearing its menacing bulk from the hidden depths into the glaring light of the tropical sun. Great swells of saltwater sloshed from the gargantuan hump, and briny froth hissed in menacing waves that radiated toward the defenseless motorboat bobbing on the open ocean.

Seemingly unconcerned, the two men in Hawaiian shirts spun their craft to circle around the surfacing form, while the driver shouted rapid Spanish into his cell phone. The dorsal appendage of the aquatic horror grew to alarming proportions as the speedboat circled tighter. Then, a startling POP! sounded, followed by a hissing sigh, like the explosion and release of a giant champagne cork. The end section of the monster's dorsal fin, four feet in length, unhinged and fell back. Issuing from this surprising revelation—over all other sounds, including the idling engines, the lapping ocean, and the screaming complaint of a motley batch of seagulls overhead—came the dulcet tones of a familiar voice singing:

> *If a man don't understand you,*
> *if you fly on separate beams,*
> *Waste no time, make a change,*
> *Ride that man right off your range.*
> *Rub him out of the roll call*
> *And drum him out of your dreams.*
> *I'm gonna wash that man right outta my hair,*
> *I'm gonna wash that man right outta my hair,*
> *I'm gonna wash that man right outta my hair,*
> *And send him on his way!*

A single, hefty figure, levitating from within the piscine anatomy, rose into view. She was wearing an enormous, frothy wig of sparkling polyester curls. A voluminous lei of assorted plastic flowers mercifully hid the otherwise naked torso, and a genuine grass skirt, embroidered at the waist band with lurid green fiber spelling, SAMOA, screened her lower half.

"Lilly? Lilly Linda Le Strange?" Cornelia didn't know whether to be gratefully relieved, or what.

Gyles shook his head from left to right, attempting denial, and searched his pockets for a cigarette.

"Why am I not surprised?" he asked with a deep sigh.

CHAPTER 23

▼

CAPTAIN NEMO'S
NAUGHTY-LASS

Inside the sight seeing submarine, *Naughty-Lass,* all was cozy and dry—perhaps a bit too cozy, with La Diva sashaying about in her grass skirt and very little else. Not surprisingly, the compact vessel could not allow for the extended height of Madame's polyester curls, so she appeared wigless as well as topless. Beneath the garish plastic lei dangling round her neck, her formidable brawn could be glimpsed, covered with adense stubble, one quarter of an inch long.

Gyles' attention was in no way focused on Lilly. Since entering the submarine he was enthralled by the view from the row of midsize windows running along both sides of the center of the sub.

"It's an entirely different world down here! Look at the colors! Those fish glow like neon signs. I've never seen anything more beautiful in my life!"

"Looks like a bunch of fish to me." Lilly jealously dismissed Gyles wonder and turned to Cornelia.

"Darling little microbe, you look a bit fried." To emphasize her point, Lilly pressed the tip of her index finger against Cornelia's bare forearm, which left a contrasting pale print against her sunburned skin.

"What you need is a little Aloe-Jojoba skin rejuvenator and a lotta anesthesia."

"Yes, you're right. I could use some lotion. After a week this close to the equator, I may have overdone it a bit."

"Come right this way. I have got just the thing for you." Lilly traipsed off toward the stern of the vessel, carrying her pile of polyester curls nestled neatly beneath her left arm from which unlikely source came muffled yapping.

"Pipe down, Pepe, you'll get yours in a minute!"

Though mystified, Cornelia thought it safer not to question La Diva further, at least not until she produced the suntan lotion.

Meanwhile, Gyles was glued to the windows, looking out at the fantastic underwater world of coral reefs, where waving forests of seaweed and schools of colored fish were dancing in perpetual motion all around the submarine.

"Yo, Gyles," said Stanley, materializing at his elbow. "Wancha to meet my good buddy Captain Nemo. This here's his tub we're in."

"Captain Nemo? Sounds familiar—you mean like in Jules Verne? Glad to meet you, Captain." Gyles offered his hand to the captain.

"Sorry, Stan," Gyles continued. "I didn't mean to ignore you, it's just that I have never seen anything like this. I mean, I got a little taste of it snorkeling one day, but way down here, there are so many beautiful fish of all sizes and shapes. Those huge schools of minnows with the neon blue stripes, wow! There must be millions of them, and when they are startled by something, they flash apart like lightening cutting through thunder clouds."

"Hey, man, no need to be sorry. I couldn't agree with you more." Captain Nemo replied with evident pride. "Ain't it cool? It's a whole new thing in Eco Tourism and deep-sea diving. Lots of tourists don't go for the hassles of scuba gear, but this is real easy for them, so I do a lot of business."

"How did you get started? This must be a considerable investment, and also require a great deal of technical schooling."

"In the Navy I was part of the Scuba squadron. That's how I know Stan, here, and Lilly, for that matter. He's … I mean … she's … well, whatever … a trip and a half. We were all in Nam together. Anyway, when I got out, I set up a scuba business for tourists in Belize, and then I added paragliding and, after years of saving, I bought this tub and had her reoutfitted as the *Naughty—Lass,* which is now the biggest draw in Aruba.

"Yo, Captain Nemo, got a prob here. Can I see you?"

The captain was called away by one of his crew, leaving Stan to fill Gyles in on the details.

"He seems like a nice guy." Gyles said.

"Nemo's oneada best. We go, way back, as he was saying, along with Al."

"Who's Al?"

"Whatcha mean, who's Al?"

"I'm sorry, is that one of the fellows who brought us here?"

"No way, man. That's Manuel and Ricardo—they run Nemo's paragliding business. You mean you really don't know who Al is? He's Lilly."

"How can he be Lilly?" Gyles was all at sea.

"I know, can you believe the fucker? A pig farmer from Kansas, but really a great guy. Saved my life, and Nemo's too. I thought 'cause you were queer and all, you knew all about that."

Stan dropped this bomb casually without malice.

"Well, yes, but I like to think of myself as gay, not queer, and anyway, that doesn't make me a mind reader."

"Albert Mellenoffsky is the name his mother gave him."

*   *   *   *

Lilly slathered on her special sauce, which, as predicted, immediately soothed the sting of Cornelia's sunburned arms. Cornelia looked around her in amazement at the tented dressing room that Lilly had created in the stern of the *Naughty-Lass*. This improvised space was separated from the body of the sub by a curtain of beach towels, whereon Donald and Daisy Duck, along with the six assorted nephews and nieces, were cavorting. Behind this terry-cloth barrier, Lilly Land reigned supreme. A dressing table, of sorts, had been created by stacks of vintage luggage. A mirror framed with a collection of gaily colored bottle caps was hanging from a puzzle of pipes that ran the length of the sub. Lilly's more-than-somewhat-battered steamer trunk stood swung open, drawers overflowing with silks and lace, sequins and feathers, all of which was cascading in a general froth around the compact space. Two folding Italian campaign chairs, popularly referred to as Butterfly chairs, provided seating accommodation, and these were further draped with gaudy bits of frumpery.

"There you go, sweet pea, that'll do ya."

"Thanks Lil, and I like sweet pea a lot better than Little Microbe."

"Darling lump, I can't help it if you are the tiniest thing in the universe! Here, have a hit of this, it'll make you more liberal."

"No, thanks. I promised the goddess that if we survived the terrorist kidnapping I would never smoke another joint."

"Suit yourself, sweetheart, but if you think those cute boys in the motorboat are terrorists, you shoulda been with me in the cab with the rumba contingent."

At this bewildering juncture, as Lilly was puffing away on her reefer, a muffled yapping resumed from somewhere close at hand.

"Land sakes, I forgot all about Pepe! Oh, darling little pooch, come to Mama." Digging into the pile of polyester curls, which Cornelia recognized as the wig Lilly had worn for her Wash That Man routine, La Diva delivered a tiny Chihuahua that yapped hysterically with addictive greed.

"OK, OK, calm down and exhale, here comes." Lilly held Pepe's muzzle gently cupped in her hefty mits and blew a pungent puff of smoke at the wee pooch. Cornelia could hardly believe it, but the dog seemed to smile, and after a moment he let out another couple of yaps.

"You greedy little dope fiend! All right then, have some more." So saying, she repeated the procedure, which resulted in a completely pacified pooch.

"There you go, back into your little bed, I wish all my patients were so easily pleased." Lilly gently eased Pepe back into the wig, from which there came a faint snoring noise.

"Before you pull another rabbit out of your hat, what the hell are we doing in Captain Nemo's *Naughty-Lass* at the bottom of the ocean?" Cornelia demanded with some pique.

"Pepe ain't no rabbit, honey …"

"Leave Pepe out of this and cut to the chase, Le Strange."

"You're getting a little testy, hon. I told you, you should have a little puffy-poo—you know it will clear your head."

"I know nothing of the sort! Will you please fill me in on what is going on here? Gyles was really worried about you and Stan, because Claude Voit was apparently grilling him about your whereabouts to the extent that he thought we should warn you."

"Your bother, my son's husband, the exclusive eleganza queen of Boston's Back Bay, was concerned for me?"

"So much so that we nearly got fried on the open ocean searching for you."

"Well, it's really a long story …"

"Lilly!"

"OK then, here it is. Urna Flamanté, who was dead—you remember, we caught her act at the Jungle Casino—is now alive and being chased by Scarface Malone, Fathead Fabiano, the CIA, the FBI, and an odd assortment of other unsavory characters. This is a direct result of her shady past and double dealing. I, who am a total innocent on this occasion, nonetheless, have gotten into deep do-do by keeping the wrong company, namely, the Lady Urna. Therefore, we are on the lam and hoofing it outta this burg and back to civilization where I will produce, direct, and star in my fabulous new show, *Naughty Astronautess.* Now does that satisfy you?"

"You know, on second thought, I think I should have a hit off your joint" was Cornelia's only reply.

✳   ✳   ✳   ✳

Darlink! Where did you come from?"

Urna Flamanté sidled up to Gyles, who was completely absorbed by the antics of a school of small squid with disproportionately large eyes, who seemed to be swimming backwards just outside his window.

"I'm sorry?" Gyles turned toward the voice behind him. "Ahh … Aruba … that is…. The Royal Palms Hotel … but Boston really." He was so startled by the vision of, and close proximity to, Urna that he stumbled incoherently.

"Urna's eyes devoured Gyles with a slow once-over, traveling from head to toe with brazen scrutiny. She had perched herself on one of the passenger benches that lined the center of the sub, just behind Gyles, so he had to turn around to see her.

Urna was rail-thin, except for her ample bosoms, which had the suspicious shape of the confections called snowballs—in other words, perfectly globular. She wore shocking-pink toreador pants that came only to midcalf, exposing sinewy ankles and feet that were shod with bright turquoise pumps with four-inch heels. Her Versace silk blouse, printed with too many colors and too many patterns, was tied in a knot just above her navel, thus exposing a surprising ripple of tense abdominal musculature. Her face seemed to float above deeply sculpted clavicle regions, like an incongruous memory of her faded past. Hanging from her over stretched earlobes were small, finely wrought gold mousetraps, firmly clamped on diminutive naked men, also in gold. Her jet-black hair stood erect in a bristle of three-inch-long spikes all over her head.

"Ooooo, Boostooon, Darlink, are you one of those big, bad Brahma bulls?"

"Brahmin, maybe, but bull I try not to sling." Said Gyles recovering his wit.

"I know a guy in San Diego with a leather sling hanging from the ceiling over his bed, if that's what you mean."

"No … I … didn't quite have that in mind."

"Well, what *do* you have in mind, Darlink?"

By this point, Urna had twisted herself into a knot halfway between cubist distortion and vaudeville contortionism, intended to be an alluring pose reminiscent of Judy Garland on speed.

"Urna! Is that extreme yoga you're practicing, or are you in the process of a metabolic upheaval like Dr. Jekyll or the wolf man?" demanded Lilly, as she sailed down the isle toward amidships, Cornelia trailing placidly behind.

"Bug off, bitch!" Snapped Urna. "I got here first. This hunk and me was just getting chummy."

"Oh, Lilly, thank God you're here … I mean … ah … here we all are! Hi, sis," Gyles fairly gasped.

"Yes." Cornelia nodded, giggling a bit.

"Say, have you been smoking pot?" Gyles frowned disapprovingly at his sister. "I thought you swore to the goddess, if we got out of here alive, no more dope?"

"We haven't gotten out of here yet." Cornelia pointed out in her defense. "I was merely trying to get my bearings."

"You've got ball bearings tumbling in your brain, Cornelia." Gyles retorted.

"Did you say balls, Darlink? Let's take a look." Urna lurched forward, eyes blazing with what might have been interpreted as lust—however, because of excessive applications of mascara and kohl, she more closely resembled a tarantula suffering from angina.

"Urna, be careful, you're liable to injure yourself. Now, straighten out and be nice," said Lilly, taking Urna by the collar and gaving her a wee, bitty shake. She then plopped herself down on a bench beside Gyles. "As I was telling Corny, Gyles," she continued, "Stanley and I are on our way back to Bean Town. The unexpected appearance of our dear Urna has really lit a fire under our collective asses, so we're dashing outta this dump, pronto. But, much of the story is classified, so the less you know the better. Now, tell me about Claude Voit."

Gyles recounted his suspicious encounter with Aruba's Minister of Tourism, and even Urna shut up to listen to this one.

"But Lilly," Gyles finished with a question, "how are you getting back to Boston? Surely, this small submarine can't make such a journey."

"Don't fret your handsome face. We're only going out beyond sight, into international waters, where a seaplane will take us to Venezuela. I'm planning to make it back in time for Valentine's Day at the Casa Romero. I feel a powerful urge for Leo's perfect margaritas and his puerco adobado. That should fire up my jets hot enough to launch this *Naughty Astronautess* into orbit!"

CHAPTER 24

▼

RETURN TO LILLY LAND

Betty the Bounder was sprawled on the overstuffed chaise that dominated the front parlor of Lilly Land. This accommodating lounger had been cus-tom-designed for one "singular sensation," the resplendent Lilly Linda Le Strange, but as Lilly had been conspicuously absent from the said domain for the better part of the winter season, Betty had moved in. Yes, fully prepared, the Bounder had brought over her cozy collection of stuffed dinosaur pillows in an effort to fill in the lonely spaces between her and the vast recliner. Betty's brand of gaunt and lanky svelteness had been accomplished by decades of strict adher-ence to the drinking-girl's diet, which consisted primarily of cheap gin and See's chocolate truffles. There had been numerous campaigns launched over the years by Lilly and a dwindling clutch of cohorts to rid the bitch of her nasty habits, but Betty proved the intractable as soon as the silly snippet was left to her own devices—back she would slide, gleefully sloshing the sauce.

Ostensibly Betty was there to keep an eye on things while Lilly languished in Aruba, a mandate Betty interpreted to include the pound of grass that La Diva had discreetly concealed in a Mickey Mouse cookie jar sitting beside her famous heart-shaped bed.

At the moment Betty was, with reserves of concentration that would have powered a high school wrestling team, engrossed in a good book, her half-glasses perched precariously on the end of her schnoz. Delicately, she sipped warm gin from a Baccarat flower vase, a remarkable accomplishment considering she also clutched, a corncob pipe between clenched teeth, from which she drew deep drafts of Lilly's aforementioned grass. Whereas the simultaneous consumption of hefty inebriants was remarkable, sipping and puffing in turn, what veered toward the miraculous was Betty's ability to grasp the story at all. Although some of the details did slip beyond her comprehensive abilities, still she caught the general drift, much like a snow fence that will eventually catch enough of a blizzard to pile up a considerable bulge. So also did Betty's mind bulge with enthusiasm and identification as she greedily devoured *Extravaganza King,* a history of Boston's musical theatre by Alison Barnet.

At a pivotal moment in the book, when Robert Barnet was about to don the raiment of Isabella, Queen of the Daisies, there was a thunderous slam-bang, followed by a shuddering tinkle of bells, noise that surely should have alerted Betty to the fact that someone had breached the garden gate. But Betty was oblivious, too engrossed by her book. Further warning that should have alerted anyone within earshot were heavy foot-falls, reverberating against the brick walls and only slightly muffled by the jungle-like growth that ran riot around the garden. But Betty's attention was arrested by the line in her book, "The gown Robert Barnet wore was yellow satin with ermine trim, and had a tucked bodice dotted with daisies." So distracted was the Bounder by this gripping narrative that she failed to take any notice of the heavy tred approaching.

The explosion that occurred when Lilly Linda Le Strange burst through the Dutch door of her Boston flat with a well-placed bump of her left hip was a distraction that even Betty could not ignore. The house trembled with complaint as the sturdy door went flying inward and collided with a five-foot-tall Mr. Peanut manikin that had been converted into a standing lamp. Lilly plunked down her burdens, a collection of vintage pigskin luggage plastered with so many hotel and steamship stickers they formed a patchwork collage. She glared at Betty in silence, simultaneously arching her right eyebrow with an expression of scornful menace.

"Oh, great! Lilly, listen, you're just in time. I've been reading this incredible book, you won't believe it, but according to this, Boston's been full of drag queens for a hundred years and more."

Betty shelved her drink on a handy occasional table made from a stuffed emperor penguin with a silver tray riveted to its head. She peeled herself off the chaise, a process that resembled a punch-drunk boxer staggering back for more punishment. But inexplicably, once the Bounder accomplished her full stature she was remarkably agile, albeit a wee bit wobbly, and she fussed over Lilly with deference and skill. Ushering La Diva toward her chaise, Betty quickly scattered the dinosaur pillows to the four corners of the parlor so the lounger could accommodate Lilly's bulk. She then yanked off Lilly's signature platform pumps. These particular lethal appendages, designed after the pylons of the Mystic River Bridge, could not be hurled any old which way. Betty carefully placed the mammoth sabots beside the Dutch door, which had survived Lilly's entrance with only a minimum of additional distressing. She then closed the door and returned her attention to Lilly, who was sniffing the crystal vase on the penguin table.

"Betty, why does my Baccarat flower vase stink of cheap gin?"

"Gee, Lilly, is that really Burt Baccarat's highball glass? I knew it was special, but not that special. Now listen, Lill, you gotta read this book, *Extravaganza King*. It's by our neighbor, Alison—you know, the gal who lives around the corner. Well, it turns out her great-grandfather invented drag!"

"Betty, you are drunk!"

No, Lill, it's true! He raised a quarter of a million dollars to build the castle in Park Square because the Boston Brahmins were a bunch of drag queens, just like George Wortheley, and they were afraid the Irish would horn in on their act and get all the plum parts."

"Betty, have you been smoking my dope? You are stoned and drunk!"

"Now, just simmer down and take a gander at this book. See, that's Robert Barnet on the cover as Isabella, Queen of the Daisies."

Betty thrust *Extravaganza King* into La Diva's mitts and deftly proffered the refilled and refired corncob pipe, now glowing with fragrant herb, a temptation Lilly could not resist. So, puffing away, La Diva breezed through the book, looking at the pictures, while Betty scurried off to the boudoir to draw a steaming tub of bubbling broth for Lilly to soak in.

Returning to the parlor of Lilly Land, Betty trailed a scarlet chiffon negligee, trimmed with fluffy marabou, over her arm. In a shamelessly affected manner, she liberally spritzed the room with an Art Deco perfume atomizer. La Diva was, however, already deeply involved in *Extravaganza King*, while at the same time blissfully puffing away at the corncob pipe, and so she was completely unaware of Betty's ministrations. Betty continued to spritz with determination, until she had saturated the air to such an extent that a thin haze began to form on the garden windows.

"Say, isn't that Poison I'm smelling?" Said Lilly, raising her eyes from the book.

"I remembered how much you used to like it, so I got this special for you from work."

"Betty, you go to work in that condition?"

"It's just Filenes's Basement, you know."

"Yes, but even they must have some standards."

"Oh, Lilly, I've been hawking the stink in that basement so long I could do it in my sleep."

"That's no excuse. Betty, I left you here to look after things and look at this joint, it's a dump."

"Oh, now, let's not exaggerate. I have, after all, been involved in important research."

As Betty proffered this reason for the relaxed state of house keeping, she thumped a few pillows and kicked the edge of the curled carpet back in place. She then wafted the scarlet chiffon negligee enticingly in Lilly's direction, but Lilly was again absorbed by the pictures in Betty's book.

"You know, Betty, you may be right," mused Lilly. "This looks like pretty hot stuff. I'm really beginning to dig Alison's great-granddaddy. He looks like my kinda guy."

"Well, darling, yours he ain't, 'cause he's dead and gone, but it's nice to know drag queens have been a part of our Boston history—and high society, at that. So, how was Aruba, Miss Thing? I see you got a tan, but what on earth is that gorilla growth sprouting all over you? Girlfriend, you need an overall peel, plucking, and waxing. But first, I have a nice hot tub waiting."

"Oh, yum! I could use a good soak."

"Yeah, well, I could use a good poke."

"Now, Betty, don't chase after lost causes, it'll give you wrinkles." So saying, La Diva trundled off to her bath, barking more orders in her wake.

"Betty, before you haul out the Hoover and suck up all your crud, bring me my cell. I hafta make a dinner reservation over at La Casa."

▼

THE SHORT SIDE OF A LONG SAD STORY

"*Buenas noches*, Casa Romero Restaurant."

"Darling lump, *Buenas noches* to you too. This here is Lilly, and I am desperate for your puerco adabado and a gallon of those perfect margaritas."

"Pardon? Would you like to make a reservation?"

"Sí, Sí! You bet I would. How 'bout eight at eight for Lilly?"

"What day would you like to dine?"

"What day? Tonight! My little muchacho. I can't wait."

"I am sorry, Señor Lilly, but this is Valentine's Day and we are all booked."

"Señora Lilly to you, bub, and you don't hafta tell me what day it is, 'cause I dashed here all the way from Aruba. Listen, lemme speak to Leo."

"Señor Romero?"

"Yes, the hot Latin number with the naturally curly hair."

"Please hold."

"Lilly sighed with impatience, an action that sloshed gallons of bubbly water close to the brink of her tub. To pass the time while she waited to plead her case to Don Leo, she scooped up a handful of suds and absently smeared the froth on her head, molding it into a fashionable do.

"*Buenas noches,* this is Leo Romero. How may I help you?"

"Leo, you divine lump! This is Lilly. I've just flown in from Aruba, if you can believe that and …"

"I am sorry, there is a lot of static on the line. I am having a hard time hearing you. Did you say, Billy playing the tuba? I am awfully sorry, but we don't have an entertainment license."

"That ain't static doll face, those is Bubbles La Reine. I'm in the tub."

"Hello? Billy?"

"Lilly Linda Le Strange."

"Oh, Lilly, I get it, but I thought you were out of the country."

"Darling, I'll be outta my mind if I don't get somma your chili chow, pronto."

"I'm so relieved to tell you … I mean … I'm so sorry to say, Lilly, we are all booked tonight. You do know it's Valentine's Day? If you had only called last month."

"Last month? I wasn't even born then. OK, OK, you win, but how about tomorrow?"

"*Sí,sí, manana*, what time?"

✳   ✳   ✳   ✳

Lilly Linda Le Strange was regally ensconced in the small private dining room at the Casa Romero Restaurant in Boston's Back Bay neighborhood. She, of course, had assumed her rightful place at the head of the long dining table which was inset with emerald-green tiles. The two long walls of this rectangular room were painted with rich, warm, earth tones. On these walls, pairs of large, decorative plates were hung at either side of a central mirror. The mirrors were held in tin frames inset with colorful tiles.

The short wall at the end of the room was covered three-quarters of the way up from the floor with hand-painted Talavera tiles, decorated with geometric designs.

La Diva munched with gusto a mouthful of the Casa's signature dish, puerco adobado, which consisted of thin-sliced pork tenderloin, butterflied and pounded to melting perfection, then marinated in a sauce of tangy orange and smoked chipotle peppers. Between bites of this blissful concoction she cooled her glowing pallet with dainty sips of Leo Romero's perfect margarita, a libation that had a lotta oomph and pizzazz.

Monique La Farge, the statuesque showgirl, ever mindful of her figure, and therefore always in a perpetual state of ravenous agitation, had already finished her dinner. This had consisted only of ceviche cocktail, a Casa specialty of delicate bay scallops, marinated in fresh-squeezed lime juice, flavored with cilantro, then mixed with diced onions, tomatoes and avocado.

Predictably, Monique had grown restless without a prominent mirror to reassure her, so she strutted about the room, practically scraping the ceiling with her wavy auburn hair. She wore her beautiful tresses loosely piled on top of her head and anchored with a red plastic hair clamp the size of a bear trap. As she pranced, she skillfully balanced a margarita cocktail, pinched between two fingers by the stem of the glass, thereby showing to advantage her long, manicured nails, lacquered with a color known as Drop Dead Beautiful.

"Monique, stop strutting around like a hooker in debt and listen up!" Lilly ordered her sometime costar.

"Lilly, when can I expect to hear the new music?" Shana Finale broke in, always impatient to start work on her choreography before Lilly had a chance to change everything from the story line to the time, place or number of characters.

"New music? Woops! I knew I forgot something."

Monique took this moment of Lilly's belated realization to plunk herself down on her boyfriend's lap—a maneuver requiring considerable talent because Butch, the boyfriend, was greedily devouring his pollo molé. He contentedly munched, while loading up his fork with more tender chicken breast dripping with dark rich molé poblano sauce made from roasted nuts and peppers ground and then mixed with Mexican chocolate. Monique somehow managed to insinuate her elegant long limbs to straddle Butch's lap, while she playfully daubed his lips with a yellow cloth napkin.

"Mo! Do you mind?" mumbled Butch, who, although usually transfixed by Monique, was at this moment more interested in his dinner.

"What do mean you forgot *something?*" Shana screeched at Lilly. "The musical score to a musical review is not just *something!*" The choreographer exploded with panic and outrage.

In Shana Finale's orderly and syncopated mind, she knew she would have to endure a little craziness in the process of creating the dance portion of *Naughty Astronautess*. This was a given when dealing with any of Lilly's productions. But, having no music at all did not auger well for Shana.

Meanwhile, Betty the Bounder returned from her supposedly innocent trip to the girl's room, precariously balancing two margaritas as she wobbled in on five-inch stiletto heels.

"Betty, be careful, you know you're not licensed to drink and walk at the same time!"

So saying, Lilly stuffed another delicious morsel of tangy pork into her trap and relieved Betty of one of her cocktails. Betty instantly experienced pangs of acute loss and downed her other margarita in one gulp.

Monique's sleek figure nestled into Butch's massive lap and she ran the palm of her hand along his bristly crew cut.

"Baby, your head feels just like my Teddy Bear."

"Mo, shift over a little bit. You're crushing my dick."

"Oh, lover man, you really know how to get a girl going."

Butch retaliated by wolfing down forkfuls of refried beans flavored with cinnamon and dark, rich molé sauce, alternating with fluffy Mexican rice that was cooked in an herbed chicken stock. He relished the tasty combinations and somehow ignored Monique.

At this juncture of family conviviality, a mysterious stranger slithered through the curtains separating the private dining room from the restaurant. The person before them wore a black trench coat cinched tight at the waist and covering the rail-thin figure down to the ankles, which showed an incongruous glimpse of fishnet stockings stretched over sinewy ankles. Old-fashioned, buckle-up galoshes covered the feet. On the head of the intruder was a crumpled fedora, pulled low over the ears. The face was obscured by mirrored dark glasses, in wire frames of the type worn by motorcycle cops, and beneath that was a bushy black beard that could only be described as ridiculous.

Everyone around the table gasped, and placed their hands on their upper chests in a posture of dismay. Not easily intimidated, Butch burped and reached for his glass of Negra Modelo.

"Darlinks! Draw the curtains and turn down the lights, I am being followed!" said the mysterious figure, reaching into the tightlybuttoned trench coat and extracting a black Luger. Everyone in the room gasped again, and Betty, ever excitable, lunged across the table for Lilly's margarita. But the bearded figure in the fedora fumbled with the lethal pistol and got an index finger stuck in the trigger guard. Growling with disgust and frustration, she yanked out the cramped digit and in the process dropped the gun. There was another collective gasp and this time Lilly's Chihuahua, Pepe, that was lodged in the upper reaches of La Diva's coiffure, woke up from her drugged stupor and began yapping hysterically. The dark figure stooped to grab the Luger from the floor, pointing it at the door draperies, which billowed out, indicating the arrival of....

"Wally St. John?" Lilly and Betty blurted out in close harmony.

Unfortunately, this abrupt ejaculation jarred the jumbled nerves of the bearded stranger and she squeezed the trigger, covering Wally in....

"Gardenia perfume, yuck!" shouted the drenched Wally. "Hey quit it knuckle brain or I'll report you to the Department of Homeland Security!"

Yes, strange as it may seem, the Luger was loaded with Jungle Gardenia perfume, which indicated one thing: that the gun-toting mama was none other than, Urna Flamanté.

Once dead and now alive, Urna's resurrection had already been explained to Lilly, although the period of adjustment required for believing Urna's hokum was still at a point where Lilly maintained her usual attitude of healthy skepticism. What for instance did ScarFace Malone see in Urna that so captivated the thug? This and other conundrums weighed uneasily on the scales of Lilly's reason, threatening to tip the precarious balance in some untoward direction. However, Lilly had been expecting Urna that evening. Now as for Wally, there was no such explanation. So, braving the worst, La Diva put it to him.

"OK, Wally what's the deal? I was under the impression from our last conversation that Fathead Fabio had rubbed you out! And if you think I'm gonna shell out for another phony funeral like Urna's, think again, 'cause this queen ain't got a pot to piss in!"

"Thas OK Lill, you can use my empty beer glass." This generous offer was made by Betty, who thought she knew what was going on.

"Betty, stay out of this," retorted Lilly. "I'm trying to get the truth outta Wally."

"Talk about lost causes giving you wrinkles ..."

"Betty, I'm warning you," growled Lilly,

She then returned her attention to the costume designer of the queens, Wally St. John, glaring at him in expectant silence.

"Now, Lilly, what's the big deal?" asked Wally, throwing up his hands in an attempt to convey lithesome innocence.

"Leme tell you, Wally, the big deal is this. I distinctly heard you being strangled over the phone when I called to ask about the coffee-percolator platform shoes you made for Urna."

"Oh, that, I was busy when you called. You *do* remember, I made that very clear. I was giving Brother Jonquil a blowjob and, well, he couldn't get enough so I had to give him somore."

"Brother Jonquil! squealed Betty. "I heard he has a donkey dick. What's it like?"

"Betty, will you shut up!"

Lilly stomped her foot, an action that shook the whole room and commanded unquestionable obedience, although the group around the table was now all agog to hear about the monk's member.

"You mean to say that Fathead Fabio was not wringing your scrawny neck, but instead you had the effrontery to subject me to your lewd slurping on a long-distance call from Aruba?"

"That's about the size of it, yeah," agreed Wally with wistful nostalgia.

"What size *is* it?" demanded the whole gang leaning across the table.

∗   ∗   ∗   ∗

Urna Flamanté sat at the long table with the green tile top, eating savory chicken enchiladas smothered with verde sauce that was flavored with fresh green cilantro. Butch poured her a Negra Modelo cerveza.

"Urna, how come you're not dead?" he asked innocently.

"Oy Veh! Darlink, it's such a long story, what I've got to worry about now is how to stay undead and shake Scarface Malone off my tail."

"You might ask Abbot Acidophilus to put you up in a cell over at the monastery," suggested Wally St John, himself a semipermanent inmate of the Holy Fryers Monastery.

"Gee, Darlink, that's big a ya, 'specially after what I just done. Could you really put in a good word for me?"

"No sweat, Urna. Jungle Gardenia is mighty stinky stuff, but it'll wear off. Now, as far as good words and you go, the Abbot's no dummy. I think you'd better appeal to his sense of outrage. Why don't you just tell him the truth?"

"Between you and Urna the truth is something no one would believe." Monique piped up with a rare perceptive comment.

"Hey, that's sorta deep, Mo." Butch was impressed.

"Don't worry about Abbot Acidophilus," Lilly assured them. "I have it from the horse's mouth, our own dear Brother Jebadiah, that the Holy Fryer Brothers are chomping at the bit for a little entertainment and fundraising."

"What's Jebadiah doin' in a horse's mouth?" Betty nudged Wally and asked, "Are the Holy Fryer Brothers practicing veterinary science? I'm glad to hear it, 'cause I took Lilly's little Pepe over to the Humane Society behind Fritz's bar to get her teeth brushed, but they wouldn't do it."

Wally stared at Betty blankly then ordered a frozen mango margarita from Eduardo the waiter.

"That reminds me Scena," said Lilly, "let's schedule a rehearsal at the Club Crazy tomorrow, first thing."

Suddenly, everyone froze, forks full of enchilada, puerco adobado and Chicken molé were suspended in midair, and, most amazingly, no one even dared to sip their drink.

"Whaaaaat?" Lilly implored the gang, who all cowered in frozen animation until their spineless fear moved them toward human sacrifice, at which point they all turned with one mind toward Betty.

"Oh, no! I ain't telling her! Not me! Listen, girls, hash this out between youse. I gotta buy me a ticket to Providence on the Bonanza bus."

Betty tried to get up from the table and flee, but Butch rested a chummy arm—bulging with more muscle mass then Betty possessed in her whole scrawny body—across Betty's thin shoulders. He thereby effectively pinned the bitch to her chair, where she squirmed with unseemly desperation.

"OK, Betty, what is it this time?" demanded Lilly, folding her arms belligerently over her chest. Pepe let out a few sympathetic yelps for his friend Betty.

"I'm waiting, Miss Thing!"

Lilly bore down on the Bounder mercilessly.

"You see, it's like this, Lill. There is a long, sad story, but I'd probably get it messed up, so lemme just say this: It's gone."

Everyone around the table began to imbibe, big time, and Wally signaled for Eduardo to keep 'em coming.

"What's gone?" demanded La Diva in a tone reserved by the Almighty to announce Armageddon. But everyone shrugged noncommittally and continued to slosh the sauce.

"You don't mean …? It couldn't be! The Club Crazy is *gone*? Arrrrrgah!"

*   *   *   *

Lilly Linda Le Strange sat on the throne in the girl's room at the Casa Romero. In truth, this receptacle could only accommodate her left cheek, but she wasn't there to use the facilities, she was there to weep.

Monique Le Farge was attempting to ease La Diva's grief with the aid of a particularly fat joint of Maui Wowie, and because the two headliners were, by nature, larger than life, and also because the Damas accommodations at the Casa Romero were as tiny as a dwarf's closet, there was not a lot of room for maneuvering. Accepting these limitations with good grace, they passed the reefer back and forth, using the sink as an ash tray.

Pepe the Chihuahua whined pathetically from within Lilly's bouffant coiffure elaborations.

"Listen to that, Lilly, the little fucker's given' ya some sympathy." Monique proffered this interpretation, attempting by association to provide some sympathy of her own.

"No, the poor little mite just wants to have a hit off the joint."

Monique smirked knowingly at herself in the mirror and readjusted the hair clamp holding her torrent of auburn waves in place.

"Would ya blow a little dope in his muzzle?" asked Lilly.

Monique did as she was bid, but not without reluctance and disapproval. Pepe sucked in the cloud with trembling greed and settled back into the protective coils of Lilly's coif for a good snooze.

La Diva retrieved the joint from Monique and puffed away ferociously, but the anesthetizing herb was not enough to keep sorrow at bay, and she sniveled in spite of herself.

"Oh, Monique, it's no good, I'm all undone."

This confession unsettled Monique's confidence and she checked her own zippers and snaps, but finding them in order, she adopted a tone of generous condolence.

"Here Poopsey, hava little smear a lipstick," she said. "I always use red when I'm blue." And she handed her friend a tube of Scarlet Harlot, which Lilly applied with perfunctory enthusiasm.

"So, the Club Crazy is really outta commission?" Lilly asked, leaning her head against the wall in a listless pose of melancholic remorse.

"You poor, exploded bombshell! the Club Crazy is way gone. Your ex-partner in crime, Mr. George Wortheley, got real mean and nasty, throwing us out on our asses the day after you crashed his party. You probably heard, that silly bitch wife of his smashed her head on the floor that night. I think she cracked the cement, so I guess he had some reason, but I don't think *she* does anymore, 'cause she's in a coma."

Following the knoted thread of Monique's story was a perplexing struggle, and Lilly was too saturated with self-pity to be overly concerned with the particulars, so Monique sailed on.

"All the fixtures and furnishings were sold at auction a month ago. Then the joint was scraped back to the I-beams and rented for office space to some outfit called The Right to Lifers. But what rights Lifers are 'sposed to have, I ain't got no idea. I thought if you landed in the slammer, that was it."

This last bit of Monique's exposition careened toward the truly demented. Lilly was trying to sort it out in her head, but she couldn't muster up the energy required to set Monique right, and besides, that was probably impossible, so she let it all slide.

"George shoulda invited me to his fucking party! How was I to know the wife would take the fall for him, so to speak? I'm really sorry for her. I read she's in Brigham and Women's. Do you know if she's still there? I wonder what she looks like. Is her face all right, I wonder? Oh God! I've really cut off my nose to spite my face this time!"

Snookums! Get a grip! This ain't no time for surgery ... besides, your honker is one of your better features."

Monique got everything so consistently screwed up that Lilly just shook her head and had another hit off the joint. There was an urgent rapping at the door, but the two friends shrugged at each other with dismissive contempt.

"Keep your panties on, girl." Monique quipped.

Lilly rose from the throne, deposited the roach in the bowl and flushed the solid evidence away. Monique got to work spraying the room with her purse-size atomizer of Cover Me with Lies, a fragrance that had worked wonders in the past, but did not promise much coverage on this occasion.

The two stellar lights emerging from the *Damas* was much like a crowd unfolding of clowns from a tiny car at the circus, except in this case there were only two of them, and, although funny they may have been, clowns they were not. At least, they did not envision themselves in that role. Both gals ducked to keep from scraping the low ceiling of the Casa Romero. Uncharacteristically, Lilly and Monique attempted to scoot unnoticed by Leo Romero, the handsome and dignified proprietor. His jaw and chin were covered by a luxurious gray beard, groomed to accentuate the strong, attractive lines of his face. He wore an immaculate tuxedo of ageless grace and perfect tailoring, and on his black silk lapel was pinned a red carnation, the national flower of Spain.

"Lilly, Monique, you look gorgeous, as always."

The two giants fluttered their collective lashes at Don Leo and tried to slink outta there before he caught a whiff of the pot smoke and called the cops.

"*Mi casa es su casa*, and I am so happy to see you and your friends. By the way, the strange ... ah ... person in the trench coat and Brillo-pad beard was a friend of yours?"

The girls nodded vigorously, but for once they exercised rare discretion and kept their traps shut about Urna. Then, with small coordinated side steps and silly little finger waves, they attempted to escape. These maneuvers were not lost on the savvy Leo, so he dispensed with further niceties and got to the point.

"I hope you'll understand when I tell you that the next party for the private dining room has been waiting for half an hour."

"Darling lump, say no more and send us the check!"

Lilly engaged Leo in a brief headlock embrace intended to convey affection, which left the usually unflappable restaurateur reeling from the impact.

CHAPTER 26

▼

THE UNKNOWN VISITOR

A tall and solidly built man, dressed in a pin-striped, navy-blue business suit rode an elevator to the third floor of private suites at Brigham and Women's Hospital. Pinned to his left lapel, over his heart, was a small, discreet American flag made of enameled gold. A starched white handkerchief was square-folded and tucked into his outside breast pocket. His red silk necktie was perfectly knotted. The man's imposing military posture exuded power and confidence as he marched down the hospital hallway that was painted with serene shades of blue-gray and golden-straw. Hanging on the walls were a series of paintings depicting comforting views of big expensive beach houses, probably intended to be Nantucket. The man approached the reception counter, where a crisply uniformed nurse stood expectantly. She took in at a glance the man's short gray hair and commanding demeanor and, responding to his assumed authority, greeted him with deferential politeness.

"Good evening, sir. May I help you? Which patient are you here to visit?"

The gentleman acknowledged the nurse's correct form with a slight nod of his head and replied, "Mrs. Rosalind Wortheley."

"Mrs. Wortheley is in the Coolidge Cunningham suite, sir. If you would please follow me, I will show you the way."

Nurse Oppenheimer did not always usher in her patient's visitors, but Mrs. Wortheley was of sufficient importance to merit special attention. And, if truth be known, she also felt a certain protective care was due the lonely beauty, who lay perfectly still and isolated beneath her Plexiglas bubble. The nurse was concerned that her patient was being neglected by her family. Other than Cornelia Chilton's several visits, no other friend had come to comfort the woman who had made a profession of entertaining so many people. There was, of course, that dress designer, Alasandro Della Snozzy, and his staff who traipsed through once a week to change Mrs. Wortheley into one more absurd outfit after another. This process seemed to be beyond everyone's understanding or control, a kind of unstoppable march of fashion fueled by too much money. Nurse Oppenheimer was especially perplexed by the absence of Mrs. Wortheley's two children who had, along with their lovely mother, been favorite subjects for photographers of the social pages around the world. Perhaps their father had considered them too young to visit the hospital. But Nurse Oppenheimer rather doubted that George Wortheley considered anyone other than himself. At least, that was the impression she got from his two brief visits during the last two months.

Now, finally, here was someone whose dignified appearance reassured her. So with deference, she gladly showed him the way and discreetly withdrew after having placed a comfortable chair by the remote Rosalind.

The man, who had arrived with such self-assured confidence, was transfixed and disturbed by the vision of the sleeping beauty before him. Rosalind was swathed in starched linen gauze, which was wrapped like a medieval wimple around her head, framing her exquisitely sculpted face. The pure, white linen contrasted with the delicate blush of her cheek. Her gown fell in flowing but studied pleats down the length of her elegant figure. The unsettling effect was of an effigy carved in the finest marble. The man was compelled to back his chair away from the transparent bubble it reflected, on its hard surface, spectral images of the surrounding room, including him. His emotions surged through him uncontrollably when he saw his distorted reflection hovering over the dreaming lady.

"I can hardly believe that is you under there," he said aloud. "I had only seen you through George's eyes before, and he could make Boticelli's Venus seem dull. That is, I never really saw Boticelli's Venus except of course in pictures. She must be somewhere in Italy, I suppose, but who knows? There are so many museums all over the world … but you don't want to hear about that crap! Oh, sorry, ma'am, I'm not used to being around ladies, real ladies, that is. But, what am I thinking, talking to you like this, you can't hear me. Although, I wish you could, because I wish I could tell you how sorry I am. It's George who should be frozen in a block of ice, not you! I didn't know you would get hurt. It's not fair."

Rosalind's eyelids seemed to flutter, and the man was so startled he stopped talking abruptly and stared at her. He took time to examine Rosalind, hoping beyond hope that she might wake up.

"Oh my God! What if she did wake up and see me?" The military man was unusually shaken by the idea, and at the same time he wanted her to wake up.

"How could anyone have skin so flawless, like unpolished alabaster, glowing from within. I'm sure if that were me, I'd be snoring. What am I thinking about, I'm a big ugly mug and she, Rosalind, is the real thing. Those lips are like the curves of a violin. I can almost hear her singing. And soft, they must be so soft, soft enough to kiss a baby's cheek. There are two kids, I think. How sad they must be. Rosalind, what are you dreaming? You must be dreaming. Your eyes are the shape of dreams knitted together by long auburn lashes. They cast a shadow fringe along your cheeks. Look at your ears beneath that hood thing they've got you up in. How did you wear those huge diamonds in those tiny ears? Dear God! I can see the pulse in your neck. Can that be? Yes, right through the gauze."

The man, so used to command, reached out to touch the sleeping beauty, but his powerful fingers were abruptly stopped by the Plexiglas barrier. He was startled and flinched, withdrawing his hand and rubbing his fingertips against the palm of his other hand. He gazed intently at Rosalind's fine nose, with its slightly flaring nostrils. There were two lines that curved down from the center of her arched eyebrows, forming a defined plane spacing the symmetrical sweep of her closed eyelids. He gently put his hand back on the smooth surface of her transparent cage.

"Sleep now, dream on, some day we will meet, and I will tell you secrets that will make you laugh."

Chapter 27

▼

Looking Deep, Taking Time to See

Gyles Chilton returned from Aruba to his home on Union Park in Boston's South End. He was relieved to be back after seven days of vacationing, and eager to see his lover Val.

He took a moment to gaze up at the brick façade of his building, examining the new storm/screen windows that had been installed while he was away. His condominium windows, on the second and third floors, seemed to be OK, and he was once again grateful for Larry Reed, the current condo president. Larry was proving to be a competent officer and a real stickler for details, which was not surprising considering that he was one of the partners of the prestigious law firm of Twine, Biddle, Chrysler and Reed.

Although there were only three units in the five-story townhouse, there were unending chores to maintain a nineteenth-century building in good order. Last year during Gyles, tenure as condo pres, it had been his responsibility to restore the elaborate cast-iron fence that contained the delightful small garden in front of Jill Anderson's basement unit. The biggest part of this project was the florid scrolling banister that ascended both sides of the exterior granite steps leading to the first-floor entrance hall. Only one side of the banister still survived the past century and a half, so Gyles had to have the missing parts reproduced. Convincing Larry and Jill that this architectural embellishment was worth a whopping thirty-five hundred dollars was even more of a problem than finding the craftsman to reproduce this excessive Victorian conceit.

Gyles ascended the stairs of the front stoop to the elaborate walnut front door, which was inset with panels of frosted glass decorated with leaf and flower scrolls carved into the thick plate glass. He let himself in and put his luggage down in the front hall just long enough to pick up his mail from the Victorian credenza that dominated the room. He muscled his way up one flight of stairs to the front door of his condominium and sighing with relief he let himself in. Dropping his bags along the way, he plopped himself down on the sofa. Leafing through a week's worth of mail, Gyles made several neat piles on the glass-topped coffee table in front of him. The last letter in his stack was addressed, "To hot lips, from lonely boy." This was the only letter Gyles opened, and he did not bother to reach for the letter opener on his desk—he just tore into it. Inside was a post card of two hunky and naked men, resembling Hercules and Apollo, in a pose teetering between wrestling and embrace. The inscription on the back read:

Hey, hot lips,

Hope you soaked up a lot of sun in Aruba because I need to thaw out from chilling too much. Come on over and let's build a fire.

Lonely Boy

Gyles smiled to himself and felt a charge shoot through his body, traveling from his upper chest down to a place between his legs, beneath his balls. Leaving everything as it was, he hurried upstairs to his bathroom, showered quickly, threw on some jeans, sneakers, and a royal blue tennis shirt, and was out on Tremont Street flagging down a cab, all in 30 minutes.

*   *   *   *

Gyles climbed into the old-fashioned Checker cab that happened along, taking no notice of the unusual comfort provided by the big old cab.

"280 Commonwealth Avenue, between Gloucester and Hereford in Back Bay," he said eagerly, as the cab took off.

"Ain't that the old Chilton house?" the cabby asked. "I heard it's been turned into a B & B?"

Gyles mentally flinched to hear his great grandfather's home referred to as a B & B, but he said nothing. Instead, he rolled down the window because he felt beads of sweat forming on his forehead. But the chilled wind of an April evening did nothing to stop his mounting excitement at the thought of Val.

"So, are you staying at Chilton House from out of town?" the cabby continued. "I hear it's terrible expensive. Then again, I hear the lady who runs the place is mighty grand, and word is out, she's a real good cook. They say Creole shrimp is one of her specialties."

Gyles began to hear too much of an old familiar story not to take notice. He examined the cabby's ID pinned above the meter—it read Charles Darling. Being both surprised and a little ashamed not to have recognized Mr. Charley right off, especially in his conspicuous old Checker cab, Gyles was rattled, but rather than show it he volleyed back, "Darling? How come we never called you that?"

"Who you calling darling, boy? Watch your mouth. Whadya think I am anyway? Just because I picked you up in the South End doesn't mean I'm that way, you know."

"And what way is that, mister? I meant your last name."

"Oh, Master Gyles, you're just up there too high to take notice of the likes of me."

Both men laughed at their unexpected meeting, which was tinged with the nervous energy of the truth in their jests.

"I am such a dunce! I am so sorry, Mr. Charley, I didn't mean to be rude, I just had a lot on my mind and I didn't recognize you."

"Salright, Master Gyles, I figured you'd be needing a lift tonight, so I was sorta hanging around. How was Aruba?"

"Wait a minute, how did you know? And what do you mean, Aruba? *I* didn't even know … and you can drop the Master Gyles business, no one has called me that since I was a boy."

Gyles was caught off-guard to find that even Mr. Charley had heard about his vacation in Aruba. He began to realize the full extent of the conspiracy regarding his recent trip, and he felt confused.

"Don't hafta tell *me* what to call *you*. It was good enough when I taught you to drive, and it's good enough now. There's a heap too many changes in this life for an old man like me to remember your dignity. So, never mind about the small stuff, I want you to take good care of your Lucy Ann and the kid. They've been working their tails off."

Gyles fell into line listening to Mr. Charley, who had been a part of his earliest childhood. It was Mr. Charley who taught Gyles, to take risks, like driving a car when Gyles was so small he had to sit on Mr. Charley's lap. Mr. Charley apparently knew Val was his lover, and this was his way of saying that he knew, and it was OK by him—just another risk.

"I'm going there now, aren't I? Give me a break, I only just got off the plane."

"I know. I missed you at the airport by five minutes. I had a fare, big guy in a black suit going to Brigham and Women's. He looked kinda familiar, like I'd recognize him in different clothes, but I couldn't quite place him. Made me wait a full hour. I wouldn't have stayed, but he gave me fifty bucks. I drove him back to your neighborhood, so then I could afford to hang out and see if you'd show up.

Mr. Charley smoothly maneuvered his cab into the reserved parking place in front of the Chilton House B & B on Commonwealth Avenue.

"Now, mind what I say, and be nice to both of them."

"Thanks for the ride."

"Think nothing of it."

"That would be difficult."

As Gyles got out of the cab, Aunt Lucy Ann appeared at the door and walked toward him. This surprised Gyles, who didn't expect such a welcome. When she reached him, she planted an affectionate kiss on his forehead.

"Gee, Lucy Ann, I only went away for week."

"Yes, child, and I can see it did you a heap of good, so off I go. You mind the house while I'm gone, and don't bother Val too much because he has his own work to do."

Having given these brisk instructions, Lucy Ann proceeded toward the waiting cab. As Gyles watched, he noticed that his aunt was dressed in a smart traveling suit of mauve gabardine with a plum-colored silk scarf tucked modestly into the neckline of her jacket. The colors of her ensemble enhanced her flawless café-au-lait skin. Her wooly silver hair was arranged neatly in a bun at the top of her head, adding even more stature to her five-foot-eleven-inch height, and a considerable amount of distinction.

Behind her came Val, carrying a vintage Louis Vuitton suitcase and matching vanity box. Gyles watched in surprise as his lover carefully placed the luggage into the boot of the cab and closed the hood. Charles Darling quietly closed the passenger door and circled the car to the driver's seat. Lucy Ann leaned out her window, proffering a cheek for Val and Gyles to kiss, which they did obediently.

"But, where are you going? I just got here" demanded Gyles.

"Bermuda, where else? I hear the lilies are in bloom."

With that breezy farewell, Mr. Charley's Checker cab merged into the flow of traffic on Commonwealth Avenue and sped away.

Gyles turned to Val in obvious perplexity and was about to sputter complaints, except Val enfolded his lover in a powerful bear hug and kissed him squarely on the mouth.

*   *   *   *

In his bedroom on the third floor of Chilton House, Val stood eye to eye with Gyles, matching his height perfectly. They kissed slowly with a sloppy laziness and then they lay in the soft indulgence of Val's bed. He looked intently at his lover's remarkable blue eyes, searching beyond the flecks of violet and gray that enlivened his iris, deep into the mysterious inner core of the man. Val wanted to sink into the center of Gyles. But like any diver in the ocean, he would have to brave the crushing pressure of deep water in order to fathom the unknown.

Love was the courage that allowed Val to dive fearlessly into the unpredictable currents surging between them. With trust, inspired by the taste of passion, he released any clinging possessiveness and all tension drained from his body. In this ethereal and formless state, he flowed into his lover's gaze. The breath they shared inflated their chests with a radiant glow that felt like waves rolling through their bodies, dissolving differences in the foaming surf that crashed on the muscled shore of their nakedness.

All fears of intimacy were dispelled by Val's compelling need to know his lover's essential being. He wanted to see into the crystalline structure of Gyles' invisible core. How would that gem split the light of their day in the sun? He desperately wanted to memorize the colored radiations that emanated from their desire and their fulfillment. With wisdom beyond his years, Val realized that his probing quest had planted a seed able to grow beyond time. Not an ordinary love but the heroic bond of men loving men.

"What do you see when you hold me with your eyes like that?" Gyles asked.

"Nothing and everything—it's like I feel you, but only for a sec, and then I'm not sure."

"What aren't you sure of?"

"Who knows, sometimes I wonder if I know you at all. I mean it's like I never saw you before, not really. It's just, I can hardly believe it."

"It?"

"Us."

"Why?"

"Because it feels so good, I'm not used to it."

"Yeah, I know what you mean ... even now, after how long?"

"One year, ten months, and two weeks."

"Wow! You know."

"Every day."

"Am I that important to you?"

"No. We are that important together."

"Oh, sorry, I didn't mean ..."

"Am I that important to you?"

Gyles paused to tease Val but also because he was afraid of his answer, and yet very sure.

"Yes, yes you are Val, with you I feel at peace and excited at the same time. When we make love, you make me sweat."

"Yeah, I know. You're sorta salty, and kinda tasty, too."

"What do you mean, tasty?"

"Promise you won't get mad?"

"Cross my heart."

Lilly makes this chicken thing that I can never get enough of. She says it has magic herbs. I never knew what that was, so I didn't ask."

"You mean, you don't know what herbs she cooked with?"

"I guess so, but I kinda don't know what that is, anyway."

"Oh, that's easy. Herbs are leafy small plants that smell good and add flavor to food," Gyles answered Val's unasked question simply.

"Yeah, well, you taste that way. It usually says a man is real hot and horny when he's tasty."

"You should know, you're the expert."

"See, now you're jealous and angry. I can't help what I know, it's what I don't know that hurts."

"How?"

"Never mind.... Well, it stings, I guess ... and aches too, but maybe not so much, anymore. Sometimes I feel dumb."

"Val, you are far from dumb. You're one of the smartest people I know. You're quick and observant. You remember so many details. I see you taking everything in and mulling over what you've seen and heard. You picked up the computer faster than a full-time geek, while I'm still struggling with the basics. You can be anything you want, and you're already fantastic ..."

"All I want right now is you, hot lips. Stick you tongue down my throat and lemme feel your hard cock."

"Oh God! I thought you'd never ask!"

Gyles laughed and wrestled with Val on the big, old-fashioned bed, tossing his weight on top of Val's solid torso. Val wrapped Gyles in his long dancers legs and lithe arms, tumbling them around once, then twice, across the rumpled sheets, until they came to the sagging edge of the mattress, where their combined weights threatened to dump them on the floor.

"No you don't, big guy, you're not getting away from me!" Val bragged triumphantly, and before Gyles knew what was happening, Val rolled them back to the center of his bed with seemingly effortless force. Now on top, he lay full-length sprawled over Gyles, and pinned his lover's arms straight out over his head. Val elevated his own torso by arching his back, and, purring like a preening lion, he luxuriantly licked the black silky hair that grew thick in the pit of Gyles, arm. Gyles squirmed and writhed with intense ticklish pleasure, but Val held tight and simultaneously rolled his hips back and forth, crushing Gyles' hard cock beneath his own, which he squeezed from inside, making his cock head swell against Gyles, flat abs.

*   *   *   *

Gyles lay back in bed with his shoulders and head propped up on pillows. With one arm he held Val close to his naked side, and with the other he held his Balkan Sobranie pinched between two long fingers. Val's breathing became slow and steady, and after a while, his hand pulled away from Gyles' hip, falling with the limp weight of sleep onto the mattress. He lightly snored, like a puppy after play. Gyles smiled to himself and took a drag off his cigarette.

He watched with fascination as Val slept. He was careful to be still so as not to disturb. But he could not help himself and, with one finger, he gently swept the silken blonde fringe from Val's eyes. He could hardly believe the beautiful, sweeping line of Val's eyelid, where black lashes, like a curving wave, trembled slightly, hinting at the dreams that secreted themselves behind the curtain of his lover's sleep.

For a moment, Gyles felt a pang of jealousy for those dreams he could not know. So he looked closer at the man beside him. After a while, he was content to spend the hours of deep night watching over his perfect beauty—we only own our love by giving ourselves away completely. At this revelation, Gyles became radiant, as the moon reflects the sun, so also did Gyles reflect Val.

"One year, ten months, and two weeks," thought Gyles.

"I guess that's long enough to consider this real. Although it all seems like such a dream to me. But, thank God, it isn't a nightmare anymore. That was the really unbearable thing, when life with John became such a nightmare or, more accurately, his dying did. Jesus, I don't even want to think about that … him … John!

"I wonder what John would make of Val? He would probably be the perfect gentleman. Although, would he really approve? Or is that me? Do I really approve of myself and Val? What was that he said, before we made love? 'Sometimes I'm not sure if I even know you.' There's brutal honesty for you. Do I know Val? But that's silly, here he is, a fairly straightforward kind of guy. Maybe a little young, but sometimes so old. I don't want him to be alone, drifting around. But, who am I really thinking of, him or me? No, it's *us*! We are a pair, and I don't want to miss this chance. I don't care how old he is. That certainly didn't matter between me and John. He was twelve years older, and what the hell did I know, then? What do I know now? Val is much savvier about the real world than I. I know some things about antique furniture … and something about … herbs."

Gyles crushed out his cigarette in an ashtray that Val had bought especially for him. It had a picture of a Tom of Finland hunk, with a hairy, barrel chest smoking a cigar and scratching his bulging basket. Gyles snuggled up close to Val and, ever so gently, licked Val's chest near his right nipple.

"Humm, tasty, a little salty and, yes, vaguely like tarragon … no, rosemary … must mean I turn him on."

Gyles fell asleep with a smile on his handsome face, and, in sleep, they both lost their differences and dreamt together.

*   *   *   *

The next morning, they were sitting over coffee and bagels in the big old-fashioned kitchen in the basement of Chilton House

"So how was Aruba?" Val asked.

"You know, I really rather liked it."

"You sound surprised."

"I am. As you remember, Aruba was not the intended destination. So how come no one told me?"

"Get real, Dude."

"That's it?"

"Yeah, that's it. If we had told you, would you have gone?"

"You see! I knew it. You did know!"

"Duh? That's not such a brilliant deduction. You woulda known too, without your usual, absent-minded professor routine. We were at the Club Café when Monique spilled the beans, and not by accident either. But never mind the ancient history. What did you do?"

"Nothing very original, I guess. The time seemed to race on by. I did go snorkeling on the coral reefs one morning, and that was incredible! There were thousands of colored fish. They all moved together in a cloud. If I stayed very still, just floating, the fish, at least the small ones, came close and enveloped me in a huge swarm. They were flowing with the currents, back and forth. Their sleek little bodies had a stripe of neon blue that glowed with an inner light. The sun reflected off the surface of the ocean and cast shadow patterns through the water onto the fish. The brighter-colored fish were the bigger ones, and they kept their distance. There were cute little mini-squid with large eyes that seemed to be swimming backward. They were curious fellows and came right up to my mask to peer at me."

"Hey, what were you smoking?"

"Well, we did run into Lilly. Did you know about that, too? Anyway, she turned us on to a joint at one point, and we may have had a toke that morning, I don't remember. But the fish would still have been just as amazing."

"Oh, I'm sure."

Val crossed his arms over his chest, holding his coffee mug tight in his right fist. He smiled knowingly, and nodded his head with smug satisfaction. Secretly, he was relieved to hear Gyles had let down his hair on his vacation. He was also happy to hear Gyles enthuse about something other than his work and antiques, which Val had become rather jealous of. Mostly, he just liked listening to Gyles talk. Because of the details he provided, Val could see the places and things in Gyles' stories that were new to him.

"The hotel pool was surrounded by an incredible garden jungle complete with bright scarlet and electric-blue macaws. That was truly an extravagant fantasy, considering that Aruba is naturally a desert island.

"Our suite at the hotel was bigger than my condominium, and actually rather tastefully decorated, with a lot of raw-silk drapes, rattan furniture, and ethnic art accessories, all very textured, world-culture casual, if that is a style. Anyway, my bed was easily the biggest dammed bed I've ever seen—although it only made me think of you, so I am glad our jaunt was only one week."

Val was pleasantly surprised by this simple statement of affection, and he felt a glow of satisfaction spread through him.

"As I said, we ran into Lilly—or more accurately, she ran into us—when she did a huge cannon ball dive into our hotel pool from an airplane, if you can believe that. Have you ever noticed that Lilly is absolutely nuts? I mean, quite apart from the fact that she might say anything to anyone at anytime, without the slightest regard for the consequences, she apparently is capable of near-suicide stunts and is constantly embroiled in one scene after another."

"So, you mean you're beginning to like her." Val stated flatly.

"I did not say that. In fact, I am appalled by most of her antics," Gyles snapped back rather primly.

His rejoinder made Val smile, because it reminded him of a grade school teacher he'd had, and this comparison completely disarmed Gyles with the result that Val felt a protective indulgence.

"Yeah, so, only *most* of them?"

"What do you mean?"

"Appalled you?"

"Well, sometimes she can be rather funny, in an offbeat way," Gyles conceded. "There was a time in the Jungle Casino when Lilly was standing on the bar, slamming her purse on the stage above and hollering for Urna Flamanté. What was it? 'Urna you get your sorry ass out here and explain yourself!' or words to that effect."

On reviewing this scene in his mind's eye, Gyles was unsure whether the incident was funny or truly appalling. He wondered if the Maui Wowie they had all smoked, and the sidecar cocktails, had unduly colored his impressions.

Val was curious to know what Lilly was doing at the Jungle Casino, whatever that was, and what on earth, or heaven, Urna Flamanté had to do with it. Considering the fact that Urna, whom he had never actually met, was supposed to be dead, how could she show up in Aruba? But Val kept his questions to himself so as to not break Gyles' mood, especially since Gyles saw the incident as funny, and he wanted to encourage his lover's lighter side.

"Yeah, that sounds like Lilly" Val chuckled.

CHAPTER 28

▼

FOLLIES DERRIÈRE

Urna Flamanté perched on a bar stool in the shadowy recesses of the Follies Derrière, a shabby cocktail lounge in Boston's overcrowded Bay Village. Her nerves were on edge to such an extent that she had literally tied her arms and legs in knots. She wore a black Burberry trench coat, belted and buttoned tight to the neck, with the stiff lapels turned up to bury her face in dark shadows. Her eyes were further obscured behind oversized, mirror glasses in wire frames.

Between gulps of her Singapore sling, she puffed madly at her unfiltered Chesterfield, as if trying to hide in a cloud of smoke.

"Hey! Urna, ya know there's no smoking in here, this is a public lounge, you know." Said Dillbert the bartender patrolling his domain with strict and serious intent.

Urna lowered her mirrored mask halfway down her prominent nose and peered about the empty bar, "Coulda fooled me." she remarked. Rummaging in her purse she extracted a tiny cell phone which she stabbed with her skeletal finger, memory #1.

"Claude? Urna! What? Yes, I know cell phones aren't secure ... yeah, well, never mind your cover, mine's been blown out by a hurricane, so what I've got to say is, nobody's secret! Yeah, that's right. Scarface is here in old Bean Town, and that means Fathead's not far behind. How do I know how he found me? Unless your people accidentally on purpose whispered in his ear. Trust you? Darlink, is a rattle-snake poisonous? "OK, let's skip the twenty questions and cut to the chase.

How would you like to invest in an Off-off-off Broadway show? Yeah, you heard right. The stupid bitch lost her backing and her theatre, now she is out on the street. So, if you want to continue surveillance, you're gonna hafta ante up.... Oh, I don't know, maybe twenty or thirty Gs. That should go far in a Le Strange production.... Whadaya mean, what's it about? Total dementia, if history is any lesson. OK, lemme think ... she actually did tell me ... now, what the hell was it? Oh, yeah, *Naughty Astronautess!* about the first drag queen astronaut.... Don't ask, don't tell? Don't be ridiculous! She's not actually joining the air force *or* going to the moon, Claude, it's a musical comedy. Le Strange won't even make it as far as Dorchester ... unless it really does take off, and Hollywood gobbles it up, but I doubt that that's in the cards ... although, who knows? If they do bite, then the sky's the limit!"

Pitching a new show always excited Urna, and as she enthused over *Naughty*, she unknotted her twisted limbs and signaled to Dillbert for another Singapore sling.

"So, what do you say? Certainly such a paltry sum is small petooties to the Pentagon's budget. Just sell another rocket to Rwanda. You prime the pump and I can scrape up the rest of the cash.... What do you care, how I do it? I'll get Scar to cough up the difference, and then you can keep tabs on Fathead and Scar's operations so your friends in Colombia can continue the supply. Then you pin the rap on the slimy mobsters and ask Congress to double last year's budget to fight the war on drugs, plus a six-figure income for the Drug Czar himself. It's a brilliant setup ... you increase the value of a worthless product by making it illegal, then you tax the stupid slob citizens to pay for the creation of an entire branch of government to rub out the business you began to begin with. It makes built-in obsolescence look like the United Way! Yeah, I know, and the Mafia is a family from Sicily, that's a cute fairytale. But if that's so, who are that bunch of Episcopalians from Connecticut, the Bush boys, who migrated to Texas, where they use the world's crude to finance their born-again barbeques? I thought you had to be smart to go to Yale ... Hey, all I'm trying to do is put on a show! The toilet seats on an aircraft carrier are a bigger line item, so what's the problem?"

Urna snapped her phone shut, lit another Chesterfield, and swizzled the sauce, while signaling to Dillbert for another sling.

CHAPTER 29

▼

PANCAKES AND POISON

Val sat perched on a barstool that was upholstered with orange Day-Glo vinyl on its puffy seat cushion. His well-defined dancer's legs, covered with blonde fuzz, were unseasonably exposed beneath tight cut-off jeans that were rolled up so short as to leave nothing to the imagination and a great deal to enjoy. A purple tank top struggled to contain his torso but was losing the battle.

"Darling lump, it seems that Mama has fucked up big time, once again!"

Lilly delivered this introspective condemnation with bitter disgust as she deftly flipped a fluffy flapjack three feet in the air, launching it from a black iron griddlepan molded in the form of a hippopotamus. The lightly browned pancake came down to rest squarely on the hippo's ass, from whence came an enticing aroma of Aunt Jemina's finest.

"I supposed I should have guessed it, but who knew George could be such a louse?"

"Uh-huh."

Val agreed, but otherwise sipped his coffee in diplomatic silence. He leaned both elbows on the pink, and, black Formica countertop separating him from "La Chef de Maison." His heavy blonde bangs fell over his eyes.

"I guess I'm whatcha call broke, and without the Club Crazy I don't know how we can possibly produce *Naughty Astronautess.*

"Uh-huh," Val repeated.

Lilly flung her culinary creation onto a stack of steaming delectables and took a slug of java from her "horse's ass" mug. This abrupt action threatened to dislodge her toque, a canvas chapeau that could, in a pinch, double as a parachute if need be.

"But, you know, I'm still determined to succeed somehow, because I *wanna fly me to the Moon* …" La Diva broke into full-throated song.

"Wow!" enthused Val.

"But where will we get the costumes?"

With this unanswered question hanging in the balance, La Diva poured the last of the buttermilk batter onto the hippo grill and pensively watched it spread into a perfect thin wheel. When tiny bubble-pores popped in the rising dough, she flung it in the air and caught it with a backhanded lunge that really impressed Val.

"Gee, Ma, you mighta messed up with the Club Crazy, but you sure can flip a flapjack!"

"Thank you, lump. Maybe I could go on that TV show, *The Iron Chef.* Wally could rustle me up some fabulous drag … but how could I pay for any of that?! Although, come to think of it, that stoned queen still owes me, big time, so I guess I could squeeze it out of him."

Lilly's musings on the subject of torturing Wally cheered her up enough to finish cooking brunch. She heaped tall stacks of blueberry pancakes on two pink Fiestaware plates accompanied by sizzling slices of Canadian bacon. In a bowl of mango slices, she added piles of raspberries, and dribbled the fruit with Poire William, and sprinkled the top with fresh mint leaves from her garden.

"Yum, yum! Ma, ya done good."

"Valisha! I thought you were learning to speak like a proper lady with that eleganza queen husband of yours!"

"Yeah, well I'm still not a well woman and this proves it."

Val cupped his substantial basket in his right fist and waged the package at Lilly.

"Valisha, please! Where are your manners? Now, sit down and stick this in your mouth." Lilly shoved a heaping plate at Val. "You know, darling," she further admonished, "man cannot live on nuts alone."

A pop shot sounded, and a plastic cork rocketed across the kitchen. Lilly poured foaming Korbell "champagne" into two plastic flutes, which she had decorated with holographic stickers of dancing rhinos wagging impressive boners.

"Nice glasses, howdja do that?"

"On my computer, with Adobe Photo Shop. It's actually Harry the Hunk's pecker, far too big for Harry but perfect for the rhinos.

"Since when did you get a computer?" Val mumbled with a mouth full of pancakes.

Lilly reached across the table, napkin in hand, and wiped a dribble of Vermont maple syrup from the corner of Val's mouth.

"It was the one good thing I got out of the schlump before I had to flee the country."

"Who's the schlump?"

"George Wortheley, who else?"

"Oh, but howdja learn photo shop? I took a class in that last semester at Bunker Hill and it was real hard."

"I'm glad to hear something in your life is hard, besides your dick! What do you mean, how did *I* learn? I do have a brain, you know. And besides, darling lump, how do you suppose Mama got this far in life? You have to keep up with the trends in order to get ahead."

"I had head this morning and that's one trend I wanna keep up forever."

"Lump! Eat your bacon and behave. You know very well I didn't mean that."

"So, how come he's a schlump if I'm a lump?"

Lilly masticated determinedly for a rare moment of silence. She swallowed with an outward thrust of her jaw, then daubed her lips politely before swigging down a full draught of Korbell.

"*You* are my own darling lump of gold. The schlump is a dumb-ass bastard!"

"Oh, yeah, I get it."

*   *   *   *

After brunch at Lilly Land, Val had gone off to work at Chilton House in Back Bay. La Diva bundled herself up in a pink mohair sweater, pleated wool trousers and sensible shoes. She referred to this outfit as her Katherine Hepburn drag. Considering the season had only progressed to mid-April, Lilly also wore a voluminous, if somewhat lackluster, mink coat. Thus attired, she sauntered out to her garden, slipping her massive mitts into a pair of gauntlets that were decorated with scenes of Minnie Mouse planting tulips.

Intent on spring cleanup, she progressed down the garden path beneath the wisteria arbor. First off, she realized that the plastic Christmas lights looped in the arbor vine were not blinking. Figuring a fuse must be blown, or some such snafu, she seized hold of the string of small lobsters alternating with pink flamingos, and gave this menagerie an encouraging tug and shake. Presto! The ensemble began to pulsate cheerfully and Lilly sighed with satisfaction. Next, she put to rights the cast-cement family of Disney characters: Snow White and her leering dwarfs, Bambi, Mickey and Elmer Fudd. Lilly carried on an animated conversation with her "Little Darlings" as she rearranged and straightened them into an orderly bunch. Leaning against the arbor was a festive broom, which was made with plastic bristles in stripes of bright yellow and turquoise. This had been a gift from Panchita, the "Mexican Hot Tamale" who had brought down the house at the Club Crazy last season with her rendition of *Ay, Caramba! I Got a Jalapeño Stuck in My Pussy!!* Lilly sighed with poignant nostalgia for those halcyon days of yore as she took up her broom and swept the arbor path.

Having thus expended her reserves of concentration and enthusiasm for gardening, Lilly hooked up her hammock and heaved her weary self into its comforting sag. Weakened by her exertions, her mood collapsed into melancholy and woe. She began to snivel and sniff until, quite uncharacteristically, the dam broke and she hollered and howled in a frightening performance.

✳   ✳   ✳   ✳

Betty the Bounder shoved the pink door of Lilly Land open with her fully-extended left leg, a feat reminiscent of her more limber days when she was so relentlessly drilled by Madame Olga Incunabulofski.

In those hopeful days Betty had promise, some of which blossomed briefly on the South American tour of the *Ballet de Bronx,* under whose auspices she created the central role of Daffnina in the avant-garde ballet, *Duck in the Muck.* She enacted the drama of a farmyard fowl who was spurned by her fellow poultry with such vehemence that she ran off with a no-account crow named Rothbart.

Unfortunately for Betty, art sometimes presages reality. Just when she was basking in the full flush of her success at the opera house in Buenos Aires, she fell prey to the honeyed words of a gaucho who ignited her combustible imagination with torrid romance stories of life on the pampas, and off they went. It transpired, however, that Lardino was a nefarious gaucho who knew nothing of the pampas and, in fact, had dissipated his youth pinching eggs from penguins in Tierra del Fuego.

After a week-long binge on maté and pulque, Betty regained consciousness in the back room of a tango parlor where Lardino had tried to pawn her off as Chin Chilla, the Inca Princess. But Betty lost her standing when the left heel of her patent leather dancing pump came down heavily on a discarded martini olive, thereby squeezing the pit of the gin-soaked fruit with such force as to project it with rocket velocity smack dab into the eye of Lardino. The rest of the evening was a mystery to all involved.

Mortified and contrite, Betty limped back to the Opera House where, much to her horror, she discovered that the *Ballet de Bronx* had sailed off without her. Left to her own devices she developed an "artistic" dance that might also be termed Hoochy-Kooch. This dance featured her extraordinary leg extensions, which earned, albeit in small increments, her fare back to Bean Town—a lengthy odyssey extended by a general lack of interest in Betty's charms and talents. Upon her return it was rumored in Reginald Pew's column in *Gay Windows* that Betty was pregnant ... but how could *that* be when Betty was no lady?

This digression will lend credence to the phenomenon of Betty flinging wide the pink door of Lilly Land with her fabled leg extension. It will not, however, explain what met her eye in that Eden of obscurity, Lilly's garden.

"Land of Goshen! I never thought I'd see the day!" exclaimed Betty with a hint of glee as she set down her load of designer shopping bags from Abruzio Della Snozzy's boutique on Newbury Street. The cheery chimes attached to the pink door tinkled and clanged, announcing Betty's entrance, but these did nothing to muffle the sobs and sniffles issuing from the crumpled Diva, swinging in the hammock beneath the wisteria arbor.

Yes, Lilly was awash in self-pity and alligator tears, a sight for sore eyes, as far as Betty was concerned, because she was stuffed full of pent-up gripes from years of La Diva's abuse.

"So, our brilliant star has lost her perpetual shine," gloated Betty. "What's up? I thought hard-hearted Hanna had been vaccinated against the blues?"

"Shut up, Betty, and get me a Kleenex!" sniffed Lilly mustering up a particle of pluck.

"Kleenex? What you need is a roll of paper towels!"

And with this smart-assed remark, Betty efficiently produced just that. Lilly attempted her usually formidable glare, but, washed out as she was, she more closely resembled a drowned platypus.

"What are you? A walking 7-11? Or are they selling designer paper towels at Della Snozzy's?"

"I just happened to hit the sale at the Osco when I went to pick up Butch's Viagra."

"Butch needs Viagra?"

"No, not Butch, but he gets it for his AA sponsor, Big Mack. Mack's on welfare and they don't pay, so Butch...."

"Betty! Hand over the paper towel before I slug you!" barked Lilly.

"Now, that's my old Lilly! You had me worried, just now. I thought it might be somum serious."

"No, Betty, nothing serious … I've lost my theatre, I'm broke, and I can't afford a subway token to Somerville … but don't you fret. I'll just strangle myself and get it over with."

"Lilly, before you do anything hasty or rash, why doncha read this book. After all, you can't say you don't have time."

"What book? *The Complete Guide to Self-strangulation?*"

"Now don't mope, Missy! It ain't gonna getcha nowhere. Here now, I showed you before, *Extravaganza King*. This is fulla brainstorms."

"I can't read that, I haven't got my glasses."

"Funny you should mention, here's a pair now," and Betty dug into her shopping bags, coming up with a pair of magnifiers still in their package.

"Don't tell me, those are for Big Mack to find his pecker after he swallows his Viagra."

"Hey Lil, that's a good one," hooted Betty, "but no, I got 'em at the Osco sale."

"I don't suppose you have a cocktail stashed in those bags? What with Butch breathing down your neck and all?"

"Darling, is the Pope Catholic?" Betty asked gleefully, extracting a Spiderman thermos from her designer shopping bags. She shook the thermos rigorously and poured Lilly a concoction disguised as Mountain Dew, but it turned out to be a perfectly balanced side car cocktail with quite a punch. La Diva glugged greedily and settled back to read *Extravaganza King*.

*   *   *   *

An hour later Betty emerged from Lilly Land where she had been "using the ladies, room," but in truth—if such a concept could be applied to Betty—she had tiptoed into the inner sanctum and purloined a joint for the rigors of her workday. Betty had to do a double shift at the Basement.

"OK, Lil, I'm off now. Chin up, and no I don't mean surgery, it's too early in the morning for that. Ciao for now!" Betty slammed shut the pink door of Lilly Land and the bells clanged and tinkled.

Lilly was soon consumed by the story of Robert Barnet and the musical reviews called extravaganzas and Mother Goose burlesques that he'd staged for the First Corps of Cadets at the turn of the twentieth century. The book, written by her South End neighbor Alison Barnet, read like pouring honey on a bun—easy, sweet and fast running. Lilly was surprised to discover that Alison was this man's great-granddaughter. Alison had never given a hint of being anything like an Extravaganza Queen herself, just a nice, soft-spoken neighbor whose ageless appearance was attractive and quietly engaging. Her great-grandfather, Robert, sounded like Lilly's kind of man. A father of five children, husband to a devoted wife, who at the same time had made a sterling reputation for himself playing Isabella, Queen of the Daisies.

Lilly read with genuine surprise about the Cadets, a private militia of high-society toy soldiers, whose original function was to protect the royal governor. Over time they had switched sides, while still retaining a proclivity for exclusive social climbing. They had conceived a self-righteous mandate to keep the hordes of Irish papists in their place. The particulars of the Cadets' politically incorrect bigotry escaped Lilly, although she did note that her shows could never get away with such shenanigans. She was more interested to read that the extravaganzas generated much of the money used to build the armory on Park Square, where apparently they intended to defend their proprietary hold on Boston. This picturesque old pile, a castlelike fortress, had a high tower and enormous drill hall. The castle had been through glory and neglect and was now enjoying a revival, of sorts, as an expensive steak house where the riff-raff rubbed shoulders with the hoi polloi. Lilly could hardly believe her eyes as she read:

> Burrage, in real life an Old Colony Trust Company bookkeeper, was a vision in violet velvet. He wore a Gainsborough hat trimmed with old rose silk, white crepe and aigrettes (feathers). Phinney, an officer of the Warren Steam Pump Company, wore dove-gray velvet trimmed with lace. The lace formed a lover's knot at the side of his skirt. His bodice had a turquoise blue ceinture (girdle) and collar. His toque of gray velvet was ornamented with a score of doves' wings. Aldrich was in ecru faille as well as real estate, his outfit topped off with a toque that had a green crush crown bordered with purple poppies and trimmed with huge bows of cream lace. "It is understood that Mr. Barnet has already received (dressmaking) offers … from ladies of quality," the *Globe* reported in 1895. It is not putting it too strongly to say that he is a genius in this line. (*Extravaganza King, Robert Barnet and Boston Musical Theater* by Anne Alison Barnet, 2004. Do yourself a favor and buy a copy today! This one's a doozey!)

Lilly snapped her book shut with a loud clap!

"Well, Mr. Barnet, this lady of quality is putting in her order, and that should starch your ruffles stiffer than a board!"

La Diva searched her copious cleavage for her zippy little cell phone. After some probing she found the warm appliance, whereon she punched out a number—having first inadvertently taken a snapshot of her left foot, an image that was automatically sent to the overlarge mailing list of her entire address book. Not to worry, she thought blithely, as she redialed.

"Hello, Filene's Basement perfume counter, we spray you stink, this is Betty, but make it fast."

"Whaddaya mean 'Make it fast'?"

"Listen, mister, I got customers here. Either spill it or zip it up! Dincha read the paper? We got a big Poison promotion going on." Betty broke off, and Lilly could hear as she addressed a customer, "Yes, madam, I know that bottle is only half full, but it's only half price, too, which is more than we can say about *your* life. Now, do you want it or not?"

"What kind of sales technique is that, you drunken sot?" Lilly yelled into the phone. "Is that the Poison I like? I want to put in an order for a case of the junk."

"Say, who is this anyway, Donald Trump, or K-Mart? ... Security! ... That lady is stuffing all my stock in her purse!"

"This is your fairy godmother, bitch, so watch your mouth!"

"Now you sound like Butch, but he doesn't know from fairies or mothers so you must be a figment of my imagination. They told me at the rehab this would happen if I went off the wagon again, but who knew they knew what they were talking about?.... No, madam, we do not give out doggie bags at Filene's, you have to take the whole bottle."

This time, even Lilly was confounded by Betty's banter and she wondered if it weren't time for another bottle of Korbell—but before she conceded the last shred of sanity to the eradicating influences of The Bounder, she made another stab.

"OK, Betty, this is Lilly, not *Mr.* anybody, so listen up."

"Not Mr. Anybody? Whaddaya think I am, a psychiatrist? Don't call me up with your identity crises, I've got enough questions of my own every time I look in the mirror. No, madam, I can't save those three bottles for you until next week! This is a one-day sale. Buy it or lose it."

"Lilly, Lilly Linda Le Strange."

"Oh, hi Lilly, why didn't you say it was you? Hey, lady, I said *sample* not bathe—put that bottle down!"

"If you have sufficiently subdued the marauding public, may I ask you for Alison Barnet's phone number?"

"Oh, yeah, sure—648-5960."

"Thanks, girlfriend, and make sure you reserve some of that Poison for me!
"Oh, Lil, doncha think you gota nuffa your own?"
Betty hung up fast, letting that message sink in.

∗   ∗   ∗   ∗

"Alison Barnet? This is Lilly Linda Le Strange, your neighbor over here on Dartmouth Place ... yes, that's right, the Star of *Glamour Galore*. So, you caught the show? Oh, thank you, yes. it was one of my favorite roles. You saw it twice, did you say? Oh, because you couldn't quite believe it, huh? Well, show biz *is* bigger than life. Now, listen, I've been reading your book, and that's a little hard to believe too well girleen, no offence, but it's not everybody whose grandfather was a drag queen. I certainly didn't have any such noble role models. What? *Great*-grand father? Well, I guess that makes it doubly amazing. What? *Not* a drag queen? If you say so, pooch, I've been known to believe almost anything. Now, here's my question. What happened to the drag?"

"I'm really not sure, Lilly, I would suppose the costumes are all gone—in any case, there are only a few Cadet military uniforms at the First Corps Museum on Commonwealth Avenue—I've never seen any of the extravaganza costumes. Yes, but my book is a history of Boston theater concentrating on the extravaganzas. No, I didn't concentrate on the costumes especially ... well, yes, I did of course describe them ... yes, there are photographs of the shows in my book. Yes, Robert Barnet did design a lot of the costumes with the help of his wife, but ... you really are going into much greater depth then I did on this facet. I did most of my research at BU—yes, because the majority of the Corps' document archives went to the university library when they sold the castle building in 1967. You know, listening to you makes me think that you should talk with Commander Jarvis. Yes, he's a member of the Corps and in charge of the collection. He would probably be able to help you better than I. However, I should tell you that Commander Jarvis can be—how shall I say it?—abrupt, even rather curt."

∗   ∗   ∗   ∗

The scheduled appointment with Commander Jarvis, the Cadet Archivist was, contrary to Alison's apprehension, a cordial and productive meeting. The commander was favorably impressed by Albert Mellenoffsky in his navy-blue, pinned-stripped business suit, red power tie, and white handkerchief tucked into his outside breast pocket. The American flag and Marine insignia lapel pins, both of enameled gold, pinned proudly over the combat nurse's heart, were testament to his military pride and trustworthiness. In addition to these favorable appearances, Commander Jarvis read with interest the credentials of Lieutenant Mellenoffsky's highly decorated combat service. True to Alison's foretelling, the ranking officer was frugal with his conversation.

"Glad to have you aboard, Lieutenant," snapped Jarvis with a brisk salute. "At ease, soldier." And with that command, he retreated into his inner sanctum.

Albert could not repress all of Lilly's sense of style, and this was a little less than discreetly apparent when the researcher pulled out a pair of pink plastic half-glasses and perched them on his nose. Fortunately for Albert, the hale and hearty commander had made note of the proffered credentials and, having fulfilled his duty, withdrew to his "command post" for a snort of corn mash and a snooze.

Left to his own devices, Lieutenant Mellenoffsky labored long and hard, combing the archives for some mention of the costumes he was searching for. Although he was not a practiced researcher, he was tenacious, slogging through bin after bin of musty-smelling documents. But even the most determined of sleuths can find their attention flags and wavers, and so did Albert's. As a break from all the dry accounts and histories, the lieutenant started leafing through an oversized ledger of architectural drawings from the firm of William Gibbons Preston. These detailed plans and elevations of the castle building were not exactly lively material, but in contrast to page after page of business documents and correspondence, the pictures were at least some relief. As he idly leafed through the pages, a detail caught his attention. He took off his glasses, rubbed his eyes, wiped his glasses clean, and stared closely at the drawing of a subbasement marked "Parade Dress—Meeting Room Access."

Albert looked around the library. From behind his table, overflowing with document boxes and crumbling books, he pulled the librarian's cart, loaded with books and files, close to himself, creating a handy blind. Concealed behind this barrier, he tore several sheets of architectural drawings from their bindings and stuffed them into his briefcase. Thanking Fred, the bored student library assistant, Albert left the library with a confident swagger.

CHAPTER 30

▼

MONSTRAT VIAM

"Hi, guys, how are ya t'night? Gotta reservation?"

Lilly Linda Le Strange was about to balk at this slap-dash greeting, not liking to be demoted to the generic "guydom" of common parlance, but in the interest of expedience, she repressed all witty retorts and replied as plainly as possible.

"Le Strange for six at seven."

Lilly had muscled her way to the head of the line crowding the entrance of Smith & Wollensky's steak and chop house at the castle in Park Square. La Diva had dragged and herded her group of five friends along the ramp leading up to the front door by elbowing everyone else out of the way. One fearless or foolish man, take your pick, who had been waiting patiently in line with his wife, tapped Lilly on the shoulder intending to protest his displacement. Lilly gave him The Glare, and he thought twice about something for the first time since his hesitant proposal to Maureen, the woman he now called, "the wife."

Having thus gained her advantage, Lilly turned her attention to the host and radiated a determined conviviality that could have easily melted an artic glacier. She smoothed the jacket of her smartly tailored, silk taffeta pants suit and heaved a self-satisfied sigh. The fabric of her outfit was printed with a snakeskin pattern—python, python to be precise—of such ferocious realism that you half expected her to morph into a writhing coil and crush the life out of a passing wildebeest. Of course, Lilly's accessories included her signature platform pumps that elevated her to an altitude somewhere in the range of six foot six, if you included the full extent of her beehive hairdo.

Looking Lilly up and down, but mostly up, the host, who was no dummy and could spot trouble at a glance, hastily shuffled the Le Strange party off to Colette, a passing waitress.

"If you can handle this one, honey, you'll get all the choice shifts." The beleaguered host muttered, under his breath.

As luck would have it Colette was no stranger to Lilly—if truth be known she was no stranger than Lilly either—and she ushered the party deftly through the first grand dining room of Smith & Wollensky's at the castle. Lilly caused more than a mild stir as she and her party traversed the Flag Room.

"So, Colette, how's your skating going?" asked Lilly. "I'm glad to see you picked up this gig for a filler, but don't let 'beef and brew' go to your head, because we'll be back in business with my new show, *Naughty Astronautess,* before long."

"Oh, Miss Le Strange, am I glad to hear that! They won't let me skate here and my bunions are softening from lack of abuse."

"Now I remember! You're the skating waitress from the Club Crazy." Cornelia chimed in.

"Yeah, and I remember you, too, the wife to that bezerko dike, Rita. I just wancha t' know that I didn't lay a finger on ya then, and I ain't gonna now."

Cornelia laughed nervously at Colette's reference to her ex's excesses of jealousy, but a tinge of wistful sadness deflected off a door in her heart, now tightly closed.

"Lay off the kid, Colette. She's a Gay divorcée now, but still hurtin,."

The original baronial décor of the Flag Room had been restored and enhanced by the design team who had refitted the castle as a chop house, a concept not too far off the mark as the Cadets had originally equipped their posh boys' club with lavish banqueting facilities. The two-story room was ringed by a balcony with a scrolled iron railing supported by an oak frieze carved with the names and dates of past commanders of the Corps. Hanging in clusters from the lofty ceiling were bronze lighting fixtures sculpted in fine detail and appearing like cabbages on steroids. Bronze flowers sprouting light bulbs dangled on thick chains from these fanciful sculptures. The focal point near the entrance was an elaborate fireplace and overmantel that stretched from floor to ceiling, decorated with pilasters, eagles, shields, scrolling ribbons, a veritable jungle of voluptuous acanthus leaves flopping about gracefully, and the famed motto of the Corps, *Monstrat Viam,* "show the way." In addition to all this grandeur, the room was hung with enough stars-and-stripes bunting and so many antique American flags that it could have been an announcement for the second coming of freedom and democracy.

"Whoo girl! Hold on! What's *this*?" Lilly reined in the progress of her party to a screeching halt as a particular series of pictures lassoed her attention. "I see the flag part of the décor, but what're all these photos?"

"Oh yeah, dintcha know? The place is chock-full of drag queens. Seems they built the joint or somethin'. That's why I took the job, 'cause after the Club Crazy, I mean, how could I do without?"

"How indeed?" Gyles murmured shaking his head in awe and wonderment at Colette's creative abbreviations.

"These are cast photographs of the extravaganza's that were produced by my great-grandfather from 1891 to 1906." Alison Barnet translated Colette's garbled reference to the photos decorating the wall by saying, "They raised about a quarter of a million dollars—over half the money required to build this building. Although some of the Cadets were impersonating women, and they were intended to be funny, I don't know if drag queen is exactly accurate."

The group portraits showed a host of festive thespians wearing elaborate costumes and posing against painted landscapes of romantic fantasy. The diverse characters they depicted ran the gamut from blushing geishas in kimono, obi, and painted paper fans to European ladies of quality, ennobled by an abundance of feathers and lace. There were also several frilly missies in tutus, tights, toe shoes and blonde wigs that frothed over hefty bare shoulders. All these "ladies" were intending to convey exotic allure and compelling charm, but instead they conjured up all the furtive camaraderie of misplaced persons discomforted by a none-too-convincing femininity.

"Quite a bunch. Looks like Pagliacci meets Pavlova," Gyles suggested, pointing to a rather forlorn clown in the back row of one picture.

Representing the male contingent in the extravaganza photos were touts, louts and cowboys in a variety of getups and distinctive head gear. Looming center stage in one picture was a Prussian officer in full-dress uniform, brandishing a saber and sporting a nifty fur cap with a flaring brush standing to attention at the crown of his head. Here and there was a sprinkling of top-hatted dandies wearing white kid gloves. One of these boulevardiers, enthroned in an elaborately carved chair, dandled a delicious darling on one knee while mysteriously grasping the hand of a formidable creature who resembled the original old maid.

The crowning glory of the extravaganza photos was a closeup of four floozies in flounces. Their white dresses were cinched at the waist in an unnatural pinch that only a wasp could accomplish. Their luxurious coifs were frizzed, waved, curled, and then curtailed beneath bonnets that resembled starched cabbage leaves. Throwing all caution to the proverbial breezes, this quartet of dainties was trimmed from stem to stern with flower garlands of shameless frivolity.

"A tad over the top, wouldn'cha say?" queried Lilly with dismissive scorn.

"I don't know, Lil, looks sorta like somea your drag," Betty said, studying the photo. "You know, that routine you cooked up last year for the fundraiser at the Holy Fryers Monastery. All by yourself, you played Mae West, June East, July South, and Augusta North. Boy, that was a doozy!" the Bounder reminisced cheerfully.

"Yes, but I didn't look like a flower shop on Mother's Day, thank you very much!"

Lilly put Betty straight, which was apt to take some doing, and for the less intrepid, might even be considered a lost cause.

"If you don't mind, Miss Le Strange, can we get on with it?" Colette urged the Le Strange party on. "I mean, you know, I gotta pick up a couple of filly minions for a deuce who just got engaged and they wame ta pop a bottle of bubbly too."

"Lead the way, Miss Thing, but do people really get engaged in public restaurants?"

Lilly had old-fashioned ideas regarding intimate affairs.

"Oh, sure, all the time. This guy got down on his knee, popped the question, and laid a rock on her the size of an ice cube! The whole dining room applauded. You probably know the happy couple, Monique and Butch?"

"Monique La Farge and Beef-Cake Butch just got engaged at a steak and chop house?" Lilly bellowed in disbelief, as Colette deftly steered the Le Strange party to a table at the center of the semiprivate Meeting Room, which was off the main Flag Room.

"Do you mind, Le Strange? This is supposed to be a classy joint—at least until you showed up."

Butch defended his honor and dignity with a fierce snarl from his table across the room. Monique was decked out to kill in a gown that Abruzio Della Snozzy had promised to Nicole Kidman until Butch threatened to break Bruzi's arm— not the most subtle coercion perhaps, but effective when coming from a two hundred and thirty pound, lean and mean bruiser. Besides, Butch paid cash and Nicole was wont to expect extended credit.

"Sorry darling, I didn't realize *you* were the boy next door."

Lilly squinted in Butch's direction, but when her gaze fell on Monique in her fabulous Della Snozzy gown, Lilly's eyes popped.

"Girleen! We *are* looking our best! You know, Monique, you constantly surprise me. You really do have talent. Congrats, to both of youse."

Monique chose to interpret Lilly's remarks as homage deserved and she basked in the attention gracefully. She raised her champagne glass in silent salute, acknowledging Lilly's wellwishes. This gesture was a bit premature, considering the fact that Colette hadn't popped the cork yet. Their bottle of Korbel still shivered expectantly in its bucket of ice, and Monique's glass was empty, but it served to flaunt the rock, or more accurately, nuptial boulder, decorating Monique's left hand.

Monique's justifiable, if somewhat ostentatious, display of the magnificent sparkler was not lost on any of the Le Strange party, who gasped in concert with emotions hovering between disbelief and envy.

"Beautiful ring, Monique, Harry Winston or Cartier?" Cornelia couldn't help asking.

"Not a chance, babe." Butch bounced back with pride and enthusiasm, "I won it from the bubblegum machine at the Ramrod. It's the thought that counts, you know."

"Funny, I never would have guessed he had any thoughts at all." Betty tossed her barb negligently.

"Not so funny, bitch, since you ain't got no brain to think with."

Butch had good hearing and wasn't going to take any guff from the likes of Betty.

Monique shamelessly clasped her beautiful hands in a prayerful pose crossed over her chest, displaying to great advantage the "diamond" in question—and while she was at it, her even more magnificent manicure, which was a top-quality job, masterfully applied at The Sound of One Hand Clapping, a Buddhist nail parlor on Newbury Street.

"They have bubblegum machines at the Ramrod with phony diamond rings?" Gyles demanded incredulously.

"Yeah," Val supplied the answer. "Ever since the 'freedom to marry' thing got passed, there's a big demand. Haven't you seen the wedding section in *Gay Windows?* It's huge. Since the net took over the personal ads, the gay press lost major bucks, but now the wedding business has taken up the slack."

"The Ramrod is an S & M bar with a leather and denim dress code in the back room dungeon—how does a Cinderella princess ring fit into that picture?"

Gyles' assumption of fastidious proprieties sometimes blinded him to the amusing irregularities of gay life. Betty explained the fine points.

"That's easy. They call 'em *Cinderfella* rings. They slip one or more of the sparklers onto their cock rings and it adds some extra grip. But Butch is kinda sentimental, so he's using his in a more traditional way."

Gyles decided that further explanations were not in order, and he turned to Alison Barnet.

"Alison, I read your book with great interest and enjoyed it immensely. My great uncle Peabody Chichester was a Cadet at the time of the extravaganzas. Did you ever come across his name in your researches? He was Harvard class of '88. At the time of the productions he had already graduated and was an officer of the Chichester Bank."

"Without my notes I can't be sure, because there were so many Cadets involved. The casts were huge. I know in 1903, for instance, the Bank Officers Association put on another crazy play. That was called *Baron Humbug* and it employed 100 of their members. So it's highly likely that your great uncle did perform with the Cadets or the B.O.A. in one or the other of the shows."

The ever-diligent Colette staggered into the room hefting a tray encumbered with a multitiered pagodalike contraption heaped with every known species of oyster, clam, shrimp, scallop and mussel that could be wrenched from the seven seas. She managed to transfer this towering pile of mollusks and crustaceans, otherwise know as Ralph Wollensky's Shellfish Bouquet, to Monique and Butch's table, a feat of no mean accomplishment. Then Colette popped the cork of the happy couple's bottle of bubbly, which rocketed off at high velocity toward the ceiling and possibly beyond.

"Whoops! Heads up, guys!" Colette barked her terse warning as she splashed foaming "champagne" every which way, including some into her customers' two glasses. The Le Strange party gawked shamelessly at this performance and snatched up their menus, intending some serious research.

"Remember everybody, the dinner is my treat as a memorial to Uncle Wisner, who pinched every penny he could for the better part of 80 years, except when thinking of himself. Let us follow his lead and indulge ourselves."

Gyles' generosity was a subtle form of revenge on his departed uncle, who had left behind so many surprises secreted away in hidden closets that his legacy was a heavy burden in need of sharing. [2]

Colette proved to be a remarkably competent server, if somewhat less polished than one might hope. Orders were placed for exotic cocktails, lavish dinners, and abundant bottles of wine, and in a flash the goods were delivered.

As Lilly swilled the last drop of her second Pink lady cocktail and began to assault her very own Shellfish Bouquet, she got to the meat of the matter, so to speak, and said in a voice intended to be heard by the whole room, "OK, so you all know why you're here, and you all know we can't get caught. We aren't going to clear out the loot tonight, so we're safe for now, but we need to find the stash before Miss Colette brings in the chocolate cake, because that big mother is gonna put me under the table."

There was a loud chorus of "Right on, Lilly!" from around the room, and to Alison's surprise all the guests at the six tables around the small Meeting Room raised their glasses and clinked.

"What does she mean?" Alison asked nervously turning to Cornelia. "I'm not being dragged into some kind of robbery am I? And what's all that about the big mother putting her under the table?" Alison was really beginning to look worried, and Cornelia reached for the Pinot Grigio and filled the historian's glass.

"Didn't Lilly tell you? No, I can see by your face that she didn't. Well, first the good news: the big mother thing is because the chocolate cake is rumored to be so big that even Lilly is anticipating diabetic shock, so that's fairly harmless.

Alison looked askance at Cornelia, who until this moment she had assumed to be one of the more sane and responsible members of the party.

"So, what's the bad news, or maybe it's better if I don't know. Perhaps I should just plead a headache and go. I'm not really so far from home, I can walk there in no time…."

Alison looked wistfully at the yellowfin ahi tuna with its dollop of wasabi-lime mayo melting pleasantly on top of the fish. Colette had just delivered this temptation, and sniffing its redolent juices, Alison's resolve to be cautious began to waver.

"It is a little complicated," said Cornelia, laying a soothing hand on Alison's arm, "but, remember when you suggested to Lilly to get in touch with Commander Jarvis at the BU library regarding the original architectural plans of the castle?"

"But all I said was that the archives are at BU and Jarvis was the man to ask about such things. My researches and the subject matter of my book have nothing to do with the complexities of the architectural designs that she was asking about or the symbology of the Corps insignia."

By this time Alison was really getting worked up. She knew quite well how unaccommodating, brusque, or even downright rude Commander Jarvis could be. Now, as she envisioned the meeting between Lilly Linda Le Strange and Commander Jarvis, she could only imagine a conflict of implacable wills. And if Commander Jarvis could be difficult, how much more so could Lilly be?

Alison was in the act of excusing herself under the pretext of visiting the ladies, room when the heavy clamp of La Diva's mitt came insistently round her delicate wrist.

"Hold on, darling lump, it's the drag."

Alison nervously glanced from Lilly, who was looming over the table and grasping her left arm, to Cornelia, who was gently holding the author's writing arm.

At a signal from Butch the entire population of the Meeting Room got up from their dinners, some still munching greedily, and began to poke and prod the walls, the doors, the display cases, and especially the oak-paneled fireplace flanked by Corinthian pilasters and crowned by a broken pediment ornamentation. Only Lilly, Cornelia and Alison kept their seats, and not altogether willingly.

"I am not your darling lump, and get your hands off me!" Alison was no push-over, and now she was pissed to boot. "I don't know what you people are up to, but count me out."

Alison shook off the hands that bound her and stood on her own two feet.

"OK, sugar, be that way. But all I'm trying to do is be the first woman on the moon, so some feminist *you* turned out to be."

Lilly's petulant complaint did nothing to mollify Alison or elucidate the issues in question.

"First of all, you're no woman. And secondly, I'm no feminist, so get that straight!" Alison's fiery retort was as shocking as a slap on the cheek.

Everyone in the room gasped and wrenched their attentions away from the mysterious search long enough to stare open-mouthed at the diminutive author and the towering drag queen. No one had actually ever said that Lilly was, or was not, a woman, but there were limits beyond which no one wanted to tread.

"OK, OK, everybody. So there's been a major event, but let's not lose our grip altogether. Take notes if you must, but let's find the drag!"

This surprisingly focused pep talk came from none other than Betty the Bounder, who with gentle solicitations guided Lilly back to her chair. While handing La Diva a half-full bottle of chardonnay to swig, she glared at Alison accusingly. In the meantime, Val stepped in to try and explain the situation to Alison.

"Sorry she got to ya, Alison, but Lilly's under a lot of strain. I know that's no excuse, so let me try to spell it out simple. Whatever your grandfather was or wasn't ..."

"Great-grandfather."

"Oh, yeah, sorry … anyway, whatever he was, Lilly knows that anybody who is that crazy about a show that he would go to any length to write it, direct it, make the costumes, and star in it at the last minute because the intended star had a hissy fit … well, Lilly thinks that your granddaddy musta kept the dra … costumes. See, no one that dependent on what Lilly calls The Mask would ever let it go. Everything else can slip through your fingers but never the … drag. Sorry, I just had to say it that way. It's a way of life, it's make believe … it's all she has."

Val's heavy blond shank of hair fell over his eyes, hiding an unexpected swell of emotion. Alison Barnet got up from her chair, crossed over to the fireplace and, moving her hands lightly over the oak panels, she somehow manipulated the moldings. There was the faint sound of a double click, and a whole section of the wall, the size of a small door, swung open. Behind the wooden cover was the steel door of a safe, cracked to an open position.

▼

CHAPTER 31

TO WHAT LENGTHS FOR DRAG?

Lilly Linda Le Strange extracted a pair of smart pigskin gauntlets from her equally smart Hermés shoulder purse and slipped the snug gloves over her own hefty digits with practiced ease. Back in the purse, she rummaged around searching for her flashlight, which, when duly found, she clicked on and flashed into the darkness before her. The narrow beam of light dimly illuminated the precipitous edge of a steep spiral staircase disappearing into the gloom below. At the sight of this deathtrap her heart skipped a beat, a phenomenon of unnatural silence in her massive chest, rapidly followed by an audible thump.

"Bite my ass!" she remarked with alarm and dismay to no one in particular. "What a depressing hole this joint is. I'd feel a hell of a lot better if I coulda left the door to the safe open, but covert is the way of the day and anyway, that little minx, Alison, was about to spill the beans, so I had ta disappear."

Mustering up measures of chutzpah as yet uncalled for, La Diva progressed, and although she tried to tread lightly on the iron steps going downward, her platform pumps clunked rather loudly.

"Oh, fuck it! Whose gonna hear me, locked in a safe embedded in this pile of granite?"

So saying, La Diva descended the stairs with determination, tightly gripping the iron railing riveted to the wall. As she descended she thought she caught a whiff wafting upward, smelling suspiciously like grease paint.

"But no one's used old-fashioned greasepaint makeup for nearly a hundred years. It's only because the clowns at the Gay Rodeo use it that I recognize the smell at all."

Lilly's thoughts raced on, puzzling over what might lie ahead. She followed the stairs circling round and round into an ominous darkness that seemed to thicken and spread, filling all unknown spaces.

Paling considerably in the darkness, she paused in midflight to rummage some more inside the comforting elegance of her Hermés purse, wherein she latched onto a nip of cheap gin that Betty had rightfully thought might come in handy. Lilly glugged the hooch greedily, attempting to bolster her bluster. After a pause, while she waited vainly for the intended effect, she continued her descent. The next few turns of the spiral descending were—whether or not due to the gin—less bothersome, and Lilly finally reached what appeared in the dimness to be a stone archway, with an expanse of limitless black space beyond that absorbed the beam of her flashlight, disappearing in a vanishing point far away.

On the brink of the great beyond, La Diva tripped—a misstep that really rattled her bones and cast her sprawling into god only knows what! Her flashlight died, her ankle twisted (*quelle surprise*, Miss Thing, with the extreme platforms already, whadja expect?) and she klunked her shin on something hard. The only thought left in her head was for the safety of her silk taffeta python pants suit, which had cost a fortune.

A blinding light ignited the room with all the cruelty of unexpected revelation, followed by a booming command.

"Freeze! Put your hands over your head and spread your legs!"

"Say, what is this? A sex thing or an arrest? Butcha know wha? Who gives a fuck! Shut up! Help me up! And who the hell are you, anyway?"

Lilly may've been down for the count, but she wasn't unconscious and was certainly not about to concede.

∗   ∗   ∗   ∗

Meanwhile, back upstairs in the Meeting Room, the assembled party had resumed their seats and with fierce concentration and little conversation were chowing down big time. Colette and her back waiter had already lugged in the first and second courses, consisting of the vast amounts of food that Smith and

Wollensky lavished on their patrons. The conscientious waitress returned again with yet another load, this time consisting of some extra sides, lobster fried rice, truffled macaroni and cheese, asparagus and crabmeat salad, etc. She even managed to slip in a double G & T for Betty, which she disguised in a Perrier bottle. Fancy Foot Freddie, the lead dancer of Lilly's troupe, who was only five, five and as skinny as a rail, had ordered a colossal lump crab cocktail which he eagerly accepted from the waitress.

Having accomplished her mission of the moment, Colette mopped her brow with an extra napkin from the busboy's station, a maneuver of questionable refinement, but hey, the gal was really truckin'. Besides she knew most of these kids from the chorus of Lilly's show *Glamour Galore* and her days at the Club Crazy, so why stand on ceremony?

"Say, how come you're all so quiet? And where's Miss Le Strange, anyhow? Her lamb chops are coagulating."

Colette addressed her concerns to the general company, but only Gyles looked up from his filet au poivre, again amazed by her special linguistic style.

"I'd better take this back to the kitchen and have 'em zap it."

"'SOK, Cole," Val interceded before Colette could remove the chops, "Lilly's just gone to the girl's room. She'll be back in a jiffy."

"If you say so, Doll face, but don't blame me if ..."

Butch had sidled up to Colette and gave her ass an appreciative squeeze.

"Hey babe you've done great and thanks a bunch, but buzz off now because we've gotta talk some serious show business."

Colette flounced off, rubbing her bum fondly. She shooed her back waiter and busboy before her and closed the oak doors separating the Meeting Room from the Flag Room. Sighing with relief at the respite, she headed for the delivery dock to bum a butt from the dishwasher, Manuel.

$$* \quad * \quad * \quad *$$

Lilly stood to attention, bound to a stone pillar. Her hands were pinned to her sides and encircled by an unconvincing cord, looking suspiciously like fancy gimp rather than strong rope. For the moment she was held immobile, mostly by the shock and outrage of having been found wallowing in the dust by an ugly gnome. This Golumlike creature had used her confusion to coax her over to a pillar. Before she knew what the little bugger was doing, he had spun his web, cackling gleefully to have snagged such a great prize. Although her ankle throbbed a bit, she was far more discomfited by the grime clinging to her python pants suit than by any real concern for her safety from the little creep.

As her eyes adjusted to the bright lights of her surroundings, Lilly saw a large room with a vaulted ceiling supported by stone pillars. The room was fitted with row upon row of old-fashioned wooden clothes racks hung, stuffed, jammed and overflowing with costumes galore! Lilly's practiced eye took inventory of the crinolines and tutus, hoop skirts, bustle dresses, petticoats, overcoats, undercoats, vests, blouses, pantywaists, corsets, and yes, a vast collection of bloomers! There were feathers and lace, flounces and fringe, silk, wool, cotton and fur! In her immediate vicinity, right across the aisle from the pillar whereon she was loosely strapped, was a rack of mysterious-looking armor. These doublets were covered with coin-sized metallic disks looking like the scales on a fish or dragon. She was utterly fascinated by this collection, and quickly estimated the number of costumes there to be more than enough to cover her chorus of *Naughty Astronautesses*. With her special gift for stretching the plausible way out of shape, Lilly saw these antique costumes in her mind's eye as space suits.

Studying the Flash Gordon fantasies in front of her closely, Lilly got the shock of her life. A skinny chump in a black Burberry trench coat cinched tight at the waist, and wearing buckle-up galoshes, squeezed from between the tight bunch of costumes. A crumpled fedora was pulled down low over the ears of the specter and the face was obscured by mirrored glasses and a bushy black beard.

"Darlink! Don't move or I'll plug ya!"

Having delivered this ridiculous line, the barrel of the black Luger in the creature's hand dripped a drop of familiar scent, Jungle Gardenia.

"Urna Flamanté!!!"

"Lilly Linda Le Strange!!!"

"Bitch! What are you doing here?" The rivals barked the exact same demand of each other.

Any reserves of patience Lilly possessed had been squandered in this escapade. She inhaled deeply in preparation to pounce, an action that inflated her girth to the breaking point and she burst her bindings, which were, as suspected, only antique costume trim.

Lilly slapped Urna once, twice, and then three times, then bopped her cohort the ugly gnome, Golum, squarely on the noggin. The two unfortunates collapsed in a heap on the dusty stone floor, and Lilly brushed off her python pants suit with dainty care.

*   *   *   *

Alison Barnet munched pensively on her yellowfin ahi tuna, and with a non-committal glance she accepted a refill from the bottle of Australian chardonnay circling the table.

"Alison, did you know all along about the secret panel beside the fireplace?" Val asked her, between bites of his prime rib and Caesar salad.

She stared into the overlarge balloon glass at the pool of pale golden chardonnay swirling around. "I've never been in this room in my life. I had no idea what was here, she said, as if in a trance.

Then she looked up in evident confusion, "Where is Lilly?" she asked.

Val glanced at Gyles over her head, shrugging his shoulders in bewilderment.

"Everybody here knows each other, why?" Alison continued forlornly.

"We didn't mean to keep you in the dark. I thought Lilly had explained everything to you …" Val said, looking expectantly at Alison, but she merely shook her head.

"We're all members of Lilly's troupe of dancers in the chorus of her shows.… Except for Gyles and Cornelia, of course. Betty is, well, Betty … I mean, she's Lilly's dresser."

"How about me, pretty boy," Monique broke in amending the narrative. "I'm no chorus girl."

Val shrugged, and continued his explanation to Alison.

"Lilly told everyone to make reservations for the Meeting Room so we could help her find some kind of secret door to a storage room. She said she needed privacy and she didn't want to be interrupted."

"Fat chance of that! I can hardly get a word in edgewise with that queen." Betty complained, slugging directly from her Perrier bottle. Butch eyed her with growing suspicion.

"Interrupt what?" Alison asked impatiently.

"As I was trying to explain before, Lilly had this hunch from reading your book that the production costumes for the cadet extravaganzas were still here. That's why she was asking you about the architectural plans, and then you suggested Commander Jarvis …"

Alison looked up alarmed, and Val backpedaled fast.

"Not to worry, they got along fine. I know it's hard to believe, but Lilly was a Marine in Vietnam."

Alison wondered if the USMC accepted drag queens in its ranks but quickly dismissed the idea as unlikely. Val could see by her expression that he was losing her and he hastened to explain.

"She was a nurse," he said and left it at that, not dragging Albert Mellenoffsky into the story.

"From studying the plans," Val hurried on, "Lilly thought she found what she was looking for when she came across a drawing for a room in the subbasement marked Parade Dress—Meeting Room Access. Last week Lilly told me she was coming over here on a ... recognition mission?" Val said haltingly, looking to Gyles for help,

"Reconnaissance possibly?" Gyles suggested.

"Yeah, that's it, she wanted to snoop around. When she came home that night she said she found it 'cause it wasn't there ... Val paused. "I was kinda busy at the time ..."

"Yeah, rolling joints, I'll bet." Betty guessed correctly.

"Button it, Betty, and let the kid talk," said Butch sharply. By this time he was pretty sure the Bounder had been sloshing the sauce. Even though she didn't have a cocktail or wine glass, he knew the cunning and baffling ways of Betty.

"She found it because it wasn't there?" Cornelia repeated, gently placing her hand on Val's shoulder. "What exactly did she mean?"

"Oh, yeah, I guess that's sorta lame, but it was exactly what she said. I had a look at the plans that she had ripped outta some book, and sure enough, the meeting room had only one entrance ... those doors," said Val, pointing to the solid oak double doors that Colette had closed behind her.

"Anyway, at the time I hadn't a clue, but Lilly musta guessed about the secret panel."

"Pretty wild guess, if you ask me." Gyles shook his head in disbelief.

"Now I get it!" exclaimed Cornelia.

"How do you mean, Corny?" asked Gyles.

"Lilly came over to my house a couple of nights ago, and she asked to borrow a book."

"Is that how she got ahold of *Extravaganza King?*" Alison asked the question that had been plaguing her from the beginning.

"Naaa, I wash ta un ho ..."

Before Betty could finish her slurred sentence, Butch snatched the Perrier bottle away from her and sniffed suspiciously.

"OK, Betty, that does it! You and me is outta here and to the nearest meetin'."

"Over my dead body, Butch! That bitch ain't gonna bungle my betrothal!!!"

Monique had risen to the occasion, all six feet nine inches, a feat aided by towering heels, really big hair and very good posture. She gave Betty a negligent slug in the jaw, sending the offending member of the party sprawling on the floor. Although Val had been hopelessly interrupted by this fracas, he turned to Alison explaining.

"Butch's Betty's AA sponsor...."

"Will you people *please*, SHUT UP!"

Miraculously, everyone obliged the usually demure historian. Further emphasizing her intent to be answered, Alison grabbed Cornelia's shoulders and gave her a stern little shake.

"What book did Lilly borrow?"

"*Nancy Drew and the Secret of the Hidden Staircase,*" was all that Cornelia could sputter.

✳   ✳   ✳   ✳

Lilly Linda Le Strange shook her head with peevish dismissal of the rumpled bodies on the floor of the Parade Dress storeroom—then she stepped over these inconvenient lumps, for once quite literally. She wanted a closer look at her "space suit" chorus costumes hanging on the rack opposite. As she fingered the goods, a musty smell of grease paint issued from the antique costumes, but otherwise the fabric was sound. Lilly could picture her hoofers with blazing colored lights reflecting like a major kaleidoscope off the large metallic sequins sewn all over each "space suit." She could also picture herself, the Naughtiest Astronautess, in the center of all this reflective glitz, singing her heart out.

> *Oh way up high, up in the sky,*
> *oh tell me why,*
> *I sure ain't lost my splendor!*
> *Bright moon.*

Mulling over these comforting thoughts and visions, La Diva poked through the clothes rack. Then, remembering Urna's unexpected entrance from this very spot, she became curious and shoved the inventory aside, creating an opening barely large enough to wriggle through. Penetrating the barrier of disguises, she stepped over a threshold into another dimension.

The door she had come through closed itself gently behind her. Turning back quickly to secure her escape, Lilly collided with her double. Yes, she had stepped through the mirror and, although not alone, she was the only one there. She hardly registered the fantastic surroundings of the room she had stumbled into, so gripped by dismay was she when she saw in the mirror her careful coif now a mussed-up mess, and dark smudges at the knees of her python pants suit. Always expecting mirrors to tell her the best, La Diva was undone by her disheveled appearance, and her sole thought was to repair the damage. Fortunately for her the room she had entered was a fullyequipped dressing room, albeit somewhat old-fashioned and more than a wee bit overdone. She readily located hair and clothes brushes and got to work putting herself to rights.

As Lilly brusquely brushed, she looked about the room. She had apparently entered through a door concealed behind a full-length mirror held in place by a fussy gold frame. Once her hair and pants were back in pristine condition, she checked the latch mechanism of the mirror door to learn how it worked. She then looked at the room more closely, seeing before her an opulent and theatrical boudoir, incorporating much Rococo frou-frou, painted, gilded, and populated by swarms of chubby little babies holding curtains of lace tinted the exact shade of flushed pink known as, "spank the baby's bottom," a sophisticated hue popular during the Belle Époque.

It occurred to Lilly that the room looked suspiciously like a stage or movie set, and one that was mighty familiar. Just when the memory of which show was about to dawn on her, the mirror door flew open.

Lilly lowered herself onto the dressing table pouf, a padded stool wearing a lacey skirt. She crossed her legs and cupped her right elbow in her left hand while she idly admired her manicure with a studied pose of overburdened patience.

"So, Urna, glad you could drop in. Is that Golum looking for "My Precious," or is it Jiminy Cricket you're hanging out with?"

"No Darlink! This here's Dildo, the Phantom of The Follies Derrière!!"

With that concise introduction, Dildo untangled himself from Urna and strutted over to a corner of his secret domain. There, from amongst a whole pile of junk, he extracted an old windup hurdy-gurdy. Dildo then donned the classic half mask of the Phantom and, cranking away at his shabby barrel organ, launched into a surprisingly melodious rendition of the most over-sung aria of the last two centuries.

"*The Phaaaantom of the opera is inside your mind....*" etc.

"Oy veh! There he goes again! Now that you're here Darlink, have you got a joint?"

Urna flopped herself down on a handy chaise, upholstered with exuberant tufting reminiscent of a Victorian coffin, and extended a needy paw. Lilly rummaged in her Hermès handbag and came up with the requested reefer. For a while the two old rivals puffed away in indulgent silence, half listening to Dildo's warbling medley.

"So, what's the story this time, Urna … are you dead or are you alive?"

"Well, you know, I'm on the lam."

"Yeah?" Lilly gestured at Dildo's domain. "And what's all this then, mint jelly?"

"Very funny, Darlink Le Strange. But, get a load of this and weep!"

Urna leapt to her feet, kicked off the buckle galoshes, unwrapped the black Burberry trench coat, and tossed away the hat, glasses and beard.

"Ha Ha!" she hollered, smacking a tambourine above her head with contra-puntal poise.

Lilly sat bolt upright and took notice, feeling like the pale moon snuffed out by the burning sun. Before her strutted a vision victorious, comprised of all beauty distilled into one radiant presence. Urna must have had a total body transplant, because gone were the lines of worry, the pallid complexion, the puffy eyes, and the drooping muscle tone. And "hello" to two magnificent bubble breasts, the skin tone of angels, cascades of lustrous blue-black hair, and the stunning appearance of a young Barbie.

"Urna! You devil!!" wailed Lilly. And for the first time in her lengthy professional career, La Diva fainted dead away as Dildo's organ swelled to monstrous proportions in double forte Phantom frolics.

When Lilly came to, it was not a revelation of joy—at least not for La Diva, now painfully aware of her mounting years and their consequences.

"Aaah!" growled the fading star.

"What kinda dope did you broads smoke, anyhow!" croaked Dildo, "Just look at the bitch. You know, Urna, this ain't no crack house."

Dildo's dour remark bounced off Urna's triumph without leaving any impression.

"This is a safe house, Urna, not a flop house." Dildo added to emphasize his serious nature. He had enough problems in his life without a corpse on his hands. His job as chief bartender at Follies Derrière, the infamous drag bar in Bay Village, was a handful already. In addition to his grueling schedule shaking cocktails eight hours a day for some of the city's most vicious queens, he had his life's work to consider. As the historian of drag, he needed order and structure to concentrate.

Years ago when Dildo had only a burgeoning collection of drag which even then bulged beyond the confines of his studio apartment, a disused hall closet before he took up residence, Dildo had stumbled upon his salvation. One evening late, actually early morning, after the show was over and the bar was closed he was desperately searching the beer-splashed basement of the Derrière for a nook to stash a bra belonging to Belinda Bustamante that he had recently pinched. Belinda was a generous sort and didn't gripe even though she saw Dildo stuff her foundation garment into his backpack.

As the desperado rummaged in the dank shadows, he came across a niche behind a wall of beer cases in the far back corner of the basement. As he explored farther he had to use his cigarette lighter to look into the darkness, and from the unseen reaches of that passage came a steady stream of cool air strong enough to blow out his lighter. Dildo realized this must lead somewhere.

Lilly peeled herself off the overstuffed chaise and shuffled haltingly toward the vanity. Bending down close to the mirror, she peered into the glass to take inventory.

"Feeling better, Darlink?"

One glance undid her. La Diva screamed with fright and agony when the transformed and glorious Urna's rejuvenated visage appeared beside her in the mirror, a stark contrast to her own fading beauty. Lilly spun around, pressing her hands to her upper chest in a gesture of maidenly upheaval.

"Don't scare me like that, you know its bad luck to talk into a mirror," gasped Lilly referring to an old taboo for actors: Never speak to each other's reflection in a mirror. But, in fact it was the loss of face that really terrified her. She had always been a better looker than Urna, for going on thirty-five years, now. How could this be happening?!

"Sorry, Darlink, you seem a little jumpy. How about a slug of Robitussin?"

Lilly dismissed Urna's over-the-counter panacea and mustered up enough courage to look at Urna closely. She took hold of her rival's chin between her thumb and index finger and firmly turned Urna's head from side to side.

"Urna! Not a line or wrinkle. What'd that doctor do to you, tie your ears behind your head?"

"Do you like it?" gloated Urna. "I got the idea from that smartass author, what's his name, you know, the one that wrote that goofy *Family Jewels*? (For clarification see the back cover, author's photograph, of *The Family Jewels*)

"Oh yeah, Iory Allison. I figured if he could get a total body transplant so could I!"

"Yeah, yeah. I know the bloke. He thinks he's running the show, but wait till he sees where this is going. Anyway, not a line or wrinkle. Is this the work of voodoo?

"No nips, no tucks, no surgery, and no doctors! That's the beauty of Buttocks."

"Not buttocks, you numskull. Botox. Whadja do to get like that? Mainline the junk?"

"I'm no junky, Darlink, and it is too, Buttocks. Made from the rendered fat of a yak's ass."

"Nooo! You finally admitted it! You're a jack ass."

"Very funny, Darlink bitch woman. You should only hope your sorry jackass looks like this." And with that Urna flashed Lilly a glimpse of her bikinied body from beneath her flimsy peignoir, displaying all the right curves and squeezables.

"OK, OK, so where do I sign up?"

"Buttocks is not for the faint of heart, Darlink."

"Listen, I've never done that before. It musta been something I ate upstairs."

"Le Strange, did you ever read *The Picture of Dorian Gray?*"

"Naaa, I don't go in for small boats. Now, give me a big white yacht and I'm with you."

Urna looked askance at Lilly, then gave up on that tack and took another more direct course.

"Darlink, let me put it in a way even you'll understand. My days are numbered."

"Well, I'm glad to hear that, but what price glory, huh?"

"Exactly! I knew you'd catch my drift. You see, they've given me only six months before my buttocks melts."

"Don't tell me, and that means you and your portrait in the closet aren't gonna look so pretty."

"Darlink girl, you *have* read Oscar Wilde."

"Only the classical comic, and then mostly just the pictures. But it's essentially a Faust story, ain't it? Selling your soul for what … Barbie's body?"

"*And* a brand-new face! So, here's the deal: I've got the theatre and I've got the backing.…"

"Yeah, well, Urna, that's terrific, and I think we may have already been through this back in that whorehouse in Nam. But still, I'm not selling my soul for a theatre or a new face. Now, if there were a diamond necklace involved, I might consider it."

"Darlink Le Strange, fellow thespian …"

"Hey, I don't kiss girls."

"Never say never, Le Strange, and remember I know your true nature and all your secrets."

"I've warned you before, Urna. One word out of you about my true nature and you will wish the inquisition had caught up to you before me!"

"Temper, temper, my Darlink."

"Cut to the chase, Miss Barbie Boobs. My lamb chops are chilling upstairs."

"Do you remember, in *I, Claudius,* when Livia wailed, 'I want you to make me a goddess after I die, Claudius!'"

"No, Urna, I don't seem to recall that."

"I forgot you don't watch *Masterpiece Theatre.*"

"I think I'm looking at it right now."

"Lilly! I want to star in *Naughty Astronautess* before my buttocks melts!"

"Oh, is that all? Why didn't you say so? You have no chance in hell, Urna!"

"Remember, my pet Darlink, you're not the only Naughty Astronautess among us!"

∗   ∗   ∗   ∗

Upstairs in the Meeting Room, the waitstaff were busying themselves with the all-important dessert and coffee service, when out popped La Diva from behind the secret panel concealed in the fancy wood work surrounding the fireplace. She vigorously brushed the detritus of the dungeon off her silk taffeta python pants suit and plopped herself down, center stage.

As soon as the headliner resumed the hostess chair, Colette whizzed over with a dinner plate fully two feet in diameter and covered by a silver dome that was intended by the manufacturer to accommodate a stuffed turkey; such were the he-man, steak house proportions of Smith & Wollensky's dinner presentations. Colette lifted the lid with a dramatic flourish, in honor of Lilly's stellar stature, to reveal a brace of sizzling lamb chops sharing the plate with a pile of mashed potatoes impressed with a crater of redolent rich gravy.

"Here you go, Miss Le Strange. I kept your chops hot for ya, but if they're too tuff now, we can redo 'em."

"Darling lump, the only thing that needs redoing around here is me!"

Having uttered this rare, self-deprecating dish, Lilly plucked a chop from her plate and, pinching it delicately between her index finger and thumb, she chomped down with serious intent.

Everyone in the company was dying to know what lay beneath them in the secret crypt of the castle. Equally compelling was the question: why on earth would Lilly, the most done to death amongst them, need to be redone? Still, the future Astronautesses and their friends exercised Bostonian restraint and asked nothing, nor did they intrude any idle chitchat. The reason for their discretion was, of course, the chocolate cake, not deference to La Diva. Everyone had ordered the huge slabs of chocolate cake the restaurant was famous for. Their unanimous enthusiasm had required two extra back waiters to haul in and distribute the goods, and this excess of confection had relegated all other diversions to the back burner. Everyone munched contentedly for a while until Lilly picked her last bone. She licked her fingers with fastidious care but rather too much noise, then she glugged a slug of Australian chardonnay that could easily have drowned an aborigine. Thus replenished, she began to feel neglected by the seeming lack of interest in her adventures. In retaliation, she cast about the dessert plates of her neighbors with her dinner fork.

"Hey, watch out, lady!" Cornelia snapped out a warning to Lilly. "Remember I'm studying Tae Kwan Do at the Wymin's Place."

Lilly's response was a studied expression of surprise and dismissal, pointing her magnificent nose upward while she glared downward at the diminutive designer sitting beside her and said, "You've got a chocolate mustache, tiny lump. I can see that in my absence standards have slumped. I thought you were a Pilgrim princess, you're suppose ta share."

"I may be a Pilgrim princess, but this is not Thanksgiving and you are definitely not Pocahontas, so lay off my chocolate cake."

Lilly stood up abruptly, powered by neglect and effrontery. She spread her arms with supplication—a reach of nearly eight feet—and demanded in rumbling tones, "and all that any of you Queens have to say is, 'lay off my chocolate cake'?"

"Oh yeah, Lil—so what happened down there?"

Betty knew a cue when she heard one, but the flat and preoccupied tone of her delivered question only revved Lilly's engines.

"To think I, who have risked everything for you," here she gestured inclusively with a leaning reach first to the left and then to the right.

"Skip the guff and spill the beans, babe." said Butch "Yo! Colette! Bring Madame Le Strange a banana split and another bottle of bubbly—oh you got it already? You sure are a cute little filly." Butch slapped Colette's ass appreciatively as her team did a swift switcho-chango job, removing Lilly's spent dinner plate and replacing it with a porcelain boat, easily the size of a bathroom sink. This receptacle was filled with an abundant selection of Ben and Jerry's, peeled Chiquita's, Bosco, Fluff, and nuts.

POP!!!

"Whoops, heads up!" Colette announced her pour, gushing foaming bubbly into La Diva's glass.

Monique poked her rapier-sharp manicure at Colette as she passed by and threatened the waitress with vulgar taunts, the gist of which were meant to convey zero tolerance for any competition for Butch's attentions.

"You're not going to believe this, but Urna's down there with Dildo, the Phantom of The Follies Derrière," announced Lilly between bites of Cherry Garcia and Chunky Monkey.

"Oh, yeah, Dill. I can see why *he* would freak you out," commiserated Betty.

"You know Dildo?"

"Sure, everybody knows Dildo." Betty dismissed Lilly's question with a wave of her hand.

"I don't!" Gyles insisted, all too primly for credibility.

"That's what they all say." Betty's stab flashed by Gyles.

"We *all* know him." chimed in the rest of the kids of the chorus with big smiles.

"Wait a minute, what kinda knowing are we talking about here?"

"Oh, Lilly girl, where have you been? Dilly has been collecting our old drag for decades," said Monique, who had had enough of the blushing bride routine. She rose up and sauntered about the room, ruffling hair and pinching earlobes, her special form of pet petting.

"The Derrière is, whatever you say for or against it, the bottom line of drag. I know, just for starters, you had your East Coast debut there. You must remember little Dilbert, the bartender?"

"Dilbert? I thought Urna said Dildo."

"Dilbert, Dildo, take your pick, it's a stage name. We all have one stuffed in a drawer beside the bed."

"Now that you mention it, maybe I do remember the little pecker. Musta been him who kept pinching my gowns and accessories when I had ta play that dump. But do you have any idea how much drag is stuffed in this basement?" Lilly's eyes swam in a sea of intoxication and envy.

"So, how come you need a makeover, Mama?" Val asked simply, interrupting Lilly's gloating.

"Oh, darling lump!" Lilly lunged for Val's blond mop and slammed the young man's head against her well-padded breast in a histrionic gesture that left him reeling from the impact. Gyles put a stabilizing arm around his lover's shoulders and gave Lilly a stern look.

"It's that devil woman, Urna."

"Urna Flamanté is no woman," Cornelia insisted. "I saw her at the Casa Romero in galoshes and a bushy beard."

"So did I," Lilly agreed, "but who did we really see?"

"You mean the skinny bitch who darlinked everybody?" Monique tossed her question out like a nasty slap.

"Hey, wait a minute, bubble brain, Urna useta be my boyfriend, just remember that." Betty blurted out a rarely remembered bit of ancient history that had still not been adequately explained.

"Yes, well," said Lilly, refocusing everyone's attention, "that was before he became a Marine officer, a CIA operative, a notorious drag queen and a gangster's moll on the lam from that dumb thug, Scarface Malone."

Everyone in the room gasped at the mention of the fearful villain.

"Now, adding insult to surgery, the bitch has gone and gotten a total body transplant, and she looks like a MILLION DOLLARS!"

CHAPTER 32

▼

RETURN OF THE UNKNOWN VISITOR

At the reception desk at Brigham and Women private wards, Nurse Oppenheimer recognized and smiled at the dignified visitor with the military bearing.

"Good evening, sir."

"Good evening, nurse."

This brief exchange was all that ever passed between them. The gentleman's demeanor did not invite casual conversation and the nurse's professional restraint was such that she did not presume to intrude. Because of the visitor's authoritative manner, Nurse Oppenheimer had never even asked his identity over the weeks he had regularly visited Rosalind Wortheley. She was just relieved and grateful that someone was a friend to the remote and lonely woman under her care.

The military man in the pinstripe suit found his way to the Coolidge Cunningham suite where Rosalind lay in a deep coma and let himself in. Taking up the unused visitor's chair, he placed it close to the Plexiglas dome protecting the patient. This week, Rosalind's outfit had been changed by Abruzio Della Snozzy to silk satin pajamas of the delicate shade of spring violets, with plum-colored piping outlining the perfect tailoring of the broad lapels and generous cuffs at the wrists and ankles. There was even a breast pocket wherein nestled a crisply folded handkerchief sprinkled with a print of flowering violets.

The towering man sitting beside the recumbent beauty reached out and gently placed his hand on the transparent dome hovering above one of Rosalind's gracefully limp hands. He stared through the barrier, studying every lovely detail of the professional beauty who was once described in the fashionable press as "A work of art sculpted by the Gods."

The visitor's eye came to rest on Rosalind's full breasts rising and falling, following the rhythm of her shallow breath. Even now, after four months of unnatural sleep, hardly stirring at all, her shape and muscle tone were softly defined, resilient, and lush. The visitor delicately stroked the Plexiglas barrier in a circular motion, reaching with his imagination into the emptiness between them. The intensity of his emotions brought him up short, and he shook himself as if to wake from a dream.

"I'm sorry, I didn't mean to take advantage. I don't know what I'm thinking. We are so many miles apart, and I never thought I'd be back here. I only intended to come once, to see for myself if you were OK, and you aren't and I'm sorry. But, now I'm more than sorry. You're asleep, but I'm the one who's dreaming. I am dreaming about you all the time. I can't get enough, and I haven't got anything, and no right to hope."

As the visitor spoke his pained and confused thoughts out loud, the sleeping beauty's eyelids fluttered and his heart skipped a beat. He reined in his weakness with a hard tug.

"No, this has happened before. She can't hear me, and even if she could…."

But he stared at her eyes anyway, noticing each soft hair of her naturally arched eyebrows and how they glistened in the defused light. Studying Rosalind so closely, her presence radiated through the false barrier and filled his solid bulk with a throbbing ache that hovered between a sob and a laugh. Suddenly he knew he had overstayed his visit.

CHAPTER 33

▼

LURKING IN THE ALLEY

Dildo and Urna faced each other across the bar of The Follies Derrière, slugging down some serious cocktails.

"How the fuck did the Le Strange bitch discover the Phantom Cave if you didn't tell her?"

Dildo was livid with Urna, figuring that she had let the cat out of the bag. His mind raced with paranoid fantasies of all those rotten queens pawing his carefully won treasure. He saw them tearing apart all the lovely gowns, like a frenzied bloodbath of sharks after a bleeding swimmer, and he shuddered with horror.

"Darlink Dill! I did not broadcast the Phantom Cave to Le Strange or anybody. Good gravy, I'm trying to dodge the crazy woman, at least until I need her."

"There you go, you drags are all cut from the same cloth! 'Until I need her, harrumph! And with an attitude like that, I'm supposed to believe you're not using Dildo?"

"Yes, now that you mention it, I could use a little cheering up, but I have to save myself for Scarface and oy veh, you have no idea what an ordeal that can be. Since I fled the island nation of Aruba with barely a powder puff to my name, I had to leave behind my collection of leather hoods. You, of all people, should understand the importance of fashion accessories. As I may have explained, Darlink Little Dildo, Wally St. John makes all my hoods formfitting...."

"Yeah, I know Wally over at the monastery. I have some choice items in my collection from him. My absolute fave is a Goth mosh pit outfit made from old body bags studded all over with a world class collection of Pez dispensers. They say it belonged to Peter the Pill Head and he kept his stash in the Pez dispensers. It was torn off his body when he split his head in a botched mosh at a Piss on Me concert at the Pig's Trough."

"Oh, Darlink Dilly, how you do carry on! It sounds like a marvel of couture. But getting back to my hoods, Wally makes 'em sans eyeholes, of course, so I don't have ta look at Scar. But jeepers creepers, what a bummer! Not only am I without my hoods, but Scar has discovered mirrors. Do you have any idea what's it like to end up in bed with a package of sliced meat bouncing back and forth between seventeen mirrors?"

Urna drained her Singapore sling with desperate need, slammed down her glass and gasped.

"I'll switch to zombies and make 'em doubles!!"

Dilbert set about concocting a new round of cocktails that, when duly assembled, he shook with the force of a mixing machine at the paint store.

"Darlink Dill," said Urna sipping delicately at her double zombie, "you've undone yourself."

Dillbert checked his fly, but finding it zipped he realized her slip.

"Not 'undone yourself,' it's 'outdid yourself,' you silly Ukrainian hussy."

"Shut your mouth, Dilly Darlink. The closest I've ever been to the Ukraine was when I took the number 43 bus from Dudley Station and ended up in East Mattapan."

"So, what's with the 'Darlinks' 'jeepers creepers' and 'good gravy's'?" Dilbert demanded hotly.

"Oy veh, can't a girl have any fun? What about diversity and multiculturalism?"

"Skip it, Urna, I shoulda known better than ta drink with the likes a you."

Urna was rescued from further scorn when her cell phone intoned the introductory bars of *Pavanne for a Dead Princess.*

"Yes, Darlink, I am here ... o, that's you, is it? What now, more mirror shenanigans? ... I know I'm on contract, you big lug.... Yes, I know how expensive Buttocks injections are, you're talking to a professional, you know. No! I don't care how horny you are, you'll have to find me first before you can have me ... I wouldn't dream of doing what you have in mind ... the bar at the Derrière? Well, yes, that might be close by ... Your limo's in the alley? Don't try anything rash, you bad boy!"

Urna frantically scooped up her ciggies and jammed them into her tiny purse—a maneuver that drenched her rouge pot with Jungle Gardenia perfume, inadvertently squeezed from her plastic Luger. She untangled her knotted legs from the barstool and fled to the beer-splashed basement of the Derrière and Dildo's Phantom Cave.

CHAPTER 34

▼

CLOVIS HAS GONE MISSING?

After the banquet at Smith & Wollensky's, Scena Finale shared a cab with Lilly back to the South End.

"What do you mean you struck a deal with Urna for a starring role in *Naughty Astronautess?* I've just finished the choreography for the whole show and there is no place between Cape Canaveral and the dark side of the moon for an astronautess with two left feet. Do you know how tricky the routines for the "Penis under Mars" scene in act one alone?"

"Scena, Scena, Scena, you make it sound as if Urna is a neophyte. If nothing else, she can do her clog-stomping routine. That's pretty impressive. I seem to remember she's got real Cajun blood in her."

"Whatever blood once oozed from Urna's marrow has been sucked dry by that vampire, Scarface Malone, and replaced by Urna with girly cocktails!"

Lilly grandly dismissed Scena 's misgivings with a wave of her hand, although she might also have been shooing away a fly. Lilly's body language sometimes slipped into arcane dialects.

"Don't swish me off, lady, I won't have it!"

"You won't have a show then, because Urna's the angel."

Lilly's simple explanation spoke volumes to Scena.

"Whatdoya mean? I don't get it … yesterday the silly bitch was dead and today she's suddenly the Bank of America's charitable branch and the National Endowment for the Arts rolled into one. You don't mean that? No! Even you're not that dumb!! *Naughty Astronautess* is going to be financed by Scarface Malone? Lilly, he's a ruthless gangster, a cold-blooded killer. I heard he ate La Freda Thrombosis for lunch two weeks ago and God knows what happened to Clovis Galicurchi."

"What's the matter with Clovis? He's supposed to be training the Gay Men's Chorus for the choral interlude, "Peckers in Deep Space," that's crucial to the plot development for the show."

"There you go, what *is* the matter with Clovis? He was last seen testing pitch pipes at the Berklee Music store when he was accosted by Madame Sonya Schnable, frantically insisting that she must audition for the position of basso profundo soloist in the chorus. Sonya insisted that she had channeled Ima Sumac with her ouija board and Ima wanted to sing again. Clovis fled from Sonya's hallucinations out into the street, where a limo, stretched beyond all sense and sensibility, lured him into its shadowy recesses."

Lilly looked at Scena with renewed interest and asked, "Huh? How on earth would you know that, even if it were true?"

"How do I know? Lilly, it's all over the city. Reginald Pew scooped the item in his column in *Gay Windows*. Reggie was trying to hock his collection of original Batman comics at Loony Tunes, which, as you know from being one of their better customers, is right next door to the Berklee Music store. Reggie tried to give his actions an upgrade by reporting in his column that he was practicing Chopin preludes on the Steinway in the window of Berklee, but that has to be a lie, because he only has seven fingers. But whatever, he claims he saw Clovis leaning into the back window of a limo on Boylston Street. This choice bit of gossip was supposed to imply that Maestro Clovis was turning tricks in broad daylight, a nasty bit of filth everyone was all too ready to believe because of Clovis' relentless fundraising efforts on behalf of the chorus. However, what was really happening was that Reggie was plucked, because Clovis rejected his audition for the chorus. Apparently, Reggie had prepared a lengthy rendition of 'Can't Help Lovin' That Man o' Mine,' but Clovis made him sing 'America the Beautiful' instead."

"Scena! Enough! I get the picture, Clovis has gone missing and without him, no Gay Men's Chorus. Excuse me while I gnash my teeth."

Lilly rolled down the window of the cab and blasted the airwaves with the anguished howl of the hound from hell.

"Arrrrrghe!"

The cabby got so spooked he slammed on the brakes and the cab lurched to a halt, slamming the two passengers against the grubby divider separating the front and back seats.

"What the fuck was that?" The cabby succinctly registered his distress.

"Don't fret, daring lump," replied Lilly, "I've just lost my choral director, and I needed to vent."

"Jeez, was that all. I thought for sure it was Osama bin Laden farting."

The cabby gave Lilly a smug grimace in his rearview mirror as Scena struggled to untangle herself from the floor of the cab where she had landed.

"*Vissi d'arte, vissi d'amore*," Sobbed Lilly, "I who have dedicated my life to art, why me?"

CHAPTER 35

▼

ASSIGNATION IN THE
PHANTOM CAVE

Betty the Bounder was feeling thirsty and blue as she dragged her heavy feet, climbing the scruffy stairs from the Holy Redeemer church basement. Butch had insisted that the gay AA meeting at the Redeemer was the right place for Betty. She, however, had her doubts, and as she pondered these misgivings she drifted away from the clumps of well-wishers hovering about the basement door, blowing cigarette smoke. As she passed through their ranks, they hailed her with slogans of relentless cheer.

"Keep coming back."

"It works, if you work it."

"Hang in there, girl."

Once curbside, Betty snapped the clamps of her Roller Blades and whooshed away down the street. The pleats of her short white skating skirt flapped in the breeze about her thighs. Her multicolor-striped leggings made her legs look like a stack of Life Savers, but they kept her snug.

Whooshing through the South End, Betty soon worked up sheen from her exertions, and after awhile, without having any thought or destination in mind, she found herself in the vicinity of that infamous gin mill, The Follies Derrière. Homing pigeons are creatures of strong habit and so was Betty. She hummed to herself that snappy tune, "What Good Is Sitting at Home by Yourself?" and figured she might as well drop by and check out the action. But when Betty came in sight of the old dive, she couldn't help noticing a black limousine belching a low-lying cloud of carbon monoxide in the alley. Since Reginald Pew's story about the disappearance of Clovis Galicurchi in *Gay Windows* yesterday, Betty was on her guard. Sensing trouble, she slithered around to the back entrance of the club, by the dumpster.

Gliding into the club from backstage, Betty made an unexpected entrance. Behind the bar, Dilbert was already more than a wee bit rankled by his encounter with Lilly and Urna, not to mention being staked out by Scarface Malone. Now the diminutive bartender got really spooked by the floating apparition invading his Derrière, so he hurled his trusty cudgel, a massive rubber doubledildo shaped like a boomerang. It lassoed Betty's scrawny neck, and over she went in a thrashing heap.

With the intruder down for the count and the schlong wrapped around Betty's neck, Dilbert recognized her for what she was—the Bounder. He figured she'd probably need some resuscitation after this unexpected turn of events, so he got to work shaking up a new batch of zombies.

After some moments of gurgling doubt, Betty came to with a shudder and groan. With the resilience of one who has come to expect the unspeakable, Betty rose to the occasion, she peeled the offending member from around her neck, and dropped it on the bar, where it jiggled in an unseemly manner.

"Hey Dilbert, I know I haven't been around for a while, and even then my tips mighta been a bit skimpy, but what kind of a greeting was that?" Betty demanded.

"I'm *so* sorry, Betty, but you scared the shit out of me," Dilbert sputtered, pouring from his shaker.

"The feeling is mutual. What's this?"

"A double zombie."

"Keep 'em coming."

Betty pulled up the nearest barstool in the empty club and knocked back her zombie.

"Did you see Scarface Malone's limo in the alley?" asked Dilbert. "He's after Urna, and she just skedaddled her skinny ass outta here."

"Scarface Malone!" Betty gasped, and grabbing the stainless steel shaker right out of Dilbert's hands, she took a deep slug.

"Hey, whadaya think this is?" Dilbert wrenched the cocktail shaker out of Betty's fist. "We've got standards here, you know."

"Sorry, Dilly, I musta forgot myself."

"'SOK, I'm just a little jumpy, that's all."

"And you have every right to be, with Scarface hanging around," said Betty, reaching across the bar to pat Dilbert's arm, intending to be soothing. But, inadvertently, it was Dilbert's wriggling cudgel that received Betty's cosseting. Her chummy little squeeze felt suspiciously rubbery, and when she looked down at what was actually in her hand, she shuddered, flinched and recoiled.

"That's not the half of it," continued the oblivious Dilbert. "That Le Strange woman broke into the Phantom Cave and now she wants to snatch my drag."

Betty wiped her hand on a cocktail napkin and took a slug off her zombie. She needed a moment to consider her loyalties before she replied. Dilbert was, after all, an influential character at the Derrière, being the head bartender and all. He was also a little creep, sneaking around dressing rooms, snitching any item of unguarded apparel he could lay his hands on. Betty had to wrestle more than once with the avid collector over the odd bauble, and once they even came to blows over Lilly's favorite designer gown. But that was water over the dam at this point, because Lilly had graduated from the Derrière many moons ago. Now, Betty could adopt a more philosophical indulgence toward Dilbert, especially if she wanted free-flowing zombies.

"Aw come on, Dilly, what are you gonna do with all that stuff anyway?"

"Do?! Stuff?! I'll have you know, Madonna offered me a hundred Gs for *some* of the choicest items. But no one's laying their dirty mitts on my collection … Not Madonna, and certainly not Le Strange. I'm saving for my retirement next year. I'm torn between South Beach, Key West, or The Castro. Ya see, I'm going to open the world's first museum of drag!"

"That's swell, Dilly, but didn't you just say Urna was here? Which way did she go?"

"Can't tell ya."

"Whaddaya mean, can't?" Betty demanded. Leaning over the bar grabbing Dilbert's flannel shirt and pulling the bartender up front and close, she growled, "What's it gonna cost me?"

"Your purse."

"Not on your life, runt! This here is an original copy of a Chanel shoulder bag. I got it at my first Filene's Basement sale, way back in '79, and even then I had to slug a nun to get it."

"Nuns don't carry Chanel shoulder bags, you silly wino. Now, if you wanna see Urna, fork it over."

Betty dropped Dilbert, snatched up her cocktail and drained the glass. Dilbert could see the struggle in Betty's eyes, so he primed the pump and poured her another zombie. Betty sipped with rueful resignation, and after being properly anesthetized she handed over her purse.

Not being totally without pity, Dilbert dumped the contents of Betty's purse into a black paper shopping bag from the Abruzio Della Snozzy boutique. An airline-sized glass nip of Beefeaters clunked amongst a Clinique compact, a canister of puce spray paint and a nonlatex dental dam.

"So, where is she?"

"Turn around, I gotta tie this blindfold on ya."

"Dilly!"

"If you wanna see Urna, you gotta wear this."

∗   ∗   ∗   ∗

Dilbert led the blindfolded Betty to the top of the slimy stairs of the Derrière basement. The Bounder's Roller Blades, like Betty herself, were inappropriate to the task and she slipped, slided and crashed down the entire staircase. After making a considerable effort to peel Betty off the dank floor of the basement, Dilbert led the way through the secret panel behind the moldering beer cases at the darkest reaches of the dungeon.

The subterranean passage that connected the basements of the Derrière to the Corps of Cadets castle was an anomaly of urban construction, owing its existence to the all-powerful Major Swan. The major had simultaneously been the chairman of the Cadets building committee and the Commissioner of Public Works for the City of Boston. Serving in these capacities, he was accustomed to getting his way no matter how wayward that might be, and in this case it was not far. Just around the corner from the castle, the major's mistress was neatly tucked into a modest brick townhouse in Bay Village. With an adroit misuse of power he connected his two interests, thereby enjoying easy access to the accommodating lady and his high-tone boys' club.

Time passed, and as luck would have it, Swan's Way, as one wag had called the mistress's house, eventually evolved into the notorious drag bar, The Follies Derrière. Following the demise of the major and his mistress, the passage suffered many years of disuse and neglect. Eventually it was entirely forgotten until that fateful evening when Dildo desperately needed to stash Belinda Bustamante's bustier, leading him to rummage in the basement of the bar.

Behind her blindfold, Betty was blissfully ignorant of the squalid passage Dildo led her through to rendezvous with Urna Flamanté. Fortunately for Betty, although the going was rough, the passage was all on one level, so she glided with comparative ease behind the furtive Dildo until they reached a double bolted and locked door.

The reunion of Betty and Urna in the seclusion and privacy of the Phantom Cave was so long overdue that neither one knew how to start or what to say to each other. Dildo seized the opportunity to contribute to the awkward moment by hauling out his hurdy-gurdy, winding the crank, and launching into that interminable old saw:

"The Phaaaaaantom of the Opera is inside your mind...."

"Dildo! Butt out! Butt-in-ski!!"

"And that means scram, punk!"

On the issue of Dilbert, Urna and Betty were in perfect accord, hastening the little bugger's timely exit with shoves and heaves. After they had closed and bolted the door behind him, Betty turned to Urna and lit into her something fierce.

"Urna, how come you're alive and how come you didn't tell me? Even when you crashed Lilly's dinner party at the Casa Romero last week, you acted as if I wasn't there. I'll have you know that when your ashes got lost in that cab going to the cemetery, I was fit to be tied."

Urna was about to interrupt at this juncture to ask for some clarification but decided it was better not to know too much of Betty's story. (See chapter 35 of *The Family Jewels* for some details of this peculiar turn of events.)

"And who gave you that phony Urna Flamanté name, anyway? When we were at the seminary together, you were just plain Joey, or at least Brother Joseph. Then, after years of absence without even a Christmas card, you turn up on your grand farewell tour Unctuous Urna Yodels with Her Uvula. All I can say about that is yuck! I thought a uvula was some kind of a female sex organ, and that you had gone and had a sex change! What a waste that would have been, 'cause I can remember way back when, in the Sacred Fart Seminary, you had a large endowment, the envy of the whole freshman class. Didn't you believe me when I told you I loved you?"

Urna, rattled by Betty's impassioned declarations, stripped of all pretence of pride or restraint, began to recognize and remember Betty as she once was.

"Dagmar Benjamin? Darlink Dag? *You* are Dagmar Benjamin? Jeepers creepers! Little Dag who dogged my every step? Who did my homework for me? Gave me cheat sheets inscribed in braille on my rosary? Beautiful Dag with all that goofy red hair? I'd never seen a guy with a red bush before. And you said the Sacred Fart Seminary? It must be you! No one else but you and me knew that name. Good gravy, forgive me, Little Dag. I searched for you after I got out of

Viet Nam. I went all the way back to Rattle Snake, Wyoming, to find you. I banged on the monastery doors until my hands bled. That monster, Abbot Oscarmyer, jeered at me from the battlements, cursing me and casting me out. He told me you were transferred to the Yukon Territory where you choked on a gristly piece of blubber and died. Oh, why did I believe him? I knew he was jealous of us. I knew he wanted your sweet virginal cherry for his own pie, well maybe not entirely virginal. Anyway, I wept."

At this moment in his spiel, Joey got down on his knees in front of Dag, pleading for his forgiveness, and Dag found himself fondling the now spiked green hair, stiff with product.

CHAPTER 36

▼

DUMPED IN THE GUTTER

Clovis Galicurchi was unceremoniously dumped outside the Tantamount Theatre on Washington St. in Downtown Crossing on the edge of Boston's theatre district. He was a bit roughed up and more than a bit outraged and riled. Maestro Galicurchi was used to giving orders and commanding instant respect from his large troupe of adoring gay choristers. His sojourn amongst the sordid lot of jeering gangsters hanging out in Scarface Malone's limo was far from his usual exalted podium and, to him, not a bit funny. As it turned out, the thugs in Malone's employ were all from one remote village in the Zelengora Mountains of Bosnia and spoke no English. Clovis, who did have a reputation as a cunning linguist in the international world of choral music and opera, was, however, woefully ignorant of the mountain dialects of the Zelengora. As a consequence Clovis got smacked upside the head a couple of times until he got the picture and joined the gang in a wee nip of Slivovitz, a potent distillate of plums.

Soon Clovis and the gang were enjoying more cordial relations. In this relatively relaxed condition Clovis began to hum a ditty he had been teaching the Gay Men's Chorus, "If I were a pig on the farm" an old Appalachian lullaby. The Zelengorian clan perked up their collective ears and, being starved for the folk ballads of their native Bosnia, enthusiastically hummed along. Clovis was, of course, a compelling teacher, and after they had consumed another bottle of plum cordial, he had the five men singing full voice in close harmony that eternal saga of porcine life in rural Georgia.

But what Clovis did not realize—indeed how could he on such a casual acquaintance—was the volatile temperament of the Zelengorians. Once cooked on slivovitz and worked up to a teary frenzy by the music, the gang got really rambunctious. One man actually fired off a few rounds right through the roof of the limo. Clovis had had it. He lunged for the door and popping the lock he rolled out of the limo into the gutter right in front of the Tantamount Theatre. Clovis struggled to pick himself out of the gutter and brush off the dust of ignominy from his person. The limo, stretched beyond reason, speed away. As luck would have it, this was the exact moment when Urna Flamantè, Lilly Linda Le Strange, Wally St. John, Scena Finale and Betty the Bounder had assembled to inspect the old movie palace as a possible venue for *Naughty Astronautess*.

"Oh, there you are, Clovis. Someone said you had been kidnapped but I knew that was bosh. I 'm so relieved you made it on time. Now there you are girls, a true professional."

Lilly greeted Clovis casually leaning over to give Maestro air kisses. "Darling lump, mind your manners!"

Before Clovis could gather his dignity or proffer any further explanations, an immaculately polished black Packard limousine rolled up to the curb in front of the theatre. Out hopped Butch in his dove-gray chauffeur's uniform with spit-polished black knee boots. He circled the vintage automobile where he stood to attention and opened the rear passenger door. Out stepped Monique in an outfit incorporating a short jacket of long black monkey hair and a cloche hat encircled with a veil like the vapors of a foggy night.

"You will never guess who I ran into at the nail parlor just now." announced Monique eagerly. All ears were trained toward the showgirl. Knowing her reputation, they eagerly expected the worst.

"I would never have dreamt it except in a nightmare, but Scarface Malone was having a pedicure in the next booth to me!"

This revelation prompted the by now classic response, caught between a gasp and a shudder, "Scarface Malone!"

"How didja know it was him?" Betty wanted to know.

"Monique, please! What did Scarface look like?" Butch wanted to know.

"Don't ask!" Urna shuddered from long experience.

"Have you ever seen Picasso on acid?" Monique's ambiguous reply was as clear as peeking through a kaleidoscope.

Maestro Clovis shuddered at the memory of his ejection from Scarface's limo.

"I need a drink!" uttered Clovis in a tremulous voice.

"Here ya go Mav." Betty obliged the Maestro with a bottle of peach schnapps she had secreted in her Lion King lunch box.

"I saw that, Miss Thing." Butch bellowed a warning at Betty.

Lilly was pissed at being upstaged by Monique. She strode toward the boarded-up entrance of the Tantamount Theatre, which was plastered with life-size photos of 1940s movie stars. There she took hold of one of the sheets of plywood by prying the edge with steel fingers. She ripped the whole thing off its frame. A terrible shattering complaint was heard around the neighborhood. Standing aside, Lilly directed the gang to pass through the break in the barricade with a sweeping gesture. Not one of them obliged willingly.

CHAPTER 37

▼

UNEXPECTED AWAKENING

The dignified man visiting the exclusive and private ward of suites at Brigham and Women's Hospital appeared as usual in a well-tailored pinstriped business suit and perfectly knotted red silk tie. The overhead lights of the reception desk sparkled briefly in his gold and enameled lapel pin, adding a military shine to that diminutive American flag. But as he approached the nurse's station where the ever present Nurse Oppenheimer was standing, she saw him reach for his hand-kerchief and mop his brow. She wondered if something might be amiss with Mrs. Wortheley's regular visitor. He had always seemed the picture of stalwart com-mand, an invincible protector. However, nurses are trained to observe not to intrude, and here on Ward A discretion was a necessity when dealing with the rich and powerful. Nurse Oppenheimer therefore focused overelaborate attention on the paperwork before her and only nodded politely acknowledging the tower-ing presence as he passed on by.

The powerful man made his own way toward the Coolidge Cunningham suite where Rosalind Wortheley languished in the fifth month of her coma. He care-fully and quietly closed the door behind himself, feeling that his heavily charged energy might disturb the sacrosanct chamber if he did not hold himself in check. Before he turned to face the patient, he paused and took a deep breath. Slowly he turned to face her, but even after this preparation he was defenseless to dodge the lightning charge that shot across the room. For him Rosalind had become a divine presence shattering the bulwark foundations that supported his pose of invincible strength. He felt as if his solid form might be dissolved by her forlorn loneliness, and most disturbing of all he wanted to yield to her melting radiance.

Lying serene and unnaturally still, isolated beneath her Plexiglas shield, Rosalind had been dressed by Abruzio Della Snozzy in a gown of sparkling gold tissue that clung to her, accentuating every nuance of her sensual body. The man standing by the door was compelled to stare at her shining auburn hair eddied about her head in graceful waves like the tide about to turn. Rosalind's mythic features seemed to him sculpted by sagas of heroic women. She was imperfectly exquisite. Her jaw was too strong, her nose impossibly refined, her lips a bit too full but saved by broad exaggerated curves, and her complexion was the color of sunset after summer rain.

The man's gaze was drawn down her long lithe form irresistible traveling over the soft curves and slight swells, leading downward toward the woman's belly, which was punctuated by the depression of her navel and surrounded by the structure of her hip bones shaped like the graceful S curves piercing the sounding chamber of a viola. The rich dark tones of that most haunting of instruments seemed to vibrate around him, and he shuddered with a thrill that threatened to drown him in the song of her inner self.

In an effort to shake the spell that enthralled him so completely, he knew he must do something ordinary and mundane. Desperately he tried to reestablish control over himself. He grabbed the back of the visitor's chair to place it, as he always had, by the Plexiglas shield imprisoning her ethereal spirit. But even this effort was beyond his strength, useless, even somehow pathetic.

Was he so accustomed to action in combat to sit beside her and weep? Was he so experienced in the chaos of war to cower in futile helplessness? How many patients of his own had he and the field doctors sewn up or literally yanked out of death's grasp? It was always the necessity of imminent death that made them think of a way back to life. Once in the midst of a fire storm, engulfed in the ruins of a frontline hospital, a soldier's breath stopped. No oxygen. No breathing apparatus. No drugs. The lieutenant nurse had grabbed the departing soul, clamped his lips tight to the dying soldier's and forced breath back into the boy—and he lived!

"What now, Rosalind, where are you? Come back, it's this way out! You haunt the dark spaces before the dawn and I alone am here calling you. I mustn't think of the distances between us. I can't be bound by the rules of this world anymore. I can no longer obey the orders of command. I too am lost in the wilderness of your dreams."

First Lieutenant Albert Mellenoffsky, three times decorated combat nurse, Viet Nam veteran and hardened fighter, gave up, surrendered and gave in. Heedless of any consequences and compelled by forces beyond his control or understanding, the lieutenant lifted the Plexiglas dome covering Rosalind. It was alive with phantom reflections of the hospital apparatus crowding the room, but now for the first time he gazed at her directly without any barrier shield. Slowly bending over the recumbent beauty he could feel a slight tingling charge of static electricity, gentle as champagne bubbles, popping on his cheek. Closer than a hero's secrets he came to her with adoration, fear and agonizing need. His pursed lips hovered over hers so soft and forgiving. His final hesitation was but a tiny gasp inhaling her breath, elixir of life, anesthetizing his last fears. Pressing his lips to hers, their kiss calmed the storm that raged inside him. They were for a moment together, beyond time.

Rosalind's eyelids struggled with blindness trying to remember the light. She heard a whisper of promised joy, and she opened her eyes to see her prince. His gentle tears washed the heavy sleep of months from her eyes as he, with exquisite care, enfolded her in his enormous embrace.

CHAPTER 38

▼

TRUE NATURE REVEALED

Urna Flamanté sat at the kitchen table of Lilly Land wearing a purple vinyl mini skirt, black patterned stockings and white go-go boots. Her waist was cinched by a breath-defying black leather belt, and her Buttocks-inflated boobs were standing to pert attention beneath a skintight black leotard. Completing the ensemble she wore wrist-length white cotton gloves and a pink pillbox hat perched jauntily on her green spiked hair. Her jewelry was all vintage Chanel consisting of numerous oversized "gold" chains strung with large beads of synthetic origins.

Urna was idly leafing through the latest *Gay Windows,* so hot off the presses the ink hadn't even thought about drying, hence the gloves. Between sips of mocha java lava from Moondeers Coffee Shack, she made vague attempts to read. Her listless wanderings through the world of print journalism brought her to that threshold of sleaze, Dreck and Dross by Reginald Pew.

"Now here is a hissing geyser worthy of my attention," thought Urna as she made a concerted effort to concentrate, but she slipped out of gear a couple of times until she realized her deficiency and fired up a joint. Hitting hard off her refer she began to focus on Pew's stink.

"Hey get a load of this," Urna's speech lurched forward without expelling any breath. "Reggie has all the latest dish on that Wortheley woman!" Urna absently passed the smoldering J with such offhanded cool that it came to rest in Betty's red fuzzy beard, where it smoldered ominously. Why the Bounder sometimes wore this mangy accessory was a universal mystery without charm, but she insisted it kept her warm and she was sticking to that story. On this occasion it nearly went up in smoke, but Val came to the rescue by tossing his glass of OJ onto the hairpiece. Betty, being a professional, whisked away the burning J before the juice put out the home fires altogether and she giggled. The Bounder was grateful to Val and disposed to be indulgent toward Urna since their recent reconciliation in Dildo's lair. Betty blotted her beard with a handy kitchen towel and thought nothing more of the incident as she sucked greedily on the joint. Urna, of course, was oblivious to the consequences of her actions concerning Betty's near immolation and read Pew's stink aloud:

> Rosalind Wortheley, wife of George Wortheley, CEO of the Essential Insurance Company, and only daughter of Mrs. Adams Cabot Lowell Untermeyer, and the adoptive mother of the Ling Ling twins, has miraculously recovered from her five-month coma.
>
> While hosting the opening of the Essential Center Shopping Mall last November, Mrs. Wortheley was struck dumb and fainted, falling on her head and rendering her even dumber, a remarkable accomplishment considering her lack of capacity to begin with. She had remained in a vegetative state in the very private and exclusive ward of Brigham and Women's Hospital in Boston until yesterday afternoon when a mysterious visitor administered artificial respiration resulting in a belated awakening. The old tried-and-true mouth-to-mouth did the trick that an army of specialists could not accomplish.
>
> Mrs. Wortheley was discovered awake and sitting up but in a dazed condition by her dress designer, that maven of haute couture, Abruzio Della Snozzy when he arrived with his staff for her weekly change of outfit. Sig. Della Snozzy's sumptuous gowns have been the only vestige of Mrs. Wortheley's former life of fashion and glamour soothing the patient during her protracted illness. A member of Atelier Della Snozzy spoke to this reporter under protection of anonymity describing Mrs. Wortheley's distracted condition when the team arrived as hovering on the frantic edge of despair. His actual phrase was "The dame was weeping and hollering and making a terrible mess outta the gold tissue sheath Della had made for her. She keeps on about 'her prince, oh where could he be?' but we all ask ourselves that question at some time or another, so we figured she was delirious."
>
> If truth be known most of Della Snozzy's clients are hovering over the edge, and it has been suggested that some of his staff are actually brain dead themselves and therefore not likely to overreact. The result of all this discretion was that no one took the slightest interest in the patient's wandering thoughts or babblings. They dressed her in a 60s Hawaiian muumuu of retro fantasia and left the client looking splendid, complete with a lei of frangipani blossoms hooked around her neck. The Esthetician Marjory Rubenstein, granddaughter of Helena and consummate genius of all makeup artists, was

the last member of the team to see the professional beauty. She was quoted as saying, "When Della and the gang left, the Wortheley dame was looking fantastic but babbling something about lost love, and well, I told her I didn't believe in love and left it like that."

Subsequent to the Della Snozzy team efforts in the cause of fashion, Mrs. George Wortheley has disappeared from Brigham and Women's. An extensive search of the entire hospital has as yet yielded no trace of her. It has been suggested by some that she hightailed it for the divorce courts of Reno...."

"That's just about enough of that smut!" bellowed Lilly belligerently snatching Urna's copy of *Gay Windows* out of her hands and tearing the paper to shreds.

Val was used to Lilly's morning distemper and continued to sip his coffee placidly. But Betty took alarm when she noticed that Lilly was dressed in blue jeans and an old white T shirt and, most alarmingly, wigless!

Urna, in her usual fog of self-absorbed oblivion, imprudently protested the destruction of her *Gay Windows* newspaper saying, "Miss Thing, that was *my* paper and I hadn't finished the article!"

"You're finished now, bub. Don't ever bring that prick or his scummy rag into my house, you embalmed corpse, and most especially don't you dare read his lies and dish in my kitchen."

Lilly stood six foot two inches tall in her bright orange Crocs. Both hands resting on her hips in an aggressive posture, she glared down at Urna, who took in the disheveled Diva in a glance and nonchalantly commented, "Looks like your true nature is coming out again, Le Strange. Better go powder your nose and have a really close shave—you look like a truck driver."

"I've warned you, zombie brain, any comments on my true nature and they'll have to scrape you off the ceiling."

Lilly uttered this threat with such venomous hissing that even Val had to wonder. He looked at Betty with a "what's up" shrug, but the Bounder was even more baffled and asked aloud, "There's nothing true or natural about Lilly, Urna, whaddaya mean?"

"Thanks, Betty, some people know where their loyalties lie."

Val wondered if Lilly intended any pun with this thanks but kept his musings to himself.

"Another peep outta you 'bout my nature, true or otherwise, and you'll be trying to pull your head outta your ass."

"There you go, Le Strange never could really hide Albert, could you? I mean how many defenseless maidens do you know who act like a lineman for the Green Bay Packers? And while we're on that subject, what are those hideous rags you're wearing this morning, Mr. *Allllbert?* Dungarees? And what's that hair sprouting all over your body? Well I'll tell you what it is, Mr. Jolly Green Giant! Testosterone! That's what it is, you're a man. A living breathing HETEROSEX-UAL MAN!!!"

An ominous silence griped the group around Lilly's kitchen. Betty began to whine and whimper like a shut-out dog. Val frowned and crossed his arms across his chest in a severe and judgmental stance. Lilly was thunderstruck, looking like a steel spring being wound tighter and tighter. At this agonizingly tense moment, there was some commotion heard coming from the inner sanctum of Lilly's boudoir. The pink satin upholstered door creaked open tentatively and more fumbling could be heard.

Then a voice with a beautiful weeping break asked, "Al, is it OK if I come out? I hear voices, who's that with you? I couldn't find anything to put on except this."

From behind the pink door appeared the most authentically gorgeous long, smooth and sexy legs ever to have immerged from Lilly Land. The three characters in the kitchen gasped with disbelief. There was no deigning these limbs were the real thing, and as the door slowly swung open there stood Rosalind Wortheley wrapped only in a man's pinstriped suit jacket which she held coyly tight around her slim waist. Val couldn't help noticing Rosalind's voluptuous cleavage beckoning beneath the gaping lapels of the double-breasted jacket, which judging by its large size must be Al's. Rosalind's wavy blonde hair flowed halfway down her back, and her head leaned to one side as if the weight of that cascade of lovely long tresses were too heavy for her to hold upright.

Urna couldn't resist, and with withering tones of scorn and disapproval she boomed and pointed first at Rosalind then at Al.

"I told you, that is a real Woman and he is her Lover!"

✳   ✳   ✳   ✳

The ensuing pandemonium that resulted from Urna's glaring indiscretion was extreme to a violent degree. She left Lilly Land feet first not stopping to "pass go or collect $200." Propelled by Al's anger, hefty biceps and a swift kick in the ass, Urna sailed through the air. Unfortunately she snagged her purple vinyl mini skirt on an old rusty nail when she was hurled over the garden wall. She landed with a dull thud in the alley where her bruised carcass lay in the mud of the dank passageway. Betty sobbed and hollered over the crumpled and near naked body. But nudity was the least of Urna's problems at the moment. The harshest reality was reserved for her face. Buttocks does not fare well under adverse conditions and Urna's condition was rattled, roughed up and dire. The dread duo, insult and injury, had this morning heaped crushing loads of misfortune on the fallen star and she began to look her age, a grim reality from which she had heretofore fled in a big hurry. The injustice of her situation struck her harder than Al's foot and she burst into that old dirge, ♪ "Nobody knows the trouble I've seen. Nobody knows but Jesus." ♫

*   *   *   *

Al chided aloud as he strutted through the garden of Lilly Land beneath the arbor where plastic lobster lights blinked with fevered agitation. He was really pissed at Urna, although having given the old floozy the boot had been a satisfying rebuke.

"How dare that old bag of bones make fun of Rosalind? Reading Pew's stink in my kitchen, indeed, what did she expect? Doesn't she know Rosalind is a goddess for real *and* in a delicate condition? I'd like to see Urna survive a five-month coma and come out looking like an angel."

The garden door of the apartment burst open and Rosalind rushed out with a bottle of rubbing alcohol and a box of Band-Aids in each hand. She had shed Al's voluminous suit jacket and was now dressed, slap dash, in a felt skirt appliquéd with poodles and a shocking-pink blouse billowing about her elegant torso and quickly tied at the waist. On her feet a pair of bunny slippers slapped loosely against her heels.

"Whoa there, little lady, where daya think your going? You know, you look kinda cute in my old poodle skirt, but that's hardly the outfit to give a press conference in."

Lilly caught Rosalind at the waist and tucked a strand of wavy gold hair behind her ear with delicate concern.

"Oh, Al, you big bully, let me go! I saw you throw that lady over the fence and I can hear her crying. I've got to help the old dear."

"That ain't no lady, honey lump, that's just Urna in a snit."

"But, Al, I saw her wearing little white gloves and a cute Jackie O pill box hat. Oh my, and look up there, her skirt is caught on the fence. My god, the poor woman must be naked and alone out in the street!"

"Poor she may be, but woman she ain't. That silly bitch is nothing more than a no account drag queen with one foul mouth, and anyway the alley is on the other side of the fence not the street. But have it your way, sweet pea, take a look for yourself."

Al waved Rosalind on past and opened the garden gate with a fierce tug that made the attached donkey bells clank and clangor. What greeted Rosalind in the alley was totally unexpected. Urna sat perched in a congealed heap on a discarded milk crate simultaneously smoking a joint and hitting off of Betty's Batman thermos bottle, full of God only knows what. Betty was haggling with Homeless Herman over some rags piling out of a bunch of shabby luggage crammed into his rusty shopping cart.

"There, you see, the three witches are getting high and shopping, nothing out of the ordinary. Now come on inside and let's get you into some decent clothes."

"But, Al, who is that bum?"

"Which one?"

"The one with the shopping cart and what's he got there? It looks like the muumuu Abruzio made for me. That gown is worth a fortune."

"Oh yeah, that's Homeless Herman, he musta found that Della Snozzy rag out in the trash and now he's trying to sell it to Betty. Herman's a charter member of the Chamber of Commerce without walls and a natural entrepreneur."

"Al, how did this Herman fellow get my muumuu?"

"That's simple, I tossed it out."

Rosalind was frequently mystified but never surprised at what the men in her life were apt to do, and she stored this particular grievance for another time. Now she sprung into action with the bottle of alcohol and box of bandages in hand and approached Urna.

"I am so sorry you're hurt, I think I may have been partly the cause of the problem and I wanted to see if I could help."

Rosalind had been out of commission at Brigham and Women's for entirely too long. Now awake she was itching to lend a helping hand if she could. She was known as a tireless organizer of charity events and worthy causes, and Urna looked to her to be out of luck and on hard times.

"Excuse me. I thought you might need some assistance?"

"You said it girly come over here with that bottle and let's take a look."

Something in Urna's manner made Rosalind hesitate, but she bravely inched forward anyway. Betty and Herman ceased their negotiations for a moment and both of them stared at Rosalind. Al stood in the doorway to Lilly land, arms crossed over his chest, ready to spring to Rosalind's defense if need be.

Urna was incapable of any form of restraint no matter who was lurking ready to pounce. She snatched the bottle of rubbing alcohol, brutally bit off the tin cap from the plastic bottle, spit it out on the ground and glugged a bunch before any-one could stop her. But stop her they did. Even Herman got in the act. Al got there first—lunging past Rosalind he tackled Urna just as the antiseptic began to burn her esophagus. Plucked her from her perch by the ankles, he yanked the tipsy tidder topsy-turvy and gave her a good shake.

Most of the alcohol made an unsightly reappearance, Urna started to hack and Al gave her a swift smack on the ass and set her down again somewhat in the manner of an old-fashioned pediatrician getting a newborn to breathe.

Betty and Herman recoiled at this roughhousing, and Rosalind was too shocked by the lightening speed of the encounter to do anything. Al took her by the hand and led her back to the relative sanity of Lilly Land slamming the pink door shut, which shuddered on impact and rang out with ting-a-ling of donkey bells.

"Al, is that … uh … person … an alcoholic or something? I've never seen any-body drink rubbing alcohol."

"Not to worry, little princess, that was a harpy on the skids and not content with mere alcoholism—she's a junky too."

The bunny slippers Rosalind was wearing got caught in the miner's cap of one of the plaster seven dwarfs who was lurking in a pile of leaves beneath the grape arbor. She teetered on the brink for a moment until Al caught her and swept her up in his arms. He cheerfully lugged her back toward his apartment where Val was staring at the couple from the open upper half of the Dutch door. As they approached the door, Val turned his back on them and withdrew. Al had to put Rosalind down to open the door. He figured this meant something was up with Val and this was one confrontation he was not looking forward to.

"Rosa honey lump, why dontcha make yourself at home. The kitchen is well stocked and coffee is ready. I gotta talk to my daugh … I mean … son Val, I guess this whole thing is a bit of a shock to him."

"OK, Al, take your time, I want to look at everything here. It's all so cute—last night at first glance I thought maybe I was still dreaming."

Lilly followed Val into the "study," a little used room leading off the living room where a surprising number of books shared the shelves with a collection of Barbie dolls posed in hooker drag doing a variety of lurid and unnatural acts.

"So lump, you wanted to say something?"

Lilly tried to act nonchalant as she flopped into a crumpled chair slipcovered in a fabric printed with ice-skating hippopotamuses. Val looked at his "mother" with contempt and disgust. He pulled a Camel cigarette from the chest pocket of his flannel shirt and fired it up, taking a deep drag.

"Oh no you don't. I'm not standing around here and watch you kill yourself with tobacco. Not in my house. Not as long as I'm your mother, you little scamp."

Lilly made the mistake of actually springing from her chair and trying to snatch the cigarette from Val's lips. But before she could complete the move-ment, Val's iron grasp clamped tight around her wrist. He held Lilly's gaze with a narrowed squint while he forced her hand away from his cigarette. The power of their wills strained the limits of their strength, bruising the old protective bond that would now always show shadow marks like dead blood.

Nothing like this moment had ever passed between the two. They had been friends in desperation against the whole world that rejected them. Unequal equals of different ages, temperaments and experiences. Lilly had rescued Val from turn-ing tricks on the street and put the boy in her shows in order to give him a little cash but more importantly to give him some confidence in himself. As it turned out, Val was a great dancer, well liked by the other members of the troupe where he felt safe and a part of the gang. Val was also a hard worker and as a performer, fully immersed in their shows no matter how bizarre or far-fetched. He believed in Lilly, and he sensed without ever saying so how much Lilly needed to be believed in. He could certainly see that Lilly needed an audience all the time. Val accepted that because Lilly was bigger than ordinary life both literally and figura-tively. After all Lilly was a star, out there, beyond the ordinary. She could project herself, above any distraction. Make the weakest of material interesting even if that was only opening a can of soup. There was never a dull moment with Lilly. She commanded everyone's attention and she got it, by shear force of will pow-ered by an insatiable need. Val knew that Lilly's thirst for love was never really satisfied. After all, who could equal such energy? Only a theatre full of hundreds of people could come close and then only for the evening. Who could ever feed such hunger?

Val thought he knew Lilly in these unspoken ways, although he would never say what he knew, that was not their way. Loneliness was an inviolable secret, and the only consolation was to believe in make-believe and make a joke of it all. This was their pact against world, their private bond.

Now the tide had turned Val had pushed Lilly's busybody bossing away and he smoked his unfiltered Camel in defiance and contempt.

"Who's she?"

Lilly flounced back into the chair with the ice-skating hippopotamuses and perversely took up her knitting, a ridiculous and forgotten project tucked into the corner of the upholstery. She had pretended to learn knitting when she had quit smoking ten years ago, and since then the remains of more than a few gloves or sox lurked in forgotten corners.

"Who's Who?"

"The bitch in your bunny slippers!"

Val practically hissed.

"Watch it punk! You know, I can get rid of a daughter just like putting out the trash."

Even Lilly winced at her rash words but foolishly did not retreat, she only went on knitting furiously.

"What do you think you're doing bringing that woman here? All you are to her is the freak of the week. Like those awful clothes she wears, Christian Le Crock and Abruzio Della Snozzy, you'll find yourself recycled at the next-to-new shop on Newbury Street. She has to chalk up her charity points at the Junior League, especially now that she's been outta action in the hospital, for what's it been, five months? My god she's gonna need a really big comeback to get the attention of the society reporters now, but after she does she'll be through with you. It's not me who's gonna be put out with the trash, Miss Thing. It's you! What do you think you are playing at? No, don't tell me, Albert Mellenoffsky the big Marine Nurse is going to recreate Rosalind the society dame into what, the bride of Frankenstein? And then you'll deliver your big line, 'She's alive'! Well guess what, dumbo? She ain't alive, Rosalind Wortheley was brain dead before she ever went into a coma. How else would she end up with you?"

Now it was Val's turn to be shocked by his own words, and he tried to concentrate on his cigarette but the fleeting blind of tobacco smoke did nothing to hide his discomfort. Lilly stared at him in disbelief, not recognizing her Val. She looked for the laid-back and totally cool friend who had always been there.

"Who the fuck are you to tell me what to do? Correct me if I'm wrong, but aren't you the street trash whore I picked out of the gutter? You have no idea who Rosalind is or is not. And you have no idea what she is to me."

"I know you've been going over to that hospital for the last month dressed up like some kind of a undertaker. Yeah, but, like Michael Jackson she slept in your bed but you didn't do nothing."

"So what if she has been in my bed? What then? What's wrong with that? I don't need anybody because why? Because I'm a freak who's supposed to listen to your love-lorn babble about that uptight eleganza queen Miss Gyles until I just want to puke? Well think again, cunt face, I am not the Elephant man. I am not an animal. I am not a sideshow freak, and I am not the doormat for you to wipe your self-righteous muck all over. I am a man and she's a woman, what's so weird about that?"

"You're not a man! You're a faggot!"

Like the trained soldier he was, Al had experience dodging bullets, and when the smoke cleared he looked across the battlefield and saw the enemy and realized this was not his war.

"No sweetheart that's not me. That's you. You're talking about yourself. And you know what darling, you're not right about that either. You're not a faggot. That's something hateful. We're not that. We're both men and we're both lovers, we just do it differently.

"I never was gay. I just wanted to be beautiful and important and looked at. That might not be the greatest career choice in the world but it's the truth, what can I tell you? Life can be so ugly and I know you kinda understand because the street ain't no picnic, but still, lump, you don't know what it's like when the world goes crazy and hate fills up even the fingerprints on your hands so you're a soldier without a name and all you can do is cause pain. I couldn't do anything for those boys from Kansas or Ohio. The war stole their bodies and their brains and their lives. And you know what? No one cared about Mom at home crying. She shoulda screamed louder.

I needed to run far away from Viet Nam and be someone very different. I needed to laugh and feel good about myself. I forgot how, but one day I met all those crazy queens and they gave me color and feathers and jewels and they made me over, and when they were through I *was* beautiful and I was laughing too.

Then I got so busy making everyone else laugh, it was like my obsession, my mission. I sorta forgot about ... love ... I thought no real woman would want me and I soon discovered that the drag queens didn't wanna hear anything about it either. So I just stuffed it. After all I had my fans and my friends and my daughter Valisha, but now you don't wanna be my friend or daughter anymore so ... That's what Urna means when she threatens me with my true nature. Urna saw it all happen. She couldn't really believe it, but then again neither could I. Urna said I was a lesbian-thespian, and who knows ..."

Then along came Rosalind, and you're wrong, Val, she's not a bimbo. We're kinda alike really or maybe not so real, see, she's been acting a part too and we've both been running alone and uphill for so long. Don't you think we deserve a break? I mean I know I bitch about your boyfriend and all, but even I can see he's hot and I guess if you put a gag in his mouth, I mean ..."

"So now what? Now Heather has two mommies maybe?"

"Maybe, things could be worse you know. You'll get double the pleasure double the fun. It's sorta like chewing gum only everyone could use a little bit more love, dontcha think?"

CHAPTER 39

▼

THE UNINVITED GUEST

Despite the dark drama of the early morning it was still a bright and sunny day with all the promise of spring. In the kitchen of Lilly Land, colorful café curtains of crisply starched linen hung in the windows adding to the general cheer of the season. These seemingly innocent window dressings were printed with Dick and Jane of grade school reader fame. On closer inspection, however, innocence was remarkably absent from the scenes depicted. These couple of old favorites decorating the fabric were playing poker with Spot the dog and Andy the cat while furiously smoking cigars and drinking highballs containing a substance suspiciously resembling rye whiskey. Dick was leading with a royal flush and raking in the dough. To complete this picture he held a smoldering stogy clamped in his bared teeth.

Rosalind Wortheley, oblivious to the finer points of the interior design, was busily engaged in her favorite pastime, entertaining. On this auspicious occasion, the first morning of her recovery, Rosalind was bustling about Al's kitchen. She briskly whisked farm-fresh eggs preparing a frothy omelet in a pink Fiestaware bowl. As the egg mixture hissed and sizzled in a copper omelet pan from William Sonoma, Rosalind added thin slices of chanterelle mushrooms and crumbled bits of Gruyère cheese. Urna Flamanté was assisting by sprinkling the perfectly browned omelets with fine chopped chives from the garden. Betty the Bounder was buttering English muffins and Homeless Herman was greedily slathering the muffins with a particularly scrumptious raspberry jam from Fortnum and Mason's.

Rosalind had been delighted to discover that, true to his word, Al's kitchen was indeed well stocked and perfectly equipped. When she discovered the Hawaiian Hula coffee in the cupboard, she thanked her lucky stars for whichever fairy godmother had sent such a man as Al to her rescue. She popped a bunch of the dark roasted beans into the Melita grinder and flipped the switch. It was fortunate indeed that Rosalind had come across the killer coffee because after the general imbibing that the assembled company had indulged in already that morning, a strong potion was needed by all. Now on their second pot of java folks were beginning to wake up. Although, far from clearheaded, Homeless Herman remarked, "You know, Rosalind, I thought that you were some kind of a helpless society dame and nothing more than a dumb broad. The way they talked about you in the paper I got the idea that you couldn't boil water."

In reply, Rosalind's musical laugh, like a gentle stream cascading over smooth stones, soothed the glaring rudeness of Herman's blunt statement.

"That's OK, Herman, when I first saw you this morning I thought you were nothing more than a bum. I guess we all have a lot to learn.

Urna and Betty exchanged raised eyebrows at Rosalind's comeback. They were beginning to get the picture, the lady was no fool and they were genuinely impressed by her unflappable grace. No one noticed Val standing in the doorway listening intently while trying to look ultracool.

"I actually didn't know much about cooking until I met Joyce. M. Gaspar, our chef at my home in Chestnut Hill, wouldn't let me into the kitchen, which he considers his own, and I suppose it is really. When I was growing up Mummy used to say ignorance is bliss whenever I expressed any interest in domestic skills. Mummy really doesn't know how to cook although she's very good at planning menus and seating plans. One day when I was a kid the plumber showed up at our front door by mistake. He asked Mummy which way to the kitchen and she had to ask her secretary.

"My husband George and I were on the maiden voyage of the *QM II* last year and Joyce was the onboard chef, giving classes in Italian cooking. I loved her from the start. She's like a glass of Asti spumante, sparkling and festive, and she's a great teacher. Joyce's husband, Ron Della Chiesa, was onboard too, lecturing on Italian opera—he's a real doll. You've heard him on the radio of course. Joyce regularly teaches at Boston Adult Education in Back Bay, but when we all got home I invited her to give me private lessons on M. Gaspar's day off. I'm afraid I haven't had enough practice yet, but now I'm looking forward to doing a lot more cooking."

Urna and Betty exchanged more raised eyebrows and meaningful glances. Betty couldn't resist adding, "I know how to bake hash brownies."

"My daughter's just like you, Betty. She's got a big sweet tooth." Rosalind enthused affectionately.

"Darlink, Betty's got something big, holy cow does she ever, but not a tooth in her head."

Urna reported nostalgically remembering distant days of youthful romps at the Sacred Fart Seminary.

"Yeah, I lost the front ones in the locker room of the ball field," admitted Betty wistfully and added more details before anyone could stop her. "Yeah, I was going down on a bat but I got shoved from behind."

"So ah ... Mama Two, is there another omelet for me?"

Val hastily interjected this request as he entered the kitchen from the doorway of the study where he had been staring at Rosalind. He was trying to derail Betty's train of thought and rescue Rosalind from the cruder implications of Betty's babble. He hadn't intended to come to Rosalind's aid—it was just a natural reaction. Although Val had just dubbed her "Mama Two," a title that would now become his own special nickname for Rosalind, he felt more like a big brother to her and as such he realized how hungry he was.

"Yes, Valish.... I mean Val ... entine. There's plenty to go around, pull up a stool."

Rosalind had at first stumbled over Lilly's nickname for Val, but she wisely left it alone and, returning the favor of a special name, she called him Valentine and he liked it, certainly more than Percival the finky name on his birth certificate.

The inmates of Lilly Land munched companionably enjoying Rosalind's breakfast until Urna did the unthinkable and everyone stopped in there tracks.

"Darlink, can I have sumore?"

Presumably a simple request and when uttered by Oliver Twist even natural but there was little natural about Urna, and her request was earth shaking.

"Whatddaya mean?" demanded the three friends around the table. Rosalind looked around at the group completely bewildered by their reaction. Without looking up from his own breakfast, Val did the explaining for Mama Two.

"Urna hasn't been known to eat any solid food for, what's it been Urna, ten years?"

"Very funny, hooker boy, I'll have you know I was eating before you were born and don't you forget it!"

"I'm not the one forgetting, mummy brain," Val shot back. The direction of these retorts was getting the combatants back to normal and as if on cue Lilly made her entrance.

"Rosalind who are you cavorting with?"

"Oh, Al, there you are. I was just about to make Urna an omelet. Would you like one too?"

"You better make three for him," muttered Betty pointing her thumb at Lilly.

"Urna Flamanté is eating? In my kitchen! I don't believe it. What do you think this is anyway, a miraculous shrine? I don't know what you're up to, Flamanté, but I wasn't born yesterday."

"We can see that." Betty muttered again.

"I thought I tossed that bitch out on her ass. Lemme at her!!"

"**Albert Melenoffsky!** Will you please shut up, sit down and tell me what you want for breakfast."

Everyone in the room gasped with horror, a reaction hitherto reserved for the mere mention of Scarface Malone! And again as if on cue the top of the Dutch door leading to the garden flew open with a force reminiscent of the big bang. The building shuddered, and a sound like the gates of hell screaming open at Armageddon reverberated through the bones of everyone present. When the dust settled a growling grumble was heard to inquire, "**Fee fi fo fum,** do I smell the blood of Urna Flamanté?"

The unseen was seen. The mystic Arcanum revealed. Sibilant secrets so awful slithered in on a miasma of heavy stench, and even a passing cockroach screamed with horror. Before them appeared a seemingly disembodied head, a talking plate of living cold cuts, Scarface Malone!

CHAPTER 40

▼

TOPSY-TURVY

Rosalind was the first to recover. She had no idea why the gang around the kitchen table was frozen with horror. It did not escape her, of course, that the uninvited visitor was a bit tough on the eyes. She could remember a time when she too was taken aback by him but over time she had grown used to the little man with the scared face who had been a business partner of her husband's on and off for years. What business that had been was never explained to Rosalind nor did she ask. If truth be known, Rosalind found Mr. Malone a welcome change from George's usual cronies at the Essential Insurance Company, who were all actuarially calculating how not to pay damages or compensations. In contrast Mr. Malone was a generous sort. He always arrived bearing lavish gifts. This once included box seats at the Metropolitan Opera production of *Rigoletto*.

"Mr. Malone, what are you doing here?"

A simple question for sure, even though it did ignore his Fee Fi Fo Fum routine, but Rosalind tended to ignore the more pithy conundrums of life. In this way she maintained a relentlessly cheerful attitude.

"Never mind me, girly. What are *you* doing here?"

Again a simple question and in many ways perfectly justified even if Mr. Malone's tone was a bit autocratic. Indeed, what was Rosalind Wortheley doing in Lilly Land? She however was far too busy for volleying questions back and forth. In fact games were not Rosalind's strong point. This lack of competitive athleticism had been a sticking point with Miss Brickhausen, the gym coach at Dana Hall, but Rosalind never did learn which end of her field hockey stick was which.

"I am making omelets with chanterelle mushrooms and Gruyère cheese. Would you like one?"

"OK, missy, but hold the chanta … whatever."

The short man with the messed up face waddled in on bowed legs and elbowed his way between Urna's and Betty's chairs. He glared at Betty, who stopped her trembling long enough to faint dead away onto the floor. Scarface nudged the limp Betty with his left foot and climbed up onto the now unoccupied kitchen chair. Once perched there with his feet swinging in the breeze, Rosalind handed him a napkin, which he tucked into his shirt collar. The napery matched the kitchen curtains with an image of Dick and Jane slipping each other aces under the card table, a singularly appropriate picture for Scarface Malone to spread across his broad and powerful chest.

Urna, in a feisty mood after her early morning belt of rubbing alcohol and half a pot of Hawaiian Hula coffee, grandly ignored Scarface and helped Val to peel Betty off the floor. Not to be upstaged, Al donned a pair of mirrored motorcycle cop sunglasses that Butch left behind. Al turned to Rosalind and demanded, "Where do you know this galumph from?"

"Now Al don't get your feathers all fluffed up. I have a past too you know."

Urna and Betty exchanged yet more meaningful raised eyebrows and Urna slipped Betty a tab of acid for her coffee. Al protested Rosalind's evasion, "Wait a minute, I'm not wearing any feathers specifically in your honor."

"Holy cow! That's the problem, Le Strange, your true nature is busting out all over."

"Thanks to you, Darlink, holy cow, that is yesterday's news. Pass me my raspberry jam and remember to leave twenty bucks cash on the table, that's imported from abroad."

"Is that so? Well this broad's been deported time and again and no one's leaving me a twenty-buck tip."

The intended meaning of this exchange escaped everyone including Betty, who had said it. Rosalind busied herself at the stove and Val helped by distributing her redolent omelets to the newcomers. After another round of Hula coffee, just when Rosalind was sitting down beside Al to begin her breakfast, Scarface Malone started to weep uncontrollably.

"Jeepers creepers, the whole world has gone topsy-turvy! exclaimed Urna, but seeing her would-be jailer dissolve into tears, she took pity on him and handed over a clean hanky drenched in jungle gardenia perfume. She murmured softly to him, "E avanti a Lui tremava tutta Roma!"

The sniveling gangster mopped his tears with Urna's hanky, coughed and sneezed with allergic reaction to the perfume and wailed, "You don't know the half of it, Urna, I'm totally broke! And those goddamned Zelengorian punks stole my limo!!"

Homeless Herman came to the rescue suggesting, "No sweat, Scar, you can go to work for me terrorizing the other scavengers so I can get all the choice items. Look at this piece of goods I picked up just this morning. Herman foolishly produced Rosalind's muumuu from a crumpled Star Market brown bag and proudly waved it in the air.

"Thank you very much, I'll take that."

Rosalind snatched her designer original with remarkable swiftness leaving Herman with empty hands. He sputtered outrage and protest, "Waddaya mean?"

"I mean," said Rosalind with a mouth full of mushroom omelet, "this is my Abruzio Della Snozzy retro muumuu, and if you want proof just look here."

Rosalind carefully wiped her fingers on her own Dick and Jane napkin. While still munching with gusto in a surprisingly unladylike manner, she pointed out the enormous embroidered label, prominently sewn inside the neck of the garment, which read Atelier Della Snozzy. Beneath this conceit, embroidered with gold thread was the name Mrs. Rosalind Wortheley.

"Pretty conclusive evidence, wouldn't you say?"

"Do you mind, missy? I'm the one having the crisis here."

Scarface reasserted his primacy by blubbering some more before he added a complaint more pertinent to the group here assembled, a surprise that no one wanted to hear, "So you see, Urna, I can't fund your *Naughty Astonautess* show. In fact, the feds are after me, threatening Sing Sing unless I spill the beans and talk."

Scarface continued to snivel while stuffing his mouth with omelet.

"Say, Urna, I thought this guy was some kind of a gruesome gangster, not an opera diva who can only squawk."

Betty's bafflement was universally shared by the odd assortment around the kitchen table of Lilly Land.

But Urna ignored Betty and fussed over Scarface, hoping that his dread revelation about going broke was only a passing fancy.

"Darlink poopsey doodles, buck up! What happened to the stiff upper lip? Whoops, forget I said that. What I mean is get a grip! For years I been spreading propaganda about your diabolical cruelty—you could at least snarl while you weep. What's the world coming to when even the bad guys turn sissy. Good gravy topsy-turvy is only the beginning!"

Urna was working herself up into a major tizzy in an attempt to snap Scarface out of his blues. This in turn got Betty's juices flowing fast and she came to Urna's assistance saying, "Never mind him, Urna, a crook with no dough ain't no good to no one."

Betty's curt dismissal of the gangster in question was more than a bit hard-hearted, and considering the fact that she had, only a minute ago, fainted dead away at the mere sight of the man, her chutzpah now was heroic but such was Betty's abiding loyalty to her old beau, Urna. In the process Betty had succinctly pointed out the jam they were all getting stuck in, and this in turn riled Al to panic. He griped, "OK, Scarface, turn off the faucet and let's get this straight …"

"God forbid!!" shouted everyone in the kitchen.

"Very funny peanut gallery, well let me rephrase the question then. Let's get the gay perspective here. What do you mean you're broke?! You two-bit hooligan. I have a show to put on!

Al loomed over Scarface while the little man wolfed down his breakfast in an unseemly and desperate manner.

"Now, Al, let Mr. Malone alone to finish his breakfast. You're only upsetting everyone and you haven't even touched your omelette. What's the matter, isn't my cooking good enough for you?"

Now it was Rosalind's turn to sniff and turn on the waterworks. She fished in the pocket of her borrowed felt skirt and came up with a hanky, which she used to daub her eyes delicately. Al couldn't take Rosalind's tears, and what's more he suddenly saw the hanky she had found in his poodle skirt was embroidered with two humping rhinos. Under the pretext of consoling Rosalind, Al enfolded her in his arms, deftly plucked the hanky with the randy rhinos from her grasp and replaced it with a hunk of paper towel snatched from the counter.

"There, there, darling lump, don't cry."

A suggestion that increased Rosalind's tears. Urna and Betty exchanged meaningful glances, rolled their collective eyes and shook their heads with exasperation.

"I am not a lump!" whispered Rosalind with petulant complaint.

"You'll have to get used to the lump thing if you're gonna survive Lilly Land. Mama One calls everyone that, Mama Two. It's supposed to be sweet.

Val interjected his explanation, trying to calm the storm so that they could get back to the Scarface mystery. Uncharacteristically Al did as he was told and resumed his seat and began eating his breakfast. Homeless Herman had been serious about his chow, scarfing up every morsel and several helpings of English muffins. Moseying over to the stove, he helped himself to more coffee and asked, "So uh, Mr. Malone did you have investments in Enron or what?"

"No, Herman, it was not Wall Street who could mess wit Scarface Malone—no, not by a long shot. It was those schlubollas George Wortheley, Claude Voit and Fathead Fabio wit their goddamned Zelengorian punks.

"I was innocently trying to make a living by booking gigs for the Jerk de Olay in Vegas. You musta heard a dem—they're the hottest act in Vegas. Anyway, the Zelens were recommended to me by an agent in Bosnia by the name of Meatball Malosovitch. Meatball said the Zelens were a troop of displaced gymnasts who had no funding because of the fall of the Evil Empire. So I took the bastards on and sent them out to Nevada in my limo for an audition. But come to find out, the fucking punks were pushing crack outta the back a my limo right here in the South End, and then they get their sorry asses busted by none other than Claude Voit. So now the fuckin' fairies on the parallel bars are putting the finger on me. They're shooting their mouths off saying I mad'em do it. The feds have seized everything including my last paper clip. So there you have it and I don't."

Rosalind got up from the breakfast table and started to make a fruit salad. She found it easier to think when her hands were busy. Val cleared the dirty dishes from the table and Betty made more coffee. The news this morning was too hard to take, and it looked as if *Naughty Astronautess* was dead on the launching pad. Urna pensively lit a huge bomber of a joint that she was saving for a rainy day but figured life couldn't get any damper so, what the hell. As the J went the rounds of the kitchen everybody got super gloomy until Rosalind piped up.

"You know, Al, I have some savings that I could invest in the show."

Val passed out the fruit salad while everyone around the table mulled over Rosalind's offer.

"Yeah, swell but what about me? I'm going to the slammer for sure when they find me here." Scarface resumed weeping and gnashing his teeth.

"Maybe there's space for you at the monastery? mused Al "I'll call over to Abbot Acidophilus. I've gotta check on Wally and the costumes anyway."

"That's nice, Al, and you know, I think Mummy's plastic surgeon could do wonders with Mr. Malone's face. That way no one will ever know who he is. I know for a fact that no one ever recognizes Mummy, until she opens her mouth."

CHAPTER 41

▼

HOME IS WHERE THE HEART IS

Rosalind Wortheley thought she might have a lot of explaining to do when the cab dropped her at the front door of her residence in Chestnut Hill. However, the only living soul to greet her on this cheery spring morning was Charlotte, the shaggy dog. True to her affectionate nature, Charlotte did not cross-examine Rosalind or demand any explanations, but after liberally distributing some slobbering kisses, Charlotte did proffer her butt to be scratched. Rosalind dutifully obliged wondering if this greeting might not presage what was to follow with the rest of her family.

After Rosalind's disappearance from the exclusive wing of private suites at Brigham and Women's Hospital, a huge city and statewide search was launched. But as testament to the combined power and prestige of George Wortheley and Mrs. Adams Cabot Lowell Untermeyer, not a peep was reported in the media, either in print or on TV. George and Mrs. A.C.L.U. did not see eye to eye on much in life, but the one thing they both avoided like the plague, even more than each other, was scandal. Their reluctant collaboration flexed powerful muscles putting the kabash on all publicity concerning the affair of the missing wife, mother and society hostess.

Ultimate power may have undue influence and some individuals are exempt from common concerns altogether. Reginald Pew's column in *Gay Windows* was so far from common concerns that even his editor had little idea what he was reporting most of the time. So Reggie's column, Dreck and Dross, concerning Rosalind's disappearance squeaked by without censure. The perfume counters of the Chestnut Hill Mall were more than enough to eradicate the miasma seeping from Pew's stink, and so society at large was kept in the dark.

As a result of this media blackout, no one had a clue about Rosalind's disappearance except for the army of city and state police, the FBI, the CIA and the Department of Homeland Security. But because none of these agencies speaks to each other, the secret was well kept. In compliance with the mandate for complete discretion, the chairman of the Republican National Committee, a crony of both Mr. Wortheley and his mother-in-law, recommended Guy Noir to head the investigation.

In an effort to be timely in a crisis for a change, a memo from the White House went the rounds suggesting that the presumed kidnapping was the work of the "Bad Guys." This declaration resulted in a temporary setback for Guy Noir because of the confusion of whom or what actually was a guy. This being the glaring and ubiquitous confusion of modern parlance, doubt gripped everyone concerned until P. I. Noir cleared up the issue of authority by commanding the go-ahead on twelve thousand wire taps all over the Boston metropolitan area. As to the mysterious visitor of high military rank who had visited Mrs. Wortheley at Brigham and Women's, that person had disappeared as if he had never existed and this at least was not far from the truth.

Rosalind stooped on her front step scratching Charlotte, who emitted gleeful grunts of approval. Around them spread the two giant wings of the mansion built of Boston brick and Indiana limestone in a tastefully correct Georgian manner. Both sides of the portico were flanked by Chinese magnolia trees in glorious bloom. Their voluptuous pale pink blossoms filled the air with soft perfume, and the whole scene made Rosalind sentimental and a bit weepy.

At that gripping moment a cab came barreling up the gravel drive throwing the odd pebble onto the weedless carpet of green lawn where drifts of Welsh daffodils sprinkled with purple and gold crocuses blossomed. The car came to a grinding halt in the deep gravel of the entry court and out sprung the children, George Jr. and Rosalind-Jane. Rosalind spread out her elegant arms in an all-embracing welcome, tears of mother love gently moistened her long eyelashes. But the kids sidestepped past their mom dodging her like a goalie on the soccer field and ran screaming after each other into the house followed by Charlotte barking like a happy idiot. Escorted from the cab like the grand dame she was,

Mrs. Adams Cabot Lowell Untermeyer leaned heavily on the arm of the young driver.

"Rosalind what the hell are you doing here!" bellowed Mrs. A.C.L.U. in her husky contralto as she flicked her lit Dunhill cigarette onto the lawn with her index finger cocked against her thumb.

Rosalind watched with dismay as the offending butt smoldered amongst the spring blossoms. She dropped her arms with disappointment and inspected the newly sculpted visage of her mother who minus the Bulgari necklace, the full-length mink coat, and the Channel suit would have looked to be about 26 years old, or four years the junior of her daughter. It was a wonder what the Rancho Miraculoso could do with unlimited funds.

"Darling, since you're here give this sexy boy twenty bucks, I haven't got a cent on me."

Mrs. A.C.L.U. was an expert in acquisitions and mergers but not at payments and dispersals. For those annoying details she depended on the slavery of her nearest and dearest or whoever might be handy. Rosalind had been shelling out since the original Mr. Adams, her discarded father, had been dispatched to Riggs Sanitarium in Stockbridge, Massachusetts, years ago, leaving mother and daughter with equal half interests in a real-estate empire that encompassed most of downtown Boston. Still "The Mother" frequently called upon her daughter for ready cash. Rosalind, inured by a lifetime of being bilked by a pro, gave the cab driver one of the twenty-dollar bills that Al had given her to get home.

As Mrs. A.C.L.U sashayed toward the house, her Escada heels sank in the gravel making forward progress a bit dicey until she repossessed the cabby's arm. Passing by Rosalind, her mother snatched the crisp bill and marched off toward the front door leaving Rosalind empty-handed.

"Darling? What are those awful rags you're wearing? Come inside before the neighbors catch sight of you. You know what an awful gossip that Connie Tredway is. She might say almost anything to almost anyone! Why, young man, you are strong. Let me feel your muscles."

The dowager with the girl's face paused before the mahogany front door to give the driver a squeeze but much to his surprise it was not his biceps that enjoyed her attentions. Beaming with manly pride, he swaggered past Rosalind tucking her money into the pocket of his tight jeans. Then he climbed into his cab and sped away.

Rosalind was staggered by the offhand way her children had brushed by her. In consequence she felt so heavy she collapsed on one of the marble benches flanking the entryway. She was quite used to the general abuse her mother dispensed, but she had expected more of the twins.

Rosalind had yearned for motherhood and she was determined to make a better show of it than Mrs. A.C.L.U. had. George Wortheley had three balls, but he suffered from a diminishing sperm count. Although the former phenomenon had been a famous anomaly of frat legend supposed to indicate super potent virility, this did not prove to be the case. After several years of rigorous attempts on behalf of Rosalind and her husband, followed by an exhausting parade of doctors and fertility clinics, the unhappy couple ended up at the door of Mother Clarissa. Clarissa was an ex-Playboy Bunny who had arrived at her middle years, some time back, without a retirement nest egg. Clarissa's lack of funds necessitated creative action, and so she had taken on the persona of Priestess of Abundance. In this capacity she made a tidy living coaching would-be parents in the ways of fecundity. Mother Clarissa, as her coterie of zaftig handmaidens called her, had assisted George and Rosalind in a Trantra Yoga marathon that resulted in Clarissa's retirement from the business altogether but no babies for Rosalind.

The only recourse for Rosalind was adoption. She resigned herself to this fate and researched the topic at length. The result of her labors, and George was not at all forthcoming in this endeavor, were the Ling-Ling twins from Vietnam. Mrs. A.C.L.U. was not amused, but Rosalind's close chum, Connie Tredway, was overflowing with condescension and concern. In her enthusiasm for the project Rosalind was oblivious to the disparaging clucks and tutus hurled about her.

She was impressed by the track record of adoptees from the South Asian country with their fabled reputation of strong genes and smart kids. George's only contribution was the names, George Jr. and Rosalind-Jane, not at all original but Rosalind had pressed him and in a pinch he had come up with the easiest solution. The kids were at the time of their acquisition reportedly nine years old and Rosalind had adored them with an amazed enthusiasm. They in turn were bewildered by the beautiful lady who whisked them away from hearth and home especially because they were neither twins nor naturally related and their actual ages hovered somewhere around early teens at the time of their adoption.

Rosalind rummaged in the pocket of Al's poodle skirt looking for a hanky. Betty the Bounder had safety-pinned the skirt with such skill you would have thought the outfit was made for Rosalind, and as a fond farewell Betty had spritzed her with Omar Khayyam's Persian Spring perfume, a rare find that had arrived at Betty's counter in Filene's Basement by mistake. Rosalind did locate a crisp hanky and was daubing her eyes with justifiable self-pity when a candy kiss fell from the hanky onto her lap. She picked up the tiny confection, which had a surprise message printed on it saying, "darling lump." This discovery completely unhinged Rosalind, and she wept confused tears as baby pink magnolia petals floated down around her in tribute to a beauty beyond themselves.

CHAPTER 42

▼

A LIGHT DAWNS FOR ROSALIND

Rosalind's reentry into the social swirl was an enterprise of utmost urgency for Mrs. A.C.L.U., George Wortheley and Connie Tredway. Each of these characters had their own agenda of self-interest driving them at such break-neck speeds as to completely disregard Rosalind's misgivings on the subject of swirling society.

But Rosalind was a changed woman since her accident and subsequent coma. This lacuna in the relentless charge of high society charity balls and other frothy concerns had provided Rosalind a respite to plumb the depths of her subconscience. In that nether—world of amorphic being a seed had been planted in the rich resources of her spirit. Now awake she wondered if her old life would do at all. It seemed so empty, dull and lonely.

But the rabid trio of social sharks, George, Connie and "The Mother," who swarmed around Rosalind churning up the waters to a visible boil, had not the least interest in or sympathy for misgivings of any kind. These three were all focused on producing the Rose Garden Summer Party, the favorite charity of Muriel Brunelleschi, the mayor's wife, who fancied herself a gardener because she had been given a potted rose bush on the occasion of her first communion. Whatever was the truth about Muriel's green thumb no one really cared. The point of the matter was to get city contracts and as everyone knows the place for those negotiations is at swanky soirees and high-society shindigs.

Connie Tredway poured Rosalind Wortheley another cup of Huqua from her Heridon tea pot. The purity of Connie's white porcelain did not match the motivations of the hostess, although the botanically accurate roses hand-painted on the hard glazed surfaces did speak of her calculating designs. Connie poured Sandeman's best into two Waterford sherry glasses and passed her neighbor a heaping plate of cucumber and 'cress sandwiches. For a moment the two beauties sipped and munched while gazing serenely at long drifts of Emperor Tulips that were the principal feature of Connie's garden this spring.

"Darling, what is that strange new perfume you're wearing? I thought you were subscribed to Guerlain's Shalimar. Is this the new you or what? I hope you don't have too many more surprises up your sleeve. You know, Rosalind, it's not good marketing strategy to change product recognition, not when your name is as established as yours."

Connie was a professional hostess determined to utilize her MBA from Wellesley with dispassionate analysis, so she said it as she saw it.

"It's called Persian Spring by Omar Khayyam, a gift from a new friend."

"New friend? How could you have a new friend? Darling, you've been asleep for the better part of the winter season. Who could you expect to meet when you're out of the loop like that? I suppose no one has told you we are at war with Persia or at least Iraq, which is more or less the same place. I just don't know if this ... Persian Spring is the right thing for you."

"What is the right thing for me, Connie?"

The wistful irony of Rosalind's question escaped Connie's mercantile analysis. But Connie was not at a loss for words, opinions or advice, especially when the matter at hand was one of her "fêtes."

"Darling, I *am* glad you asked that because I have just the project to get you up on your feet and back in business. Muriel Brunelleschi's garden party is this June and I want you to be on my committee. Oh I know the Brunelleschis are impossible and she doesn't know a Rosa Reversa from a Rosa Centiflora, but her husband is the mayor so we all have to lend a hand, in the interests of business. I happen to know that your George has a lot riding on this event in the way of insuring the city's pension fund. Anyway, Muriel is a power to be reckoned with and I must tell you, and this is in strictest confidence, well, it was Muriel who had Columbus Park overhauled and torn up and you won't guess why. Muriel didn't like Rose Kennedy's garden getting more attention than her own home-grown charity in the Fenway. I mean why the woman has to pick such a marginal place is beyond me. Maybe she wants us all to get mugged by those dreadful pansies who lurk in the bushes all around there, who knows. But I can tell you, I told

Chief Donavan in no uncertain terms at the Policeman's Auxiliary banquet last month that he must deploy an absolute army of boys in blue to the Fenway before, during and after Muriel's event so we can all be safe, at least for one night.

"Anyway, the Parks Department gleefully tore up the Kennedy garden at Columbus Park and had no intention of replacing it. But then the senator got wind of it and put up a terrible stink. The outcome was that the Rose Kennedy Memorial Rose Garden was actually expanded and completely replanted which has, of course, made Muriel furious, and now she is hell bent on election to raise as much money as she can squeeze from the good citizens for her project. So you can see how important it all is and how much we need you. Since you've been out of commission for so long and everything was so touch-and-go with you, I just know that everyone will flock to the place just to get a glimpse of you."

Rosalind studied Connie as she prattled on, wondering if what Connie said about "pansies in the bushes" was true. This made her think of Al and his Lilly Land and all the interesting characters she had met there. She didn't think police protection was at all necessary against those people. In fact she longed to be back with them. Al was a great deal more attentive to her than George had ever been and Al was very sexy in the sack. George, after all, had "dressed up" too. She had been bewildered when George first revealed his secret and asked for her assistance. But when she thought about it she realized that "dressing up" was both fun and powerful, so why not. After all, it did turn him on and they were trying anything to have kids. Rosalind never held this against her husband. On the night of the Essential Mall opening, it was not such a big surprise to see George in one of his outfits—that was not the problem. What had actually happened was Rosalind's heel got stuck in between the boards of the speaker's platform and she had lost her balance and fallen.

It was George's neglect of her that made Rosalind so miserable. All through the process of their trying to conceive, George made her feel as if it was Rosalind's fault. But after numerous tests, that turned out to be not the case at all. He also gave her the impression that the whole process was grueling work. Now after her return home Rosalind realized how lonely she was. For a long time she drew comfort from her love of the twins, but it seemed now as if they had grown up with lightening speed, she didn't yet realize their true age, and they had their own busy lives.

"Rosalind! Are you listening to me? I was telling you about the football field."

"Football? I thought you said rose garden, although I must admit I don't quite know where the Fenway rose garden is ..."

"There you see, you weren't listening at all. The Fenway rose garden is right across the Muddy River from the Museum of Fine Arts. And they leave the lights on the football field all night and the whole place is in a blaze of light. It will spoil the atmosphere and ruin the decorations. I want them to turn off those dreadful lights during our event ..."

"Wait a minute, did you say there is a lit football field next to the rose garden?"

"Yes, but don't get stuck on that detail. I intend to talk to the commissioner and get her to turn them off."

"No, don't do that!"

Rosalind surprised herself with the vehemence of her reaction and shocked Connie.

"You don't have to bite my head off, Rosalind. Are you sure you're all better? I mean what is your actual prognosis?"

"Me? I never felt better and, Connie, yes, I will be on your committee. In fact I want to head the entertainment committee. I've got an idea that will make Rose Kennedy as dull as yesterday's *Herald*. If Muriel wants a really big show I think I know just the person to give it to her. Now leave everything to me but don't turn out the lights."

"OK, OK, you're in, but stop being so mysterious all of a sudden. What have you got in mind?"

"Have you ever seen inner planetary space flight?"

Connie was sure Rosalind had flipped and that was fairly near the truth.

CHAPTER 43

▼

LURKING IN THE BUSHES

Under cover of the gathering gloom of June twilight that was rapidly descending about the Fenway Rose Garden, a spectral shade crept out from beneath the tattered yew hedge surrounding the joint. The figure in question was disguised incongruously as a Spanish matador complete with a red satin cape beneath which could be glimpsed a dim twinkle of light reflecting off a polished blade of Toledo steel. The matador's creeping posture accentuated his unusually short stature as he progressed on all fours in an odd sideways shuffle reminiscent of a salt-marsh crab.

"Fuck with me bitch and I'll fix your wagon! The nefarious intruder hissed as he skirted the area of party tents hovering about the entrance to the garden.

"No one can snatch my drag and get away with it! I don't care how big your tits are."

This whispered threat and cryptic dismissal hovered on the chilled mist coming off the Muddy River that oozed slowly by the edge of the surrounding parkland.

"After I've done with you, we'll see how far you can fly, fatso!"

A diabolical cackle escaped the skittering shadow but was cut short when his stubby legs caught on a tent rope sending the midget matador sprawling on the damp grass. Stung by the collision and fearful of having run his pink silk stockings, the figure rocked back and forth in repressed fury finally blurting out, "Psshaw!"

While thus preoccupied he thought he heard something rustling in the dense underbrush bordering the river and his hackles bristled. He instinctively assumed a fighting posture fingering a peculiar cudgel in his left, throwing hand. The noise came again stronger now working itself into a thrashing racket that was articulated by the vaguely familiar exasperation,

"Holly cow, Darlink, this is not a pretty pickle!"

Spooked beyond control by an excruciating moment of déjà vu, the creeping matador let fly his secret weapon just as the fumbling figure in the reeds came staggering out of cover. The impact of the double-headed boomerang took down the intruder with a thunk when the wiggly rubber thing wrapped tightly around its neck. An unnatural silence oppressed the dark park until somewhere in the distance the fading scream of a city siren, like a dying banshee, split the night. The matador took this opportunity to check the condition of his silk hose and finding no snags went to retrieve his lethal appendage. As he approached the groaning pile near the bushes, it unexpectedly sat up, fumbled in its clothing, and came up with what appeared in the half light like a bottle, which it desperately sucked on. Miraculously the concoction in the bottle gave a jolt of life back into the rumpled thing on the riverbank. The matador watched from a distance as the figure pealed the cudgel from around its neck and gingerly holding it between two fingers held it up to the defused light of the surrounding city. A scream of horror and revulsion announced the recognition of the double-headed weapon wriggling in its grasp.

"Dildo? Yuck! Darlink, you measly runt! How dare you?

The matador who was, of course, none other than Dildo of Follies Derrière fame recognized the distinctive squawking of Urna Flamanté. The figure huddled on the edge wore a mohair chenille suit that Dildo immediately recognized as vintage Chanel. His palms began to itch with greed because his collections sorely lacked any of the French designer's signature couture.

"Hey bitch, too bad about your face and all, but I warned you against any more surgery. It's like a wicked addiction you know," Dildo greeted Urna.

"Buzz off, barf brain, and keep your phony pecker to yourself. Holy cow, you could have strangled me!"

Urna hurled the double-headed dildo boomerang back at the gloating matador, who instinctively held up his gleaming sword to deflect the oncoming weapon from cumming on him. Incidentally the sword turned out to be a Knights of Columbus relic that had never seen any part of Spain much less Toledo. Nevertheless, it did have a sharp point that impaled the flying prosthetic genitals just in the nick of time.

"Nice catch, Darlink, now go roast your whinnies by yourself and leave this innocent girl to get on with her business."

"So that's it, is it? Business huh? You lousy trollop, turning tricks in the bushes again."

"I am not turning tricks in the bushes, jesz Louise, whaddaya take me for? If you must know, I am looking for my lost ear, rings."

"Oh, right. That's a bunch of bull if ever I heard it."

"Well Darlink, in that outfit you should know bull when you hear it. But while we're on that topic, what the fuck kinda dip-shit drag is that anyway?"

"This is my Zorro outfit, ain't it cool? I am a bold renegade who signs a Z for his name, a Z that stands for Zorro. I'm gonna fix the Le Strange bitch once and for all."

"Zorro was a bullfighter?"

"Well, maybe not but it's the closest thing in my collection that's Spanish and maybe he …"

"Listen, lame brain, Zorro was Mexican. You better stick to Robin Hood, you know, green tights and a jerkin."

"Hey, who you calling a jerk? Have you looked in the mirror lately? What are you anyway, Coco Chanel after the funeral?"

This convoluted rigmarole rambled on for a while, and in the course of their mud-slinging Urna worked up a powerful thirst and had to take a hit off her bottle, which was neatly tucked beneath the garter belt. She haphazardly passed the jug to Dilly who took a swig and soon they were draining the supply together. Now, feeling slightly more companionable as a result of some particularly vicious vodka, Dilly inquired casually, "Whaddaya mean earrings?"

"Now you're talking, it's like this, the Le Strange bitch as you so succinctly put it has called a rehearsal here tomorrow, so I came over today to scout out the joint because I was gonna sprinkle some thumbtacks into the contraption she's gonna be shot outta. But I got a bit distracted by this hunk over by the war memorial and we retired to the bushes for a quick one."

"Yuck! A quick one with you? What kinda hunk would do it with you?"

"Listen Darlink, lip shits, I didn't kiss him or anything, holy cow, it was a quick blowjob, all right? And anyway the real issue is my earrings. I took them off because they were slapping me in the face when lover boy was pounding away. They were a gift from Scarface Malone who came dashing over to my room at The Chandler Inn earlier tonight. He was frantic about the damned earrings. So I says, earrings? You two-bit thug …"

"You said that? To his face?"

"Darlink, 'course I did, what's left of it, the face I mean ..."

"What *is* left of it? I hear he's a sight."

"Listen, who's telling this story, Darlink?"

"Sorry, so go on already."

"The upshot of Scar's tale was that the earrings are the keys to his safety deposit box that has all that's left of his now vanished fortune after having been busted by Claude Voit, which is a whole other story. Well, after getting a mouthful of boner the last thing I was thinking of was his crappy earrings but now I'm frantic because all this rough-housing has reeked havoc with my Buttocks and the injections cost a fortune ..."

"Yeah, well your ass was never your strong point."

"At least I've got one."

"Not nearly enough, you half-assed midget."

At this juncture their exchange degenerated into a minor hullabaloo until Dilly said, "Listen, I'll help you look for the blasted earrings if you give me your dress and help me with a certain plan I have cooked up for the Le Strange woman."

"My dress? This is a genuine copy of a fake Channel!"

"OK, but it was worth a try. I didn't realize it was just a knockoff. How 'bout just helping me out with my scheme.

"So spill the beans already, let's hear it."

CHAPTER 44

▼

DRESS REHEARSAL

For the veterans of Glamour Galore Productions no one was greatly surprised that the final dress rehearsal for *Naughty Astronautess* was a wee bit slow in getting off the ground. The interminable and grueling rehearsals throughout the month of May had been seriously retarded by a number of setbacks, not the least of which was the lack of a coherent script. Madame Le Strange was a grand artiste and as such she depended heavily on inspiration, a nebulous ingredient composed of whispering muses and heavy hits of Maui Wowie. Furthermore, when the muses were silent La Diva was apt to retire to her boudoir and soak in the tub beneath mountains of frothy bubbles. Eventually she would get around to placing pen to paper, but this was frequently as a last resort only. The real kicker behind La Diva's posterior struck when she discovered that Urna Flamanté had taken the bull by the horns and wrote her own "Damed" script. Adding chutzpah to hubris, Urna had the temerity to distribute her opus to the entire company. Even in her rage Lilly had to admit that some of "Urna's stuff was sorta OK," and after considerable and heavy editing, consisting of crossing out Urna Flamanté and replacing it with Lilly Linda Le Strange, the show got on the road, so to speak.

Thus it was that the *Naughty* dress rehearsal was finally commencing on the very day of, and if you can believe it, the very afternoon of the Fenway Rose Garden Party, and even more compelling it was the *late* afternoon.

"OK boys, drag that thing over here and aim it high. I want to fly clear over the rose garden."

But, Lilly, it's not as easy as you think. This motha weighs a ton or more." Paddy O'Punk complained.

The leader of the radical gay activists, The Ninja Fringers, wore his usual green plastic carapace strapped to his front and back as well as knee, elbow and wrist guards of the type made for Rollerblading. All of his protective armor was fitted over spandex body stockings of submarine green, and his identity was further obscured beneath a sleek helmet fitted with a tinted Plexiglas visor.

Paddy had been sprung from the slammer after languishing for several months in the Charles Street Jail. It was determined that no credible charges could be trumped up to hold O'Punk and the several Ninja Fringers who had been nabbed at the opening ceremonies of the Essential Center opening. To her credit Lilly had coughed up the dough and paid the fines pending against Paddy and his crew. This act of largesse was, however, not an act of disinterested charity. In fact Lilly needed help and little muscle with the production of *Naughty Astronautess,* so the Fringers were recruited.

"And I thought I was the fairy around here. Look, it's got wheels so what's the beef?"

"Hey Darlink, Le Strange, fairy you are not, and about the beef, good grief, you're wearing it."

Urna Flamanté was sometimes a stickler for accuracy, and with foolish bravado laced with more than a drop of gin, she added, "Your true nature is oozing out all over the joint."

Lilly's theatrical temperament was tipped over the brink by Urna's bitchery.

"Oh Urna, so glad you could make rehearsal. Now as my understudy you get in the cannon and we'll blow you out to see if you hit the target squarely. Paddy, stuff that walking corpse into the rocket and wind up the spring."

"But, Lilly, I told you it weighs a ton!"

"You activists are all alike—when it comes down to the grunt work, it's not in your contract. Give me that thing and watch me."

Lilly snatched the trailer loaded with the circus cannon that Paddy and his dozen Ninja Fringers were struggling to avoid. With the deafening grunt of a Sumo wrestler on the verge of a hernia, Lilly dragged the rocket launcher onto the football field of the Fenway playing ground.

"Wait a minute! Wait! Just one cotton-pickin' minute! I have been up all night for weeks slaving over this contraption, so just hold it still while we slide it on."

"Wally! I told Abbot Acidophilus to chain you to the monastery grill until the rocket launcher was finished! How did you get out?"

Lilly could be a strict disciplinarian when one of her shows was in the offing and production time for *Naughty Astronautess* had stretched beyond everyone's patience. As a result, extreme measures had been enacted especially in the case of Wally, whose attention span was apt to wander. But there was no one else who could transform a circus cannon into the Twinkle starship. To wit, Wally had been judiciously dosed with a potent brand of Ecstasy guaranteed to inspire his creative juices and left to create.

So here now was Wally with Brother Jonquil and Brother Jebadiah, both good friars dressed in sackcloth and sandals, and the three of them were struggling with a flaccid plastic sleeve that looked suspiciously like a huge condom.

"What is this? A safe sex demo? Act up on your own time, Wally, I've got to launch a rocket to the moon!"

"The moon?! Holy cow! No way, Darlink. I ain't being shot outta no cannon going to the moon. Ah ah. Not this girl. And while we're on the topic of contracts, let me tell you I am no one's understudy! No, no, Darlink, I am a star in my own right, and what's more I have my own original material to sing, a serious ballad entitled, 'Don't grab my balls if you want me to sing.'"

"That's just swell, Urna. I knew you could be counted on to be prepared. OK, boys, gag her and throw her into the cannon."

Having given this brisk order, Lilly turned to Wally and in a dangerously pleasant tone said, "Now, Wally, as long as you're here show us whatcha got."

Urna Flamanté, being no one's pride or joy, was mercilessly set upon by Paddy and his Fringers. They bound the hapless headliner with bungee cords, stuffed her mouth with a red bandana and tossed her into the oversized barrel of the circus cannon.

Meanwhile Wally and his cohorts struggled to shove their prophylactic disguise over the gaily painted circus cannon in an effort to transform the behemoth into some semblance of Apollo Nineteen. The Fringers eager to appear helpful, as long as they didn't have to actually lug Lilly's "space ship" anywhere, leaped to the aid of Wally and his crew. In a flash the heavy plastic sleeve was slipped over the erect tool. Next Wally inflated his creation with a handy leaf blower on loan from Friar Tuck, grounds manager of the monastery. Miraculously the thing took on the exact shape of the Apollo Space Shuttle, completely accurate to every detail except for the nose cone, which Wally had coated with a particularly lurid shade of pink glitter.

CHAPTER 45

▼

TRIAL AND ERROR

A desperate but muffled protest could be heard from the depths of the Twinkle starship. In fact it was a scream of abject terror.

"Someone musta grabed her balls 'cause she's singing up a storm," Lilly remarked casually as she lit the fuse of the Twinkle starship with her steel Zippo.

"But, Miss Le Strange, how can that be, woman don't have balls?"

For a man of the cloth Brother Jonquil had an unnatural curiosity about the mysteries of the flesh. And none knew this better than Wally, who had been servicing the good brother throughout his sojourn at the monastery. But Wally had left brother Jonquil in the dark, no matter how satisfied, and so the brother's curiosity had been perked about balls and the like.

"Urna's got more than balls up her sleeve or in her panties for that matter. But I was referring to her ballad 'If you want me to sing grab my balls.'"

"Hey, Lil, you got it ass backwards, 'If you want me to sing *don't* grab my balls,'" Gary Gardenia interjected, trying to untangle the mangled title of Urna's ballad. Brother Jonquil and Lilly gazed with surprise at the cute Ninja Fringer who had recently been reunited with his hero Paddy O'Punk and the gang. Brother Jonquil was particularly intrigued by Gary's proclamation, but not having heard Urna's original statement, the monk willfully misconstrued the boy's meaning and was about to pursue the subject deeper when a tremendous flash and bang grabbed everybody by the balls, with or without them.

Wally's rocket stayed in place and Urna was hurled into space, an action that tore the gag from her mouth allowing a full articulation of the performer's innermost feelings at that moment:"AAAARRRGHE!"

Urna flew through the ether at a terrifying velocity. Her Jackie O pillbox was ripped from her head, but professional that she was, her Carol Channing wig stayed firmly affixed to her skull even though every strand of peroxided hair trailed behind her, straight out.

Lilly concentrated with professional zeal, marking the pattern of Urna's flight from the barrel of the canon up, up, above and over the rose garden in a smooth arc flying through the air with the greatest of ease. Unfortunately Urna's skirt got snagged in the topmost branches of a crabapple tree, tumbling this naughty astronautess directly into the yew hedge that surrounded the garden. An agonizing crunch and crash was heard. The spectators all cringed at the sound except for Lilly, who was carefully studying the trail of Urna's flight. She adjusted the aim of 'Apollo' by use of the handy crank on the side of the space ship, and rubbing her hands together with anticipation she bellowed, "OK boys haul Urna outta the bushes and drag her back over here. I think I have the right settings now."

Lilly casually ordered the Fringers to reload Urna back into the cannon. But Paddy's conscience balked at the apparent cruelty he and the Fringers had inflicted on Urna. When they plucked the performer from the yew hedge, she was a real mess. But somehow she had managed to retain both of her Ferragamo spike heels. These lethal appendages were, however, no longer attached to their original source—the rest of the shoes had been torn to shreds. But the most disturbing aspect of Urna's dishevelment was her panty hose hanging in tattered shreds from her ears.

"You know, Lil, I sorta think maybe this Urna broad has, like, had it."

"Then have it your way, O'Punk. I think I've got the settings right now anyway, and considering the time, I'll have a quick little blastoff and then we can all break to put on our faces before the lights go up on SHOW TIME!"

Urna was now in a state of shock that rendered her speechless even beyond her usual 'Darlink.' As a result she was dispatched in a wheelbarrow from the rose garden to the Fenway Clinic across the Muddy River to recharge her batteries.

"You see flying's easy really when you apply the scientific method," Lilly told Wally, who was fingering Brother Jonquil's package in an effort to soothe his artistic temperament.

"But, Lilly, what setting are *you* going to use?" gulped Wally.

"Whaddaya mean? The settings are already calculated. Why do you think I sent Urna aloft?"

"Don't ask me, I figured your diabolical nature was coming into play," Wally conjectured.

"Watch those cracks about my nature, buddy, or you'll end up beside Urna at the Fenway Clinic."

At this dramatic moment Rosalind arrived in a conveyance hard to believe. She was regally ensconced in a Yellow Ducky bicycle rickshaw peddled by one sexy hunk in bright yellow chamois short shorts and a white cotton tank top that was stretched to the limits by bulging shoulders, shapely pecks and rippling abs, all to die for. The driver was Val. The Yellow Ducky, his newest enterprise with which he intended to ply the streets of PTown this coming summer.

Rosalind was transformed from a slave of contemporary fashion in perpetual dreary black to the heights of romance. Her outfit this morning was an exact copy of Garbo's breathtaking crinolines as seen in the country scenes of the movie *La Dame aux Camèlias,* and Rosalind was if anything more ravishing than Garbo.

"Yoo hoo, Albert." chortled the besotted Rosalind wafting a lace hanky, of all things.

"Ros, you divine lump, what luck, I was just about to blast off on a test run, you'll bring me luck"

Everyone assembled snapped to attention at the arrival of the mythic beauty—and Officer Patrick Shannon exclaimed, "Sweet Jesus, 'tis an angel for sure."

No other comment was necessary because the truth had been told. Rosalind signaled Val to stop beside the Twinkle star ship where she descended from the Yellow Ducky with the studied grace of a ballerina.

Just at that moment when everyone's attention was focused on the professional beauty, Clovis Galicurchi, maestro of the Gay Men's Chorus and his bus load of happy songsters came to a lurching halt on Park Drive beside the long bank of bleachers that bordered the playing field. The rickety old school bus let out a ferocious backfire fart, sending noxious fumes skyward. The warblers piled out stumbling all over one another in an effort to evacuate the bus before that old rattletrap exploded. The only maintenance that Clovis and his crew could afford had been to spray-paint the thing pink. This made for a festive appearance but little in the way of safety.

On the brink of blastoff Lilly paused. Even for La Diva the appearance of eighty-five dandies dashing out of a dilapidated pink school bus deserved some attention. The warblers had eschewed their usual somber black tuxedo drag for more festive costumes appropriate to the season and occasion. They were all dressed in identical rainbow-striped jackets, white linen trousers, pink sox, and white buck shoes, all toped off with stiff-brimmed straw boater hats, sporting rainbow-striped headbands around the crowns.

Clovis gathered his clan on the bleachers and discreetly piped them a pitch somewhere around B flat. The chorus tore into a snappy rendition of the "Easter Parade" while one of their ranks came forward. This shameless ham had donned Minnie Mouse dancing shoes with boxy half-heels in addition to his barbershop quartet costume. Prima Donna as the soloist was known, bounced into action. Climbing up to the highest rung of bleachers, he launched into a frenzied tap dance routine that dropped everyone's jaw.

"Albert, who are all those ... fellows, and why are they singing "Easter Parade" in the middle of June?"

"Good question my sweet. The most prominent among them is a character called Clovis Galicurchi, if you can believe that. He is rumored to have been the music therapist at a high-security Gulag in Siberia before the fall of the Communist Regime. How he got to Boston is anyone's guess, but he has real talent for squeezing blood from a stone and actually gets pretty decent performances out of the chorus. Now with any luck Prima Donna, the would-be dancer of the lot, will break his neck and the rest of those hooligans will shut up so I can get on with my launch."

As if to fulfill a prophecy Prima Donna staggered in the midst of his pinwheel turn and came tumbling down into the chorus, who all screamed and fled leaving Prima alone in a thrashing heap.

Al took up his handy megaphone and bellowed, "OK, Galicurchi, that was terrific but this event is a garden party not the Easter Parade, so scrap the Lawrence Welk cuteisms and give us "Peckers in Deep Space.""

Lilly was referring to the opening number for *Naughty Astronautess*. The rumor was that the lyric for this song had first been glimpsed scratched into the men's room wall at the Widener Library at Harvard. This source explains the literary direction of the ditty.

From the distance across the playing field, Clovis could be glimpsed in an unseemly temper ranting, raving and pounding his fists against the bleachers. The chorus may be a bit skittish and apt to scatter when set upon by Prima Donna, but when Clovis' ire was irked to such a degree as it was now, the brotherhood knew they would have to tow the line. So with quick dispatch the boys reassembled, straightening their boaters as Maestro dragged himself back up onto the podium, a heavy plastic milk box, and gave the boys a down beat:

Peckers in Deep Space

Charlie called from Chelsea, then his cell phone broke up
Ted turned up in Tanzania with a whopper case of gonorrhea
Ned wrote to say, he really wasn't gay.
I've got those Monday morning blues on Sunday afternoon.

So I went to Starbucks for some java
I got real buzzed 'cause the stuff's like lava
Now I got an itch to rocket off the globe.
I've got those Monday morning blues on Sunday afternoon.

Don't dilly dally, take the quantum leap, and blast off
I'm on the Ttwinkle starship and boy what a trip
Rocketing 'cross the Milky Way is sorta like a real good lay
I've got those Monday morning blues on Sunday afternoon.

But prepare yourself for a lotta weird stuff,
Cell phones are outta range, TV is totally strange
And there's not much to do between Mars and Uranus
I've got those Monday morning blues on Sunday afternoon.

Light-years are so long I'll have to brake out my bong and play with my
    schlong
Peckers in deep space might while away the hours
But then what's to do? I don't have a clue
I've got those Monday morning blues on Sunday afternoon.

"Al, am I hearing right? Peckers in deep space? I'm not sure that Muriel Brunelleschi will appreciate that sentiment."

Rosalind had given Al free reign to create a show-stopping medley to be compiled from his new show, *Naughty Astronautess*. She had also shelled out $30,000 to cover expenses for the production. Until this moment she had assumed and hoped that *Naughty* would be only a little naughty, and given Al's track record with *Glamour Galore* this was a pretty safe bet. Rosalind had reasoned to herself that the urban sophisticates migrating between endless grazing pastures of charity events needed a bit of oats to flavor their feed and grab their limited attention.

Last year Sonia Schnable had appeared at the Myopia Hunt in her full-length red fox fur coat thrown rakishly over her impeccably tailored Pinks. After enjoying a brace of stirrup cups, Sonia had weaved her way toward her mount only to be set upon by the pack. With memories like these claiming legendary status amongst the idle rich, Rosalind figured what better way to get people's attention than with one of Al's ditties.

But listening to "Peckers" Rosalind got cold feet. She had to admit the chorister's eight-part harmony was impressive. She also had to concede that the GMC had startlingly clear diction. "I'll have to brake out my bong and play with my schlong," came through loud and clear. Most remarkably the well-rehearsed chorus had managed to squeeze all the lyrics, cadences, rhythms and mismatched rhymes into their song, and the refrain, "I've got those Monday morning blues on Sunday afternoon" actually did have some merit. But merit or no, Rosalind had an inkling that Muriel would not appreciate lines like "*Rocketing 'cross the Milky Way is sorta like a real good lay.*"

Rosalind turned to Al and suggested, "I am beginning to see Clovis' point. Maybe 'Easter Parade' would be cute."

"Darling lump! What are you saying? I have finally pried space suit costumes outta that dwarf from hell, Dildo, over at The Follies Derrière. My chorus can't be gentlemen songsters! We are astronautesses aiming for the sky. Yikes, outer space is hanging in the balance!"

"Oh Albert, I can see it means a lot to you, but isn't there any other song they could sing?

Rosalind took Al's arm in the most shamelessly fawning manner, leaning heavily against his sturdy bulk, her white crinolines enveloping his tweed trousers, her taffeta petti coats whispering seductive swishing sounds. Predictably Rosalind's feminine wiles caught Al's attention and he wavered in his resolve long enough to change direction.

Ever the pragmatist, Al took up his handy megaphone again and bellowed, "OK, Clovis, that was more to the point. I'm sure the fans will eat it up at the theatre, but the producer says scrap it for the garden party. Let's hear the finale of Act One, 'Moon for Miss Begotten.'"

Clovis was doubly plucked by what he considered Al's untoward directives and resumed ranting, raving and pounding his fists against the bleachers. Fortunately the distance across the football field absorbed most of the details of Clovis' tantrum, and after a while of misspent passion he again raised his baton.

This time the men of the chorus outdid themselves with a blast of harmonic hoopla that no one could resist.

Oh moon for Miss Begotten you must be made of cotton, 'cause all that fuzz has blurred your features, makin' you look like outer space creatures.

"OK, Clovis cut!" But even with his trusty megaphone, Al's booming voice was not nearly loud enough to interrupt Clovis' gang, and the boys sang on:

Oh moon for Miss Begotten, some say you're really rotten. We know you have a dark side, which may explain low tide, but don't get bent all outta shape, nobody's perfect.

"Clovis! Shut the fuck up!!" Al cranked up the megaphone to superloud shout and blared out his command across the football field.

"Sorry 'bout that, sweet pea, but enough is enough, already, and the boys actually did sound great, dontcha think?" Al's perfunctory explanation to Rosalind was less than charming, but this astronautess was not called naughty for nothing and besides, he was anxious to get back his all-important test flight. When you're eager to blast off, niceties may fall by the wayside.

Clovis did not take this latest interruption easily in stride. In fact the beleaguered maestro resumed ranting, raving and pounding his fists against the bleachers with such vehemence that the chorus, who were a high-strung lot, offered up Prima Donna to administer mouth-to-mouth resuscitation. Prima was not at all prepared for an act of mercy involving such intimate contact, so he substituted the service of extreme unction instead.

"Well, Rosa, it looks like Maestro has had a meltdown. He apparently has a few wrinkles to iron out, but that's dress rehearsal for you. In the meantime let us resume the countdown."

No one bothered to argue with Diva Le Strange.

At this dramatic moment when all hope for a brief dress rehearsal was cast to the proverbial breezes, Connie Treadway came strutting over the lawns of the Fenway playing field. The committee woman was incongruously clad in a black Armani cocktail dress and English rubber boots of the type affectionately known as Wellys. She had acquired these tony galoshes from the farm shop on the Chatsworth Estate while touring with the Royal Oak Society last summer.

Clip board in hand, Connie barreled down upon the *Glamour Galore* cast. From the side of her face a tiny mike broadcast her strident voice over the powerful PA system around the party venue.

"YOU PEOPLE THERE! CLEAR THE AREA. THIS IS A RESTRICTED AREA. RESERVED EXCLUSIVELY FOR THE MAYOR'S ROSE GARDEN PARTY."

As may be imagined, this first meeting between Lilly Linda Le Strange and Connie Treadway did not go at all smoothly. In fact total disaster was momentarily diverted by a totally unexpected aspect of Rosalind that shocked the *Glamour* crowd momentarily into mute horror. It was her dress.

Connie's nerves were stretched well beyond the limits of her precarious sanity by the manifold responsibilities of trying to outdo Muriel Brunelleschi as chairwoman for the garden party at the Fenway Rose Garden. When she caught sight of Rosalind in the midst of this collection of "street trash," she hit the ceiling. However, being outdoors on the Fenway playing field, there wasn't even a ceiling to contain Connie's wrath. "ROSALIND WORTHELEY, WHAT IS THAT REDICULOUS COSTUME YOU'RE WEARING? AND WHO ARE THOSE AWFUL PANSIES YOU'RE WITH?"

When Connie used the P word, a gasp of horror went up from the assembled company around the playing field and an ominous universal growl shook the earth of the Fenway neighborhood. But heedless of warning Connie charged onward, "WHAT ARE YOU **DOING** WITH THESE *CREATURES?* JUST WHEN I NEED YOU? REALLY, ROSALIND, HOW COULD YOU? GET OVER HERE RIGHT THIS MINUTE AND CHANGE INTO SOMETHING DECENT. THE MAYOR AND MURIEL WILL BE HERE ANY MINUTE! DO YOU WANT ME TO BE THE LAUGHING STOCK OF BOSTON?

Connie's mike amplified her ranting to supersonic decibels and all eyes snapped to stage center, which now spotlighted the humbled beauty who uneasily cast her gaze down wistfully playing with her lace handkerchief. This made Rosalind all the more lovely by virtue of her complete absence of malice.

Albert Mellenoffsky, veteran combat nurse from the front lines of Vietnam and even fiercer combatant on all the drag stages of every cheap dive across the country, was not about to let his divine lump, the lovely Rosalind, be insulted by this "anorexic scarecrow." Lilly was a quick thinker in adversity. She barked an order that compelled all to tremble on the brink.

"PADDY O'PUNK, AIM THE TWINKLE STARSHIP AT THAT BITCH AND FIRE, NOW!

Rosalind tossed aside her own embarrassment and quickly took control. She leaned up to Al and gave him a passionate kiss on the lips, wiping away tears of gratitude from her eyes. This elicited a hearty cheer from the *Glamour* gang, and the Gay Men's Chorus broke into the Harvard football anthem "Fight for the right and send Yale to hell." Rosalind standing on tiptoe, whispered into Al's ear as she held his face with both her elegant hands before reluctantly turning away and approaching Connie. As she passed the starship she directed Paddy to turn the barrel away from the intruder, pointing it back into the sky. When Rosalind approached Connie, she firmly disengaged the chairwoman from her microphone by simply unplugging the wire at her waistband. Then she took Connie firmly by the arm and marched her away from the Naughty Astronautess.

CHAPTER 46

▼

MURIEL'S PRIDE AND JOY

By the time Muriel and Bruno Brunelleschi arrived at the Rose Garden Party in the Fenway, the event was already in full swing. Three party tents of increasing size hovered around the west lawn of the park, all lit from within and glowing like uranium in giant Tupperware bowls. The Lester Pomeroy band was pumping out a plethora of irresistible tunes that had the guests clicking their fingers and tapping their toes. At least one dowager was squirming in her seat and itching for a dance. An army of black-clad caterers slithered amongst the congealing crowds, passing out a steady river of booze. A phalanx of reservists pushed silver trays laden with exotic hor's d'oeuvres architecturally arranged in vertical piles and composed of foodstuffs from six continents, all out of season in Boston. The flower arrangements on each of the overdressed tables were the special creation of Mr. Jon, Winston's top designer. These over generous thickets consisted of tropical foliage gathered from a remote bend on the Amazon River interspersed with black orchids and night-blooming cereus. Not a rose was in sight until Muriel arrived on the scene with "The Witches' Cackle." She had nestled the bush in a cute little red pull wagon commandeered from the Back Bay Montessori School where her housekeeper's daughter, little Maria-Isabella, was enjoying a scholarship funded by Cardinal Singh funneled through the Barbadian branch of Catholic Charities.

*　　　*　　　*　　　*

There had been a time, maybe 10 years previous, when Muriel would have been toiling all day at the Rose Garden then dash home, throw on a dress and her trusty straw hat decorated with silk roses and race back, dragging Bruno behind her. Once there Muriel, of course, assumed her rightful place at the head of the reception line beside her husband, the mayor. But that was before Mayor Brunelleschi had been reelected for a second term and triumphant third term.

When Bruno Brunelleschi was returned to the city hall on a landslide victory, Muriel breathed a deep sigh of relief. In fact some said that it was the first breath Muriel had dared gasp for the better part of a decade. Whereas the lack of oxygen may have turned Muriel "a whiter shade of pale" it did not, mysteriously enough, tint her vital juices anywhere near the desired shade of patrician blue that she toiled so furiously to accomplish. During Muriel's arduous trek from the bottom floor of a triple-decker in the outer reaches of Dorchester to a sumptuous Federal townhouse nestled into Beacon Hill's exclusive Louisburg Square, she had been synched into a corset that successfully inhibited all of her naturally expansive nature. But having arrived at the apogee of political and social accomplishment in the city of Boston, Muriel had discarded her restrictive girdle and whereas she did not let it all hang out, she had calmed her over-zealous sense of responsibility toward charity events. Now the gracious Lady Bountiful got to where she was going when she damn well pleased.

One of the unexpected perks of Bruno's high office had been an invitation to the investiture of the Lord Mayor of London. It was rumored that this social plum had been anonymously arranged by Mrs. Chandler Hennery Agassiz, whose husband had been the mayor elect's unseated predecessor. Mrs. Chad, as she was known to one and all in the sacred regions of the Chilton Club and the Cricket Club of Chestnut Hill, was a force to be reckoned with. It was also rumored, although this may be merely vicious gossip, that Mrs. Chad had arranged this tony invite intending Muriel to "slip in the mud on her boots" and fall flat on her capacious butt, thereby laying an egg in London. Such was Mrs. Chad's regard for Muriel Brunelleschi.

The investiture of the Lord Mayor of the City of London at the Guildhall was an event of great pomp and ceremony and Muriel deemed this time ripe for a new hat. Never one to do anything by half, she went directly to Mrs. La Freda Jones who supplied a splendid array of millinery creations to an eager clientele of Baptist matrons at her Chapeaux Boutique on Tremont Street in Boston's South

End. At that emporium of froth and fury Mrs. Jones and Mrs. Brunelleschi engaged in a serious powwow, pouring over all the back and current editions of *The London Hatter, Royalty Rides Out,* as well as *Accroutrement du Mode.* This last publication lavishly illustrated all the aristocratic high jinks of England, Europe and several other continents. It was in *du Mode* that they discovered a creation so exalted that it had graced the noggin of no less a personage than the Dowager Duchess of Dungarees, who had been setting society on edge since her debutante days during the depths of the Depression in the 1930s.

Muriel, thus regally appointed beneath her exact copy of the duchess' zippy chapeau, did not slip, slide or hesitate when she breezed through the reception line guarding the entrance to the Guildhall. She, of course, hadn't a speck of mud clinging to her Bali heels as she alighted from the Rolls onto the plush red carpet and up the well-swept marble stairs of the palace. Muriel was well versed in the ways of reception lines, having survived hours of handshaking and small talk during her husband's career. She had developed a knack for welcoming total strangers by putting them at their ease with a motherly look of kindness as if to say "You are the most fascinating creature on earth."

So with the confidence of a veteran tempered by genuine good spirits, Muriel was, in due course, presented to the reigning Mrs. Lord Mayor, who was holding the place of honor as the keystone in an arch of august pomp and circumstance. The circumstances of this intended brief moment were unexpectedly extended when the two women came eye to eye with each other. The buzz of the room halted abruptly and there was an unnatural silence. Muriel and Lady Chumly had on the same hat. They stared at each other dumbfounded, each lost to her own surprise, until after an agonizing moment of international unease they both began to giggle, and Bruno Brunelleschi, close on the heels of Muriel, blurted out in a thick Dorchester accent, "Never mind, you look just as good as my misis."

Muriel, always happy for Bruno's support, took his arm and they curtsied and bowed at the same time.

The reports in the international press glowed with universal praise for the gallant mayor of Boston and his 'Missis. The two were the toast of the town and in due course received an invitation to tea at The Mansion House residence of the lord mayor in the City. Mrs. Chandler Hennery Agassiz was livid!

*　　　*　　　*　　　*

Since her sojourn in London those several years ago Muriel had not felt the need to hurry anywhere and, whereas the Rose Garden Party was a cause dear to her heart, she was, in the maturity of her husband's career, quite content to allow the committee ladies to take full command. Besides, she had been delayed that very afternoon at Winston's nursery, Chestnut Hill. She was having a tough time deciding on an appropriate rose to donate to the garden, and as a consequence she had made every one of the half dozen managers hovering about her nuts. They had all exhausted their repertory of laudatory adjectives until what should catch Muriel's eye but a yellow rose of rare and precious beauty called, of all things, *"The Witches' Cackle."* Unfortunately this special-order specimen was reserved for none other than Mrs. Chandler Hennery Agassiz, and that did it for Muriel. She would not take no for an answer. She had found her prize and she intended to have it. But as she lay hold of the thorny bush there ensued a brief but vigorous tug of war between the mayor's lady and senior assistant manager of Winston's nursery, Chestnut Hill. Muriel however did not give a hill of beans for the puffed-up junior executive and exerted all her pith and brawn in the effort. The result was a foregone conclusion. "The Witches' Cackle" was duly dispatched to Muriel's Beacon Hill abode.

CHAPTER 47

▼

COMMITTEE LADIES FALL
OUT OF LEAGUE

When Rosalind got Connie out of earshot of the *Glamour* gang, she let her have it in no uncertain terms.

"Listen Connie, I know you're trying hard to do a good job, and maybe following Muriel with the chairmanship after all these years is a tough act to follow. But that does *not* give you license to ride roughshod all over everybody's feelings. I don't care what you think of the gay community, or anybody else for that matter, but keep it to yourself. If you didn't know before, let me be the first to inform you. The Fenway is a traditional gay neighborhood, and these folks have slaved for months to put on a show that will make you a lot of money and the talk of the town. So give us a break!"

Rosalind surprised herself with the vehemence of her retort and was rather exhilarated by the experience. She pulled down the pointed bodice of her dress and straightened her neckline. Then she perched her gloved hands on her tiny waist, elbows bent outward in a posture of belligerent defense. Rosalind stared at Connie with stern rebuke.

"Have it your way, Rosalind, but you better deliver the goods, and from what I could see of that bunch out there...."

"Connie! Stow it!"

Rosalind was not taking any more guff from the likes of Connie Treadway.

Connie, momentarily subdued, really gave short shrift to Rosalind's concerns and at that very moment caught sight of far weightier matters.

"Look sharp now, Rosalind, here comes Muriel but what is that thing on her head? Oh my God! It's that ridiculous hat she cooked up to wear in London at the lord mayor's investiture. Do you know where it came from?

Rosalind gave Connie a vacant stare.

"Oh, of course you don't, since your accident you are about as informed as a freshman at Wellesley. Well, Muriel went to that La Freda Jones woman. Why do those people have such impossible name—La Freda—I mean, really! Do you know where the shop is? Tremont Street in the South End, not exactly Newbury Street or Saks. Muriel is always trying to be such a relentless democrat except when she goes house hunting, then she ends up on Louisburg Square. I wonder if Mrs. Jones is invited to dinner there. Thank God Mrs. Chad didn't come to the garden party this year. I don't blame her really, I mean if my Skip lost so much as a round of golf to the likes of Bruno Brunelleschi, I would just die! And high office is really a lot more important than golf, don't you think. Although Chandler Agassiz would like us to believe otherwise, he is just putting a brave face on it. Lord almighty, look how that woman can ruin a perfectly good dress too...."

"Muriel, how wonderful you look in that cute little hat, I know we've seen that one before, an abiding favorite I see, but what is this? Darling, you are too _cute!_ A yellow rose, is this for the garden? And that wagon, how do you think of these things, Muriel? It's just pure genius. Good evening, Mayor Brunelleschi."

Connie reserved her more restrained and dignified greeting only for Bruno. The Mayor in turn looked over Connie's head trolling the turbulent sea of humanity for any big fish he might be able to hook. Connie's brand of gushing condescension toward Muriel and therefore himself was at this point in his career like a pesky mosquito to be brushed away without notice. But he would make sure that the rapacious Skip Treadway and his construction company came under painstaking scrutiny when bidding for city projects from now on. Reluctantly the mayor brought his attention down to Connie's level.

"Hello, Connie, this event certainly has escalated far beyond anything my Muriel ever planed. I trust the Rose Garden will benefit adequately. Hello, Rosalind, glad to see you back in action. I love that dress you're wearing, it really suits you. I am happy to see a pretty gal properly dressed and not traipsing about in her slip. Bruno conspicuously glanced at Connie's abbreviated cocktail dress and went on, "How's George doing? Ready to underwrite the entire population of Massachusetts I'll bet, well, I can only help him with Boston I'm afraid."

Connie was infuriated by Bruno's dig about her Armani frock and she only barely managed to suppress a tart comeback. She feared Bruno had overheard her remarks about Muriel and she figured that was the implied message in his reference to the Rose Garden finances and his elaborate compliment to Rosalind. But being a trained warrior in the perpetual conflict of high society, steeped as it is in the interests of big business, she didn't quaver. She quickly dismissed her apprehensions without a smidgeon of remorse when she remarked, "Your trust is well founded, Mayor. To date we have raised $150,000 for the operating budget alone and with generous donations such as this," Connie made a flourishing gesture toward Muriel's rose, "our acquisitions fund will be immeasurably enriched."

"I knew you would like it, Connie, it's called 'Witches' Cackle.'" Muriel piped up with this seemingly innocent pronouncement, and Rosalind had to resist blurting out 'fifteen love.' While Bruno smirked with pride at his missis' rejoinder, he took her arm and steered her toward safer harbors leaving Connie with their donation.

"Didn't I tell you? Those people don't know their place. Do you know how much money Skip and I have raised for that rat? Big buckaroos, that's all I can say."

Rosalind was deeply uneasy with this conversation and longing to be away from Connie. She heard too much of her old self in the chairwoman's vitriol and she was greatly relieved to catch sight of Cornelia and Gyles arriving.

"Connie, will you excuse me, I want to thank Cornelia for visiting with me during my illness."

"Sure thing, but how do you know she was even there? Maybe she just had flowers delivered. Mummy and Skip told me not to bother because you were in a coma. I...."

"Yes Connie, I see now how much you care, but if you will excuse me ..."

"I'm sure I don't know what you mean, Rosalind, you *do* know I am very busy. I have many committees and responsibilities as well as a husband and two children. But, never mind, you're probably still a bit affected by your problems. I see your George appears to be on the straight and narrow these days. There's nothing like a shock to make a man of our men. They can be such, well, such boys sometimes."

Rosalind tried not to listen as she drifted away from Connie's hissing insinuations.

But before she could catch up with Cornelia and Gyles, she was waylaid by an even more formidable opponent, George Wortheley.

"Rosalind, old girl, glad I caught up with you, Listen what gives? I haven't seen you in weeks and now Eben Chichester tells me you're filing for divorce. Now let's just put the brakes on here for a moment. Just to begin with, I would appreciate it if you did not drag that snotty Brahmin lawyer, Chichester, into our private affairs. Now, I know that he is related to your old flame Gyles Chilton, and I suppose that this is the way you all close ranks. But just remember your mother's first husband, who may or may not be your real father, was a has-been Beacon Hill grandee when we got married. You and your family didn't have a pot to piss in then, so where does Chichester get off giving me attitude."

As George fumbled in his jacket pocket for a cigar, he took a look at Rosalind for the first time. He was rather taken aback. He had seen his wife dressed by all sorts of designers from Abruzio Della Snozzy to Christian Le Crock, and although he paid the bills willingly he really thought he deserved better. But now he couldn't figure out what she was wearing or why. It did not escape him, however, that tonight she looked sensational. As he stared at her the wind blew a strand of wavy blonde hair from beneath her broad-brimmed hat, which Rosalind caught and tucked back into place. This demure gesture so unguarded and natural made him realize he may loose a great prize if Rosalind actually did decamp.

"Oh listen Ros, I know I've been busy lately and not such great company, but you have the twins to keep you busy and I gather you are the entertainment chairwoman for this event. Well honey I'm proud of you."

Rosalind was jolted out of her embarrassment by George's stab at reconciliation and the phrase "too little, too late" came rushing to her mind. But Rosalind realized she must deflect George's attentions and not engage him in arguments with any complaints or criticisms. George was after all the master of hostel buy outs and corporate takeovers, and she knew he was only interested in what wasn't his. So she sidestepped the issue altogether saying, "George I know we must talk, but as you said I am the entertainment chairwoman this evening and the curtain is about to go up. Please find yourself a seat, I think you may recognize some of the performers. Oh here comes Connie, she's the big boss tonight and she has been scolding me already, so be nice to her, if you can, and as I said, we'll talk later."

As Rosalind walked briskly away from George she muttered under her breath, "Much, much later."

Connie caught up with George Wortheley and took his arm.

"George, thank god you're here. I don't know what has gotten into your wife, but since that hit on the head last year ... well have you had her checked out?

Some of the people she is associating with, I don't mind saying, you're not likely to meet any of *them* at the Wellesley Country Club. Now I know of this marvelous doctor in Stockbridge at Riggs? Dr. Chilblains? Have you ever heard of him? Well, he did wonders with Charlie Stanton's wife De-De. Since she's got back, she is so docile and amusing too. The only hitch is that she has a tendency to set off car alarms now. It has something to do with residual charges from Dr. Chilblain's electric shocks."

George shuddered involuntarily at the implications of Connie's suggestion. And whereas even George would hesitate to send Rosalind to Dr. Chilblains, he did begin to see Connie in a more valuable light and he wondered if he might not use such a ruthless gal like her on his staff. This idea gave George a little itch and he excused himself saying, "I see what you mean, Connie, and I will think it over. But before I join the party I think I'll take a stroll and smoke my cigar."

"Don't go far, George. The mayor was asking after you and I know you'll want to say hello. And George, be careful in this neighborhood, heavens only knows what kind of trash is lurking in the bushes."

Unlike Connie, George knew exactly where the trash collected. He lit his cigar with sensual anticipation, twirling the stout and fragrant rod in his lips as he strolled confidently forward led by a now insistent itch.

Rosalind snagged a full tray of bubbling champagne flutes from a passing waiter and cheerfully offered drinks to all and sundry as she made her way across the party tent toward her childhood friends.

"Hi you two!" Rosalind piped up perhaps a bit too perky. "I've brought us all some drinks. Here we are, one for Cornelia, one for Gyles and two for Rosalind."

She quickly parked the waiter's tray on a nearby table and took a big gulp of her champagne. Gyles shot a quizzical glance at Cornelia, who in return shrugged back in complete mystification. These gestures did not escape Rosalind, who nonetheless took another swig, polishing off her first glass of bubbly. She handed her empty glass to a passing waiter, daubed her lips delicately with the back of her hand and said, "I know, I know, not a lady like thing to do but I needed that. I have just escaped Connie Treadway and not entirely unscathed either. I can't tell you how embarrassed I am. To listen to her is a lesson in scorn. She must be frightfully unhappy to be so snobby and awful. I am so afraid that I used to sound just like that."

Gyles was surprised by Rosalind's contrite tone partially because of his harsh judgment of Rosalind over the years. He thought of her as perpetually self-absorbed and purposefully obtuse. What he just heard her confess was like a lightning flash of explanation. He never considered the glamorous and wealthy socialite known universally as a professional beauty could possibly be "frightfully unhappy" herself.

Cornelia had always harbored a soft spot in her heart for her old school chum. In fact it had started out as an intense schoolgirl crush but that was ancient history. Even now when Rosalind was difficult Cornelia was not totally exempt from her glamorous appeal. And yes, as Rosalind matured she had adopted a pose of being a "flippity jibit" without regard for the effect of her words. But mostly Cornelia saw this as a disguise.

"Promise me one thing, you two, that if, no probably when, I sound like Connie Treadway you'll knock some sense into me. Cornelia *please*. Gyles, I know you'd like to, so here is your chance."

Gyles raised his glass toward Rosalind as a sign of agreement and they all clinked together, but before they had swallowed their toast Betty the Bounder appeared as if from nowhere tugging at Rosalind's sleeve and entreating her to follow with a mute gesture of "come along."

Betty was all dolled up in her version of respectable Boston matron and had thankfully left off her bushy red beard, so at a quick glance she did not appear to be a complete outrage. Although true to self she did pluck the champagne flute from Rosalind's hand and down the remaining sauce in one gulp. That was at least in character. Then the unlikely pair went off on their mysterious mission leaving Cornelia and Gyles with their collective jaws hanging in disbelief.

"What's gotten into her? She seems completely changed and positively glowing I might add, and it's not just her dress although that sure helps along with that hat, which she uses to full advantage peeking out beneath it like an eighteenth-century courtesan."

Gyles surprised himself with his positive reassessment of Rosalind.

"It's a mystery to me, but at a guess I'd say she's in love." mused Cornelia.

"With George?"

"He is her husband, after all, and love knows no bounds but still I find that hard to believe. She didn't appear to be even mildly enthralled with him just now when they were speaking. And he didn't even try to kiss her when they met. Perhaps there is someone else."

"Talking of someone else, how on earth does she know Betty?"

"Good question, how does anyone know Betty?"

"Indeed."

CHAPTER 48

▼

NEW ARRIVALS STIR UP
THE ACTION

The three large party tents and two smaller service tents set up for the garden party effectively corralled the west lawn by the Fenway Rose Garden protecting the invited guests from the general run of humanity who might stray too close to the exclusive gathering. Surrounding this restricted area an army of police on time and a half overtime mustered around their patrol cars, motorcycles, horses, a paddy wagon and yes even bicycles, forming a steel ring of security. The group who gathered within this seemingly impenetrable force, ostensibly for the charity of a public garden, had little faith in their fellow citizens and rather hoped they might simply disappear, thereby adding a new wrinkle to the triumvirate of Christian virtues.

The precautions of Connie Treadway and Police Commissioner Chuck Snarler were of small consequence to one of such unassailable stature as Monique Lafarge. Monique quite literally towered above her fellow citizens no mater who they were. The entire constabulary force of Boston was known to fall back with awe in the presence of such radiant glamour. At one event recently an otherwise unflappable officer was heard to remark, "Get a load of her, vavoom ain't hardly enough."

Monique was at first cool to Lilly's latest brainstorm concerning the preview of *Naughty Astronautess* at the Fenway Garden Party. But she knew a good part to play when she heard one, and the more Diva Le Strange fleshed out her vision to Diva Lafarge, the more she began to dig it.

Butch eased his polished and gleaming 1938 Packard limousine onto the west lawn by the Fenway Rose Garden and glided slowly forward toward the specially designed rose arbor that disguised the metal detectors guarding the party compound. Inside the landau Monique sat serenely beneficent beaming at her passengers with amused indulgence. Her companions were fairly giddy with anticipation regarding their part in the evening's festivities.

A clog of cops guarded the gate and glared at the vintage automobile, trying not to look too interested or impressed. They assumed the car had clearance just by the strength of its ostentation. The invited guests were arriving in a steady stream, The men wore light sports jackets or seersucker suits and the occasional Panama hat. The women wore colorful sundresses or loose slacks and, of course, splendid hats of all descriptions. One of the more fetching examples was Rosalind's broad-brimmed bonnet trimmed with swan's-down dyed a subtle shade of lavender. Connie Treadway was the one somber note in a black Armani cocktail dress that looked like an inconsequential slip but cost a fortune. It showed to disadvantage her knobby shoulders and inconsequential bust. As a concession to the evening she had perched a black velvet ring on the back of her head. Some vague wisps of net veiling trailed over her expensively mussed-up hair, which looked like the hairdresser's revenge.

Butch sported his classic chauffeur's uniform of dove-gray double-breasted jacket and jodhpurs above immaculately polished black knee boots. His eyes were shaded from view by the patent leather visor of his cap. When he extended his gloved hand to assist Monique from the stately conveyance, the parade of guests stopped to take note.

Monique had outdone herself in a vintage 1930s silk crêpe frock stained like the clouds at sunset in enigmatic shades of delicate pink and lavender. This miracle of couture was cut on the bias and clung to her attenuated figure down to a handkerchief hem at mid calf, the points of which were waited by paper-thin gold coins that tinkled faintly with her slightest movement. Her cascade of auburn hair was set in tight waves and tied in a lose bun at the back of her neck Her long swan like neck was encircled by an oyster-colored silk ribbon supporting a moonstone and pearl brooch. Around her hovered an elusive scent of heliotrope entwined with honeysuckle.

The usual migrating crowd of socialites arriving at the garden party suffered the deepening shadow of Monique's eclipse. They were annoyed and surprised to find themselves thus relegated to second place, but still they couldn't keep themselves from shameless gawking at the pack of borzoi hounds, casually ambling from the cushioned recesses of the vintage Packard. Monique gathered the dog's Hermès leads in her white-gloved hands and urged her charges forward through the gate. No one bothered to check her invitation or question her appearance there, except two inconsequential figures hovering on the sidelines dressed as waiters.

"Get a load of the Ice Queen from Hell. She musta stolen that lot from the local ASPCA But did you see that dress? It must be an original Erté. I wonder if there is a way I could ..."

"Good gravy Darlink, whaddaya ya gonna do? Peel the rag off the bitch while Frankenstein's brother, Butch, stands by and watches. Come to your senses even if the hulk would pass out from a OD of steroids, now she's surrounded by the hounds from Hell. Jeepers creepers, I'll bet those monsters know how to snap the neck of a baby. And you, little Dilly, are not what I'd call a tower of power with or without your famed boomerang. So come on, let's pass out these fucking hor's d'oeuvres and get on with our plan."

The next conveyance to confound the constabulary was none other than the limo stretched beyond all bounds in which the Zelengorian fraternity had lately rampaged the countryside, otherwise identified as Scarface Malone's getaway car. The absurd length of this vehicle precluded it's coming any closer to the festivities than the access road of Park Drive. However, that was close enough to cause a stir amongst the valet parkers whisking their charges off to parking limbo. One of those scruffy youths employed in this auto-cosseting service was heard to exclaim, "What the fuck!"

Not an overly articulate comment but one that elicited agreement from none other than the redoubtable Mrs. Adams Cabot Lowell Untermeyer, who had arrived in her Lincoln Town Car just ahead of the roadhog limo. Mrs. A.C.L.U., feeling a bit pinched by the Zelengorians breathing down her neck, handed the parking boy a fiver, much to her drivers, annoyance, and barked, "You said it kid, *who* are those vulgar people? I thought this was polite society. Here's a five spot, go get your teeth cleaned and look for a real job."

The valet looked from the driver behind the wheel of the Lincoln to the sashaying posterior of Mrs. A.C.L.U. scratching his head and frowning, a fateful hesitation that allowed one of the more agile of the Zelengorians to wriggle half out the driver's window and snatch the boy's tip.

"Hey man, what the FUCK?" repeated the boy with a slightly different inflection this time.

Just then the third rear door of the stretch limo popped open and Clovis Galicurchi briskly bounded from the vehicle followed close at heel by one of his gentlemen songsters. This fellow's rainbow striped jacket and white linen trousers appeared more than a bit rumpled and his boater hat dangled down his back, held precariously by an elastic chin strap stretched all out of shape. On his feet he wore Minnie Mouse dancing shoes with boxy half-heels that were scuffed up something terrible.

Thus Prima Donna made his entrance, such as it was, but unfortunately the silly slob went flying when his too square heel caught in a wrinkle of AstroTurf covering a tangle of heavy electric cables. Prima was undone by this faux pas and began to curse and carry on in what he mistook for Zelengorian expletives but turned out to mean "Fuck me quick, I'm on fire!" The Zelengorian gang heard Prima's lament and, happy to oblige anyone speaking their mother tongue, trundled out of their limo hot to trot.

Fortunately for Prima, his escort Clovis Galicurchi, came to the rescue plucking the flailing performer off the plastic grass and setting him upright just as the gang were about to pounce and mount. Clovis, as you may remember had experienced the Zelengorian outrage before, and had survived their extreme abuse by teaching the thugs to warble "If I were a pig on the farm," an old Appalachian lullaby that had been reluctantly discarded by Aaron Copland as being too graphic. The Zelengorians were not inhibited by such scruples. They actually loved the ditty. Thus the tenuous acquaintanceship between Clovis and the Zelengorians had been cemented. The thugs, generous to a fault, when not engaged in extortion and general mayhem, had offered Maestro a lift any time he might be in need. Being a man of no malice, Clovis took them up on their offer and hitched a ride to The Rose Garden Party. He figured that the stretch limo would enhance his prestige and also keep him safe from the pink school bus, which had proved to be a trifle unreliable. Why he brought Prima along with him was a mystery, especially after Prima's dress rehearsal crash down. The dish on the street was that Clovis was hot for Prima, but even vicious gossip can sometimes go beyond all credibility. It is more likely that Clovis was using the dancer as a human shield against the Zelengorians.

Thinking fast, Maestro Galicurchi whipped around to face the oncoming foe. He held up his elegant white baton, which in reality was a spray-painted chopstick from Sung No Good Chinese restaurant, and gave the quintet an upbeat and cue. The gang came to an abrupt halt. Remembering the porcine ballad Clovis had taught them, they began to sing, an effort at first sadly gone astray, until Maestro corrected them with his pitch pipe, blowing a tone somewhere around F sharp. As the first haunting melodies of "Pig" got going, Prima not to be outdone joined in the impromptu performance and gave them a bit of the old softshoe. Thus gaily occupied the mismatched minstrels intoned as Prima tripped the light fantastic while an astonished audience of socialites stared with horror and disbelief at the warbling thugs and the dancing songster.

Just as the Zelengorians were deep into the refrain, "a pig in mud is no joke," the pink school bus loaded with the Gay Men's Chorus arrived and came to a grinding halt with a flatulent retort that sounded to all the world like a nuclear explosion. But the impassioned Zelengorians were so swept away by "Pig" they didn't even notice being surrounded by 85 boys in barbershop quartet outfits until it was too late. Yes, if truth be told, the choristers had had enough shilly-shallying around. They had, at this point, clocked in more than three months of rehearsal time on *Naughty Astronautess* and if that meant they had to wear silly stripes, well so be it, but no lousy punks from Bosnia were going to distract their maestro. The result of this encounter was a melee that would have put the Green Bay Packer linemen to shame.

Mrs. A.C.L.U. was standing at the rose bower gate about to enter the party when she was distracted from her purpose by all the hubbub behind her. She turned to glare at the unseemly ruckus, and at that exact moment the pack of Russian wolf hounds came running out of the rose enclave dragging Monique behind them on a tangle of Hermès dog leashes. The grand dame was knocked over and blithely trampled by the borzois, which hadn't the restraint of Boston breeding to inhibit the universal appeal of 85 boys in rainbow stripes and silly hats. In a word the dogs were besotted.

The borzois had dashed out to join in the ruckus with the choristers and the Zelengorian gang. The choristers were there to rescue Clovis Galicurchi from the Zelengorians. Clovis was there to rescue Prima Donna, and no one among them gave a rat's ass about Mrs. A.C.L.U., and who could blame them?

Officer Patrick Shannon stooped to aid the fallen lady, or at least she assumed that was what he was doing. Actually his eye had caught a peculiar glint of metal reflecting the last rays of summer twilight. Officer Shannon was scooping up the mysterious bits from the long grass beside the rose bower gate and puzzling over them when the gnarled grasp of the crumpled dame clamped down on his beefy mitt.

*   *   *   *

Lurking on the sidelines of all the commotion at the entrance gate, a diminutive flunky in ill-fitting black waiter drag was toting a tray loaded with fried oysters squired with tiny plastic swords. He was whispering to an equally suspicious character who resembled an ordinary vampire, except for the tray of pickled sea urchins balancing on her left hand.

"Urna, I think that cop, Shannon, just scarfed up what looks to be your keys or earrings or whatever they are." whispered the first waiter.

"Good gravy, could it really be?" exclaimed the other.

"Yeah, from the grass by the front gate and handed them to that Untermeyer dame." Dilbert added excitedly.

"Holly cow. Where?" Urna demanded.

"What? I don't know. She was down in the dirt by the front gate—musta been looking for them herself." Dilbert snapped back.

"How does she know about my earrings?" Urna was edging toward panic.

"How do I know how she knows? All I can only tell you is what I seen, right? OK, I gotta get back to passing out these fucking hor's d'oeuvres. That Traedway dame has been eyeing me and I don't wanna blow my cover." Dilbert slithered off into the crowd proffering his oysters.

"Officer! I am Mrs. Adams Cabot Lowell Untermeyer! I have been severely injured by that pack of rabid dogs. Call me an ambulance immediately."

Mrs. A.C.L.U tugged at Officer Shannon's arm. But her demands were nothing compared with the ruckus going on between the Boston Police, the Zelengorian gang, the Gay Choristers, Prima Donna, Clovis Galicurchi, and the now frazzled Monique le Farge.

Connie Treadway was distracted from her conversation with Jed Mousebaine, the newly elected DA, by the crescendoing din of serious fisticuffs coming from the front gate. Lester Pomeroy and his jazz orchestra were used to loud parties, but even they were having a hard time drowning out the hubbub.

"Jed, will you excuse me a minute please. I have to check in with Rosalind Wortheley about the entertainment."

Little did Connie know what a stir the entertainment was already causing until she came round the corner of the first tent and saw what appeared to be a reenactment of the Battle of Bull Run in full swing. She stopped dead in her tracks, paralyzed with horror by what she saw. It was not every day you could see a Bosnian bruiser slug a Boston motorcycle cop in the gut and then stomp on his boot. And that was but a tiny incident in an altercation that threatened to get seriously out of hand.

Connie stood ramrod straight, hands on her hips, fuming to such a heated degree that wisps of steam were actually rising from her carefully messed-up hairdo. Just then Rosalind appeared on the scene looking for Al and his astronautesses. But in her haste she ran smack dab into her mother, whom she didn't even recognize because the grand dame's face was pulled so taut by Dr. Glimerglass, she looked like a total stranger. On impact with Rosalind Mrs. A.C.L.U. went down for a second time bellowing in outrage an epithet so lewd and scathing that all the combatants shut up and froze in glacial dismay.

Gripped by this foreboding calm, like being caught in the threatening eye of a hurricane, no one amongst them could utter a peep until one powerful voice could be discerned wafting toward the garden party,

> ♪Love comes in many packages
> But it's not often delivered to your door.
> You hafta weigh it right 'n slap on enough stamps
> then wrap it in brown paper and string
> but that ain't gonna hide the sting.
> I've got those boo hoo blues,
> 'cuz I lost my shoes when we ran outta booze.♪

The only person capable of singing such utter hogwash came into sight lolling about in the padded recesses of the Yellow Ducky rickshaw. Lilly Linda Le Strange was gearing up to exclaim the next scintillating stanza of "The Boo Hoo Blues," when she caught sight of the bizarre scene before her. Even though La Diva was used to center stage, she was somewhat disconcerted by the frozen fracas.

"Darling lumps, what gives?"

A question seemingly fallen on deaf ears, as no one moved an inch. The brakes on Val's bicycle ducky squeaked a sharp complaint as he parked his festive vehicle on the Rose Garden lawn. By this time Al had picked out Rosalind and the fallen Mrs. A.C.L.U.

"Holy shit! It's the mother-in-law!! I knew I shoulda eaten another hash brownie before I came over here. Well here goes nothing."

Lilly Linda Le Strange was encased in full astronautess garb consisting of a silver lamé space suit and authentic helmet adorned with exuberant Mylar eyelashes firmly affixed to the smooth shield of her Plexiglas visor. She hefted her mighty girth out of the rickshaw and sauntered over to where Rosalind was caught in suspended animation.

"Lumpy-poo, poopsey darling, speak to me doll-face, it's me, Al."

Albert Mellenoffsky shoved back his visor, puckered up and planted an excessively affectionate smooch onto the voluptuous lips of his adored Rosalind. The crowd came unglued gasping in unison and poopsey darling collapsed in the arms of her Naughty Astronautess.

Al was terrified that Rosalind was suffering a relapse of her coma, and in a panic he administered a small hit of poppers to the fainting beauty. Her large eyes shot open in a flash and she shuddered from the rush of the poppers.

"Oh Albert, there you are, I've been looking all over for you."

"Not to worry, my pet, here I am."

There was no denying the truth of this statement, for Albert/Lilly even towered above Monique in his specially designed space boots adding a lofty five and a half inches to his already six-foot-two stature. Rosalind, not a tiny parcel herself, was dwarfed in the arms of the space explorer.

At this point in the proceedings the Gay Men's Chorus were beside themselves with excitement when they glimpsed their hero, the Naughty Astronautess. They immediately abandoned their rescue efforts on behalf of Prima Donna and Maestro Galicurchi and flocked to surround the romantic couple. Inspired by the excitement of the moment, they broke into an a cappella rendition of "Peckers in Deep Space." But before they could intone that fateful lyric, "light-years are so long I'll have to brake out my bong and play with my schlong," Clovis came to the rescue when his artistic temperament was pushed over the brink by one of Monique's borzois trying to hump his leg. Maestro exploded into an unseemly temper ranting, raving and pounding his fists on the sod where the horny hound had pinned him.

Rosalind flinched as the amorous pooch went flying from the impact of Galicurchi's kick. The hairy monster indiscreetly barreled into, and then ricocheted off, the wobbling Mrs. A.C.L. U. Then all hell really broke loose.

The term "screaming banshee" comes to mind regarding the war cry that erupted from the lips of the grand dame and some of the less crusty cops blushed in response to her primal scream. But being men of action, pledged to preserve the peace, they pounced on the now dazed borzoi flailing about the fallen lady before any more damage could be inflicted.

While the constabulary forces were thus distracted, Val rushed in where wise men never try, scooped up Rosalind and Al and peddled like the devil into the party compound making a timely retreat. The eighty-five choristers, some of whom had been roughed up good by the Zelengorians, got bored with the scuffle and scurried after the fleeing Yellow Ducky. Connie Treadway was left fuming at the gate. Monique, having regained her savoir-faire, gathered up the borzoi's leashes and sauntered by Connie saying, "Miss thing, your hair is on fire and you forgot to put your dress on."

Connie was beside herself.

CHAPTER 49

▼

BACKSTAGE VISITATION

Backstage at the Rose Garden was a nifty tent especially designated for the cast and crew of *"Naughty"* who had all been rounded up and put under wraps by Connie's minions. Police Commissioner Chuck Snarler wanted to book the lot of them, toss them all into the clink and then throw away the key. But cooler heads prevailed when Muriel asked District Attorney Jed Mousebaine to intervene on behalf of the performers. Muriel hadn't actually seen the altercation but she had seen the results. When Muriel saw Connie Treadway's usually unflappable cool heated up to the boil she had an irresistible urge to test the limits of steel nerve to contain the explosive forces of steam power. In other words Muriel couldn't wait to see Connie lose it altogether and blow her top, big time.

Such was the executive power wheeled by Muriel who decided to visit the performers backstage for a closer inspection before the performance. Rosalind, as entertainment chairwoman for the fete, took it upon herself to act as liaison between the artistes and Madam Mayor. She wisely enlisted the strong arm of Scena Finale, choreographer and stage manager for *Naughty* and between them everybody was lined up for introductions.

"Muriel Brunelleschi, may I introduce the star of *Naughty Astronautess*, Lilly Linda Le Strange."

"So you are the famous Lilly, I read all about you in *Gay Windows* and I was particularly intrigued by the pictures of your garden. I believe the reporter called it Lilly Land?

"Pleased to meetcha, you darling lump." declared Al, pumping Muriel's hand with vigor more necessary than a mere howdy do.

Muriel yanked her hand away from Al's overenthusiastic pumping and inquired with a twinkle in her eye, "I've been called many names in my time, to my face and behind my back, not all of them meant to please, but I must say I rather like the idea of being a darling lump."

"Not just *a* darling lump but *my* darling lump! There is a difference you know. Now take Rosalind for instance. She is a supreme darling lump—you can see that just by looking at her. I mean, when was the last time you saw anybody wearing a hat trimmed with lavender mirabou? And a hoop skirt to boot. But there she is a stunner!

"Now let's take a peek at you, I'll bet my panties that that stunning creation perched on your noggin was created by none other than Mrs. La Freda Jones from the Chapeaux Boutique on Tremont Street. Am I right or what? What's more, I know it is an exact reproduction of a hat worn by the Dowager Duchess of Dungarees. I just love La Freda, don't you? Why if I had patuties to spare, I'd have La Freda make every hat I own. Unfortunately I live by my wits, which have been in doubt even by me sometimes, so alas I can not always afford the luxury of La Freda. But never mind all that highfallutin La La, let's meet a few of the more important players in tonight's drama."

Al hooked Muriel and Rosalind's arms around his own powerful limbs softened by shimmering silver lamé and the three proceeded down the lineup nodding and chit-chatting with all and sundry.

$$* \qquad * \qquad * \qquad *$$

In the meantime the sinister element were busy at work corroding the good will so laboriously generated by Al and Rosalind.

"Holy cow Darlink! I knew you were a despicable toad but this takes the cake. Even I could never dream of such destruction. You mean you actually replaced the spring-loaded mechanism of that infernal Twinkle starship with a real rocket launcher? How on earth?"

The diminutive waiter with a peculiar sideways gate was passing a tray of cocktails in the dance tent. Something about this shabby character caught the eagle eye of Connie Treadway and she studied this person carefully from across the dance floor. She saw the "waiter" in question talking to an even more disturbing-looking member of the catering staff. This second "waitress" was of average height, but that's where all pretence of normalcy faded. The waitress in Connie's sights was rail thin, wore black lipstick and most fantastically appeared to have shrunken heads sewn to the epaulets of her jacket. Connie gave Chuck Snarler a wink and a nod pointing out her prey and then moved in with caution, trying to catch what the mysterious duo was saying.

"With lighter fluid, Miss Thing. The bitch will burn and I can retrieve all my lovely drag."

"Oh Dildo you little devil. But good gravy what will happen? How come that slime bag Wally St. John didn't get wind of it?"

"That stupid junky is no match for me. I put Quaaludes in his martini. Why do you think I'm doing this dumb waiter job. Not to make tips, that's for sure.

Connie thought she had heard enough and seeing Snarler moving in fast to apprehend the suspects she beat a hasty retreat to locate the sabotaged Twinkle starship.

CHAPTER 50

▼

INTO ORBIT

Against all odds the show must go on and no one knew that more than Lilly, especially with the likes of Connie Treadway and her cohort Chuck Snarler nipping at La Diva's heels.

Having made nice to Muriel, introducing her to all and sundry in the cast, Lilly even went so far as to promise Muriel a personal tour of Lilly Land. Although how Muriel got hold of that ancient copy of *Gay Windows* wherein Lilly had given an extensive interview and tour of her home and garden was anyone's guess. It would appear that Muriel was a lot better read than anyone would have thought.

Be that as it may, Lilly finally ushered the mayor's wife and Rosalind out from the confines of the backstage tent and urged them to take a seat front row center hoping that that would settle down the crowd so the curtain could go up.

Maestro Clovis Galicurchi had escaped fairly unscathed from his latest ruckus with the Zelengorians, except for a minor tear between the two tails of his coat, which had been expeditiously mended by Prima Donna. Prima had at first tried a juicy wad of gum provided by one of the Ninja Fringers, but the goo wouldn't stick to the fine material so Prima resorted to a magic strip Band-Aid and that did the trick nicely.

Maestro tapped his chopstick baton for attention and the orchestra, composed of the Bronx harmonica band and an assortment of pickup musicians provided by that notorious talent scout Fruity Freddy, started to play. The musicians in question had been culled from Freddy's files of desperate choices, which assured their enthusiasm if not their competence. The 85 strapping lads composing the Gay Men's Chorus began their performance by humming along with the orchestra.

The Overture for *Naughty Astronautess* got off to a spirited rumba kind of rhythm that borrowed some embellishments from the more obscure preludes of the visionary Russian composer Scriaban. Woven into these dense cadences and sweeping flourishes were references to, if not outright plagiarisms of, Günter Schuler's Jazz Quartette. After a spell of these precocious orchestrations, the tunes for the major songs from *Naughty Astronautess* were introduced and interwoven contrapuntally developing into a rondo ending in the spurting climax of "Peckers in Deep Space." Fortunately for all concerned the lyrics for these ditties were as yet unknown to the assembled public.

*　　*　　*　　*

While Clovis was softening up the audience with his harmonic hor's d'oeuvres out front, Lilly was putting the finishing touches to her makeup and costume backstage. As Betty the Bounder handed Lilly her signature "silk" hanky, a shank of polyester sheeting that measured 6x6 feet, the technicians crowded around La Diva. This team of high-tech nerds on loan from Wentworth Institute was making sure that the special effects camera imbedded into Lilly's space helmet was all in order and broadcasting to the giant screens on either side of the stage.

To the credit of the *Glamour Galore* technical staff the temporary stage, set up on the Fenway football field adjoining the Rose Garden, was composed of building scaffolding draped with miles of black plastic. This marvel of improvised genius was accomplished on a very tight budget. Mirrors were used on the launch pad set, all arranged in radiating pinwheels. These were nothing more than 2x4-foot cheap closet mirrors from the CVS, 540 of them. The big-ticket items of the evening were the sophisticated audio-visual equipment consisting of a blinding barrage of theatrical lights, colored laser beams and a killer sound system. The final ingredient cooked up by the "Wentworth Nerds" was the afore, mentioned high-quality movie screens and projection equipment that were to broadcast Lilly's flight above the Rose Garden and when not thus engaged they reverted to a decorative psychedelic light show reminiscent of lava lamps and melting marbleized paper.

"OK Lilly, now when you are airborne like sorta remember to face downward toward the tents and Rose Garden 'cause then the audience will like to see and hear everything. And remember this device is so wicked powerful it will pick up every last pimple on anyone it sees from fifty yards away."

From the mouths of babes come predictions of unimaginable truth and momentous ramifications.

"So where the hell is Wally?" screamed La Diva "I have to make sure his space-ship is ready for blastoff."

"Better not get your skirt in a ruffle over Wally, Lil, everything will be just fine.

Now, doncha wanna have a feather or two for your helmet? I got the hot glue gun all fired up here. So which will it be, pink ostrich or turkey tail?"

"No, I don't want any of your mangy feathers, Betty! This is an authentic space suit just like the ones at NASA Betty, don't you raise that left eyebrow at me, queen, and where the hell is Wally anyway?"

"Never mind Wally, Miss Thing, there's your music queue, now get out there and knockem dead, merde, break a leg and all that rigmarole. Hey, Lilly, how about a hit of peach schnapps? You know, one for the road."

On the way out of her dressing room Lilly slugged greedily from Betty's schnapps bottle. The junk had such a kick to it Lilly shivered from helmet to space boot, and she had to check to see if it weren't really paint remover, you never knew with Betty. But no the label had a lurid picture of a drunken Burger-meister, so Lilly figured it might be authentic, albeit revolting. She tossed the stuff over her shoulder and marched off toward the stage. As luck would have it the discarded jug flew through the air and came to rest squarely on the head of Wally St. John, whose rumpled body was concealed beneath a pile of costumes in a corner of the backstage tent. Wally didn't even groan from the impact so deep was his stupor from Dildo's deadly Quaalude martini, and needless to say in this condition he had not made a preliminary, much less final, check of the Twinkle starship.

As a Naughty Astronautess Lilly Linda Le Strange was typecast. This star had strayed light-years from her intended constellation to the extent that a whole new mythology had to be concocted in order to describe the peculiar configuration of heavenly bodies wherein La Diva resided.

When Lilly made an entrance she could upstage a cast of thousands with only a flutter of her eyelashes, and people were known to gasp audibly at her audacious interpretation of even ordinary lyrics. Her voice, an undisguised bass baritone, had a timbre that could move lumberjacks to tears and fell a forest simultaneously. Lilly also had elegance and style in every inch of her body down to the last digit of her sizable pinky, which indecently was never extended in as a menacing claw but rather flowed with the grace of a Balinese dancer. But her real abiding talent was to radiate like the August sun at noontime, love, for the thousands of fans beyond the footlights, that anonymous crowd who were to her more precious than life itself because in their eyes she could be beautiful, and it was all because she firmly believed in make-believe.

> ♪ *Hold on to your seat fellas 'cus MaMa's 'bout to blast off.*
> *I've got me a ticket on the Twinkle starship*
> *and boy whata trip,*
> *We're gonna slip off the planet right into the glitzy galaxy.* ♫

> ♫ *If you give up your seat on the shuttle*
> *you'll inevitably be in a muddle*
> *And then who's to say*
> *you might even be gay*
> *and boy what trouble that would be.* ♪

> ♫ *So don't miss out, come join me*
> *We're off to uncharted space*
> *It's sorta like smoking*
> *A full bowl of hash*
> *And then you get thrown out with the trash.* ♫

At this point in her ballad Lilly was joined onstage by a throng of chorines who moved to the innovative choreography of Scena Finale, a stylistic dance leaning heavily on Doris Humphrey and Busby Berkley. But what made this spectacle irresistible was the set, which was composed of mirror panels arranged in radiating patterns that rotated slowly so that the dancers were reflected in a kaleidoscope of bouncing light. Adding to all this glitz were the astronautesses' space suits, all covered with reflective scales on the tunic and silver polka dots on outerspace-blue tights. These vintage marvels had been purloined from Dildo's secret costume cave beneath The Follies Derrière, much to Dilly's dismay. Although no one could at first fathom why Lilly was so enamored of these "old rags," as Wally St. John ruthlessly disparaged Dilly's treasures, once the dancers were incased in their shining armor and gyrating to Shana's brand of hoochy cooch the effect was spectacular with beams of laser light bouncing off every reflective curve of the dancers' shapely bodies, who also sported oversized Plexiglas bubble helmets wired with individual head mikes and bouncing spring antennae.

♫ *We're off to outer space and there's room in the trunk. If you wanna join us jump aboard* ♪

This refrain was sung in twelve-part harmony by the boys of the Gay Men's Chorus with such earnest zeal and infinite variations that the whole effect was mesmerizing. The assembled audience who had not an inkling of what was going on was none the less transfixed by the spectacle.

Lilly sashayed to the music, firing off her "space gun" toward the night sky. This toy pistol was the type that sprays colored sparks and makes neat grinding noises, the later effect not being Maestro Galicurchi's liking. But fire she did and then in a moment of inspired improvisation Lilly broke into a coloratura descant of "We're off to outer space."

The choristers and the chorines worked up a frothy climax. The timpani section, which had shamelessly stolen every pipe and plastic pail idea from the Blue Man Group, set a dizzying pace, close to frenzy, at which juncture the back wall of the stage spread open. The black plastic sheeting was gathered into columns of wrinkled drapes, and slowly from the spacious distance of the blazingly lit football field in rolled the Twinkle starship.

Next came the Ninja Fringers making their head-over-heels Kong Fu acrobatic flips on to stage center. The brotherhood had been carefully rehearsed to load Lilly onto a crane device that would levitate her at a stately pace to the mouth of the waiting cannon barrel, now disguised beneath Wally St. John's remarkable blowup likeness of the Apollo space shuttle. As if the presence of a dozen bouncing acrobats in cartoon Ninja turtle costumes was not bizarre enough, the next bunch to crowd the teaming stage was Monique La Farge and her pack of borzois representing the blastoff committee.

But the brevity of the public good will was soon to be all too apparent.

In the meantime Lilly was in her element, which consisted of more hyperbolic hysteria than could be imagined by ordinary mortals.

♪ *Hold on to your seat fellas 'cuz MaMa's 'bout to blast off.*
I've got me a ticket on the Twinkle starship
and boy whata trip,
We're gonna slip off the planet right into the glitzy galaxy. ♫

At the conclusion of her verse, Lilly, then raised by the crane to the level of pink glitter nose cone, plucked that plug from the space ship and climbed in feet first. Because the barrel of the circus cannon was cocked at a rakish angle, La Diva disappeared with a whoosh accompanied by the timpani section augmented by the Ninja Fringers who, lost to the excitement of the moment, began beating contrapuntal rhythms on their turtle shell body armor with clenched fists.

Over all this frenzy onstage could be heard an order of compelling pluck issuing from the depths of the Twinkle starship.

"O'Punk, get over here and light my fuse!"

Paddy came to his senses long enough to pluck a stainless steel Zippo from the codpiece of his spandex tights and fired up the fuse. Sparks flew all over the place, swiftly burning down toward the Twinkle starship. Everyone watching was so cranked up with anticipation that no one bothered to cringe or flinch. The explosion, when it came, was far beyond all previous blastoffs. There must have been an extra dose of gun powder in the barrel, and somehow the spring that actually powered the launch had been wound double tight.

The effect all this had on the Twinkle starship was completely unexpected and the thing somehow became unhinged from the cannon beneath so that, although the Naughty Astronautess was launched first, fast on her heels came Wally's blowup rocket.

There is just so much punishment rubberized sheet plastic will take and the Twinkle starship had been stretched way beyond its thermodynamic engineering. The result was yet another explosion, but this time it had nothing to do with gun powder. The thing popped, big time, flinging scraps of plastic rocket ship all over the place.

Remarkably in all this studied chaos, the one piece of equipment that did function perfectly was the "Wentworth Nerds" TV camera imbedded in Lilly's helmet. This device recorded and broadcast with supernatural clarity Lilly's flight: over the audience sitting on the edge of the football field, over the Rose Garden surrounded by its hedge of yews and ring of tall crabapple trees, over the adjoining War Memorial with its impressive twelve-foot-tall bronze angel with wings outspread, over the overgrown and reed-chocked banks of the Muddy River, ending with a tsunami splashdown right into the center of the Muddy

River featuring an accumulation of muck that even made snapping turtles decry, "Yuck! This junk stinks!"

The audience was composed of Boston's highest echelon of society mavens ruthlessly clawing their way up the tawdry ladder of success. This bunch had never seen anything like *Naughty Astronautess,* and in a town crammed with institutes of higher learning, the lessons about to be broadcast on the high-definition screens, flanking the stage, were of a nature so outrageous that even though shocked in the extreme no one could tear their horrified gaze away.

Lilly bobbed to the surface of the Muddy River gasping for breath and desperate for a cocktail. She sputtered frantically not being at all conversant with the Australian crawl or for that matter even the dog paddle. The closest she had ever been to total submersion was in the depths of her bubble bath. Consequently she was all in a panic until she discovered the river was only waist deep and she began an awkward lurching trek toward the shore.

Lilly's predicament caused mixed reactions in the viewing audience. Rosalind was beside herself with worry.

Her mother, Mrs. A.C.L.U., plunged a hypodermic full of some godforsaken concoction right through her Prada skirt into her thigh and sighing with relief remarked with typical candor, "Serves the fat fairy right. I hope he drowns."

*   *   *   *

Dildo and Urna were gloating in the wings as they watched the demise of Lilly. "That'll teach the Le Strange woman to mess with Dildo!"

"Darlink little runt, you are unspeakably diabolical."

"Thanks Urna, coming from you that means a lot. Come on, I'll give you a lift on my bicycle over to The Follies Derrière for a nightcap."

"Jeepers creepers, little Dilly, sounds like just the ticket, but I sorta promised Betty we'd hook up after the show. Do ya mind if she tags along?"

"Long as she doesn't try to pinch my drag, like her boss, Le Strange, did. She can stand on the rear wheel extensions." Dilly was in an agreeable mood with sweet taste of revenge drooling down the corners of his mouth. "But what do ya see in that two-bit drunk, anyway?"

"Holly cow, you know how it is, Darlink, we went to school together. And after our reunion in your Phantom cave, I don't know, I think I have a soft spot in my heart for Betty." Urna sighed remembering adolescent romps at the Sacred Fart Seminary.

"I'll bet you've got a soft spot for her but it ain't your heart, 'cuz you ain't got one a dose." Dilly giggled at his lame joke.

*   *   *   *

Muriel was at first delighted with the snappy tunes and high jinks of the show and even more delighted to see Connie Treadway seething with rage. However her motherly concern was alarmed by the missfired starship, and when a piece of Wally's exploded rocket flopped onto the crown of her La Freda Jones creation she nudged Bruno and began to pack up. But just as Muriel was gathering herself in preparation to make a hasty retreat, Bruno compelled by what he saw on the oversized screen, grabbed the wife by her wrist and yanked her back onto her chair.

"Bruno Brunelleschi, what do you think you're doing—Oh my God! BRUNO! DON'T LOOK AT THAT! GET ME OUT OF HERE, NOW!"

CHAPTER 51

▼

A SHOOTING STAR GOES KERPLOP!

Muriel's screamed reaction was echoed all over the Rose Garden party as it registered to the uninitiated what unspeakable abomination was being enacted before them. No one could move fast enough toward the exits. Some of the more determined actually ran to the parking boys madly waving their tickets with sizable bank notes in hand.

Yes, due to the miracle of modern media magic, the scene revealed to one and all at the Fenway Rose Garden Party deserved a quadruple XXXX rating, and the paying public party goers were not the only ones blown into next Thursday. Lilly was dumbstruck.

When La Diva bobbed to the surface of the Muddy River, her ordeal was just beginning. Although not deep the Muddy River was just that, muddy, and struggling along in soggy platform space boots did not make forward progress any easier. On two occasions Lilly fell back into the water and thrashed around a bit. As could be expected in this environment, a muskrat passed by and farted in protest to Lilly's intrusive ruckus.

With concerted effort Madame Le Strange reached the reed-choked bank of the river. Unbeknownst to Lilly this was that notorious hinterland that for decades had concealed the nefarious exploits of oversexed studs having man sex.

A lot of other unsavory dramas are enacted there as well, but the motivating force is unleashed desire and anonymous sex.

The Nerd's camera attached to Lilly's helmet was equipped with ultraviolet night vision and consequently could and did record everything that Lilly saw and heard. So when La Diva grabbing at straws parted the underbrush, it was not little Moses in a basket who was revealed.

Not even close.

Rather it was George Wortheley on the bottom of a sex pig-pile doing exceedingly unnatural acts. The seven and a half other men involved—one guy was so submerged in body parts as to be only half present—were engaged in activities that Lilly could not even have dreamed about in her darkest nightmares.

This may be hard to fathom but our hero as you have learned, probably much to your perplexity, was unexpectedly and relentlessly heterosexual even though he had dabbled in the gay lifestyle for many years: "Some of my best friends are Gay." He himself was nonetheless a straight man and as such had limited experience in the matters of the flesh. If truth be known, in a locked box tucked beneath his heart shaped bed draped with pink chenille, Al had a randy collection of *Hustler* magazines.

So when Lilly's eyes, both natural and mechanical, beheld what George and his buddies were up to, he was appalled but transfixed.

George as always was so self-absorbed that he was completely oblivious to the intruder, but one of his momentary companions catching sight of Al growled, "Come on, Daddy, whip it out, let's see your man meat."

The suggestion brought Lilly to her senses to the extent that she hauled herself up out of the muck double time and staggered back toward the party place. As she left she could hear the unmistakable shout of George, "AAAHHH I'M GOING TO POP! AAAAH OH FUCK YEAH AAAHHH YEAH!!

Rosalind, sitting in the front row, could not avoid witnessing the whole debacle. When George's closeup zeroed in on that part of him she dearly wished never to see again, she called out, "Not again, George, how could you?"

She promptly fainted dead away, but this time Bruno Brunelleschi, seated beside her, came to the rescue and caught the limp beauty in his hefty arms.

Val, who was standing arms akimbo observing this spectacle from the sidelines, was not in the least surprised to see George or any other man do almost anything in the serious effort to get his rocks off. Val nonetheless was sorry for Rosalind and spoke to Gyles standing beside him' "Mama Two sure has some big trouble now. I'm going to scoop her up and give her a ride home."

"But Val, where can that be tonight?" Gyles pointed out a detail that was a real problem for Rosalind.

"Val, go over there right away. Pick up Rosalind and take us to my house in your Yellow Ducky. The night air may revive her. The poor darling will need someplace to hide out for a while and she can do that just as easily at my house."

Cornelia was genuinely concerned for Rosalind, and because she had not always been the model of charity where her old school chum was concerned she now saw a way of making recompense by offering sanctuary.

Lilly, dripping and bewildered, the supreme sophisticate with unflappable cool had been blown out, blown up, and blown away. The first sight she registered when whipping the fetid waters of the Muddy River from her visor as she stumbled back toward the party place was Dildo peddling a rusty old Raleigh bicycle with Urna Flamanté riding on the handlebars and Betty standing on foot extensions of the rear wheel axel, clinging tightly to Dildo's waist. As they passed, all three screamed, "Tough luck ass hole!"

And as a parting gesture they tossed an empty bottle of peach schnapps in Lilly's direction, which on impact with the concrete walkway shattered into a million threatening splinters.

The next group to pass going at top speed was Val and the Yellow Ducky. Nestled into the comforting embrace of Ducky, a limp Rosalind was being comforted as much as could be by Cornelia. The two women looked especially vulnerable and because of that, bound to each other, this made Al feel like a complete fool.

Something inside him lurched to a halt as he stared longingly at the departing pedi-cab. He felt as if his whole skeleton was being ripped from his body. What would be left without Rosalind? Nothing. He realized that the greatest joy of his life was running away from him, horrified and revolted. His darling Golden Lump, gone. Al collapsed on the lawn, his legs not able to bare the pain of loss.

After that hordes of party goers streamed away from the Rose Garden as fast as possible. At curbside the valet parkers were frantic to retrieve all the cars simultaneously.

But not to be upstaged Mrs. A.C.L.U. had gone into metabolic shock, and three ambulances had been dispatched and duly arrived to confound the fleeing party goers. The old dame, now way beyond the help of any cosmetic surgeon, was being shoved into the more aggressive of the medical street sweepers when she held up a gnarled mitt motioning Al to approach.

"Rosalind's going to get vaginal herpes from sleeping with the likes of you."

To his credit, Al slapped the bitch hard enough to make her shut up. The paramedics were shocked but not surprised. Even a few minutes with Mrs. A.C.L.U. was enough to harden the most compassionate. They hastily loaded their charge into the screaming ambulance and speed away.

As Lilly staggered away from this latest horror, she was almost run over by the caterer's truck fleeing the premises. As they swept past he glimpsed their name and logo sprawled across the speeding vehicle: "DIAMONDS, where parties last forever." The lie of this statement cut deep into Lilly's wound and she wondered if she would make it back to her dressing room.

But when she got there the dressing room tent that had been so crowded only a short time ago, had been evacuated and cleaned out. Not a stitch of drag and not even the lowliest chorine was left. The most crushing blow was that even Betty had decamped, not even leaving a cheap tube of lipstick to comfort the fallen star.

Lilly stumbled out of the dressing room and came round to the stage where the naked circus cannon pointed its once proud barrel down to the bare stage. Behind this forlorn giant, black plastic hung from the surrounding scaffolding in torn remnants rustling in the chilly night winds.

Our Naughty Astronautess exhaled a deep sigh of despair and with considerable difficulty unscrewed her space helmet and yanked it off her head. Turning the thing upside down a quart of mucky water poured out splashing onto the stage, and when the last drop had dripped a small frog leaped out and came to rest in the center of the puddle. He blinked and looked up at Lilly beside him and said, "Ribbit, Ribbit."

"You don't say, and I thought no one would ever speak to me again. Not that I did anything mind you. It was that *worm*, George Wortheley."

"Ribbit, Ribbit."

What do I want? I want the creep to leave me alone."

"Ribbit, Ribbit."

"Listen darling you oughta expand your vocabulary. Howss 'bout a song.

> ♫ *When you wish upon a star*
> *makes no difference who you are*
> *unless you happen to be*
> *a big schulobola like me*
> *then you better watch out 'cause*

when a shooting star falls
she sure goes kerplop. ♪

"Ribbit, Ribbit."

"Miss Le Strange, oh Miss Le Strange."

Lilly looked down at the frog, thinking at this point almost anything might be possible.

"Miss Le Strange, Lilly Linda Le Strange?"

"Say, listen buddy, doncha know that name's copyrighted Lay off it, woncha, unless you happen to have ten bucks, then fork it over and use it all you want."

Lilly squinted at the gathering gloom looking for a body to the voice and hoping that it really wasn't the frog talking to her."

"Miss Le Strange? I'm Herbert Bunge, from the William Morris theatrical agency. Perhaps you've heard of us?"

From where the glittering audience had lately fled came a man carefully weaving his way between the fallen and overturned folding chairs. He wore a smart Burberry's raincoat over a three-piece tweed suit, and in one hand he carried what surely must be a Hermés attaché case in one hand and a tightly feruled umbrella in the other. He picked his way gingerly amongst the debris toward Lilly. Upon reaching the foot of the stage, Mr. Bunge said, "Miss Le Strange, my card."

And sure enough it read:

Herbert Bunge

William Morris Theatrical Agents

NY, NY

Lilly stared at the natty man in complete wonder and for the second time tonight she was dumbstruck.

"Miss Le Strange, I caught your show this evening and whereas I understand this particular performance did not go off without a hitch, nonetheless it was a remarkable performance. We at the agency have had our eye on you, Miss Le Strange, and it has not escaped our attention that your show *Glamour Galore* had an extended run which in our opinion would have rivaled *The Mouse Trap* if allowed to continue along its natural path.

"Miss Le Strange, I think you will be interested to know that the Risney Corporation has engaged my agency to offer you a contract for their upcoming reality show called Queen for a Gay. The format details have not actually been ironed out yet, but the offer is for a six-month pilot series at the attractive figure of seven and a half million dollars plus a ten-percent share in the profits provided you endorse their video game."

"Darling lump, for seven and half million bucks I'd endorse midget mud wrestling!"

After Lilly's latest Faustian impetuosity, Mr. Bunge's attractive figures were temporarily drowned out by a deafening roar approaching in the dark night sky. Lilly was desperate to hear the guy out, and although she could see Mr. Bunge was still talking she couldn't hear a word or read his lips either—such was the din hovering directly over them.

The racket steadily increased stirring up a whirlwind storm that wiped the tattered black plastic hanging around the stage into a diabolical frenzy. Mr. Bunge had to hold onto his Burberry and his briefcase to keep from being blown away altogether. Lilly cringed fearing true karmic retribution had finally caught up to her. But at the same time she was pissed like hell at the interruption to her dream come true. She craned her head to look up and see what the disturbance was all about just in time to be spotlit from above by a blinding beam of light. In true biblical form a voice from above boomed out over a powerful bullhorn.

"Yo Lil! Hey babe I caught your act on the news just now and I thought you might need a little pick-me-up. Hold on a sec. I can't land right there with all those tents and trees. I'll circle round to the ball field and touch down."

"Stanley! My old buddy from Nam.!!

Lilly shouted out to Mr. Bunge, pointing up to the sky, but the gentleman mimed that he couldn't hear a word.

Stanley Potsdam, one hunky number in a tank top and tight jeans had arrived at the opportune moment. His Eye in the Sky traffic chopper shot back up into the darkness and circling behind the stage he gently landed on the 34th yard line of the Fenway football field.

Lilly grabbed Mr. Bunge's gloved hand and made a mad dash toward the roaring chopper. Stanley awaited them beside the Eye with two hands held stirrup fashion for Mr. Bunge. Once aboard Stanley outfitted the little fellow with headphones and a helmet, fastening a safety belt over one shoulder. Lilly had already crawled and wiggled into the copilot's seat and was buckling the chin strap of her helmet when without further ado, Stanley shot up into the night sky and, making a broad sweep over the darkened area along the Muddy River, the Fenway Victory Gardens and surrounding parkland, they zoomed toward the glass and steel towers of downtown Boston all lit up with a million lights.

"Stanley Potsdam, I wancha ta meet my most divinest new lump, Mr. Bunge."

"Hey man, welcome aboard the Eye. Any friend of Lilly's gotta be sterling, so sit back and enjoy."

"Good evening, Mr. Potsdam.

Mr. Bunge scrutinized Stan in the rear view mirror of the chopper and inquired, "Mr. Potsdam, have you ever had a screen test?"

"Screen test? Hey man, the only thing they screen me for is booze and drugs, but not to worry, I am clean as a nun's bum." Stan turned to Lilly, "So where to, babe? Not back to Aruba I hope."

"No Stan, not Aruba. I think our first stop should be The Big Apple. Is that where this Bill Morris guy is, Mr. Bunge?"

"Oh yes, Miss Le Strange, New York City, that would be most convenient."

"After that Hollywood, here we come! But y'know Stan, first off I gotta call a lady about a missing item." Lilly's tone veered off in melancholy direction that worried Stanley.

"Hey babe what's gone is gone. You gotta let it go. *This* is the dream you've been waitin' for, ever since I've known ya. The silver screen is calling!" Stan was all too familiar with the perilous exploits of La Diva and tried to cheer up his friend. "What can be so important compared to that?"

"Oh, Stan, if you only knew, it's my Lump of Gold. This time my heart was torn out down there."

The roar of the chopper covered the silence but couldn't fill in the enormous gap opened by Al's confession. What more could he say?

Al mumbled to himself, "Somehow, I'll make it up to her. I know she liked my poodle skirt and no one else does, so that's gotta mean something. What I need now is a bubble bath and one big fat diamond necklace!"

The End

978-0-595-47804-0
0-595-47804-2

Printed in the United States
200386BV00003B/145-171/A

9 780595 478040